A TIME OF
BLOOD

JOHN GWYNNE

A TIME OF
BLOOD

Of Blood and Bone

BOOK TWO

MACMILLAN

First published 2019 by Macmillan
an imprint of Pan Macmillan
20 New Wharf Road, London N1 9RR
Associated companies throughout the world
www.panmacmillan.com

ISBN 978-1-50981-298-1

1 3 5 7 9 8 6 4 2

A CIP catalogue record for this book is available from the British Library.

Map artwork by Fred van Deelen
Typeset by Palimpsest Book Production Limited, Falkirk, Stirlingshire
Printed and bound by CPI Group (UK) Ltd, Croydon, CR0 4YY

Visit **www.panmacmillan.com** to read more about all our books
and to buy them. You will also find features, author interviews and
news of any author events, and you can sign up for e-newsletters
so that you're always first to hear about our new releases.

For James,
Remembering all those times when books have meant so
much to us. I think Arabel's Raven *was at the heart of it.*
I hope you enjoy this one as much as we enjoyed
those stories together.
Love you, son.

ACKNOWLEDGEMENTS

Welcome back to the Banished Lands. It's a place I love to write about, although not one that I'd necessarily like to live in. As with all of my books, this has been a team effort and there are many people to thank for their help along the way.

First of all I must thank my family, that is, Caroline my wife, and my children Harriett, James, Ed and Will. Without their love, support and understanding, this book, and all the others that have gone before, would never have happened. They are the reason I write.

Thanks must go to my wonderful editor and agent, Julie Crisp. I think few people know the Banished Lands as well as she does, and it would have been a different place without her. Probably a happier place, with less death.

Also, the always lovely Bella Pagan and the team at Tor UK. Their passion for the Banished Lands and hard work on my behalf is deeply appreciated.

And of course, a massive thank you to Priyanka Krishnan, my editor at Orbit US, and the fabulous team there.

Jessica Cuthbert-Smith, my copy-editor, has once again both educated me and saved me from countless errors. Her eye for detail is incredible.

Thank you to my small band of readers. I am ever grateful to those who give up their time to enter my world again, and your thoughts and comments are always deeply appreciated.

Caroline, my best friend, your questions always cutting to the heart of matters.

Ed and Will, my first readers, who love this world as much as I do, and whose passion for this tale and the new characters has been so encouraging.

Sadak Miah, you wanted dragons. The phrase 'be careful what you wish for' comes to mind. Kareem Mahfouz, who's passion and enthusiasm for all things Banished Lands is a constant source of inspiration to me. You're a force of nature and it's always a pleasure to chat with you about Drem and the gang, as well as fantasy in general.

And Mark Roberson, who has been a constant in the world of the Banished Lands. His love of epic fantasy and history has always been so helpful.

And finally, I must thank you, those of you who have taken the time and money to step back into the Banished Lands again. Without you there would be no more adventures in my world. It is a constant source of joy and encouragement that there are people out there enjoying the world of the Banished Lands, and this tale of Riv, Drem, Bleda and the others. If you have contacted me with your thoughts on the story so far, thank you. It is always wonderful to hear from you.

I feel that I should say something about the title of this book, the second of three in the series. *A Time of Blood* is not a subtle title, but upon finishing writing this instalment, I felt that it was perfectly fitting. Make of that what you will.

I hope that you enjoy it, and that for a while you will feel like you're journeying with our heroes and enemies in the Banished Lands.

Truth and Courage,
JOHN

Cast Of Characters

Cheren Horse Clan

Jin – daughter of Uldin, King of the Cheren. A ward of the Ben-Elim, raised in Drassil. Betrothed to Bleda of the Sirak Clan.

Uldin – King of the Cheren and father to Jin.

Gerel – Jin's oathsworn guard.

Sirak Horse Clan

Bleda – son of Erdene, Queen of the Sirak. A ward of the Ben-Elim, raised in Drassil. Betrothed to Jin of the Cheren Clan.

Ellac – A one-handed warrior of the Sirak. Bleda's guard.

Erdene – Queen of the Sirak. Mother of Bleda.

Mirim – oathsworn guard of Bleda.

Ruga – oathsworn guard of Bleda.

Tuld – oathsworn guard of Bleda.

Yul – first-sword of Erdene.

THE DESOLATION

Drem – a trapper of the Desolation. Son of Olin.

Hildith – member of Kergard's Assembly. Owner of a mead-hall.

Land of the Faithful

Alcyon – a giant who resides in Drassil.

Aphra – sister of Riv. A White-Wing of Drassil, captain of a hundred.

Avi – Fia's son.

Balur One-Eye – father to Ethlinn, Queen of the Giants. He resides in Drassil.

Ert – veteran sword master of Drassil. Trainer of the White-Wings.

Ethlinn – Queen of the Giants. Daughter of Balur One-Eye.

Fia – a White-Wing of Drassil.

Jost – a White-Wing of Drassil.

Lorina – a White-Wing of Drassil and captain of a hundred.

Riv – sister to Aphra. A training White-Wing.

Sorch – a White-Wing of Drassil.

Vald – a White-Wing of Drassil.

Order of the Bright Star, Dun Seren and other Garrisons

Byrne – the High Captain of Dun Seren. A descendant of Cywen and Veradis.

Cullen – a young warrior of Dun Seren. A descendant of Corban and Coralen.

Cure – title for the captain of Dun Seren's healing school.

Fen – one of Keld's wolven-hounds.

Flick – a talking crow of Dun Seren.

Grack – one of Stepor's wolven-hounds.

Hammer – a giant bear.

Kill – title for the captain of Dun Seren's warrior school.

Keld – a warrior and huntsman of Dun Seren.

Rab – a white talking crow of Dun Seren.

Ralla – one of Stepor's wolven-hounds.

Shar – Jehar warrior.

Stepor – a warrior and huntsman of Dun Seren.
Tain – the crow master of Dun Seren. Son of Alcyon.
Utul – Jehar warrior. Captain of Balara's garrison.
Varan – a giant of Dun Seren.

BEN-ELIM

Hadran – loyal to Kol. Riv's guardian.
Kamael – from the garrison of Ripa, supporter of Sariel.
Kol – one of the Ben-Elim of Drassil.
Meical – once High Captain of the Ben-Elim. Now frozen in
    starstone metal, sealed with Asroth in Drassil.
Sariel – Lord of the Ben-Elim garrison at Ripa.

KADOSHIM AND THEIR SERVANTS

Arn – acolyte of Gulla, from Fritha's crew.
Asroth – Lord of the Kadoshim. Frozen within starstone
    metal in the Great Hall of Drassil.
Claw – Gunil's giant bear.
Elise – acolyte of Gulla, daughter of Arn.
Gulla – High Captain of the Kadoshim.
Morn – a half-breed Kadoshim. Daughter of Gulla.
Fritha – priestess and captain of the Kadoshim's covens.
Gunil – a giant, brother of Varan.

THE BONE FELLS

Dun Murias

ARDAIN

Dun Vaner

Dun Taras

Dun Cadlas

Dun Seren

Dun Kellen

River Rhenus

Uthandun

River Afren

THE DESSOLA

Mihi

Dun Carreg

Badun

The Darkwood

River Tarin

Baglun Forest

THE LAND OF

Dun Crin

Tarba

Dun Bagul

Narvus

THE
BANISHED
LANDS

PANOS

'Dark blood drank he, from the demon welling'

Völsunga Saga

A TIME OF BLOOD

CHAPTER ONE

DREM

The Year 138 of the Age of Lore, Wolven's Moon

Drem looked up from his horse's steady gait. Through the stark branches above he glimpsed the sun sinking into the mountains ahead, a pale glow behind snow cloud and leafless branches. In a matter of heartbeats twilight was settling upon them like a shroud.

We must stop soon, else the horses risk snaring a leg.

He glanced to his right, saw Cullen riding with his cloak pulled high, face hidden in shadow. Ahead of them, Keld looked as if he had no thought for stopping, the scarred huntsman loping through the trees much like his wolven-hound, Fen.

Grief drives him, and hate.

And fear, if he is human.

Drem blinked, trying to dispel the image of Gulla the Kadoshim, twitching and jerking upon the blood-soaked table in the mine, then rising transformed, teeth long and gleaming, eyes red as coals.

It felt like a dream, no, a nightmare, even though it had been less than a day and night since it happened. Too-vivid memories of the battle at the mine leaped out in Drem's mind like rabid beasts: images of Gulla sinking his teeth deep into the throat of one of his acolytes, of feral *things*, part man, part beast, snarling, clawing, of winged half-breeds screaming their malice, of Fritha, beautiful and cold as the ice-laden forest,

I

black sword in her fist. And Sig the giantess, friend to his father.

Friend to me.

And now she is dead. Because of me.

A restless anxiety was growing within him. So much had happened in so short a time, giving him little chance to feel anything; instead he had simply reacted, mostly just trying to stay alive. Now, though, they had been travelling all night and most of the day, and he had had time to think.

So much change. I wish I was with Da, that we were trapping together, out in the Bonefells, just the two of us. And now he's gone as well.

As dangerous as that lifestyle had been, it was familiar to Drem, an old cloak, and it had fitted him well. All of this was so different, so new. He felt agitated, like when his legs ached and he just needed to get up and walk around, except that he couldn't do anything here to help himself; there was no way he could return to the familiar that felt so comforting to him.

His hand crept to his neck, looking for the steady re-assurance of his pulse.

One, two, three, he began to count.

'Camp,' Keld said as he emerged from the darkness, raising an arm and smashing a hole in a frozen stream with the butt of his spear.

A good spot, Drem thought, noting the spread of trees about them, the stream, huge boulders to the right, sheltering them from the cold wind that hissed out of the Bonefells, as well as providing a measure of protection from predators.

On two legs or four.

In silence they set to making camp. Cullen took the horses, hobbling them, removing saddles and rubbing them down. Drem found a spot for a fire and, drawing his hand-axe from his belt, began chopping through the thick rind of ice, then scooping away the softer snow until he reached the frozen ground beneath. He gathered stones, chopped kindling from a dead lightning-blasted oak and prepared a small fire. Before he set to lighting it, he trimmed thin branches from a willow beside the stream, spent a while weaving them into a latticed fence, then staked it along one side of the fire-pit he'd dug. A screen against any eyes that might be following them from the east.

Some tinder from a pouch at his belt, flint and striking iron for sparks, some cold breath upon it and then fragile flames were clawing in the snow, hissing and hungry.

A shaking of the ground made Drem look up, one hand reaching for the bone-hilted seax at his belt. A shadow the size of a boulder shifted within the trees, but Drem's grip relaxed as Hammer, the giant bear, lumbered into their small clearing.

Hammer was Sig's battle-bear and had borne them from last night's chaos, carrying Drem, Keld and Cullen away, crashing through tree and shrub, no thought or time for careful steps or hiding their passage, just a driving knowledge that they had to escape, to put as much distance as possible between them and Gulla.

Hammer had run to exhaustion, bringing them back to Drem's hold in less than half the time it would have taken them on horseback. There they had dismounted, removed the saddle, harness and battered mail shirt from Hammer's body, packing it away in paniers and saddlebags. They'd tended to the wounded bear and fed her some foul concoction that Keld said was called *brot*, then led Hammer and fresh horses into the darkness, knowing they could not wait until dawn.

They had agreed to head west, using the cover of the forest to screen them from eyes in the skies, avoiding the town of Kergard, and then to turn south when they reached the western rim of the Bonefells. Drem had voiced his worry for the townspeople of Kergard but knew there was little they could do to help them. No one in the town had believed him before, and besides, he did not know if there was anyone in Kergard left to save. To Drem's horror, scores of the townsfolk had been at the mine, secret acolytes of the Kadoshim, including Ulf the tanner, a man Drem had once thought of as a friend.

So, they had committed themselves to speed. Pursuit from the mine was likely, and they had to use every moment given them to reach Dun Seren and the Order of the Bright Star.

Drem had led to begin with, his knowledge of the terrain making him the obvious choice to steer them through the darkness. With the rising of a pale sun they had mounted their horses and Keld had taken point, his wolven-hound Fen scouting ahead. Hammer had followed them, grumbling doleful growls, taking herself deeper into the woods, though never quite out of sound or sight.

She feels grief for Sig, just like Cullen and Keld. More, maybe. They were rider and mount for more years than Cullen has drawn breath. Probably longer than Keld has lived, too.

Keld strode to the bear, unbuckled the saddlebags she was carrying, then checked over her wounds and patted her neck. She rubbed her huge head against the huntsman, almost knocking him from his feet.

'Ah, lass, we miss her, too,' Keld muttered, tugging on one of the bear's ears. She seemed to like it, a mournful rumble escaping her throat.

Fen loped into the clearing, eyes glowing in the firelight. The slate-grey hound dropped a hare at Keld's feet.

'A hot meal for supper, then. Thank the stars, I've had enough of *brot*,' Cullen said, his obvious pleasure at the thought infectious.

Keld skinned and gutted the hare and set it on a spit over the fire, fat dripping and hissing. A flapping of wings came from above as a white crow descended from the branches, landing on Cullen's shoulder.

'I was wondering where you were, Rab,' Cullen said to the crow.

'*Rab watching, protecting friends,*' Rab squawked, then hopped from Cullen's shoulder to the pile of guts and offal that had been stripped from the hare. He pecked noisily.

'But the love of slime and foul things drew you back to us,' Cullen observed.

'*All must eat*,' the bird croaked as it swallowed an eyeball.

'Fair point,' Cullen said.

The dead can't eat, Drem thought, his mind filling with his father, Olin, and Sig, grief a wave rising within him, whipped high by the winds of exhaustion. His body ached, everywhere, a thousand cuts and bruises from the fight at the mine, and from before that. He raised a hand to his throat, rubbed at the scar where he'd been hung from a tree in his courtyard, twice. A memory of Fritha's face. Sweet, kind Fritha, with her blue eyes and freckles, a face he had trusted. Thought he'd begun to love.

He didn't feel like that now.

I hate her, will see her dead for what she's done.

A deep anger uncoiled in his chest, buried deep beneath the pain of loss and exhaustion of the last few ten-nights, distant but never gone. Much of the anger was aimed at himself, at his stupidity for staying, for the choices he'd made, choices that had led to his father's death, the loss of the Starstone Sword, the death of Sig.

The enormity of it all threatened to engulf him.

'Drem, catch,' a voice called out, snapping him from his reverie. Cullen had thrown something to him. Instinctively, Drem caught it, a long bundle. It was his sword, still in its scabbard and belt.

My father's sword, mine now. He looked at the worn leather hilt and scabbard, drew it a little, stared at the four-pointed star carved into the blade, just below where it met the cross-guard. *My da, a warrior of the Order of the Bright Star.*

So much of his world had changed in such a short time; he was still reeling upon the shifting ground of his life.

'Come on,' Cullen said, drawing his own sword from the scabbard at his hip.

'What, are they near?' Drem asked, panic whispering in his belly as his eyes searched the shadows.

'No, lad,' Cullen said with a grin, though he was younger than Drem. 'The sword dance, while our supper's cooking.' He paused, looked more serious for a moment. 'I've known grief,' he said, 'know what it can do to you, here.' He tapped a finger to his temple. 'I can see it in you now. The sword dance always helped me, mayhap it'll help you, too.'

The sword dance. Traditional training for the Order. Drem had rarely touched a sword in his twenty-one summers of life. While a trapper's life required being intimately accustomed to the use of spear, knife and axe in order to survive in the wild, a sword was a warrior's weapon, used to fight other warriors. There weren't many warriors to be found in the great wild of the Desolation and Bonefells. Only four or five moons had passed since Olin had first introduced Drem to a sword and begun to teach him the rudiments of its use. Since then Drem had killed with it. A terrible knowledge, one that he felt deep in his bones, an aching sadness that weighed upon him. Drem hated to fight, he disliked the use of violence. But these were violent times, and as his da had said, better to be the one that lives than the one that dies.

With a sigh, Drem followed Cullen to a clear space. Keld looked up from the fire-pit to watch them.

'Stooping falcon,' Cullen said, raising his sword two-handed above his head.

Drem drew his own blade, dropping the scabbard in the snow, sending long, distended shadows stretching across the glade.

Stooping falcon, he heard his father's voice whisper in his head.

Drem licked grease from his fingers; the weight of a hot meal in his belly spread some warmth through him. He blew a long breath out, savouring the feeling. Beside him Cullen smacked his lips and Keld threw a bone to Fen, who plucked it from the air and crunched it into splinters.

'I can't believe Sig's gone,' Cullen whispered, staring at the flames. Drem saw a tear cutting a line through the dirt and grime on Cullen's face. 'All my life she's seemed immortal, solid as the stone and timber of Dun Seren. She was a legend even before joining with my great-grandfather to found the Order.' He bowed his head.

Keld grunted something as he sat with a whetstone, five or six knives laid out before him, as well as three hand-axes and his sword.

'*Poor Sig*,' Rab cawed mournfully from a branch above them.

'I'll take Gulla's head and drink mead from his boiled skull while I stand upon a mound of his dead half-breeds and aco- lytes,' Cullen snarled. Drem was learning that Cullen was not one to hide his feelings, whatever they were.

'*Rab will peck Gulla's other eye out*,' Rab cawed.

Cullen smiled up at the white crow.

'Aye, lad, Sig was the best of us,' Keld said quietly. 'More than that, she was my friend, saved my life more times than I can remember.' He paused and spat on the fire. 'She'll be sorely missed.' A silence fell amongst them, filled with the grate of whetstone on steel, the crackling of flames, the creak and scrape of branches. 'You'll have your vengeance, my friend,' Keld said, eyes fixed on the flames of the fire. Drem didn't think that the huntsman was talking to him or Cullen.

'I'm sorry,' Drem whispered.

Keld and Cullen just stared at Drem.

'For sending my message to Dun Seren, bringing both of you and Sig here.' He put his head in his hands. 'I wish it had been me that died, not Sig. Wish I'd left when my da said we should run, wish I'd never laid eyes on Fritha. If not for me, my father would still be alive, Sig, too.'

'You didn't kill Olin or Sig,' Keld grunted. 'It was that winged bastard Gulla and his brood.'

'But if—'

'No,' Keld snapped. 'Everything's easy looking back at the path you've trod, and it's a fool's game to try.' He looked up from the blade in his lap, eyes fixing Drem. There was something wild in his gaze, untamed. 'You've no guilt or shame in this, Drem. Think on this: what would be happening now if we hadn't witnessed that foul ceremony last night?'

Drem frowned, thinking about that. 'Gulla would be transformed, still. A Revenant, Fritha called him.'

'They wouldn't be needing to spend half a day burying their dead, or torching them, and that's a fact,' Cullen said.

'*Cullen and Keld are mighty warriors,*' Rab muttered. '*And Drem,*' the crow added, bobbing his head at Drem.

Is that crow trying not to hurt my feelings?

'Aye, true enough,' Keld agreed. 'Gulla turned some of his acolytes into the same corruption as him,' he said thoughtfully. 'This is part of the Kadoshim's plan, part of the Long War. So, I'll ask you again, Drem, what would be happening now?'

'He'd be raising his army,' Drem told them. 'Sig said the Kadoshim are too few to win the war against the Ben-Elim, that they need numbers, warriors.'

'That's right,' Keld said, 'and their acolytes are not enough. They've been experimenting at that mine, using dark magic to make those Feral beast-men, and now these new creatures, Revenants. Once Gulla has what he needs, he'll fall upon the Banished Lands like a plague.'

Drem shook his head. Part of him had known this, but in the madness of battle, the grief at losing Sig and the following exhaustion of flight, the weight of it had not settled in his mind. It was starting to make sense now.

'Without you, we would not have known anything about it,' Cullen said, squeezing Drem's shoulder.

'Aye. Long have we searched for Gulla, High Captain of

the Kadoshim. He is second only to Asroth, and you led us to him. You've given mankind a chance,' Keld said. 'Course, they may still catch us and leave us bleeding out in the snow, or those Feral things might end up gnawing on our bones and sucking out our marrows, though I'll take a few of them with us before I'll let that happen.' Keld patted his axe lovingly, face twisted in a maniacal grin. 'But at least we have a chance now, and that's because of you. Olin would be proud.'

Drem felt a flare of warmth in his chest at that, though edged with the grief that every memory of his da brought with it.

'Though he wouldn't be so proud of that,' Keld said, nodding at Drem's seax.

'What?' Drem said, putting a hand on the bone-hilted knife at his belt.

'Oh, dear Elyon above,' Cullen said.

'Can you even take it from its scabbard?' Keld asked.

Drem tried, but it was stuck. He looked closer, saw blood had crusted black on the scabbard, thick where the bone hilt met leather. He tugged and twisted the seax free. It was a big knife, more like a short-sword, as long as his forearm, the blade thick and single-edged, curving on the sharp side to a tapered point.

'Ach,' Keld said with a disgusted twist of his lips. 'You should have a ten-night on latrine duty at Dun Seren for that.'

Shamefaced, Drem set to scouring the blade clean, taking a pumice stone and oil from a pouch on his belt. There were new notches in the blade, testament to the battle at the mine. Blood had congealed in the pits of the steel. Drem scraped it away, scrubbing hard with the pumice.

'Can I see that?' Cullen asked beside him.

Drem passed him the seax. The hilt was worn and smooth from Drem's grip, a perfect fit for his fist.

Cullen hefted the weapon, noting the weight, gave it a twirl in his fist, firelight gleaming red. Then he looked closer at the blade, with Keld leaning in as well. Cullen passed the seax to the huntsman.

'Did Olin forge this?' Keld asked.

'Aye, he did,' Drem said. He remembered his da in the smithy at Kergard during their first winter in the Desolation. That had been five years ago.

Keld drew his thumb along the blade's edge, blood welled. He let a few drops land on the flat and smeared them in. '*Nochtann*,' he said, and the steel of the blade seemed to shimmer and ripple.

Drem blinked; carved runes were winking into life along the blade. He leaned forwards, staring.

'Where did they come from?' Drem muttered.

'They've always been there.' Cullen smiled.

'Aye, lad,' Keld said. 'Olin put them there, when he forged it.'

'How? Why have I never seen them?'

'We learn more than swordcraft at Dun Seren,' Keld said with a wink.

'I haven't, yet,' Cullen said sullenly.

Drem shook his head. He'd had a lot to come to terms with over the last couple of moons, foremost of which was the fact that there was much more to his da than he had ever known. It still hurt that Olin had kept so much hidden from Drem, but he knew it had been to protect him. Only when he had helped his father forge the Starstone Sword had he seen the depth of Olin's mystery; he'd carved runes and cast spells of power over the new-forged blade. It had been quite a shock.

'I've learned my letters, but I can't read that,' Drem said. 'I don't understand. What language is it? What does it say?'

'It's the first tongue,' Keld said, 'spoken once by giants and men alike, but now you'd call it Giantish. It says *dilis cosantoir.* Faithful protector.'

My da tried to protect me his whole life. And even now, from the grave, his protective hand lingers.

Drem felt his eyes mist and, for a moment, almost sensed that his father was sitting beside him at the campfire.

'They are more than words,' Keld said. 'That blade will never break, and I'm guessing it's never needed much sharpening.' He gave the seax back to Drem.

'Now that you mention it, no, it doesn't,' Drem said. He looked at the seax with a sense of wonder, and as he watched, the runes faded and disappeared. He cast his whetstone along its edge a few times, but that was all it needed, then set to cleaning the scabbard of dried blood. After that he worked on the hand-axe at his belt, the misery that had settled upon him during the day's journey a little eased by Keld and Cullen's words, and by the thought of his da.

The three men settled into a companionable silence. Hammer the giant bear sat and then lay down. Within heartbeats she was snoring like an avalanche in the Bonefells.

'How long until we reach Dun Seren?' Drem asked.

Keld rubbed a hand over his newly shaved head, a ruse both the huntsman and Cullen had used to infiltrate the acolytes at the starstone mine.

'Took us two ten-nights to get here,' he muttered, 'but it'll take us longer going back, using the forests and Bonefells to hide us from anyone tracking.'

The thought of Kadoshim and Feral beast-men sent a shiver through Drem. Last night's fight had a dreamlike quality to it, parts of it blurred and ethereal, other parts too vivid and blood-bright. He shook the thoughts away, fingers reaching to his neck, searching for the drumbeat of his heart, which always gave him a sense of calm.

'Whatever it takes, we must get back to Dun Seren,' Keld said. 'Our High Captain Byrne must hear of all that's happened. Gulla, Revenants, Feral beasts, a Starstone Sword.'

'Aye,' Cullen agreed. 'And she must be told about Gunil.'

'Gunil?' Drem said.

'Aye,' Keld grunted. 'The giant that fought for Gulla. He

belonged to the Order once, was brother to Varan, the giant lord of the Jotun Clan. Varan was killed over sixteen years ago and Gunil was thought to have been slain, too.' Keld was silent a moment, lost in thought. 'Gunil and Sig were . . . close.'

And Sig fought him at the mine. That must have hurt her. Drem felt the spark of a cold anger in his gut, another wrong that needed to be put right. He put Gunil on the list of those he would make answer for their deeds.

'Why does he fight for Gulla?' Drem asked.

Keld shrugged. 'He was always . . . guarded, secretive. But I never suspected him of being a traitor.' He grated his teeth and patted his axe. 'It's something he'll have to answer to my axe for.'

'We have to reach Dun Seren,' Drem said. 'We cannot fail.'

'Aye,' Keld agreed. 'I've been thinking the same thing. Rab, I want you to set wing for Dun Seren. Tell Byrne what has happened, about Sig, and what we've seen. And tell her to send a few swords out to meet us. We'll probably need all the help we can get.'

'*Rab can't go*,' the crow squawked, sounding horrified. '*Rab watching you, Rab protecting you.*'

'And a fine job you've been doing,' Cullen said. 'But it's more important that Byrne knows what's happening.'

'*Rab know.*' The bird's head bobbed. '*But Rab not want to leave friends.*'

'Come back to us when you've spoken to Byrne,' Cullen said. 'Lead those she sends to help us.'

'*Yes, Rab will bring help*,' the crow cawed, sounding somewhat appeased.

'Good,' Keld said. 'Leave in the morning, as soon as the sun rises.'

Drem woke to the gentle sensation of snow falling upon his face. He sat up, pushing off one of the thick cloaks he'd packed when they had stopped briefly at his hold. Dawn was settling about them, darkness shifting to grey. Hammer was gone, and Keld's bed mat was empty, the huntsman nowhere to be seen, but Cullen was curled and snoring beneath a bearskin cloak. Rab was roosting beside the red-haired warrior, his head tucked under a wing. As Drem stood and stretched, a myriad of aches clamouring for his attention, the crow poked his head out from under his wing and studied Drem with a bright, intelligent eye.

'Rab remember Olin,' the bird said. 'Olin kind to Rab.'

Drem blinked at that; the thought of his father talking to crows was a strange one.

Though it shouldn't be, not after all I've learned of him.

'He was kind to me, too,' Drem said.

Keld appeared from the trees, his wolven-hound a blurred shadow deeper within the forest.

'No sight or smell of any pursuit. Still, we should be away.' Keld nudged Cullen with his boot and tutted. 'He's a good lad to have at your back in a scrap, but he'd sleep and snore his way through the world's ending.'

'I'm wide awake,' Cullen's muffled voice came from beneath his cloak. 'Just resting my eyes.'

'Rab, you should be for Dun Seren, now.'

'Rab go search first, make sure friends are safe from Kadoshim.'

'Aye, go on then.'

They broke camp as Rab flew into the canopy above, were saddled and ready to go by the time the white crow returned to them.

'Rab see nothing behind,' the bird cawed.

'Good,' Keld said. 'Be on your way, then.' He looked into the trees behind them, sniffed. 'And fly fast.'

Cullen sat up and threw the crow something – a remnant saved from last night's meal. The crow caught it with a snap of his beak.

'Farewell, Rab's friends,' the crow squawked as he flapped into the air, spiralled higher and disappeared through the branches above, the sky a snow-glare beyond.

'Let's be off, then,' Keld said.

Drem stamped his feet and rubbed his gloved hands to-gether, then climbed into his saddle. With a clink of harness the three men set off into the snow.

CHAPTER TWO

RIV

Riv sped through the sky, wings beating, wind ripping tears from her eyes, the joy of it bubbling in her chest. She passed through a bank of cloud, whooping as she overtook a flock of geese.

I am free up here, away from the world and its turmoil. Here all is so simple and clean. A moment's thought, and her wings were snapping in tight to her body and suddenly she was looping and diving, away from the clouds and the dull gleam of the sun, down, towards an endless canopy of green. She flew back, towards a range of hills cloaked beneath the immeasurable green of Forn Forest, ancient trees rising up to meet her. A little closer and a gap in the forest became visible, a road growing clearer, upon it small figures on horseback riding towards her.

Her sharp eyes counted a dozen riders, amongst them the distinctive shape of her friend, Jost, tall and thin, and not the greatest figure on horseback.

He looks like a sack of grain tied to the saddle. Riv grinned.

She spotted another rider galloping well ahead of the others, a league at least, and Riv's grin widened.

Bleda.

Flying towards him, lower and lower until she skimmed the road, racing her own shadow, the trees of Forn Forest rearing tall either side of her. Bleda called out to her, but his words were lost in the roar of the wind. With a twist of her wings she decelerated and turned, diving into the treeline, the world immediately shifting to shadow. Twisting and turning, spiralling through winter-sparse branches, the muscles in her back aching as she demanded more from her new-found wings, the sharp sensation of scratches opening along her shoulders, one across her cheek. She didn't care, lost in the pounding of her heartbeat, and then with a burst of leaves and twigs and laughter she exploded back onto the road, right in front of Bleda.

He was an expert horseman and reined in, his knees moving, squeezing, bringing his horse out of a gallop as if it were a manoeuvre he practised a dozen times each day before highsun, but even though Riv didn't hear the words she saw the curses spilling from his lips, which made her laugh all the louder.

She hovered above Bleda, grinning as he frowned up at her, his sweat-streaked horse blowing great plumes of air in the cold.

'You should not fly so far ahead, it is not safe,' Bleda said.

'You should ride faster, then,' Riv answered, still grinning.

'Huh.' Bleda snorted and leaned in his saddle, patting his mount's shoulder. 'My mare is fast, but she is not the wind.'

'I am, though,' Riv said.

'Aye,' Bleda agreed, 'you are as fast as the wind.' He smiled then, his normally impassive face yielding to the assault of her smiles. 'How does it feel to fly so fast? The gallop, it sets my heart free, so to fly as you can . . .' He shook his head with envy.

'It is wonderful,' she agreed, a pulse of her wings as she descended, feet touching gently upon the ground.

'You are doing much better,' Bleda commented. 'I remember the first time, you almost broke your knees.' He laughed at the memory, swaying in his saddle.

It had hurt; Riv had returned from her first flight, ecstatic from the experience, but she had misjudged the speed of her landing and ended up a crumpled heap on the floor, spikes of pain jolting through her legs. Still, she had had much to come to terms with in little time. All her life she had just wanted to be a warrior, to join the elite White-Wings of Drassil and serve the Ben-Elim and their holy cause. With the coming of her wings all had changed, not least the fact that she must be a half-breed, which meant there was a death sentence hanging over her head. None of that dampened the joy of flying, though.

'I can understand the joy you feel, and the freedom,' Bleda said, straightening and wiping a tear of laughter from his eye. 'But you should still stay closer. You are not the only one in the Banished Lands with wings. And you have enemies.'

'I do.' Memories of Kol's scarred, handsome face, blond hair bound tight, white wings arching behind him, slaying Israfil, the Lord Protector of the Ben-Elim. Then turning his blade upon Riv's mam as she tried to protect her. Riv could still see her mam's lifeless eyes, glazed and vacant, felt a physical pain in her chest as the image wormed its way through her.

I swear I'll take his head.

'Even if I flew closer, what could you do, if I were attacked by Ben-Elim in the air?' Riv shrugged.

Bleda patted the double-curved bow that sat in a leather case strapped to his saddle, fingertips brushing the feathers of a bundle of arrows in a quiver harnessed beside the bow.

'I can do a lot,' he said, no trace of pride or braggart about him, just a flat statement of the truth.

Riv didn't doubt it, having seen him in action.

'I shall fly closer, then,' Riv said with a shy smile and dip of her head. 'But, in the meantime, I'm hungry, so let's eat something while we wait for the others.'

'They were right behind me,' Bleda said, frowning as he twisted in his saddle to look back along the road that snaked its way through the hills.

'You were over a league ahead of them.' Riv snorted. 'They'll be a while yet.' She took the bridle of Bleda's mount and led them to a patch of grass on the roadside shaded by towering trees, the ground thick with purple heather and thyme. They rooted through Bleda's saddlebags and sat with a loaf of bread, a round of cheese and a skin of cold spring water. A companionable silence settled between them, Riv taking a long draught of water and watching Bleda eat.

He broke a small piece of bread from the loaf, set it to one side and pulled a little eating knife from his belt, cutting a slice of cheese and placing it neatly on the bread, then with obvious pleasure ate it. She smiled to herself, thinking how once not so long ago she had thought of Bleda as cold-faced and cold-hearted, his dark skin and almond-shaped eyes making him seem almost a different species. Now she hardly noticed any of that, except to think how pleasant he was to look at.

'What?' Bleda said, feeling Riv's gaze.

'You look like you're enjoying that.' She shivered and with a rustle of feathers wrapped her wings about her.

These things have more than one use, she thought, *though they do take a bit of getting used to.* She shifted her weight, releasing one wing tip that had been stuck beneath her backside.

'It's good,' Bleda said. 'Here, try some.' He went through the same ritual and gave it to Riv.

'Mmmm,' Riv said as the cheese and bread crumbled in her mouth. She leaned back, shifted a wing and rested an elbow in a patch of purple-flowered thyme. A gentle, earthy smell wafted up.

'I used to hate the forest,' Bleda said, looking around. 'It could not be more different from my home, the sea of grass. Once this felt suffocating to me.' He looked from the trees to Riv. 'Now, I am starting to like it.'

'You are so different here,' Riv said. 'Different to when you were at Drassil.'

'My cold-face, you mean?' Bleda asked.

'Aye. And other things.'

Bleda looked at her in silence a long moment, then drew a deep breath.

'My Clan are trained to mask our emotions from before we can speak,' he said, 'but that is not all that we are. The face of stone is for our enemies. No, that is not quite right; it is for anyone who is not kin, anyone who cannot be wholly trusted. We are taught to keep this guarded –' he placed a hand over his heart – 'taught to appear strong, to show no weakness. But there is more to the Sirak than the cold-face.'

'I see that now,' Riv said.

'We are a passionate people,' he continued, 'and amongst my kin I laughed much, until . . .' He fell silent, eyes distant. Riv knew what he was thinking about, that dread day when his brother and sister had been slaughtered, and he taken from his Clan by the Ben-Elim, to be a ward as surety against his Clan's rebelliousness.

Bleda took in a long, shuddering breath and shook his head, looked back at Riv.

'I have been at Drassil for so long, a stranger in a strange land. But look at me now; I cannot seem to stop smiling,' Bleda said. 'Even after all that has happened.' He looked at Riv with sympathy in his eyes. 'Amongst those we trust, my Clan will smile and laugh, cry and fight.' Bleda paused, thoughtful. 'But it is not a gift for all to see. It is a privilege, earned by trust.'

'You used to annoy me,' Riv confessed, smiling sheepishly. 'How nothing would bother or excite you. It's not normal.'

'You used to annoy me.' Bleda grinned back. 'How *everything* seemed to bother and excite you. That's not normal, either.'

They both laughed then, warm and genuine.

'Thank you,' Riv said and impulsively plucked a flower of purple thyme, thrusting it at Bleda.

'What for?' he asked.

'For saving my life. In Drassil.'

Bleda's expression turned serious. 'You're my friend,' he

said, gazing solemnly at her. 'And . . .' They sat like that a long moment, the silence lengthening, Riv feeling that Bleda was about to say something else. The world about Riv faded, shrinking down to Bleda's face, the gleam in his dark eyes, the curve of his lips. For one timeless moment she felt the urge to lean forwards and kiss him. A jolt of shock at that thought, a tingle of excitement mingled with fear.

Crows squawked, a raucous explosion as a handful burst from branches looming over Riv and Bleda.

Bleda looked over his shoulder, at the road.

'They will be here soon,' Riv said and Bleda nodded.

'And?' Riv prompted. She wanted to know what he had been about to say.

'And . . .' His expression shifted, a softening around the mouth and a crease at the eyes. 'This world would be a darker place without you, Riven ap Lorin,' he said, using her full name for the first time. 'And definitely more boring.' He took the flower of thyme and inspected it between thumb and forefinger, twirling it. 'Ouch,' he said. Then smiled. 'It's like you. Prickly.'

The sound of hooves grew loud, and then riders came into view, a dozen others coming up to them and reining in. Two young men were at the front, their short-cropped hair and black cuirasses with white wings embossed upon them marking them out as White-Wings – and Riv's friends. The tall and skinny Jost bumped along in his saddle, with the bull-like Vald beside him, his broad and muscled bulk as dissimilar to his friend as a mastiff to a lurcher.

From the corner of her eye, Riv saw Bleda carefully put the flower she'd given him into a pocket in his cloak.

Ten of the twelve riders were Bleda's warrior-guard from the Sirak Clan of far-off Arcona, oath-bound to protect their young prince with their lives. They were of a similar appearance to Bleda, all dark-skinned with fur-lined deel tunics and baggy breeches bound with strips of cloth from ankle to knee. Curved bows like Bleda's hung from their saddles, and short curved swords were strapped across their backs. Where Bleda's black hair was long and unruly, they all had shaven heads apart from a single thick-bound braid. Until recently Bleda had always had close-cropped hair, as had Riv, emulating the appearance of the White-Wings, Drassil's elite warriors. Riv brushed a hand over her own fair hair. It had grown since the day she had collapsed in the warrior field as her wings had begun to grow, and now it was almost as long as Bleda's. As she thought about it, she was surprised to realize that she had no urge or desire to cut it back to the White-Wings uniform style.

The Ben-Elim control me no longer.

'Finally – thank Elyon above,' Vald said.

'Aye,' Jost agreed wholeheartedly. He stood up in his stirrups and groaned, rubbing his backside. 'Arrgh, but my arse feels like Balur One-Eye's pounded on it with his war-hammer. Why do you have to fly so damn *far?*'

Riv just grinned at him.

One of the Sirak riders guided his mount to loom over Riv and Bleda, an older man, grey-haired and looking like a wind-blasted tree, skin dark and cracked with deep lines. Ellac, the captain of Bleda's honour guard. His reins were wrapped around a leather gauntlet strapped to the stump of his wrist, his right hand lost in some long-ago battle. He was frowning.

Riv felt her smile wilt; something about the old man was intimidating. A glance at Bleda and she saw his cold-face was back in place.

'You should not fly so far out of our range,' Ellac said to Riv, his tone flat, as if he were stating an uncontested truth.

'I was just telling her that,' Bleda said.

Thanks a lot, Riv thought.

'And *you* should not ride so far ahead of the rest of us.' Ellac turned his flat gaze upon Bleda.

'I just told Bleda that same thing,' Riv said.

Give as thou receive, Riv intoned silently from Elyon's Lore.

Bleda's mouth twitched.

'You should not disregard your kin so,' Ellac said to Bleda, holding his gaze, the hint of humour in Bleda's face nowhere to be seen now. He hung his head.

'The blame is mine,' Riv said, a pulse from her wings as they spread wide helping her to rise effortlessly to her feet.

'Not yours alone,' Ellac said. He sucked in a deep breath. 'It is over a ten-night since you awoke,' he said to Riv, 'and closer to a moon has passed since Kol slew Israfil. The world is changing, and we are still here.' He looked up at the silent forest about them, branches soughing in a cold wind, crows cawing from the shadows of Forn. 'When you awoke, you said we would make things right.'

'I did,' Riv said, remembering that moment, the rage coursing through her at the memory of her mam's death, of Kol's murderous rebellion. 'We will.'

'When? How?' Ellac said bluntly.

'Soon,' Riv snarled and burst into the air, wings beating powerfully, the blast of it rocking Ellac in his saddle. She rose quickly into the sky, a tight spiral.

'No, not again,' she heard Jost groan.

'Back to Fia's cabin,' Riv shouted down to them, and even as she sped into the wide sky she felt a weight settle upon her shoulders.

'I *will* make things right,' she snarled at the birds and clouds.

I just wish I knew how.

Fia's cottage came into sight, a wisp of smoke guiding Riv long before she saw the slight thinning of trees that marked the old woodsman's cabin. Her flight home had not been a good one, in her head. Ellac's prodding had set her to thinking about the future, but also about the past. A myriad of questions swirled through her mind, all of them impossible to answer.

Who is my father?

Her mam and sister had always told Riv that her father's name was Lorin, that he was a White-Wing warrior who had served under Dalmae's hundred. That he had died in battle during a campaign in the south, before Riv was born.

But that must have been a lie. My father was Ben-Elim. My mam lied to me.

She felt a bloom of rage at that thought, born of hurt, but frustrated and shame-tinged as well. Frustrated that she could never ask her mam the truth of it, and ashamed for feeling such anger towards her mother, who had died trying to protect her.

But she lied to me.

Did Aphra know? Perhaps, she was no bairn when I was born, already seventeen summers and a warrior in the White-Wings herself. Has she lied to me my whole life, too?

Riv pushed that thought away. All her life she had idolized her sister, respected her as the pinnacle of what she dreamed of becoming: a warrior, a leader, wise, respected and loved by all within her command.

Aphra, my sister, where are you now? Did you fight Kol? Are you languishing in a dungeon, or is your head on a spike? Do you need me?

A glance over her shoulder as she swept into her descent showed Bleda and the others riding close behind her.

Riv landed in a swirl of fallen leaves and forest litter, stood there in silence as the leaves settled about her.

A timber cabin sat there, half-wrapped in ivy, and about her were scores of small, stone-built cairns, the burial ground of her kin, of the countless half-breeds born during the last hundred years to Kol and the other Ben-Elim loyal to him. A terrible secret silenced by death.

Silenced by murder.

And that is what should have happened to me. My mam must have kept my birth hidden, somehow, or I would have been executed and buried alongside these little ones.

When Riv had first seen the child-sized cairns she had

thought the deaths had happened naturally, during birth. Fia had told her differently: that the Ben-Elim insisted on their offspring being left to die, their dirty little secrets hidden beneath cairns of stones.

The injustice of it set red spots of rage dancing before her eyes. With a deep breath, she mastered it, mostly.

Fia strode out onto the wooden porch and raised a hand in greeting. She was tall and fair-haired, and also a White-Wing, weapon-wise and as tough as they came, second in command to Aphra, Riv's sister. She held a baby close to her chest, a boy, and he was the reason that Fia was here, why she had left the White-Wings and was hiding out here in the wild snarl of Forn Forest.

Because that baby in her arms is a half-breed, just like me, and Fia has chosen life for him, not death and a cold stone grave.

Riv looked around her, taking in the cabin and moss-covered graves.

How many have come here on Kol's orders, to kill the seed he or his comrades have sown in so many bellies? Fia was just one more in a long list. Her baby is supposed to be in a hole in the ground by now.

Riv smiled at Fia, proud of her courage and strength to defy the Ben-Elim. That was no small task for a White-Wing of Drassil. The Ben-Elim were considered all-wise and powerful, treated almost like gods, respected and adored. Not so long ago the thought of defying them would have felt inconceivable to Riv, a terrible crime.

I don't feel like that anymore.

The thud of hooves as Bleda and the others cantered into the glade.

'It's time to talk,' Riv said to Fia as the dozen riders dismounted.

'We cannot stay here forever,' Ellac said.

Riv, Bleda, Fia, Jost, Vald and Ellac were sitting upon logs in a loose circle between the cabin and the cairns. Bleda's Sirak guards were either tending to the horses or lurking in the shadows, ever vigilant.

'We are safe here,' Fia said.

'How can you be sure?' Ellac asked. 'If you are here, then surely the Ben-Elim must know of it.'

'I have told you before,' Fia said impatiently. 'The Ben-Elim do not know of this place. They are too high and mighty to wish to know the details of what happens here, or even where *here* is. They only tell us to leave Drassil before any sign of our babies show, and to return when . . .' She glanced at the small graves.

'So how did you know to come here, then?' Ellac said.

'It is a secret amongst us White-Wings. The ones who . . .'

'Consort with Ben-Elim,' Ellac finished for her.

That is why Aphra told Bleda to bring me here, Riv thought. *A secret place, known only to her and a handful of others.*

But what if Aphra is being put to the question . . . tortured?

'Aye,' Fia nodded curtly.

'Huh,' Ellac grunted. 'Even so, we cannot stay here forever.' His eyes fixed on Riv.

'I know,' Riv muttered.

'Away from here history is being made; the world is changing.'

For the worst, I don't doubt.

'I said I would make things right,' Riv said, and she meant it, her words rising on a swell of anger.

'But what does that even mean?' Jost asked. 'What *is* right?'

'And once you've figured that out, how do we do it?' Vald put in.

Those are the questions I've been asking myself, a thousand times a day.

'It seems to me that you should be thinking more on how you are going to survive the next moon,' Ellac said. When Riv didn't answer, he continued, 'I am old and have no use for long words and fine-flowered sentences. I will speak the truth as I see it.'

'I've gathered that,' Riv grunted. 'Go on, then.'

'We are too few to fight the Ben-Elim. And I am thinking you will find it hard to be making new friends anywhere within the boundaries of the Land of the Faithful. The Lore of Elyon – the Lore that you have lived by, and that rules this land – declares you an abomination, fit only for the executioner's axe. Am I wrong?'

An abomination. Riv felt a chill shiver through her – part shame that not so long ago she would readily have called for the execution of any Ben-Elim or Kadoshim half-breed. She had believed Elyon's Lore unquestioningly.

And now I find that I am one of those half-breeds. Am I an abomination? Do I deserve to be slaughtered like a feast-bull? Is my blood polluted, corrupted?

'Careful.' Vald growled, resting a hand upon the hilt of his short-sword. 'That's my friend you're calling an abomination.'

'Are you an idiot?' Ellac snapped back, staring flatly at Vald. 'I am not calling her that. *Your* Book of Elyon calls her that.' He paused, looked from Vald to Riv. 'A person is made by their heart and their wits.' He touched his one hand to his chest and then to his temple. 'And by the deeds that they do. Their choices. Not whether they have pale skin or dark skin, wings or no wings. One hand or two.' A twitch of a smile threatened to crack his cold-face. He looked Riv up and down. 'I like your wings, maybe even wish I had some of my own.'

Riv found herself liking Old Ellac.

'You are right,' Fia said, 'Riv is named as an abomination by Elyon's Lore, as is my son.' She hugged her baby more tightly to her chest.

'So we are surrounded by a thousand leagues filled with those who would see you dead,' Ellac said.

'Sounds about right,' Riv acknowledged.

'We could take you to Arcona,' Ellac said. 'The Sirak would give you safe harbour.'

Riv looked at Bleda and he nodded.

This is his idea. Bleda must have talked of it to Ellac. They would take me to their homeland, put me under the protection of their Clan. They must know that would start a war. We were all there when the Ben-Elim crushed the Sirak, putting their heel upon the neck of Bleda's people. Riv felt a rush of emotion, that Bleda would risk so much for her, for their friendship. *And Ellac obeys his wish. A loyal shieldman indeed.*

'What, and invite a war with the Ben-Elim?' Riv snorted. 'We all remember how that ended last time.'

'We have learned from the past,' Ellac said. 'We will not be so easily defeated next time.'

Next time. Does he know something I don't?

Riv sucked in a long breath, thinking over his words.

'I could not do that. Would not,' she said. 'Win or lose in a war against the Ben-Elim, many of your kin would die. They will not die for me. I'll not have that on my shoulders, too.'

What should I do? All my life I have obeyed orders, followed where I've been led, my heart's desire to be a White-Wing, to do the bidding of Elyon's Lore and the Ben-Elim. Following, obeying, is so much easier than choosing, than determining what is right.

What should I do?

She felt a frustrated anger bubbling, wanted to scream with it, but settled for grinding her teeth instead.

What are my options? To run, to Arcona or somewhere else, to live a life in hiding? And what of my friends, of Bleda, Vald and Jost? Would they run with me? Should I let them? Wouldn't that be condemning them to a lifetime of misery? Should I choose to go back to Kol, swallow my pride and ask his forgiveness for the sake of my friends. Perhaps he has changed, now he is safe from Israfil's judgement.

Riv's mind was filled with an image of her mother lying in

27

the dirt a handspan from Riv, blood trickling from her mouth, eyes empty, Kol standing over her, his blade red.

'No,' Riv snarled, all thoughts of running, hiding or begging forgiveness evaporating in the flames of her anger. 'I will not run, I will not cower in hiding here, and I will not crawl back to Kol. He slew my mother.' The long years of obedience to Elyon's Lore and the Ben-Elim were snuffed out by one deed. And suddenly it all fell into place, the answer clear as her friends before her.

Kol must die.

'Kol is a poison that must be cut out. I'm going to kill him, and then I'll see what has changed with Israfil's death.' She stood, a ripple of her wings, as if she intended to go and carry out her words then and there.

And there is another reason I must go back to Drassil. To find Aphra, to save her, if she still lives, and if I can.

And to ask her if she knows who my father is.

She looked at her friends sitting around her. 'I'm not asking you to join me. I don't want you to; the only death I want on my hands is Kol's.'

Jost and Vald shared a look. Riv saw on their faces what was going through their minds: the ties of friendship, conflicting loyalties tugging in different directions.

They have spent their whole lives dreaming of becoming White-Wings, just like me. The thought of striking one of the Ben-Elim, openly talking about killing them, it would have been unthinkable a moon ago. And they have much less to lose than I. They don't have wings, will not be spat upon and executed as an abomination.

Her gaze shifted to Bleda, who was sat staring at the ground.

He is a ward of the Ben-Elim, held as surety for his Clan's obedience. It may already be too late for him, by his act of killing Adonai, but there is still a chance that he could make things right with the Ben-Elim and avoid dragging his people into a war they could not win.

I will go alone.

Bleda stood, eyes meeting hers.

'I'm coming with you.'

'No,' Riv said. 'It is too dangerous.'

Bleda blinked at that, a look of pain momentarily sweeping aside his cold-face, as if Riv had slapped him.

'I am not afraid,' he said.

'I don't think you are,' Riv said, 'it is I who am afraid. I fear for you. For all of you. I will not have your deaths on my conscience. I will do this alone.'

'You do not have the exclusive right of vengeance,' Bleda said. 'Kol slew my brother and sister, threw their heads at my feet.' He closed his eyes a moment. 'Even if you were not my friend, we have a common enemy in Kol. We are bound by that.'

'And don't think we'd just let you go flying off into danger without us,' Jost said, rising alongside Bleda.

'Aye. We are closer than kin,' Vald said. 'Riv, the winged shieldmaiden. You've guarded my back more times than I can count.'

Vald and Jost stood, a statement.

'I've no love for Kol,' Fia said, standing with them. 'He would have had me murder my bairn and bury him here.'

'I follow my prince,' Ellac said, though he did not stand.

Riv stared at them all, emotions swirling through her like a winter storm. Love, fear, relief, worry.

Footfalls thudded in the forest litter and one of Bleda's guards appeared from the shadows.

'People approach us,' he hissed, an arrow loosely nocked at his bow. 'One has left them, is coming this way. A woman, a White-Wing.'

A woman.

They all stood, Riv staring at the Sirak warrior. Fia burst into motion, running to the cabin.

'Shall I kill her?' the Sirak asked Bleda.

'No,' Riv hissed, fear and hope flickering in her belly. Bleda gestured for the warrior to hold.

Riv waited a score of breaths, then a score more, tense as a bowstring.

Now another figure was stepping from the shadows, a woman, short-cropped dark hair, wrapped in a bearskin cloak, beneath it a black cuirass with white wings embossed upon it.

'Aphra. Thank Elyon you live,' Riv said, taking a few steps towards her sister.

Something in Aphra's eyes made Riv stop.

'I am sorry,' Aphra said.

And then shadows swept across the glade, the sound of beating wings, and Ben-Elim were swooping from the sky.

CHAPTER THREE

FRITHA

Fritha stared at the blood on her hands.

She was sitting at the end of a pier, feet dangling, the slate-grey waters of Starstone Lake lapping beneath her boots. A sword rested across her knees, its hilt plain and leather-bound, sweat-stained, the blade a dull black beneath the gore crusted upon it.

Snow was falling, gentle as a sigh, flakes settling upon her stained hands. She watched as the snowflakes melted, fascinated as the congealed mess on her palm softened and leaked into each snowflake, spreading like a dark poison through pure white veins.

'Blood on the snow,' Fritha whispered.

A memory of screams filled her head, terror and pain, of shouting and cries for help. A tumbling cascade of memories racked her and she screwed her eyes shut, but still saw her newborn daughter's face looking up at her, pale and blood-spattered, eyes glazing. Fritha groaned and hunched over, rocking, clasping the sword in her lap as if it were the fragile, lifeless bundle she had cradled on that dread day.

The day her life had changed.

'No,' she snarled, and forced herself to sit straight and still. With a grimace, she pushed the memory back into the dark places of her mind. She ran a hand across her head, the stubble-growth of her shaved hair rough on her palm. With the edge of her snow-damp cloak, she scrubbed frenetically at the blood on the blade of the sword upon her lap, as if she were attempting to scour and erase that unspeakable moment from her memory.

It didn't work. Nothing ever worked.

Heavy footsteps on the wooden quay sent tremors through Fritha's body. They grew louder and stopped behind her.

'Gulla calls for you,' a voice said, deep and rumbling.

Fritha ceased her scrubbing, and with a deep, shuddering breath she sheathed the sword, then stood slowly and turned to face the giant, Gunil.

He towered over her, head and shoulders larger than the tallest man, a mass of leather and fur, a war-hammer slung across one shoulder. He bore the scars of last night's battle: a long, scabbing cut across his angular forehead and numerous rents in his leather armour. One shoulder was bandaged, his left arm slumped, fresh blood still seeping into the linen. It was a grievous wound, Fritha knew, for she had tended it, cleaned and packed it with honey and yarrow, then seared it with a white-hot knife. Sig the giantess, warrior and champion of the Order of the Bright Star, had given Gunil the wound, a spear cast that would have killed him had it been half a handspan lower.

'How is it?' Fritha asked.

'A wound,' Gunil grated, as if it were only a scratch, not a hole almost the size of Fritha's fist. 'I live.' The giant shrugged, a ripple of muscle. For a heartbeat his eyes flared, a hint of pain-tinged madness glimmering deep within, suggesting at a wildness that scared even Fritha, but then it was gone.

'Gulla,' Gunil repeated to her.

Fritha nodded, pulled her bearskin cloak tighter about her shoulders and strode past him, boots crunching on the shingle beach as she made her way towards the mining complex built on the lake's shore.

Dawn was recently come, a pale gleam behind thick cloud

that blanketed the sky. The ground was muffled in snow, to Fritha's right a row of open-fronted, barn-like buildings ranged in a line. The sound of hammering and sawing echoed. To her left a great pyre of heaped driftwood. A body lay upon the pile, a figure stood beside it, broad and squat, leathery wings furled tight across a muscled back. It was Morn, half-breed daughter of Gulla, new Lord of the Kadoshim.

Fritha's eyes lingered on the creature of two worlds: part human, part Kadoshim. Her dark hair was shaved short to her scalp, just as Fritha's and the secret many that followed the Kadoshim. Morn's head was bowed, but Fritha could see the streaks that tears had channelled through the blood and grime thick upon her face. Her brother, Ulfang, lay upon the piled wood, his wings wrapped around him, a sword resting upon his chest. He had been slain during the fighting last night, by Drem. Many died last night, including Sig. Fritha felt a twist in her belly at the thought of the giant, a measure of pride that her hand had dealt Sig her death blow.

Sig, vaunted champion of the Bright Star, just food for crows now, because of me.

Fritha had stared into Sig's eyes as she'd slowly thrust her blade deep, seen the pain, the flutter of life as it had left the giant. But the death had not satisfied Fritha as she had hoped it would; it had done little to fill the gaping hole inside her that screamed to be slaked with death and torment. Perhaps it was the way the giant had died that had marred Fritha's pleasure – not begging or screaming. Sig's last words had been a defiance, even if they were little more than a whispered breath upon her lips.

'Truth and courage,' Fritha repeated to herself, then spat on the snow as if the very words tasted foul.

All part of the Great Lie.

Morn thrust a flaming torch into the pyre, the falling snow hissed and steamed as tongues of fire crackled and writhed. Smoke billowed, in heartbeats the stench of burning wood and flesh mingled, swirling about the lakeshore, and Morn lifted her head and howled her grief to the snow-laden sky.

Fritha walked past Morn in silence, Gunil's heavy footsteps crunching behind her as they passed through an open gateway in a stockaded wall, entering the mining complex. Lines of smoke still blackened the sky, timber frames charred and collapsing as she strode across the complex, making her way through a sprawl of buildings to the open square where the ritual had taken place, where Gulla had been changed, transformed.

Become the first Revenant.

Fritha shuddered at the memory of it, feeling a mixture of fear and exhilaration as she remembered the giant bat being nailed to the table, the excitement she'd felt coursing through her as she'd held a blade to Gulla's throat, the jet of blood. And then Asroth's severed hand, the power of his blood.

We did it.

I did it.

The courtyard opened up before her; a fresh layer of snow covered the gore-spattered ground. At the northern end stood a thick-legged table, long and broad, pools of blood, bodies and dismembered limbs still scattered across it. They were testament not only to last night's battle, but also to the many moons of laboured experimentation and muttered spells that had been undertaken, the transformation of men and beasts into something . . . *more*. Fritha felt a flush of joy just looking at it, for she loved her work. To transform, to create.

One of the results of those experiments prowled past Fritha, something part man, part beast, a creature of tooth and claw, hunched and muscled, limbs elongated. A Feral being. It glanced at Fritha, paused as it bared its teeth, long and blood-crusted, nostrils flaring on its muzzle as it drew in her scent. A tremored growl as it recognized her and paced closer, dropping its head to her.

Fritha reached out and stroked the Feral's cheek.

'My baby,' she whispered, and the Feral pushed against her

hand, a moment's affection, and then it was loping away and disappearing into the shadows.

Fritha walked around a mound of piled corpses, acolytes fallen in the battle, limbs twisted together in a macabre embrace. Their bodies steamed in the winter cold. Too many to count, though Fritha thought over a score of their number lay there, and still more were being carried in from the edges of the camp, a trail of the dead marking where Sig and her companions had carved a path to the stockade wall and made their escape.

How could they slay so many?

Four against many – over fifty acolytes and a score of my Ferals.

Sig and her companions had wreaked such havoc amongst them last night: three men, a giant bear, a wolven and a talking crow. They had fled into the night while the giantess Sig stood and bought them time with her sword.

Fritha shook her head, could still hardly believe it, though the growing pile of the slain was a stark reminder that her mind had not exaggerated last night's events.

The dead tell no lies.

A crowd stood gathered about a figure beyond the table, tall and dark-haired, wings furled behind his back.

Gulla, Lord of the Kadoshim.

Fritha strode purposefully towards him, and shaven-haired acolytes parted for her. This was the first time she had observed Gulla clearly since last night; even he had not gone unscathed. A bandage wrapped his once-handsome, sharp-angled face, covering the ruin of his eye-socket where one of the Bright Star's talking crows had taken an eye. But it was the ritual which had marked him most: his whole body was transformed, taller, limbs elongated. His muscles coiled like rope about his frame, each striation and fibre visible, veins pulsing, and a shadow seemed to edge him, like a dark halo. Fritha's eyes were drawn to Gulla's mouth, which appeared wider, the hint of too many teeth behind stretched skin, and the tips of two sharp canines protruding from his lips. Across his throat was a raw scar, scabbed and weeping a translucent pus, where Fritha had cut his throat and slain him, all the while speaking her spells of blood and bone.

And now he is reborn, the first Revenant – a new creation for a new type of war.

'My Lord,' Fritha said as she reached him, dipping her head.

'Priestess,' Gulla said. Even his voice was changed after last night's ceremony. Where once it had been deep and resonant, now it was a whispered hiss, as if Fritha heard it inside her head, scratching within her skull.

Men and women stood about Gulla, seven figures gazing at him with something akin to worship. Last night they had been human, but now, like him, they were something more. Gulla had turned them, drunk their blood and transformed them into a new creation. Into a weapon.

A weapon that will change this world.

They stood about, all of them trembling like newborn colts, as if they had not yet learned to master their bodies. One of them took a juddering step forwards. He had once been Ulf the tanner, one of the lords of Kergard, a large town west of the mine, built upon the banks of Starstone Lake. Now he was Ulf the Revenant, one of the Seven, disciple of Gulla.

'Hungry,' Ulf hissed. The others behind him grunted their agreement.

Gulla smiled.

'We did it,' Fritha said, feeling a smile spread across her own face.

'Aye, Priestess,' Gulla said. 'You did it. I never doubted you.'

Did you not? Even when I held my blade to your throat? she asked silently. *I doubted myself, for so long. But no more.* She looked at the great table, stained black from the lifeblood of a thousand experiments, her eyes moving to the cliff face behind them, set with iron bars and shadow-filled cages. Caves burrowed deep into the cliff, home to a hundred more cages, where other of her experiments lived. And bred.

Soon they will multiply. Where there are ten, there will be a hundred, where a hundred, soon a thousand.

A dull thud resounded, a puff of dust as cage bars rattled and ground at the stone they were set into. A Feral glowered out from the darkness behind those bars, then wrapped its teeth around thick iron and wrenched at it, trying to chew its way through the bones of the earth. Blood mingled with saliva and froth as the Feral heaved and tore at its cage, but the bars held.

Fritha smiled at it, like a mother at a mischievous child.

Not all of my experiments have been so successful, not all of my children can be trusted to prowl amongst us.

Her eyes returned to Gulla, full of a new, unholy fire.

But you, you are my greatest achievement.

Thus far.

'There will be no stopping us, now.' Gulla grinned. 'They will head for Dun Seren.'

'They will,' Fritha agreed.

'They must not reach it. Our enemies cannot learn of . . .' He paused, fingertips brushing his fangs, caressing. 'Me,' he finished.

'They cannot,' Fritha agreed. 'It is too soon, too early.'

A gust of wind and beating of wings, and Morn swept down from the sky, landing amidst them with a swirl of fresh-fallen snow. Fritha tasted ash and ice.

'I will hunt my brother's killer,' Morn said, muscled shoulders hunched and twitching as she glowered up at Gulla, as if daring him to deny her.

Drem, you mean, Fritha thought, remembering the young huntsman who had cast the spear that sent Ulfang crashing from the night sky. A shiver of emotion rippled through her at the thought of Drem. He had been her neighbour for a time.

And my friend. The word sounded strange, even in the veiled darkness of her mind.

37

She had seen something in Drem's eyes when he'd looked at her. Not desire, or greed, or lust; that she was used to from men. There had been something deeper.

Friendship.

Something kind.

In Drem, Fritha had seen someone searching for a kinship, for meaning, and for a time she'd thought she was the one to give it to him. She'd hoped to win him over, to show him how life was not black and white, that there was more to the Kadoshim than the nightmare tales spoken of them around fires in the dead of night. But it was not to be. Last night Drem had tried to kill her, had sworn that he would.

All things come to an end, Fritha thought bitterly. *He could have been mine, should have been mine.*

But Drem had chosen a different path, one that would involve slaying her, if his words last night were anything to go by.

We all make our choices. And truth be told, I cannot blame him. I did cause the death of his father.

It had been Drem's father, Olin, who had found and forged the Starstone Sword that Fritha now wore at her hip. The taking of it had meant Olin's death.

But I spared Drem, when I could have cut his throat or had him carved into a thousand pieces. That should have counted for something.

'Ulfang will be avenged,' Gulla continued. Something shifted across Morn's face, part snarl, part smile, and she flexed her wings and bent her knees as if to take to the air and begin the hunt that very moment.

Fritha snorted. *Grief has clouded her wits. It will take more than one half-breed Kadoshim to put the heads of Drem and his companions in a sack.*

'But not alone,' Gulla said, a hand snaking out to grip Morn's shoulder. 'Gunil and his bear will accompany you, and Fritha will lead.' The Kadoshim's eyes shifted to her. 'Fritha, gather your followers, gather your Red Right Hand.' He paused, a twitch at the corners of his mouth hinting at a smile. It was the name Fritha had given to those acolytes and Ferals that she had led into Drassil, who had fought for her and helped her to cut Asroth's iron-encased hand from his frozen arm.

Morn glared at Gulla, mouth spasming, but Gulla held her gaze.

'I share your pain, daughter,' Gulla said, 'but you cannot accomplish this alone, and I would not lose you also. Fritha will command. Together you shall hunt them, and together you shall end them.'

Morn's mouth twisted, a growling sound leaking from her throat, but she dipped her head in submission.

'Will you not lead us, my Lord?' Fritha asked.

'Me? No,' Gulla said. He looked at the seven Revenants surrounding him, his firstborn. 'I am for Kergard; I have an army to build.'

CHAPTER FOUR

BLEDA

Bleda reached for his bow as Ben-Elim swept down from above, great winged silhouettes blotting out the sky, too many to count. Fia had disappeared inside the cabin, Jost and Vald were stumbling to their feet and running to Riv, who stood frozen, staring at Aphra. Ellac was standing, shouting orders, a curved sword in his one hand, and then a group of Bleda's honour guard were running into the glade and arrows were hissing from the shadows, up at the Ben-Elim.

There was a cry of pain and one of the winged warriors crashed through branches and plummeted to the ground, landing in an explosion of twigs. The Ben-Elim staggered to one knee, an arrow lodged deep in the meat between neck and shoulder. Before Bleda could blink, Ellac was there, sword rising and falling, the Ben-Elim collapsing back to the ground, blood staining the gravestones red.

A hiss from above and Bleda was diving at Ellac, smashing into him and sending them both sprawling as a Ben-Elim's spear thrummed in the ground where Ellac had been standing. Bleda scrambled to his feet, pulled Ellac up and drew his bow from its leather case. In a heartbeat he had it strung with an arrow drawn, searching for a target.

The Ben-Elim who had cast a spear at Ellac made that easy for Bleda. A dark-haired warrior, white wings and chainmail shirt gleaming in winter sun that shone in splintered shafts through leafless branches. He landed gently, a pulse of his great wings checking his descent. On one arm he carried a long shield, and with his other hand he was drawing a sword from his hip and striding towards them.

Bleda loosed without thinking, straight at the Ben-Elim's heart, but with a shrug of the Ben-Elim's shield arm the arrow thumped into linden-wood, the Ben-Elim not breaking his stride. Bleda blinked, surprise and shock mingled, drew another arrow, loosed. Again, the Ben-Elim caught it on his shield, though the impact rocked him back a step.

A dozen paces separated them now. Bleda felt a worm of panic threading through his veins. Drew and loosed, aiming low this time, in the same heartbeat Ellac was rushing with a wordless battle-cry, sword raised. Bleda's arrow punched into the Ben-Elim's calf, dragging a grunt from the warrior and causing him to stumble, lowering his shield. Ellac swung, the Ben-Elim deflecting the blow, a clash of steel, sparks as they traded blows, then another arrow from Bleda plunged into the Ben-Elim's throat. He stumbled back, choking and spluttering, blood jetting. Ellac's sword chopped into his skull and he collapsed bonelessly.

An impact in Bleda's back sent him flying, crunching to the ground, his bow spinning away. He tasted leaves and dirt, rolled to look up at a Ben-Elim standing over him, wings furled, a spear raised high, then he thrust, driving straight for Bleda's chest.

MOVE. For a moment he was frozen, unable to do anything except watch the bright steel of the Ben-Elim's spear speed towards his heart.

Then in a blur of feathers and mail the Ben-Elim was gone, Bleda was lying on his back, gasping like a landed fish. Feathers drifted down around him, some gleaming white, others a soft dapple grey.

Dragging himself upright, Bleda watched Riv rolling with the Ben-Elim, an incomprehensible whirlwind of limbs and wings. They separated, the Ben-Elim stepping away, making room to swing his spear, a flash of horror and disgust as his eyes took in Riv and her wings. Riv snarled and leaped, bursting through the guard of the Ben-Elim's whirling spear, and her muscled arms grabbed at him, pulling the Ben-Elim close as she headbutted him; a breath later, her knee was crunching into his groin. The Ben-Elim sagged, dropped to his knees and Riv grabbed his head in both hands, with a savage twist snapping his neck.

For a moment Riv held the limp corpse in her grip, veins bulging in her neck, nostrils flaring, then she let it fall to the ground. A scream from the glade, another voice – Vald? – bellowing for help, and Riv was snatching up the dead Ben-Elim's spear and bursting into motion, half running, half flying as she sped back into the fight.

Bleda ran for his bow, snatched it up, saw Vald was standing over Jost, furiously trading blows with three Ben-Elim. Bleda knew he only had moments: Vald's sole weapon was his short-sword, standard issue of the White-Wings. It was deadly in a shield wall with no space to swing or manoeuvre, but the Ben-Elim bearing down on Vald were armed with spear, shield and sword, and Vald would not retreat from his fallen friend.

In an explosion of blood, a spear-point burst through the chest of one Ben-Elim, Riv standing behind him, lifting him from the floor and casting him away like a skewered rat. The other two halted their attack on Vald, frozen for a moment at the sight of Riv, gore splattered, wings spread. Then Fia rushed from the cabin, sprinting across the glade, White-Wing shield on one arm, another slung across her back, short-sword in her hand. She thrust a shield at Vald, shrugged the other from her back and with a crack of timber their shields locked, both of them standing over Jost.

One of the Ben-Elim turned on Riv, but he fell with Bleda's arrow sprouting from his neck, the other Ben-Elim beating his wings, jabbing a spear at Vald and Fia and retreating out of range.

A quick glance showed Bleda that some of his guard still stood, though he spied at least four dead or dying on the ground. Silhouettes of Ben-Elim still choked the sky, swirling down upon them.

'With me!' Bleda cried, running to Riv and the others, Ellac and his surviving guards following. Jost was groaning upon the ground, a wound on his head had blood sheeting across his face. Bleda and his guards formed a half-circle about the fallen warrior, guarding the backs of Fia and Vald, their bows aiming upwards.

Can we survive this?

Bleda saw the Ben-Elim were carrying large war-shields, making arrow-work harder still, even without the snarl of branches that helped to deflect the flight of arrows.

The Ben-Elim have learned from their last encounter with us Sirak. I have never seen them bearing shields before.

'Come, winged ones,' Bleda hissed, 'and we'll make a song from your dead that will make even my mother Erdene proud.' Beside him Ellac barked a laugh, the tide of battle and blood sweeping away his cold-face. The old warrior snatched up a shield from a fallen Ben-Elim and gave some cover to Bleda and the other guards, brandishing his sword at any who flew close, and Bleda and his men let loose volley after volley into the sky above them.

A handful of Ben-Elim tumbled from the sky, splintering branches in their fall, but more continued to spiral down through the trees to join the attack.

Spears rained down upon them, the warrior to Bleda's left was pierced through the chest, transfixed as the spear-point punched deep into the ground. Bleda loosed, his arrow deflected by a branch and skittering away. Drew and loosed again, this time a Ben-Elim crashing to the ground, an arrow piercing his eye.

Then a noise filtered through the din of battle, through the snap and whir of arrows, through the screams and clang of iron and steel, the beating of wings.

A steady, rhythmic drumming.

Shapes formed amongst the trees before Bleda: warriors emerging, men and women, all with close-cropped hair, clad in mail and boiled leather, white wings embossed on huge rectangular shields upon their arms. They were advancing, clashing swords upon shield-rims. Bleda recognized faces amongst them.

White-Wings. Aphra's hundred.

And Aphra led them.

Another of Bleda's guards fell, a spear in the belly, blood gushing from his mouth. Bleda nocked another arrow, felt too few feathers left in his quiver, loosed at the approaching wall of White-Wings, his arrow punching into wood. Muttered a curse.

The White-Wings emerged into the glade, tightening their formation as the trees cleared, forming a circle around Bleda and the others, relentlessly marching closer. Bleda saw the gleam of steel, knew that when the White-Wings were close enough their short-swords would end this fight in moments.

'HOLD,' a voice cried out. The White-Wings snapped to a sudden stop, shields a solid wall around Bleda and his companions, separating them from the attacking Ben-Elim.

The Ben-Elim ceased their attack, some spiralling in circles above, others landing on think branches, silent as predatory hawks.

Aphra stepped out of the line, eyes fixed on Riv, who was drenched in blood, hovering above Jost, Vald and Fia. She alighted before her friends, facing Aphra, and Bleda saw a host of emotions sweep across the warrior captain's face.

'Riv, stop,' Aphra said. 'There need be no more bloodshed. Please, lay down your arms.'

'You brought them here, led them to me,' Riv said with a snarl, gesturing up at the Ben-Elim.

'Of course I did,' Aphra said. 'This is the Land of the Faithful. The Ben-Elim rule here, and for a thousand leagues in every direction. There's been a change of leadership, but they still rule. I want you back with me, and that means back with them.'

'They slew Mam,' Riv said, a tremor of emotion shaking her voice. 'Kol slew our mam.'

'I know,' Aphra said, 'and my heart is broken. But you still live. You and I, we are kin, we are all that each other has to hold onto in this world, and I'd not lose you, too. I've lost –' she paused, clenched her jaw for a moment. '*We've* lost too much already. I wanted to find you, bring you home. Please, Riv, come home.'

'Home? To the place where my mother was murdered?'

'She was not murdered. She fell in battle, died a brave death, as all warriors hope for.'

'She needs justice.'

Aphra sucked in a long, shuddering breath, her gaze shifting to take in Riv's wings, and she exhaled long and slow. 'I knew something was happening to you, to your back, but this . . .'

A ripple ran through Riv's wings, one dappled feather coming loose, drifting to land at Bleda's feet.

'Please, Riv, come home.'

A silence stretched, then a beating of wings from above. Bleda looked up to see the Ben-Elim parting, a winged warrior descending from high above. Blond-haired, handsome, gleaming in a coat of mail, a ragged scar stretching from forehead to chin.

Kol.

He landed gently in the space between Riv and Aphra, his eyes fixed on Riv. On her wings.

'This cannot be,' he said hoarsely. 'Dalmae, when did she—?'

'Do not speak of my mother,' Riv growled.

'Dalmae, your *mother*, tried to kill me,' Kol snapped a sharp retort.

'Kol,' Aphra interrupted, 'you swore to me, gave me your oath. Riv will not be harmed.'

'Aye,' Kol said, 'but I never knew this.' He looked at Riv with disgust. 'Elyon's Lore . . .'

'Which you have broken a thousandfold already,' Aphra hissed.

'I know, but *this*, we have spent a hundred years ensuring this did not happen.'

Bleda glanced at the cairns in the glade.

'How did this happen?' Kol continued. 'Who did Dalmae—?'

A burst of motion and wings, and suddenly Kol was sprawled upon the ground, Riv standing over him. 'I said, DO NOT SPEAK OF MY MOTHER!' she screamed, spittle flying, muscles twitching and spasming in her face and body.

Oh dear.

Bleda had seen that look before: Riv's face contorted, enveloped within a red rage, when she had saved him from a beating, single-handedly laying waste to half a dozen opponents. It was as if she became someone else.

'You dare,' Kol hissed as his legs lashed out, kicking Riv's feet from under her, at the same time his wings beating, lifting him gracefully back to his feet.

Riv half fell, but her wings pulsed and she regained her balance.

'You're not fighting an old woman this time,' Riv yelled as she hurled herself at Kol.

They came together with a concussive crash, muscle, bone and wings slamming into each other, the two winged warriors such a maelstrom of fury and speed that for long moments Bleda was unable to track what was happening.

They separated, Kol rolling on the ground, Riv rising into the air, spear raised high.

Ben-Elim moved above Bleda.

'No,' Kol snarled, palm raised to his kinsmen. Blood dripped from a cut above his eye. 'She's mine.' Slowly he stood, gripped the hilt of the sword scabbarded at his hip, with a hiss of steel drew it, raised it high in a two-handed grip. 'Come, then,' he called up to Riv, 'and have your revenge, if you can.'

'NO,' Aphra screamed, throwing herself at Kol. 'You swore Riv would not be harmed.'

At a signal from Kol, two Ben-Elim swept forwards and grabbed Aphra, dragging her away. Aphra's cry of dismay was blotted out as with a screech of fury Riv all but fell from the air, a beat of her wings propelling her, then tucking in tight as she drove downwards, spear aimed straight at Kol's heart.

The Ben-Elim stood motionless as the speed of Riv's dive sent fallen leaves and forest litter swirling around him.

He's dead, skewered like a rat in a barrel, Bleda thought. And then, in a blur of motion, Kol was no longer there, a simple sidestep, Riv yelling, wings stretching wide to stop herself ploughing into the ground. With a beat and contraction of wings, she turned in the air, landed feet first, stumbled, spear hissing through the air, still searching for Kol's heart.

There was a loud crack as Kol's sword sliced, Riv stumbling backwards, her spear chopped in two, one half in each hand. She looked at each half of the shaft, then with an incoherent howl launched herself at Kol, arms windmilling, both shafts striking at him. The Ben-Elim retreated before her, sparks flying as he deflected the spear-point, grunting as the shaft crunched into a shoulder, leaning back as the spearhead sliced through air, grazed his lip, the speed and fury of Riv's assault almost overwhelming him. Then, somehow, Kol was in the air above Riv, slashing down. Riv gave a cry of pain as Kol landed behind her, a boot sending her sprawling face-first to the ground.

Riv rose to her hands and knees, one hand still clutching half of the spear shaft. Bleda felt a fist clench and twist in his gut as he saw blood leaking from a gash in Riv's shoulder. Her wings beat, helping her turn, but Kol was upon her, his sword slashing, the spear shaft spinning away, a boot in Riv's face sending her crashing back to the earth. Kol stood over her, sword raised high.

'Give your mother my wishes,' he said.

Bleda drew his bowstring, aimed straight at Kol's heart.

A blow to his arm and his arrow fell to the ground, Ellac's boot stamping and snapping the shaft.

'It's a fair fight, my Prince. Kol did not allow his own to intervene. Don't dishonour her,' Ellac hissed, his one hand gripping Bleda's wrist.

'To the Otherworld with honour,' Bleda hissed. 'It's Riv.' He yanked at his wrist, but as much as Bleda struggled, he could not pull free; Ellac's grip was like iron. There was a frozen, terrible moment as Kol's sword slashed down at Riv.

'NO!' someone screamed: Aphra, leaping forwards and grabbing Kol's forearm, hauling him off balance. 'You cannot.'

'She's a wild animal,' Kol snarled, blood dripping from his lip, one eye purpling and closing. He shoved Aphra away, a buffet of his wings sending her stumbling and falling to the ground. 'She must be put down like one.'

'No, she's not,' Aphra said, weeping now, holding Kol with her eyes. 'She's our *daughter*.'

CHAPTER FIVE

FRITHA

Fritha paused at the treeline. The boughs were heavy and bending with snow.

The meadows were painted white, and beyond them rose the palisaded walls of Kergard, the most northerly town of the Desolation. Flames and black clouds of smoke belched from Kergard's heart, and on the cold wind Fritha heard screams. Figures moved on the palisade, pinpricks from this distance. One tumbled over the wall and rolled down a slope as something else leaped after it.

'My father has waited a long time for this,' Morn said behind Fritha.

'This is only the beginning,' Fritha breathed, a flutter of excitement in her belly at the thought of her long-awaited vengeance being fulfilled, at the sounds of Gulla and his Revenants building their war-host. Though the sounds echoing from within Kergard's walls were terrible, it was not death and slaughter that was taking place.

Well, death of a sort, but then rebirth, the people of Kergard made new. Made better.

Gunil grunted from above her, sitting upon his great bear, Claw. Both giant and bear were wounded, bandaged and in pain, but Fritha knew it would not hinder them. Behind Gunil another thirty fur-wrapped figures stood, acolytes that had followed Fritha from the south. They were hard men and women, all of them in some way scarred by the hand of the Ben-Elim, their own grudges and grievances setting them on the same path as Fritha. They had followed her into the heart of Drassil, where she had cut Asroth's frozen hand from his entombed body, and stood alongside her and fought Ben-Elim and giants. She did not doubt their courage or loyalty.

Together we are Asroth's Red Right Hand.

Her eyes met Arn's, a dark-haired, hook-nosed man with streaks of grey in his beard. He'd been with Fritha the longest, he and Elise, his daughter who stood beside him. Almost since the beginning, close to six long years since the death of Fritha's bairn. They had found Fritha upon her knees, weeping in a pool of her own child's blood. Fritha pushed down the memories, refused to entertain them, just acknowledged the years of hardship, the myriad moments where she had stood with Arn and Elise against the Ben-Elim, fought together, protected each other's backs.

'Come,' Morn said, 'I can hear my brother's voice in the wind, his blood calls to me. He must have his vengeance.'

Fritha looked at Morn.

She has always been mercurial, but has her brother's death unhinged her?

'Aye,' Fritha said and turned away from Kergard, walking around the bulk of Gunil and Claw and through the parting ranks of her followers. She looked west, where the forests that spilt down from the slopes of the Bonefells met the scarred plains of the Desolation. Her gaze shifted to marks in the snow at her feet and she dropped to one knee. Snow had been falling all night and most of the day, but not heavy nor deep enough to mask the tracks of a full-grown war bear of Dun Seren. Fritha dug a gloved hand into the snow, scraping the fresh layer away to reveal red stains in the ice beneath. She smiled and scooped up blood and ice.

Drem and the others, they have fled west, sticking to the woodland to give themselves cover. Wise, when a Kadoshim half-breed will be searching for them from the skies. But it will not help them.

Even if they were able to hide their tracks perfectly, Fritha knew she would find them. She rose and strode into the wooded shadows, where a score of shapes padded in the darkness, snuffling and growling. Her Ferals, the most manageable of her experiments, men, women and bairns taken from Kergard spliced together using blood magic with a wolven pack that had come south, fleeing the harsh winter of the Bonefells.

She crooned a command and one of the Ferals approached her with its crouched, loping gait. It was all muscle and patches of fur, yellowed teeth and claw. Fritha lifted her cupped hand with the blood from the bear to its muzzle and let it take a few deep, snorting breaths. Then it lifted it head to the wind, snuffling deeply, and howled. The other Ferals raised their heads and howled, too, a sound that echoed through the eerily muted forest, rising in volume and pitch until it enveloped Fritha's senses. It filled her with a deep, heartfelt joy.

'Ah, listen to them,' Fritha said, smiling at Morn and Gunil, who did not seem to share her pleasure at the sound.

The howling died out and the first Feral set off at a loping run, the others close behind, quickly becoming ethereal shapes in the snowbound twilight of the forest.

'Come, Morn, you will have your revenge soon enough,' Fritha said and set off after her pack, her acolytes falling into step behind her.

Morn leaped into the air, wings powering her up into the snow-heavy sky, and Claw rumbled a growl, moving into a lumbering, limping stride.

Drem, I will find you soon, you and your new friends, and then you will regret spurning the offer I made to you.

CHAPTER SIX

RIV

Riv sat at a table in the woodsman's hut, staring at nothing as Fia stitched a deep gash in her shoulder. Fia's baby, Avi, lay in a cot close by, snoring gently, oblivious to the momentous events that had happened around him.

Will Kol kill him, now, bury him beneath a cairn alongside his kin? My kin.

Will he execute me? Kill my friends?

Voices outside. Riv glowered at the door.

The battle was all something of a blur to her, a scarlet haze of blood and rage. That had faded now, replaced by exhaustion and shock, but she knew the red mist lurking in the dark places of her mind was still there, a hidden monster veiled in shadow. She had a vague memory of the world freezing at Aphra's announcement, Kol's sword hovering, his face twitching. She had felt her breath leave her, the adrenalin of the fight abandoning her, draining her strength and leaving her empty, drooping like a windless sail. Then hands reaching for her, lifting her, half-carrying her to the woodsman's hut. There was blood under her fingernails, on her clothes, her wings, the stench of it in her nose, the copper tang of it in her mouth. Her body ached, a score of cuts and grazes. A few deeper wounds, like the one Fia was stitching for her. She didn't care about any of it, hardly felt the pain of Fia's hooked needle weaving in and out of her flesh. All she could focus on was . . .

She is our daughter.

Nausea churned in her belly.

Our daughter.

Raised voices outside, angry.

Is that Vald? What are they doing to my friends? Bleda? Jost?

The anger stirred and she half rose from her stool, realized that her wrists were chained behind her back. She snarled, flexed her arms, knew that she could have snapped ropes, but chains . . .

They just might take me a little longer.

Fia gripped her wrist.

'Please,' Fia whispered. 'Wait. Go out there now and you will get us all killed.'

Riv stared at her, took a long, shuddering breath and sat back down, involuntary twitches passing through her wings, an expression of her mood.

The door opened and Aphra walked in, eyes fixed only on Riv.

She is our daughter . . .

Everything I know is a lie. Aphra, who are you? Are you truly my mother?

Dalmae was her mother, Aphra her sister, whom she had bickered with, admired, loved, fought with, teased, and worshipped more than a little.

Not anymore.

'I am sorry. *So* sorry,' Aphra said, a tremor in her voice. Tentatively, she reached a hand towards Riv.

Riv flinched away and Aphra's hand jerked back to her side.

Fia tied off her stitching, bit off the thread, dabbed in some honey and bandaged the wound.

'There is so much to say, to tell you,' Aphra said.

'Aye. Of how you've lied to me, all of my life,' Riv grated through locked jaws.

A tear welled in Aphra's eye, spilt onto her cheek.

'All I've done has only ever been to keep you safe,' Aphra whispered.

'Safe? That hasn't worked out too well,' Riv observed. She pointedly looked at the fresh-stitched wound on her shoulder, the mass of cuts and grazes all over her body, the blood, everywhere. 'Mam murdered.' She passed a slow ripple through her furled wings. 'Me an abomination, at the top of the execution list.'

The door opened again and Kol entered. A fresh wave of hate and rage swelled in Riv's chest at the sight of him, a new tension filling the air, the presence of imminent death a palpable thing. Two Ben-Elim followed Kol and remained standing at the door as he limped towards them. Riv felt a moment of satisfaction as she saw one of his eyes was swollen closed and mottled purple with bruising, a scab forming on his lip.

He stood before the table, looking between them. A murmur from the baby in his cot drew Kol's eyes. Fia took a step, placed herself between Kol and the bairn. Kol stared at Fia a long moment. 'Adonai's child?' he asked.

'He is. His name is Avi,' Fia said defiantly.

'He should be cold and in the ground,' Kol said, a sneer curling his lip as he stared at Fia's baby. 'You knew the price when you joined with Adonai. I made it clear to you.'

'You did,' Fia said, 'and I agreed because I was a fool, infatuated with Adonai, blinded by the radiance of you Ben-Elim. I felt I was being loved by a god.'

Kol smiled. 'In Elyon's absence, we are the closest you mortals will ever come to a god.'

His arrogance makes me want to vomit. Or kill him, thought Riv.

'So why have you not fulfilled your part of the bargain?' Kol asked, looking genuinely confused. 'You may love us, but consequences such as . . . this –' Kol gestured – 'cannot see the light of day. Israfil would have had our heads, and yours. He may be dead, but there are others amongst the Ben-Elim who share his puritanical ways.'

'Love changed my mind,' Fia said, eyes flickering to Avi and back to Kol.

Kol gave Fia a disgusted look and took a shuddering breath. His gaze shifted to Riv, to her wings. He shook his head.

She glared at him, tested her chains. They were infuriatingly strong.

'We have much to talk about,' Kol said. 'Sit down, all of you,' he muttered. 'And you, behave yourself,' he said to Riv. With a grimace of pain, he sat, facing all three of them.

'So, Aphra, explain *our daughter.*'

'It's plain enough,' Aphra said, her eyes dipping to the floor. An indrawn breath, shoulders straightening, eyes rising to meet Kol's.

His mouth twisted. 'That cannot be, I would have known –' His eyes narrowed and he snapped his fingers. 'When Dalmae took you on campaign to the Agullas Mountains?'

'Aye.' Aphra nodded.

'Lorin?' Riv said. All her life she had thought the White-Wing had been her father. She had asked Aphra to tell her tales of her da, so many times.

'Lorin was not your father,' Aphra said, looking at Riv. Aphra drew in a deep breath, as she had when Riv was about to leap into the icy waters of the river Vold, north of Drassil. 'He was my father, but not yours. Kol is your father.'

Riv just stared at Aphra, unable to squeeze words past the constriction in her throat.

'And Dalmae?' Kol said, leaning back with his arms folded across his chest. 'What was her part in all of this?'

'It was all my mother's – your grandmother,' Aphra directed to Riv. 'It was all her idea.'

My grandmother. Another new fact that felt startlingly, shockingly, wrong.

'We were on campaign in the Agullas Mountains,' Aphra

was saying, 'fighting an uprising of rebels who wanted the land of Tenebral reformed, wanted to split from the Ben-Elim's Land of the Faithful. My father, Lorin, was slain during an ambush. We were grieving, Mam and I, and at the same time I knew that your seed was growing in my belly, had known before we left Drassil. The grief of losing my father . . . I was a mess, felt at my wits' end, and it just spilt out. I told Mam everything. About you, Kol, about the coterie of Ben-Elim that you had gathered to yourself, those that shared your . . . tastes. The secret meetings, the mock campaigns you took us on.'

'There are many of us,' Kol said with a twitching smile, a quick glance to the two Ben-Elim standing guard at the door. 'And even more, now that Israfil is no longer around to take our wings or our heads.' His smile withered. 'But how did you hide it? Even amongst Dalmae's hundred, tongues would have wagged. Your belly . . .'

'Mother handed her command down, gave it to her second, and said we were taking my father's body back to his kin in Ripa. Which we did, but then we left and lived alone in the forests around Balara for some months.' She paused, looked at Riv. 'They were happy times. And then you were born, which was my greatest joy.' Her hand reached out again, hesitant, stopping at Riv's dark look. She sucked in a long breath.

'Then we went back to Dalmae's hundred, where she told them she had been pregnant with Lorin's bairn. They rejoiced for her, and just like that, I had a new sister and was no longer a mother. Except in here.' She put fingertips over her heart.

'Lie upon lie upon lie,' Riv growled.

'I had to,' Aphra said to her desperately, 'it was that or see you murdered. You just heard Kol talk of the agreement between us privileged few who were invited to partake of the Ben-Elim's greatness. We could love the Ben-Elim, but if we ended up with child, then we had to eradicate that . . . consequence, as Kol put it. That was no choice at all for me.'

'It is not much of a sacrifice to make.' Kol shrugged.

'You may have become flesh,' Aphra growled, 'but you are not acquainted with that quality that makes us human. Love. Bonds of family and friendship.'

Kol snorted. 'Whatever frail, pathetic emotion guided you in your deception, you did it well. I never knew or suspected a thing,' he said, blowing between his teeth.

'You could not,' Aphra said to him. To both of them she said, 'Else Riv's corpse would have been out there lying beneath a cairn alongside all of the others. I could not, would not, do that.'

'There is still time for that,' Kol said, shooting Riv a flat look.

'Like to see you try,' Riv growled, rattling the chains that bound her wrists.

'You are an abomination, Elyon's Lore demands your execution,' Kol snarled.

'Yes, but I am *your* abomination, the get of a sin that you have committed, for which the same Lore demands that you should be executed, too.'

Kol and Riv glared at one another, hatred leaking in waves from both of them, their malice towards one another almost a physical thing. Then he did something that took Riv by surprise. He leaned back and laughed.

'A fair point,' he said. 'Fortunately for me,' Kol continued, 'I am now as good as the Lord Protector of the Land of the Faithful, so I do not have to be so rigorous about maintaining a Lore that would see my head on a spike. You, however, are a problem. Lore or no Lore, there is no hiding your wings.' He took a moment to consider them. 'You could never pass for a Ben-Elim, they are dapple grey, not white, and of course,' he added, 'you're a woman.'

Riv blinked at that; all of the Ben-Elim were male. She felt abruptly so alone, a half-breed, but also the only woman to have wings.

The joy of flight is a blessing, but in all other ways I am cursed.

57

Kol shook his head. 'Even forgetting your wings, your gender and your . . . heritage, you have slain Ben-Elim, taken the lives of the Faithful—'

'As have you,' Riv interrupted.

'Ah, all this one does is keep pointing out my shortcomings. I am not perfect, true,' Kol said, shaking his head and spreading his arms wide.

Is he enjoying this?

'But you have slain *my* followers, out there in the glade,' Kol continued. 'There must be a price for that. And you are a problem that I can only see is best solved by taking your head and burying you in a ditch.'

'There are other options,' Aphra said.

'Yes. I could bury you in a ditch,' Riv said bitterly to Kol.

Aphra slammed a fist on the table. 'Shut up, Riv,' she said. 'You're not helping.' She took a deep, shuddering breath. 'I am *trying* to save you.'

'Don't bother, liar,' Riv retorted.

'Life is not as clear as you see it,' Aphra said. 'You would be hard-pressed to find someone who has not lied, at some point in their life. All lie, it is the why that is important.'

'Israfil never lied,' Riv said.

'And look where that got him,' Kol said.

Riv turned her glower upon him.

'It has been a dark, confusing time. Sometimes there is no easy or obvious path.' Aphra sighed, rubbing a hand across her forehead, squeezing her temples.

'Seems simple enough to me,' Riv said. 'Israfil was the Lord Protector, Kol schemed and murdered him. And my mother.' Her lips twisted. '*Grand*mother.'

'The impetuosity of youth,' Kol observed, 'when all is so clear, so easy to judge.'

'Riv, please see, please think. I have lived sixteen years with you, a path of joy as I have watched you grow, and sadness that I could not hold you, as I yearned to, always stepping aside, to be the sister, not the mother. But that was better than not having you at all, always so much better.'

'But you've lied to me.'

'Yes, I have,' Aphra said, 'to keep you alive. You would do the same, too, for someone you loved.'

Riv felt something shift in her then, the words crashing into her like a battering ram at the doors of her heart. A swell of emotion that for a change was not rage. The doors held fast, but something in them had cracked, a hairline fracture through her rage and resolve. She ground her teeth, angry with herself for feeling even a moment of weakness in her hatred, for the lies Aphra had told, the terrible damage she had wrought. Yet part of her understood, knew that there was a logic to Aphra's actions.

But it has all led to Mother's, to Dalmae's death. To Israfil's death. To changing everything.

'I hate you,' Riv said to Aphra. Then looked slow and cold at Kol. 'And I want to *kill* you.'

Kol threw his head back and belly-laughed.

'Tell me something I don't already know,' he said when his laughter eased enough that he could speak.

'The way forward,' Aphra said doggedly.

'Aye,' Kol nodded. 'As much as this is all very entertaining, I have a realm to rule, and it is not simple, believe me. You think *this* is complicated? You should try ruling the Banished Lands for a day.' He pinched the top of his nose between finger and thumb. 'Technically, I am not even ruler yet. I have not been officially named Lord Protector.' He smiled at them. 'But I will be. So, Aphra. You said that I have options. The obvious one is to kill Riv, Fia and . . . *this*.' Kol gestured with a hand at Avi in his cot.

'Do that and you will have to kill me, also,' Aphra said, and for the first time there was no diplomacy in her voice. Just a fact.

Kol stared at her, his face shifting to something cold and aloof. Calculating.

'I could do that,' Kol said.

'Aye. But you would have to kill my hundred, as well.'

'Yes. A difficult task, and one where I would take losses. But, again, I could do that.'

Aphra nodded. 'In doing so you would be killing an ally and losing a hundred swords that would stand beside you in the difficult days ahead.'

Kol dipped his head, an acknowledgement.

'And then there would be the matter of the parchments I have written,' Aphra continued, 'that will be sent far and wide, telling of what you have done, including fathering half-breeds.'

Kol's lips twisted, shifting to fury.

'You would threaten me?'

'As you did me, to join you against Israfil, told me it was in my interest to support you, that I would die if I did not. This is no different.' Aphra's hands didn't move, but Riv could see the threat of violence rolling from Aphra in waves.

'I did not threaten you. I told you Israfil would execute you if he found out our secret.'

Aphra snorted. 'It was a threat.'

Kol shrugged, dismissing the point. 'Where are these parchments?'

'Safe,' Aphra said, 'with people I trust. The first place they will reach is Dun Seren. The Order of the Bright Star would find it all most interesting.'

'You would jeopardize the war against the Kadoshim?'

'I would not care. I would be dead, and all that I love would be dead.'

'Humans.' Kol sighed. 'Always ruled by your emotions.' He drummed fingers on the table. 'And the alternative?'

'Change things.' Aphra shrugged. 'A new order, where the boundaries between Ben-Elim and humankind are not so . . .

fixed. That is what you are doing now, anyway. This would just be more obvious.'

'Yes, you have that right,' Kol said, looking at Riv's wings.

'You have carried out a coup, killed Israfil, taken the lordship of the Ben-Elim for yourself. You are in charge, now.'

'Yes, but it doesn't mean I can do *this*. Not all of the Ben-Elim are behind me; my power is not consolidated yet.'

'It will be. You have a thousand Ben-Elim declaring their support for you already. The rest will follow. You said yourself, now that Israfil is dead, more will be happy for your *new way* to begin. You and your kind will be enjoying the pleasures this world of flesh gives, having relations with humankind, as you have already been doing for a hundred years, but more openly. But there will still be consequences, there will be more bairns born, more than ever before. You cannot keep it all a secret any longer, or do you plan to kill them all?'

'No,' Kol said, 'but I was planning on taking the steps on this path slowly, a gentle slope into change, not a cliff-leap to jagged rocks and possible execution.'

'Better to just do it, get it over with and enjoy the fruits of your victory.'

He rubbed his stubbled chin thoughtfully. 'And there is Elyon's Lore,' he added.

'Is it really Elyon's Lore? Or is it the Ben-Elim's lore, fashioned to create a world that suited the Ben-Elim? To establish the boundaries that you wanted, the obedience you needed to fight the Kadoshim?'

Kol raised an eyebrow. 'Good point.' He smiled. 'Clever as well as beautiful.'

I cannot believe what I am hearing.

Aphra is proposing Kol change the doctrines that have ruled our lives for a hundred years.

But if they are a lie, made up to keep control, then why not change them? Why follow them at all.

'You change Elyon's Lore as you are changing everything

else,' Aphra said. 'You would not need to declare it to the world, just quietly remove those parts from the texts. What is it you have often said to me? People are sheep. So, you lead, and everyone else will follow.'

Kol inhaled, long and slow, then turned his eyes onto Riv.

'And what do you say to all of this, *daughter*?' he asked her.

Riv wanted to punch him in the face for that, though at the same time she felt some strange reluctance seep through her limbs.

Daughter.

He's my father.

And I hate him.

'What do you want of me?' Riv said, her gaze flitting from Kol to Aphra.

'That you refrain from trying to kill me, if I take those chains off,' Kol said.

That will be hard.

'To understand,' Aphra said.

'He killed Dalmae,' Riv whispered, sparks of hatred fizzing out of the fiery rage within her.

'Yes, he did. It was a battle, she died. My heart is broken for her loss, a thousand times over. But I would not lose you, too.' Aphra's hand reached out, touched Riv's leg, and this time Riv did not pull away.

Part of her understood Aphra's logic, knew that there was sense and truth in it, and now there was a part of her that wanted to hold Aphra, to hug her and squeeze her and never let her go.

But the other part of her wanted to punch, smash and stab something.

No, not something. Kol.

I just feel so angry, more than I've ever felt before. Kol was a hero to me, someone I admired, no, revered, respected as a warrior, a leader. Kol is nothing like the man I thought him to be. He is a liar and a murderer.

I can understand what Aphra is saying, how she has been caught in a place with no way out, has made choices for those she loves. For me.

And she's right, I would do much for those whom I love. But would I do anything, as Aphra has for me?

'What of Bleda?' Riv said slowly. 'Of my friends, Vald and Jost?'

'What of them?'

'They are only here because they have chosen to help me. They should not be harmed for that,' Riv said, trying to hold back the rage that she felt at Kol's indifferent response.

'They have made poor choices.' He scowled. 'Slain my Ben-Elim; that cannot go unpunished.'

'Bleda's oathsworn lie dead out there, too,' Riv growled.

Hurt Bleda and I shall break these chains and wrap them around your throat, make your eyes pop from your skull.

'Punish Bleda and you risk war with Erdene and the Sirak,' Aphra added. 'You would win, but how easily? And do you need a war right now, with the Kadoshim stirring, and your position needing consolidating?'

A silence.

'No, I do not need a war,' Kol conceded.

'People die in battle,' Aphra said. 'Afterwards there is reconciliation. Pardon them all, for the sake of peace, grant an absolution to all who have fought in these troubles.'

'Peace, absolution,' Kol echoed. 'My instinct is to exterminate all who have caused me grief, but there is much wisdom in what you've said. Aphra, for a pretty human, there is some wisdom in that skull of yours.'

Aphra said nothing, just looked at Kol.

'And you,' Kol said, turning to Riv. 'Would you cooperate? Not attempt to kill me? Swear your oath to me?'

Another silence.

All I have thought about is killing you. But I do not have to do it straight away.

'I will not try to kill you,' Riv said sullenly.

Not yet, she promised herself.

'If Bleda and the others are not harmed,' she added.

'Your oath,' Kol said, more firmly. 'I must have your oath, swearing fealty to me. Loyalty and obedience.'

How can I swear an oath to him? Bind myself to him? I would truly be giving up my vengeance. Turning my back on Dalmae.

But she is dead, gone, as Aphra said. And Bleda is alive, Jost and Vald are alive. But for how long?

'Your friends will thank you,' Kol said.

Riv drew in a deep breath, felt she was about to leap into a pit of adders.

'And my oath.'

Kol held her eyes a moment longer, then nodded to himself. 'Good,' he said. 'Then swear your oath, and seal it in blood.'

CHAPTER SEVEN

DREM

Pine trees thinned, a glare of sky and swirl of snow making Drem blink as they rode out of the twilight cover of the forest into a small clearing. Reining in his horse and twisting in his saddle, he looked back. Cullen dismounted and led his horse to a stream that frothed and foamed its icy way down from the Bonefells that reared above them, brooding guardians of the north. Keld was ahead, but he paused, too, with a click of his tongue guided his horse back to Drem. Fen loped after him. Hammer was somewhere off in the trees.

'What is it?' Keld asked.

Drem squinted and stared into the distance. For some time, they had been climbing steadily into the foothills that preceded the Bonefells, trees turning from oak to pine as they gained altitude. The cold, ice-laced air felt thinner, Drem's chest burning when he drew in a full breath.

'Not sure,' Drem muttered. Something had made him pause and look back. 'There,' he said, pointing.

A day and a half had passed since they'd said farewell to the white crow, Rab, and now they were high above the plain that Kergard sat upon. With a jolt, Drem realized that they were not far from the place where he and his father had once been attacked by a great white bear. He worked it out: only five moons had passed since that fateful day when they'd found a lump of starstone rock beneath the elk pit Drem had been digging. It seemed like a lifetime ago, and a different world. Certainly he felt like a different person. Drem's hand drifted up to the bear claw hanging around his neck. He'd chopped it from the white bear as it rampaged past him. Then his da had hauled him onto his shoulder and carried Drem to safety.

It feels as if Da's whole life was spent saving me or protecting me. He rested a hand upon the bone hilt of his seax, something about it comforting after what he'd recently learned. *In some ways he still is.*

'I see it,' Keld said.

A flare of red firelight, bright in the all-white, just a flicker far in the distance, then it was gone, cut off by a curtain of swirling snow.

'I think that's where Kergard should be,' Drem said, though it was hard to tell.

Cullen joined them, drinking from a fresh-filled water skin. He pushed the hood of his fur-lined cloak back, and looked up at the sky, snow dappling his cheeks. He stuck out his tongue, snowflakes landing and melting upon it.

'Ah, but I love the snow,' Cullen said. His red hair was starting to grow back in tufts and clumps on his head.

Keld just shook his head.

As Drem stared into the distance, more flickers of firelight appeared, scattered across the plain south of Kergard.

Keld was staring, too.

'What is that?' Cullen asked, seeing the flare and flicker of light on the plain.

'Kergard burns,' Drem said.

'Aye, and a dozen holds south of Kergard,' Keld added. 'Gulla is hiding no longer.'

Drem felt a frustrated anger radiating through him. There were people down there that he knew, had traded with, had lived alongside, and Gulla and his horde were murdering them.

Or worse. He shivered as he remembered Gulla and his Revenants.

'We could help them,' Cullen said.

'Too many of them, even for you,' Keld said, glancing at Cullen. 'But we can help those further south, by getting to Dun Seren and telling Byrne what is happening.'

'Let's be on with it, then,' Drem said, a sense of futility and frustration burning in his belly.

Hammer emerged from the trees, bending and snapping branches. She scratched a paw on the ground.

Fen growled, head cocked to one side, ears twitching.

'What is it, lad?' Keld asked, one hand resting on an axe-head at his belt.

Out of the snow and wind a sound reached them, an ululating howl, rising and falling on the wind.

'Wolven?' Drem breathed, knowing instantly that he was wrong. The sound was similar, but twisted somehow. Deeper, more frantic.

More howls, in the distance, yet not far away enough for Drem's liking. Shapes moving amidst the trees much further down the slope. The shadowed bulk of something bigger behind them.

'Ferals,' Keld said.

A hiss as Cullen drew his sword.

'What do we do?' Drem asked, wings of fear fluttering in his belly.

Keld stared into the trees. Drem, following his gaze, saw more shapes solidifying than he was happy about. A dozen, more.

'I think we can take them,' Cullen said, a fire in his eyes as he bounced on the balls of his feet and gave his sword a lazy turn with his wrist.

We are clearly outnumbered and cannot win.

'We run,' Keld said. 'Quick, help me with Hammer's harness and saddle.'

CHAPTER EIGHT

FRITHA

Fritha's breath was loud in her ears, her heart a drum in her chest. She was surrounded by snow and ice, but her leathers and furs were warm, her bearskin cloak a weight upon her shoulders, and she felt exhilarated by the thrill of the chase. She was close to catching Drem and his companions, she knew, the behaviour of her Ferals spurring her on. They were as excited by the hunt as she was, snapping and growling, some bounding on ahead up the steep incline, only returning reluctantly at her stern summons.

They're excited, like hounds scenting their prey, close to the kill.

'We are close,' Gunil said. He was striding beside her, Claw lumbering behind.

An ear-splitting roar echoed through the forest, sending crows flapping and squawking from branches, making Fritha and her crew pause in their tracks.

That was a bear.

'Best mount up,' Fritha said to Gunil, then without checking to see if he obeyed or not, she broke into a loping stride, her acolytes increasing their speed with her, the remaining Ferals bursting with the urge to run and kill, looking from her to the sounds filtering down to them, like hounds pulling on a leash.

A bright light was glaring through the treeline. She drew a short-sword at her hip, felt more comfortable with it than the

Starstone Sword, which she left in its scabbard, and barked a command. Her Ferals leaped into a sprint while she and her acolytes spread into a wider line after them, Arn and Elise either side of her. She heard the crash of Gunil and Claw somewhere behind.

Then she was bursting from the treeline into a small clearing, snow swirling, obscuring her vision.

The snow was churned, a mess of hoof- and paw-prints, boots here and there.

They stopped here, to rest, water their mounts?

Fritha turned a circle, saw flickering pinpoints of firelight far below.

Gulla's work.

Gunil and his bear lumbered into the clearing, the giant holding his war-hammer across his lap.

'They're gone,' he said.

He has a talent for stating the obvious.

Fritha gestured, and Arn and Elise spread wider, searching for tracks. Elise raised a hand. 'There.' She pointed. She was fair-haired, like Fritha, and of a similar age, twenty-five summers. Arn said they looked like sisters, which may have been why they had become so close, so quickly. That and the grief they shared. Elise was small-framed, fragile-looking to someone who did not know her, but Fritha knew better, knew the strength in her sinewed frame, but more than that, her strength of mind, more determined than a huntsman's hound.

Seeing your mother hung from a tree will focus the mind, or break it, Fritha thought.

Elise was pointing to bear- and hoof-prints that led into a stream, then continued on the far side back into the cover of trees, though the woodland grew thinner here.

There's still not much chance of tracking them from the skies in this snowstorm.

'With me,' Fritha called, her Red Right Hand gathering

around her. 'Gunil, Morn,' she shouted. Thumping steps, a draught of wind, and Gunil and Morn joined her.

'The chase is on,' Fritha said. 'They are running now, no thought for stealth. We are the wolven, they the elk, we shall run them to bay.' She paused, looked again at the tracks of the bear. 'They're fleeing up, into the Bonefells, maybe hoping to lose us in the snarl of the wild. They are wrong.' She gave a cold smile.

'*Anseo*,' Fritha called, and the Ferals stopped in their sniffing and snuffling around the glade and loped over to her. One of them whined.

'Ah, my children,' Fritha said, stroking one's gore-crusted jaw. 'You'll feast soon, on bear and horse and man-flesh. Now, though, we hunt.'

The Feral threw its head back and howled, the others joining in. Then they were crashing across the stream, bounding after the tracks. Fritha lifted a hand and her acolytes followed.

'Gunil, Morn, wait,' she said. 'Gunil, can you kill their bear? It bested you at the mine.'

'Sig is dead.' Gunil shrugged. 'We will kill it.'

'You are both injured.'

'We will kill it,' he assured her.

'Good. Morn, stay close.'

'I'll fly as I please, you wingless worm,' Morn snarled.

'You'll fly close, or Gulla will hear of your recklessness and disobedience,' Fritha said.

Morn's face twisted, a curt nod. Her knees bent, and she launched into the air, though Fritha saw she stayed circling overhead.

Good.

'Now, let's finish this.'

Fritha wiped sweat from her eyes and raised a fist, drawing to a halt, sucked in deep breaths and uncorked a water skin. Half a day they had been chasing Drem and his companions, ever up into the Bonefells, the tree-clad hillslopes shifting into narrow gullies, granite cliffs and shingle ridges. Her chest was heaving, legs burning with the exertion. She was no soft weakling – a lifetime of training on the weapons-field had honed her body to flint, and what had happened afterwards had honed her spirit to that same knife-edge hardness, but life with the Kadoshim was not one of outright military campaigns, and so her body was feeling the pace.

Not every day I try to outrun a Dun Seren war bear.

But they were gaining; drops of blood fresher, Fritha guessed from wounds sustained during the battle at the mine.

The ground was changing, rockier, less sure underfoot, so the fact that Drem and the other two were mounted was giving their quarry less of an advantage. The rocky terrain was also making it harder to track them, though.

She put two fingers to her lips and whistled, summoning her Ferals back to her. They seemed as fresh as when the day had begun.

The snow was lessening, glimpses of broken cloud and sky were appearing; the sun was sinking towards the horizon. Two paths stood before Fritha. A narrow ravine leading up into the mountains and a wider path that sloped downwards.

Morn alighted upon a boulder.

'Report,' Fritha said.

'They are in the ravine,' Morn said. 'It runs for several leagues.' Fritha had sent her ahead to scout the way, a test of Morn's new-found obedience.

'And this path?' Fritha asked, pointing at the one that sloped downhill. 'Can you reach the ravine's exit by following it?'

'It drops back into woodland, but yes, you can reach the ravine's exit that way.'

Good. A flush of excitement.

'Take ten of my Ferals.' Fritha called out names, summoning her most obedient children, the ones she knew would follow her orders, even when she was out of sight. 'You will have to move fast. Lead them to the ravine's exit, hold our prey there. We shall be close behind.'

Fritha drew her short-sword, signalling for her followers to fan out behind her as she set off into the narrow ravine. Soon the Ferals with her began to behave oddly. They'd grown excited, started snapping and slavering, but now they were hanging back, following rather than leading.

Drem, where are you?

Granite cliffs reared to either side of her, the ravine narrowed so that only three or four men could walk abreast.

It's a good spot to make a stand, especially if you've a giant bear to fill the hole. They should be here, fighting, making use of this bottleneck. Of course, they are not to know that Morn and my Ferals will be creeping up and stabbing them in the back.

But there was no sign of them. There was little snow here, the arch of rocks keeping the ground clear, and no soil or foliage to search for evidence of their passing. Then she saw movement ahead, figures shifting around a boulder. Something about them looked wrong.

Fritha swore under her breath.

They are my Ferals.

They were gathered around a shape, the distinct sound of flesh tearing echoing up the ravine to Fritha.

The outline of Morn appeared atop the boulder. In her grip she held the bridle of a horse.

Fritha ran forwards, trying to control the anger she felt that Morn and her Ferals had slain Drem and the others. She wanted him as a slave, or at least the pleasure of seeing him die. As she drew closer she saw her Ferals were gathered around two dead horses, their muzzles and claws red as they feasted.

Something's wrong. There's no bear, or people.

'Where are they?' Fritha called up to Morn.

'I was about to ask you the same question,' the half-breed called down to her.

'They are not here,' Gunil pointed out.

Fritha cast him a dark look.

'Stake the horse,' she ordered Morn. 'It will feed my Ferals later, but now we must continue our hunt.'

'*Anseo*,' she called, and the Ferals looked up from their feasting, muzzle-red. Some of them loped over to her, others went back to their meal.

'*Laithreach*,' Fritha growled, and the others pulled themselves from the horses' carcasses, reluctantly joining Fritha.

They retraced their steps, Fritha's Ferals given the lead. Soon they came to a spot where the ravine wall was overgrown with scrub and brush, the dark gleam of granite behind. The Ferals started snapping and whining, one scrabbling into the brush. Arn and Elise stepped forwards; Elise used her spear to dig and pull at the undergrowth. It came away, revealing a boulder, barring the path into a new gully.

'The huntsmen of Dun Seren,' Arn said to her, 'always with a trick or two when you think they're finished.'

'It won't save them,' Fritha said. 'Their horses are gone, all of them are mounted upon the bear. How long can it carry them, wounded as it is?'

Arn grunted his agreement.

'Morn,' Fritha called, and the half-breed took to the air, winging over the boulder. In a few heartbeats she was back.

'They went this way,' Morn confirmed. 'Moved the boulder to block our path.'

'Gunil,' Fritha snapped.

The giant dismounted from Claw, gave a command as he put his shoulder to the boulder. His bear moved up alongside him, pushing into the boulder, dipping its neck and putting its weight against the rock.

Giant and bear pushed together.

Nothing happened.

Veins bulged in Gunil's neck, a fresh bloom of blood

appearing in the bandage about his shoulder. The bear shook, straining, its back legs scrabbling for purchase in loose stone.

With a grinding creak the boulder shifted, moved minutely.

Fritha ran to the rock, put her back against it, her acolytes following, Morn, too.

The boulder rolled free, up a gentle incline, then down a short slope, crushing shrubs and trees.

A new path opened before Fritha, this one leading down, twisting out of view in less than a hundred paces.

'On,' she said, breaking into a run.

A sound ahead, Fritha straining to hear over the pounding of blood in her head and the drum of feet around her. The new passage had bent and turned a downward path, opening up as they made their way into a valley between the mountains of the Bonefells. Somewhere ahead Fritha could hear the rush of water, which made other sounds difficult to distinguish, but there was *something*.

A shadow flitted across the ground: Morn, flying low.

'They are ahead, so close,' the half-breed called down to her, turning a half-loop in the air, 'a quarter-league, no more.'

Fritha picked up her pace.

The ground levelled, widening. Pine trees appeared, heavy with snow that gleamed bright in the low, sinking sun.

Not much left of daylight. Must catch them now, I'll not stumble upon them in the dark and lose the advantage.

Another burst of speed, Ferals about her growling and snarling. Some were hanging back, unease appearing to pass amongst them. Fritha grunted a breathless encouragement to them.

Soon, my children.

Behind her she heard Claw rumble a growling protest, heard the rhythm of his stride falter, Gunil commanding the bear on.

Fatigue is affecting all of us.

The sound of a river grew closer, and then she saw them. A great bear, powering beneath high-boughed trees. It was limping, still moving at a staggering pace, but not the smooth rolling gait of a healthy beast. Figures were sitting upon it, one looked back, pale-faced and dark-haired, and saw her.

Drem, it is so good to see you again. Perhaps I shall turn you into one of my Ferals, or let Gulla make a Revenant of you. If I can stop Morn from ripping your head from your shoulders, that is.

She grinned, her triumph so close she could almost taste it.

Then she frowned and spat.

What is that smell?

CHAPTER NINE

DREM

'I can see them,' Drem cried to Keld and Cullen, both men sitting in front of him upon the saddle on Hammer's back.

'Come on, Hammer,' Drem breathed. But the bear was flagging beneath them, her strength fading. And there was something else, a hesitancy in her gait; she was casting her head about, taking in deep, snorting breaths.

Drem looked around, saw only open-spread trees, the ground dense with a litter-bed of pine needles. They were deep into the Bonefells, now, but a region that Drem had never trapped in; Olin had always taken him north in the trapping season between spring and winter.

A foul smell hit the back of Drem's throat.

Hammer skidded to a halt, rearing and lowing. Keld, Cullen and Drem were thrown from the saddle. The soft spring of the needle litter that coated the frozen ground broke Drem's fall.

He climbed to his feet.

'What in the name of the Otherworld is that stench?' Cullen spat.

Drem looked about. Dimly through the trees behind them he saw the speeding approach of their pursuers, Ferals and men, behind them the silhouetted bulk of a giant bear.

We need to move.

But Hammer was standing, blowing great gouts of steaming

breath. Another wave of the smell crawled into Drem's mouth, acrid and foul. They were in a wide clearing, dotted with a few thin-trunked trees, most of the snowstorm held at bay by the lattice of pine branches above them. The occasional snowflake drifted down. All around them were mounds. They were tall, not quite the height of a man, wide at the base and tapered. Some were gleaming with ice, frozen solid, but a few on the outskirts of the mounds were steaming. Drem walked close to one, saw something protruding from it, angular and sharp-edged. He looked closer, something shifting in his gut as he realized what it was.

A bone. A big one, that looks as if it belonged to an elk. This is the dunghill of a predator.

Cullen came and stood beside him, wrinkling his nose and prodding at the mound.

I wouldn't do that, Drem thought.

Cullen's finger cracked the ice and a smell fouler than anything Drem had ever experienced, far worse than rotting meat or any tanner's chemical vat, escaped the mound and assaulted their senses, snaking into his mouth and nose like grasping fingers.

'Dear Elyon, no,' Keld whispered. 'We have to get out of here.'

'What is it?' Drem asked.

'Draigs.'

Draigs!

Drem had heard of the great beasts, and every trapper had spoken or dreamed of catching and skinning one, but they were a thing of legend, a mythical beast that only the hardiest of heroes could slay, like Maquin Oathkeeper, hailed as the greatest warrior that fought in the War of Wrath. Drem had never thought there was much truth in the tales, and certainly the last draigs he'd heard of had been hunted and slain a hundred years ago. Serpents on legs, some called them, most vicious and deadly of the Banished Lands predators, and that was quite a crown to hold.

'Come on,' Keld said, dragging at Cullen's arm.

A shadow flitted across them. Drem, looking up, saw a blur swooping above them, leathery wings spread wide.

'There's no time,' Drem cried, pointing at the half-breed, then gazing back into the trees.

Ferals were surging towards them, a dozen at least, only a few hundred paces away, and behind them were Kadoshim acolytes, shaven-haired and grim-eyed.

Keld shared a look with Drem and Cullen, gave a short nod.

'This is it, then. Let's see how many of these bastards we can take across the bridge of swords with us,' he growled. 'With me.' He ran to Hammer's side, unstrapping a long linen bag, pulling a bow of ash from it, reaching inside a pocket for a bowstring. In heartbeats the bow was strung. With a hiss, Cullen's sword was in his fist and he was taking a round shield from where it was hung upon Hammer's harness, the white, four-pointed star, sigil of the Order of the Bright Star, painted upon it. He slung it across his back, pulled the leather buckles tight, offered another shield to Drem.

'I've never used a shield,' Drem said.

'I'll teach you when we get back to Dun Seren.'

We both know that's not going to happen. Drem resisted the urge to say it out loud, knew that it would not be the most encouraging thing right now. Instead he put a hand to his neck, finding the reassuring beat of his pulse.

Keld had laid out a handful of arrows on the ground before him. He crouched down, drew a knife across the palm of his hand and clenched a fist, blood welling between his fingers.

'*Cnámha an domhain, tabhair dom do neart,*' he intoned, letting his blood drip upon the arrowheads.

The steel seemed to shimmer and ripple, and then Keld was standing, one of the arrows nocked. He drew and loosed,

almost straight up. There was a shriek as the half-breed
swerved, the arrow grazing her wing. She twisted in the air and
rose, disappearing into the treetop canopy.

Keld didn't wait, had nocked and loosed at the pack of
Ferals swarming towards them, only a hundred paces away
now. His arrow pierced one's belly, punching out through the
creature's back and hurtling on, slamming into another Feral's
shoulder, hurling it against a tree, where the arrow sunk deep,
almost up to its fletching, pinning the Feral.

That's impossible, Drem thought.

The first Feral, with a hole in its belly, stood and stared,
then slumped to its knees.

Hammer growled beside them, huge claws raking the
ground.

'Hold, lass,' Cullen whispered to her.

Fifty paces away.

Drem drew his seax and a hand-axe, thought about using
his father's sword, but his seax felt comfortable in his hand, and
the memory of his father's runes carved upon it helped to
steady his beating heart.

I would have liked to learn to use Da's sword. Maybe I will.

If I live long enough.

Keld drew and loosed, an arrow slamming into a Feral's
shoulder and on out of its back, sending the creature crashing
to the ground. It regained its feet and ran at them. Drem saw
the one with an arrow-hole in its belly was back on its feet,
staggering towards them.

Not a comforting sight. They are hard to kill.

Twenty paces.

Another arrow, this one finding the throat of an acolyte. He
fell backwards in a spray of blood.

Keld dropped the bow and drew his sword and axe, rolled
his shoulders.

Cullen laughed.

'Stay close to me, lad,' Cullen said to Drem as he set his feet.

I wish he'd stop calling me lad.

'Truth and Courage,' Keld and Cullen bellowed, Hammer roaring, and the two warriors ran at the onrushing enemy. Drem stood a moment, hesitating, fear squirming in his belly. Drem was no coward but he knew this was likely to be the time and place of his death.

I don't want to die.

Then he saw Fritha, deep amidst her acolytes, and behind her the looming shape of a bear, a giant upon its back.

My father's murderers. Sig's killers.

Fear shifted to anger.

Bellowing a wordless cry, he ran after his comrades.

Keld and Cullen crashed into the Ferals, a sword-swing from Cullen sending a head twirling through the air, blood jetting from the severed stump. Keld was slicing and stabbing, ducking and spinning, constant motion, and then Drem was amidst it all. A Feral came at him, all red jaws and yellow fangs, and without thinking he knocked raking claws away with his axe and stabbed his seax into the man-beast's mouth, the point bursting out through the back of its neck, severing its spine. Blood erupted as Drem ripped his blade free, the Feral collapsing, twitching.

A blow to his side, sending him reeling, a moment to register it was an acolyte that had fallen into him, a woman with hair shaved to her scalp, a deep wound in her thigh, from Keld or Cullen, he did not know. Drem hesitated, weapons raised, and she stabbed at him with a spear. He jumped back and she followed, favouring her wounded leg, short stabs at his chest and belly sending him reeling, one slicing along his side, cutting through fur and leather, grazing his ribs. He swung his axe wildly, connected with the shaft, hacking the spear-point off. The acolyte snarled and swung the spear like a staff, Drem ducking, chopping into her knee with his axe, stabbing up with his seax as she dropped, the blade punching into her belly, blood hot and sticky, gushing over his gloved fist, leaking under the sleeve of his wool tunic. He shoved the dying woman away, stood over her corpse, gasping deep breaths, looked for Fritha.

Hammer roared, joining the fray, a sweep of her paw sending men and Ferals flying, one Feral impaled upon a tree branch. Another claw-swing sliced through an acolyte's belly, a slither of intestines falling about his feet. Screaming. Then the other bear was there, the giant upon its back, acolytes and Ferals leaping aside to allow it to get to Hammer.

The two bears met with a resounding thud, the ground shaking, teeth clashing, claws lacerating. Hammer crouched under a blow from the bear, swiping one paw up like a pugilist's uppercut, claws raking across the other bear's neck, her jaws lunging, sinking into her adversary's head. A roar of pain from the creature.

Hammer's as fierce and battle-skilled as Sig.

But Sig wasn't upon Hammer's back.

The giant swung his war-hammer. With a sickening crunch it smashed into Hammer's shoulder and she released the bear's head to bellow her pain. She snapped at the giant, but he was swaying back out of reach, bringing his hammer high for another blow. His bear swiped at Hammer, sending her stumbling backwards, her leg giving way where the giant had struck her. She collapsed to the ground, crushing an acolyte in her fall, a great explosion of pine needles and forest litter.

Drem tried to get to Hammer, slashed at an acolyte in his way, sliced a Feral across its hamstring, but there were too many between him and Sig's bear. He cast about wildly, hoping that Cullen or Keld would reach her, protect her.

He caught a glimpse of Keld, the huntsman beset by a handful of Ferals and acolytes. Even as Drem watched, he saw Keld draw his blade across his palm, hurling a fistful of his own blood at the swarming enemy before him.

What is he doing?

'*Fola de mo chorp, a bheith tine, sruthán mo naimhde*,' Keld bellowed, and as his blood splattered across faces and torsos it hissed and burst into tiny sparks of flame. Ferals and acolytes fell away screaming, the stench of scorched flesh filling the glade.

Keld stood there, enemies writhing in agony about his feet, and then to Drem's horror he saw a Feral leap upon Keld from behind, both of them going down, the Feral's claws slashing, arcs of blood in the air. They rolled. As they stopped, the Feral was on top, rearing back with its misshapen jaws wide, claws rising. Keld lay still upon the ground.

'Keld!' Drem yelled, trying to carve a way to the huntsman, but there were too many between them.

'CULLEN!' Drem bellowed. 'Keld is down.'

Cullen was close, beset by five or six attackers, using his knife like a shield, his sword leaving bloody arcs. His eyes flickered to Drem, but then he was staggering, defending against a barrage of blows.

A slate-grey blur caught Drem's eye, speeding through the melee: Fen the wolven-hound hurling himself at the Feral upon Keld, its claws held high, blood upon them. With a snarling howl, Fen slammed into the Feral, both of them rolling away, the wolven-hound on top, pinning the thrashing creature down, jaws finding the throat. A savage wrench and blood jetted, the Feral's feet drumming on the ground. Fen leaped back to the prone form of Keld, stood over him protectively, crouched, teeth bared in a bloody snarl.

The giant and his bear approached Hammer. She was trying to regain her feet, but the bear pounded her with a paw, Hammer's leg giving way again, sending her tumbling back to the ground. The bear stood over her, the giant upon its back hefting his war-hammer.

Drem swept a sword away with his seax, chopped hard into the head of his attacker, denting the iron cap upon the acolyte's head, who collapsed bonelessly, then Drem charged, barrelled into a knot of acolytes pressing about Cullen, sending a handful of them flying, and saw open space between him and Hammer.

The giant upon his bear's back was raising his war-hammer.

A hot pain across Drem's back and he was thrown forwards, onto his knees. He twisted, saw a Feral standing over him with blood dripping from its claws.

Without thinking, Drem twisted, kicking at the creature's ankles, saw it stumble, at the same time he was rising, stabbing with his seax, piercing the Feral's eye, its momentum as it fell driving the long knife deep until Drem felt the tip grate on the back of the beast's skull.

He shoved the twitching creature away, swivelled on his feet and threw his axe.

It struck the giant bear in the chest, sinking deep, the blade disappearing. The bear reared onto its back legs, roaring, the giant on its back thrown from his saddle, vanishing from sight. The bear crashed back to all fours, bellowed a challenge at Drem.

I'm coming, Hammer.

There was a blow across Drem's back, a flare of pain lancing through the wound the Feral had just given him, a face full of pine needles as he stumbled and fell. Something was gripping his cloak, pulling him, lifting him.

His feet left the ground and he was rising, above the battle, an aerial view showing the carnage painted in blood and gore.

'This is for my brother,' a voice grated in his ear.

Drem took a moment to register the strength that had lifted him high into the air. He squirmed, his cloak knotting in the half-breed's fist. Red-hot pain seared along his waist as a knife-thrust that had been intended for his kidneys scored a red line. Another twist and he was facing the half-breed, his face so close to hers he could smell her stale breath. Her eyes blazed their hatred at him and her fist drew back for another stab of her knife.

Drem jerked with his seax, blocking the blade, and

headbutted the half-breed across the bridge of her flat nose. Blood and cartilage burst, spattering his face, and the half-breed reeled back, wings sagging.

He headbutted her again, harder, saw her eyes roll back into her head, her wings folding, her grip upon his cloak going slack and he fell away from her, saw her begin a slow plummet back to the ground.

Then he realized he was falling, too.

A moment of weightlessness and panic as he spun his arms, saw the ground rushing up to him. He landed on Hammer, fur and flesh breaking his fall. She was trying to rise again, the other bear advancing on her, the giant nowhere to be seen.

Drem rolled off Hammer, still gripping his seax. He shifted it to his left hand and, drawing his father's sword, set his feet between Hammer and the other bear.

Blood sluiced down its chest, soaking its fur from Hammer's claw-gouges and Drem's axe, though the wounds had not gone deep enough, not reached any vital organ. It opened its jaws and roared at him, spittle flying, the power of it sending him staggering back a pace.

He shook his head and set his feet again.

'Come on, then, death,' he snarled at the bear, 'but I'll give you a scar or two to remember me by.'

Two figures stepped around the bear: the giant, raising a hand and giving a command to the bear, and beside him, Fritha.

Something in Drem stirred at the sight of her, fair-haired, a scattering of freckles beneath the blue eyes that stared only at him. A memory of how she'd made him feel, *before*. A bear-skin cloak was thrown back across her shoulders, dark-boiled leather armour covering her torso. She held a short-sword in her hand, dripping red.

Whose blood is that? Which of my friends?

He saw the Starstone Sword scabbarded at her waist, had a vivid memory of how she had taken it, of kneeling beside his father in the snow, holding his da's hand as he coughed blood.

He took an involuntary step towards her, checked himself.

Fritha looked at his stance, sword held high, seax low.

'Scorpion's tail and iron gate combined,' Fritha said with amusement. 'Your new friend's teaching you the sword dance?' Drem said nothing. 'Come with me, I can teach you more than those blind idiots at the Order.'

'Step a little closer,' Drem said, 'and I'll show you what they've taught me.'

'I offered,' Fritha said. 'Either way you're coming back with me; of your own will or in chains.'

'There's a third option,' Drem said and lunged with his sword.

CHAPTER TEN

FRITHA

Fritha swept Drem's lunge away, the calculating part of her mind noting how he overextended as he lunged, but at the same time she saw him check and adjust his balance, a natural shifting of his feet and legs that showed him to be a natural fighter, and she knew that in time he would make a skilled swordsman.

If he were given the chance to learn.

She was annoyed with herself. Why had she just offered him the chance of joining her, when he had already spurned her once? She'd had every intention of crushing him and dragging him back to Gulla as a prize. But there had been something in his eyes as she'd approached him, just for a moment. It had reminded her of the way he had looked at her once, all innocence and trust, that she had found so endearing and fascinating. For a heartbeat it had taken her back to another time, the time *before*, when life was not all about the dark beating heart of revenge. That look in Drem's eyes had faded in a flash, though – if it had ever been there at all – replaced by something all too well known to her.

Blame and hatred.

Who is he to judge me?

She strode at him, swayed as he chopped down at her with his sword, parried the stab of his seax and stepped in close, within his guard, elbowing him in the mouth and sending him reeling.

She paused a moment, pointed her short-sword at Drem's heart, then followed after him, saw the flicker of his eyes that betrayed his next move, caught his sword-strike on her blade, sparks grating as she rotated her wrist, cutting his forearm, and he cried out, dropping the sword. He swung at her with his seax, but she caught the blow easily, deflected it wide and countered, cutting a red line across Drem's chest. He stumbled backwards, tripped and fell. She kicked him in the gut, put a boot on his chest and levelled her sword at his throat.

'Chains it is, then,' she said.

A deafening roar filled the woodland.

Fritha paused, looked up. She'd heard a lot of roaring this past day, mostly from giant bears, and that was loud enough to rattle her brain in her skull. But this sound was different. Not a bear. For one thing, it was louder, which didn't give her much comfort. There was also an edge to it that set the hairs on the back of her neck standing on end.

She looked about the clearing. Everyone who was still standing within it was frozen, like her, searching for the origin of such a terrible sound.

Then she saw it. A monstrous shape emerging from the shadows. It was huge, not quite as tall as Claw, but wider and longer. It was serpentine, reminiscent of the lizards Fritha had seen sunning themselves in the south, but a thousand times bigger, with green-brown mottled skin, like a snake's. Its belly was low to the ground, set upon four immensely powerful bowed legs, splayed feet with claws like the curved swords the Horse Clans of Arcona wielded. A long, wide tail swayed behind its bulk, but Fritha's eyes were drawn to its head. A broad, flat skull, its muzzle long with a square-tipped jaw full of razored teeth that dripped with thick saliva or ichor. Its eyes were small and black, gleaming with a primal fury.

Is that a draig?

Spiders crawled down her spine.

The creature paused, surveying them all, petty intruders within its realm. It opened its vast jaws and roared again, trees and branches shaking, setting the ground to trembling, vibrations passing into Fritha's boots, up her legs.

Then it charged.

For something so vast and squat it was incredibly fast, surging forwards on its muscular legs, scythe-like claws sending great gouts of snow and earth arcing into the air.

For a timeless moment Fritha was frozen, fear and awe immobilizing her.

Drem shifted beneath her, his arm knocking her boot off his chest, sending her stumbling away. He leaped to his feet, pushed her hard in the chest and she crashed to the ground, rolling in the pine needles.

And then the draig was between them, a surging leviathan of muscle. It barrelled into a knot of Fritha's acolytes, sent them careening through the air, powerful jaws clamping upon one, a ripple of its sinuous neck muscles and her acolyte was severed in two, only his legs and hips remaining.

'TO ME!' Fritha yelled, staggering to her feet, unsure if anyone had heard her, her natural instinct to order the shield wall, but she'd commanded that all shields be left behind on this hunt through the wild, thought it was unnecessary weight that would have slowed them down.

Arn and Elise ran to her; a handful more joined them.

The draig's head snapped around, eyes fixing upon something. Fritha saw it was the wolven-hound that stood over the form of Drem's companion.

The huntsman of the group, that is how the Order of the Bright Star work: always a captain, a huntsman with wolven-hounds, and a few fresh warriors.

The huntsman was moving sluggishly, the wolven-hound crouched over him, snarling and snapping at the draig.

The draig clearly didn't like that challenge to its supremacy.

88

It broke into its scuttling run, Fritha's acolytes frantically leaping aside as it charged. Fritha felt a jolt of shock when she saw that the wolven-hound did not bolt and flee like everything else in the draig's path. Instead it gathered its legs beneath it and burst into a run *at* the draig, not away. Bounding and leaping, the wolven-hound twisted in the air, avoiding the gaping mouth with snapping jaws by a hair's breadth, skidding along the draig's head, its claws raking from muzzle to skull, finding purchase, the wolven-hound's fangs sinking deep into the draig's neck. It hung there, back legs scrabbling, ripping bloody rents in the draig's scaly skin.

The draig bellowed, head whipping round, jaws snapping, trying to reach its assailant, tail lashing in its pain and rage, crushing the ribs of an acolyte unfortunate enough to be in its trajectory.

A savage shake of the draig's body, and with a tearing and rending of flesh, the wolven-hound's fang's tore free from the draig's neck, the creature swiping a claw at the hound as it fell through the air, punching it flying, crunching into a tree. The crackle of breaking bones. The wolven-hound whined, fell to the ground and did not move.

The draig cast its head about for its next victim.

An ear-splitting roar and Claw was lumbering to attack. The two beasts came together like a thunderclap, the force of it knocking men and women from their feet. Bear and draig slashed, raked and bit at one another, their vast bulks heaving, straining, claws gouging bloody streaks through fur and scale and flesh, jaws seeking purchase, snapping, biting. Claw cried in pain, staggering back, blood leaking from a myriad of wounds, the draig mercilessly ploughing forwards, a strike of its claws across the bear's head sending it crashing to the ground.

Gunil bellowed a challenge and charged, his war-hammer swinging in a loop, crunching into the draig's ribs, the sound of splintering bone, a scream from the draig, its tail whipping at Gunil, sending him reeling, clutching his side.

'TO ME, TO ME!' Fritha screamed over and over as she lurched into motion, knew that one by one the draig would defeat them all.

As she broke into a run her Ferals gathered about her, only a handful of them still living. Arn, Elise and a few others were already with her. Others, hearing her call, came stumbling and staggering as they approached the draig.

Claw was back on his feet, growling, a heavy paw-strike lashing the draig's head. Gunil staggered back into the fray, swung his hammer, howling with the pain it caused him, and crunched it into one of the draig's clawed feet, pulping flesh.

Fritha barked a command and her Ferals swept forwards, some leaping onto the draig's flanks, clawing and biting, others slinking under the vast bulk of its belly, raking, teeth sinking into meat. Her acolytes spread wide, some with spears stabbing, drawing blood, others darting in with swords, slashing, stabbing, leaping away. Fritha sheathed her short-sword, drew the Starstone Sword and slashed with it, leaving a black, smoking line of charred flesh across the draig's flank.

The draig roared its frustration as Fritha and her crew worried at it like a wolven pack bringing down an elk. But it was not dead yet. A swipe of claws disembowelled a Feral. An adder-like dart of its head, and the draig snatched up an acolyte who had lingered too long to attack, eviscerating her with a shake of its powerful neck. Elise and Arn stabbed with spears, and it spun to face them, Arn leaping away from a swipe of its scythe-like claws, Elise stumbling, trying to protect herself with her spear, the draig smashing it to kindling, hurling Elise like a straw doll through the air.

And then a winged shape swooped from above: Morn, sword in her fist, alighting upon the draig's back, between its shoulder blades. She set her feet, raised her sword high and stabbed down, the blade sinking deep.

The draig bellowed in agony, reared up, Morn's wings beating, somehow managing to keep her balanced atop the writhing draig, and she twisted her sword ever deeper. Acolytes and Ferals rushed in at the creature's exposed belly, stabbing, slashing, Gunil and Claw pounding at the draig with powerful blows.

With one last roar, the draig toppled onto its side, claws lashing out, taking the head from another acolyte. Morn appeared upon it, wrenched her sword free, stabbed in a frenzy, arcs of blood. Fritha stepped in, set her feet and swung her sword, opening up a huge wound upon its belly, blood and intestines spilling out, a stench erupting, sending Fritha reeling.

One last shudder, a strangled growl, and the draig died.

A sudden silence followed, punctuated by Fritha's ragged breaths, the groans of the injured, then Claw roared his victory.

'Fritha.' A choking breath.

She cast about, saw Arn kneeling beside Elise, cradling her. Fritha ran to them, knelt beside her friends, saw tears in Arn's eyes.

Elise was deathly white, one arm shattered, her leg twisted in an unnatural angle, and bone protruding from her side, her ribs smashed. The acolyte coughed, speckles of blood stark and vivid on her too-pale chin.

'Help her,' Arn said.

Fritha checked Elise over, knew what Arn was asking of her. *The earth magic. Words of power.*

Fritha looked into Arn's eyes. 'You know I am no adept, my knowledge is limited—'

He grabbed her wrist. 'It's *Elise*. Just try. Help her, please.'

A long breath sucked in.

Then another thought broke through her worry for Elise. *Where's Drem?*

'Staunch the bleeding and clean her wounds,' Fritha said, standing. 'I will be back soon, will do what I can.'

She looked about wildly, couldn't see him, saw that the Order's huntsman was no longer sprawled upon the ground.

Where's the bear?

'FIND THEM!' she screamed, searching the glade, saw the dead scattered everywhere, the tall dunghill mounds, but no Drem, no bear, no warriors of the Order. Her Ferals loped away, but there were so many overpowering scents that they seemed confused, bounding off in different directions.

'This way,' a voice cried from above. Morn was swooping through branches, heading away from the battleground, west.

Fritha followed, found that she was limping, a pain in her leg, and saw a gash through her leather breeks, blood leaking. She ignored it.

The roar of a river growing louder. A shape moving in the distance.

Sig's bear.

She used her last strength to reach the riverbank, a handful of acolytes running past her, flitting through the trees ahead.

An explosion of water, falling upon her acolytes like a wave, scattered them like leaves.

Fifty paces and Fritha was with them, staring past them.

A wide river roared and foamed, turbulent with snow and spinning broken sheets of ice, floating like icy rafts upon the waters. She saw the bear in the water, two people clinging to it, another lying sprawled upon one of the ice-sheets. Within heartbeats the river had sped them all around a bend, out of view.

Her eyes searched for paths, saw that in a few hundred paces the shallow bank she was stood upon gave way to rearing granite cliffs. The only way to follow them was to leap into the river.

Fritha shrieked her frustration to the sky.

So close. I was so close. And I cannot return to Gulla empty-handed. My position is not so secure that failure will not damage it. There are many others willing and waiting to take my place.

'They have escaped us,' Gunil said behind her.

That's not helpful. She resisted the urge to turn around and stab the giant.

'For now,' she muttered.

'Fritha,' Gunil said to her. She tore her eyes away from the bend in the river where Drem had disappeared.

'What?' she snapped, looking over her shoulder to see the giant looming over her. She had not heard his approach, which was worrying.

Breathe. Focus. This is not over yet; there are many leagues between here and Dun Seren.

'You should see this,' the giant said to her, and without waiting, turned and walked back into the woods. She noticed he favoured one leg, and his right arm was held tucked tight to his ribs. Her leg throbbed, and she paused to cut a strip of cloth from her cloak and tie it high, above the wound. She counted heads as she followed Gunil back to the clearing, was appalled at the result. Thirteen of her Ferals still standing, sixteen of her Red Right Hand, though she would be hard-pressed to find one unharmed from their battles.

Little more than a score left, when fifty of us set out after three men, a bear, a hound and a crow. She ground her teeth in anger.

Arn had carried Elise to the edge of the clearing, laid her down with the other injured where the healers amongst them were doing what they could.

I will join them soon, do what I can.

The draig lay with the dead scattered about it. Fritha walked to it, ran a gloved finger along the line of its jaw, traced a curved fang.

Oh, how I wish we could have captured you, taken you back to Gulla in a cage. The creatures I could have fashioned from your flesh. But I need life to fashion life, not dead, butchered meat and congealed blood.

Some of her men were already seeing to the butchering, skinning and finishing off the gutting of the dead beast, cutting claws from its feet, extracting teeth from its jaws.

We need these trophies, else no one would ever believe us.

Deep wounds raked one side of the draig's head, puncture wounds a little further along on its neck, inflicted by the wolven-hound. Fritha remembered it standing over the Order's hunts-man, protecting him, hurling itself at the draig.

Such fierce loyalty . . . She shook her head. *I want that, need that.*

'This way,' Gunil said, leading Fritha on, past the dunghills, deeper into the trees. They dropped into a small gully, with banks rearing either side of them, thick with knotted tree-roots. Gunil paused at the entrance to a cave, tore a strip of linen from the tunic beneath his leather vest, wrapped it around the butt-end of his war-hammer and struck sparks with striking iron and flint.

Holding the makeshift torch aloft, he strode into the cave, revealing a tunnel that sloped gently downwards. It was tall and wide; Gunil did not need to duck his head. Fritha followed, the smell stale and unpleasant, but better than the dunghills. Torch-light flickered on uneven walls, thick ridges scoured into hard-packed earth, and Fritha realized they were made by draig-claws.

This was its den.

A little further on and the tunnel opened into a wider chamber. Something crunched under Fritha's feet: bones, a carpet of them as thick as the pine needle litter above ground. Some smaller – badgers, foxes – others much larger, elk, what resembled a bear. She spied other shapes amidst the bones, occasionally a human skull. A ribcage here, spine there, another creature, a large skull with long canines. Fritha recognized the anatomy of a wolven; she'd carved enough of them up, fused them into something else. They strode on, towards a shadowy shape at the centre of the room.

Gunil and Fritha stood before it, Gunil raising his torch high. At first glance Fritha thought it was a head, not yet fully decomposed, but as she stooped to see it better she saw it was too symmetrical, devoid of mouth, eyes, jaws. Roughly oval in shape, there were colours swirling across it, hues rippling, like inks spilt into water.

Fritha felt a smile spreading over her face, the sense of frustration and defeat that had settled upon her like a shroud suddenly lifted, evaporating.

'A draig's egg,' she said into the darkness.

CHAPTER ELEVEN

BLEDA

Bleda sat on his horse, staring ahead at the warriors marching on foot in front of him. Three score White-Wings, all polished leather and bright steel. Colossal trees reared high on either side of the narrow road, branches looping and latticing above them. He twisted in his saddle and looked back over his shoulder, saw another two score of the black-and-silver clothed warriors marching behind. Shadows flitted across him, shapes skimming along the road they were following and, looking up, he saw Ben-Elim circling high above, yet still beneath the canopy of Forn's great trees.

He drew in a long, slow breath, mastering the emotions that were roiling within him: anger and fear, confusion and revulsion, as well as the fatigue and sense of sorrow that he'd noticed settled over him after a battle, the knowledge that lives had been snuffed out, men and women that he had talked with, eaten with – suddenly gone. It left a hollow place within him. And of course, there was Kol and the Ben-Elim.

They say we are pardoned, welcomed back into the arms of the Faithful, but I feel more like a prisoner being marched to my execution. And no one asked me if I wanted to be welcomed back.

He had sat outside the woodsman's hut when Riv had been hauled inside, as stunned as the rest of them by Aphra's revelation.

Riv is Kol's daughter.

Obviously, he had known that one of the Ben-Elim was her father, but Kol! He did not know how he felt about that.

Bleda and the others had laid down their weapons. Bleda had no heart to fight on with Riv a prisoner, fearing what Kol might do to her, and he knew that continuing to fight was futile – they were too outnumbered – so he'd chosen to save the lives of his surviving bondsmen. Only three of his ten guards still lived, and Old Ellac, who seemed immortal. The dead had been buried beneath cairns back at the woodsman's hut, alongside over a dozen Ben-Elim and White-Wings.

Vald and Jost rode with Bleda, Ellac and his three men, which surprised Bleda a little. He'd thought they would be back marching with the White-Wings, especially as it was Aphra's hundred, the very unit that Vald and Jost had trained with all of their lives. To see them riding alongside his men was another reminder that so much had changed, that life was abruptly, unalterably, different, and he was clearly not the only one to feel that way.

Jost had a wide bandage wrapped around his head, dried blood crusting on it. He was swaying a little in his saddle, and not just because he was a poor rider; he was still concussed from the blow to his head, a clump from the butt-end of a Ben-Elim's spear that had bled for half a day.

When Bleda had seen Kol stride into the woodsman's hut he had thought the end must be close, his hand finding the secret dagger hidden in his boot, though he hadn't really known what he was going to do with it.

Save Riv, kill Kol, maybe. Or at least try. Or kill myself, rather than let Kol have the pleasure.

I am surprised that any of us are still alive.

It had been a long time later that Kol had emerged, and Bleda had been stunned to see Riv walking out into the glade with him. Riv had stood with her head down while Kol had made a speech about the time for bloodletting and vengeance being over, and as the new Lord Protector he wanted to build a new world of peace and harmony. He would start that right now, by forgiving and absolving Riv and her companions of any wrongdoing.

Bleda had almost fallen over with shock.

While Kol spoke, Bleda had looked only at Riv, tried to catch her eye. He saw that she had a wound on her shoulder, freshly stitched, and that she was clenching her right hand into a fist, blood welling from between her fingers, dripping on the ground.

When did that happen?

Only once had Riv looked at him, when Kol had been speaking of forgiveness and moving on together, and she had nodded at him, as if agreeing with Kol's words. And urging him to agree, also.

What happened in that hut? How can she be going along with this? She was going to Drassil to kill Kol, and now she is making peace with him. Is it part of some plan, or is it because Kol is her father? Has that changed how she feels about him? He slew Dalmae, is a murderer.

He felt confused, angry, bewildered, and deeply worried for Riv.

Feeling and recognizing all these emotions now, he had come to the strange realization that for the last moon or so, he had been . . . happy.

Despite the shock of Kol's coup and the flight in the dead of night into the endless twilight of Forn, despite living in a woodsman's hut, shorn of the comfort and luxuries that being a prince, even if he was a ward of the Ben-Elim, had given him. It had been a long time since he had felt able to relax his cold-face, to allow his feelings to emerge from the depths where he kept them so well controlled and hidden. And he knew there was a reason for that.

Riv.

Somehow, she had managed to pick, chip and bore a hole

through his guard, fracturing his protective shield. He felt as if he had stepped out from a dark place into the light of the sun.

And now it was over, his cold-face shifting back into place, but beneath it emotions boiled, foremost of all worry for his friend.

Where is Riv?

He searched the skies, looked front and back again, but could not see her.

And now they were going back to Drassil, five or six days' travel through Forn before they would see the giant walls of the Banished Lands' greatest fortress. It was not a sight that Bleda was looking forward to.

A horn blast rang out. Aphra was standing at the head of their column, a fist raised, the signal to make camp for the night. They rippled to a halt and then two winged shapes flew over Bleda and his companions: Kol and Riv. They alighted in a swirl of leaves beside Aphra.

Riv did not so much as glance at Bleda or her friends.

Darkness, as thick and dense as a wall, loomed about Bleda. He was sitting beside a fire with Ellac, as well as his three guards: a man named Tuld, taller than was common amongst the Sirak, and two women, Ruga and Mirim, sisters whom Bleda struggled to tell apart. All had injuries from the fight at the hut, but most of them were superficial, only Mirim having a deeper wound in her thigh. Ruga was checking on it now, cleaning it with boiled water that had been left to cool. All three of them were shaven-haired, apart from the long braids that marked them as Sirak warriors.

Bleda was tending to his bow, for a moment lost in the memory of its making, so long ago; his brother had helped him craft the weapon. It was one of his most treasured memories, recalling a time when the world seemed stable and solid, and also exciting, with so much promise for his future, and he had been sure of his place within it. He remembered his brother's voice, teaching him to sand the sturgeon glue with rough shark skin, his brother's arm around his shoulders, the both of them laughing.

But now he is dead.

Now, all was in flux.

He could not just go back to Drassil and resume the life he had been leading; it felt impossible. His eyes searched out Kol, sitting at a campfire with a handful of his Ben-Elim and some of Aphra's White-Wings. Kol was drinking from a skin, laughing.

He is king, now, the Lord Protector of the Banished Lands. The man who slew my brother and sister, and shamed my mother. He has slain Israfil, slain Riv's kin, and yet he sits there drinking and laughing.

'What do you think has happened to the rest of my honour guard?' Bleda asked.

Ellac had led one hundred Sirak warriors from Arcona to Drassil as Bleda's personal honour guard, and only ten of them had been about him on the chaotic night that he had saved Riv from the madness of Kol's coup. It was those ten warriors who had accompanied him into Forn Forest, and now seven of them were dead.

Your sacrifice will not be forgotten.

'Who can say what Kol has done with them?' Ellac shrugged.

Bleda felt a dark mood settling upon him, struggled to stop it from showing. He mourned the loss of his guards, felt the weight of responsibility for their deaths.

'Ellac, Ruga, Tuld, Mirim,' he said, and they all looked at him.

'My thanks,' Bleda said.

'For what?' Ruga asked, frowning.

'For keeping your oaths, for standing with me.'

Ellac snorted. The other three were looking at Bleda with quizzical looks.

'You are our prince, and we are oathsworn to you,' Tuld said, as if that explained everything.

'Aye, and Erdene would take our right hands if we failed you,' Ruga said, a fleeting smile wrinkling her cold-face.

She probably would.

'You are brave and loyal,' Bleda said, 'and I will not forget it.'

Footsteps. Bleda, looking up, fire-blind for a moment, saw two forms approaching, both tall, one thin, one broad.

'Mind if we join you?' Vald said.

Bleda looked up at them. 'Of course not,' he said, shuffling to make room for them around the fire.

'Why are you not with your people?' Ellac asked.

'Doesn't feel right,' Jost said. 'We've been trained as White-Wings, but today was the first real battle we've seen, fought in, and we stood with you, not them. You stood with us, against them. That should mean something, not be forgotten.'

'Kol your Lord Protector said that enmity was all behind us,' Ellac said. Bleda saw he was staring keenly at the two young men.

'A world of difference between saying something and it being real,' Vald muttered.

'There is,' Ellac said flatly.

A shifting in the air, an unseen wind, and then dark shapes were descending, solid shadows dropping out of the night, taking form.

Kol, a few Ben-Elim with him, and Riv. Bleda felt a lurch in his chest at the sight of her. They alighted at the edge of Bleda's firelight, shadow and flame casting them in hues of red and black.

Riv stood a step behind Kol, her eyes taking in Vald and Jost with Bleda and his guard, meeting Bleda's gaze for a lingering moment, then looking away.

'A token to prove that I mean what I say,' Kol said. He gestured a hand, and one of the Ben-Elim stepped forwards, carrying a heavy bundle in his arms, wrapped in a wool cloak. He dropped it on the ground before Bleda, and weapons spilt out – the curved swords of the Sirak, knives, quivers of arrows, spears. Vald and Jost's short-swords were there, too. The weapons that had been confiscated after the fight at the cabin.

'Take them back, wear them freely,' Kol said. 'A sign both of my forgiveness for your past deeds, and of the trust I am giving you, for the future.' His eyes flitted to Riv, then back to Bleda and his companions.

Is this for Riv's benefit? I do not trust him.

Nevertheless, Bleda stepped forwards and picked out his quiver and arrows, his weapons-belt with scabbarded sword and knife, and slung them over his shoulder. The others followed Bleda's lead, apart from Mirim, who sat with her wounded leg stretched out straight before her.

'My thanks,' Bleda said. Six years living and surviving amongst the Ben-Elim at Drassil had taught him to keep his emotions closely guarded, and always to be polite, never to give cause for offence or to betray his thoughts.

Ellac sat and silently drew his sword, lay it across his lap and, fetching whetstone, scouring pad and oil from his belt pouch, set to cleaning black patches from his blade, the blood of Ben-Elim, no doubt. Ruga and Tuld did the same, Ruga passing sword and quiver to Mirim.

Kol watched in silence, firelight shining red in his eyes. When the weapons had all been reclaimed he nodded, looked at Bleda.

'Remember the kindness I am showing you, and the faith I am putting in you,' the Ben-Elim said.

'I will,' Bleda said.

I will remember this, and all else that you have done.

'I will, *Lord Protector*,' Kol said.

A moment's silence, stretching. Bleda felt his companions' eyes on him.

'I will, Lord Protector,' Bleda said quietly.

'I like the sound of that.' Kol grinned and leaped into the air, white wings snapping wide, his guard following. Riv paused, knees bent. Her wings beat, lifting her.

'Riv,' Bleda called out, and she hovered, looking down at him.

He just stared at her, felt his cold-face slip as he gazed into her eyes, so many things that he wanted to say, questions to ask.

Riv must have read them upon his face, but she did not land and talk to him, as he'd hoped. She looked down at him, her expression shifting. Grief, sorrow, shame, anger – always anger with Riv – all finally washed away by some kind of stony resolve that was not too different from Bleda's own cold-face.

'It is for the greater good,' she said, and then with a pulse of her wings she disappeared into the darkness.

Bleda sat with the others, a subdued silence settling over them all, just the rasp of whetstones and crackle of fire as they tended to their weapons.

All except Ellac were sleeping when Bleda unrolled his sleeping blanket and lay down upon it. The old warrior was sitting and gazing into the fire like some oak-carved statue.

'What is it?' Bleda said to him, leaning up on an elbow.

Does he think me weak, for not standing up to Kol, for calling him lord?

Ellac looked at him, but said nothing, then looked back to the fire. With a sigh, Bleda lay down, rolling over with his back to Ellac. Sleep took a long time to come, despite the soporific crackle and pop of the fire as it slowly faded. He reached inside his cloak, found what he was looking for and pulled it out carefully, opening his palm in the dying fire-glow.

A large feather, dapple grey, and, folded within it, a purple flower of mountain thyme. He lay there looking at it, thinking, until sleep claimed him.

Drassil was ahead of them; tall and foreboding, banners snapping in the breeze from towers and walls, the silhouettes of

Ben-Elim circling lazily above it. Six days of riding it had taken them to reach the ancient fortress, and Bleda felt his breath coming faster, a tension in his shoulders as he rode through the huge field of cairns that spread across the plain before the western gates.

Kol ordered horns blown as they crossed the field of cairns, and horn blasts echoed out from the gate tower in response.

All cannot go back to how it was – it must not. The world is changing.

'My mother must know of what is happening here,' he whispered to Ellac, leaning close to the old warrior, who was riding beside him.

Ellac looked at him, his heavy-lidded eyes unreadable, though Bleda had the distinct impression that Bleda was appraising him.

'I sent word to her the day we took Riv from Drassil,' Ellac said. 'My Prince,' he added.

Over a moon ago, closer to two. Then word should have reached her in Arcona by now, or soon will. Did Ellac do it to help me, or report on me? Is he my mother's spy?

'Good,' he said to Ellac.

With a heavy creak and grinding, Drassil's gates opened. Kol and some of his Ben-Elim flew over the gatehouse, more horns echoing out from the vast walls. Aphra led her White-Wings marching through the gate tunnel. Bleda followed, the clip of his horse's hooves echoing on the stone, and then they were in the courtyard, a small host arrayed to greet them: Ben-Elim and White-Wings, all manner of stablehands and servants. And then Bleda saw others, dark-skinned warriors with shaved heads and long warrior braids, for a moment thought they were the remnants of his warrior-guard that had not accompanied him into Forn Forest. But then he saw their deel tunics were blue, not grey, and realized that they were of the Cheren Clan, not the Sirak.

And he saw a young woman standing at their head,

dark-haired, straight-backed and strong-shouldered, her features fine and sharp.

Jin.

A weight like a lead ball fell in the pit of Bleda's stomach as he remembered.

I have not thought of her for over a moon.

Jin strode forwards, two of her warrior-guard at her shoulder. She stopped before Bleda, looked up at him as he dismounted.

'Welcome back to Drassil, my betrothed,' she said.

CHAPTER TWELVE

DREM

Drem clamped his jaws together, trying to stop them from chattering as he knelt on the forest floor and peered through a carefully manufactured screen of pine branches and shrubs. After crawling from the freezing grasp of the river, he had shivered involuntarily for a whole day and night. Even now, another day on from that, he had to fight the occasional spasm that rippled through his jaws. Cold had seeped into him, deep as his bones, and did not want to relinquish its hold.

They had spent close to a whole day and night in the grip of the river, sheer granite cliffs rising either side of them, Drem lying upon a thick-slabbed sheet of ice, Cullen and Keld upon Hammer's back as she swam at first, and then spent her energy on trying to stay afloat. Cullen had managed to tie Keld to the huge saddle across Hammer's back and then cast a rope to Drem, who had tied it about the hilt of his seax and stabbed it deep into the ice raft he'd been clinging to, so that they would not become separated through the dark of night.

It had felt like the longest night of Drem's life, too terrified of rolling off his makeshift raft or losing his friends to sleep. He had been sure that death was only ever a handful of heart-beats away.

When dawn had spread its pale glow across the river, he'd seen that the cliffs had given way to steep-sided slopes of shingle and pine, and as the day had worn on eventually shallow riverbanks appeared. Hammer paddled her way towards dry land, forging across the white-foamed current. The bear had crawled and scraped her bulk out of the river, then stumbled and limped to the granite boulder she was still slumped against now. Cullen had dragged Drem in by the rope and together they had cut Keld from Hammer's back and laid him out on the ground. He'd been unconscious and had remained more or less in the same state since then. Drem and Cullen had immediately set about making a fire and shelter, both knowing the cold was likely to kill them far faster than any pursuit from Ferals and half-breed Kadoshim. They had stripped their clothes, Cullen chopping bundles of coppiced willow branches while Drem had shivered and shaken his way through, dragging out spare cloaks and hide blankets that had been bundled into Hammer's saddle bags and stitching them together. Even half-frozen, fingers, toes and lips turning blue, it had not taken them long to fashion a hide shelter and scrape a fire-pit, banked with stones from the riverbed and lit with wood from a dead pine tree.

After a stuttered, shivering conference, both Drem and Cullen had been confident that the river had carried them so far and fast that, unless their enemy built rafts and followed them down the river, there was at least three days' safety between them and their pursuers.

Apart from the half-breed.

Mustn't make a sound now. He put a hand to his jaw and physically clamped it shut, his eyes scanning the surrounding woodland through his latticed hide, looking up to search the treetop canopy.

Where is she?

Cullen was crouching in another hide in the shadows of a stand of pine, not more than thirty paces away from Drem. The sound of the river was a constant background roar in Drem's ears, unhelpfully masking other sounds. They were too close to the riverbank where Hammer had dragged them ashore. Drem could see the bulk of the bear through the trees, a deeper darkness beyond the rough tent he and Cullen had built and where Keld still lay. Hammer was slumped beneath the shadow of a granite boulder. If there was any trouble Drem doubted the bear would be any help, she had hardly moved since she had staggered from the river.

Hammer's done enough for us.

A rustling in the trees above and Drem shifted, quickly and quietly, tightening his grip on a rough javelin he'd carved.

A wood pigeon, that was all.

Cullen said he saw her, the half-breed, flying along the river.

Maybe she won't come this way.

But Drem was sure that she would. He remembered her voice in his ear, the look of hatred.

This is for my brother, she had said.

Don't think she's the type to give up.

He stared at the path that led through the trees to the river. If the half-breed had led Fritha and her acolytes here, if they'd built rafts and floated down the river, then that path was the only approach to their makeshift camp.

Lot of 'ifs' there.

A twig cracked, drawing Drem's eyes. A shadow in the darkness, solidifying into a figure. Squat, muscular, carrying a spear, wings arching over its back.

Drem felt his heartbeat quicken. He'd sat in hides a thousand times, hunting elk and other beasts, and never felt the worry of it.

Hunting half-breed Kadoshim is different, though.

His hand reached to his neck, found the comforting beat of his pulse.

The half-breed trod carefully through the pines. Boughs hung low over her head.

Harder for her to fly here. That's in our favour.

Drem focused on breathing long and slow, resisting the urge to burst from his hide and hurl his javelin.

Wait. It's all about the timing, my da used to say.

She was close, now, fifty paces, her head swivelling, searching the gloom. Close enough for Drem to see the purpling bruising across her flat nose and eyes, from where he'd head-butted her.

Good. Though I came off worse in that meeting. The knife-cut along his waist burned with every movement.

Drem could see the fabric of her wool tunic, taut and stretched over the musculature of her arms, a thick neck above her leather, fur-trimmed vest.

Then she saw their tent, the patchwork of loosely stitched cloaks and blankets. The half-breed froze for long moments, staring at it, scanning the woodland around it.

Take the bait.

She took a step towards the tent, then another, and another, her spear-point coming down, levelled in front of her.

Drem shifted the grip on his javelin, slow and steady.

Just like hunting. Wait for the moment, then stand and throw. One move.

The half-breed was a dozen paces from their makeshift camp, and by now she must be able to see the shadowed outline of a figure inside the tent, a bulge pressed up against the fabric. Little did she know that it was a branch wrapped in a cloak. Drem remembered the rush of pride he'd felt at Cullen's praise for this trap. The bait, the lure, the hides, all Drem's idea, drawn from his hunting skills. It had just been obvious to him, what he thought anyone would have thought of.

Nevertheless, Cullen had been impressed and, as Drem was finding out about the red-haired warrior, he had not been reticent about verbalizing how he felt.

Five paces from the tent, the half-breed started to raise her spear, preparing for a stab at the shape in the fabric.

When she lunges is the moment. A few more paces and she'll be perfectly placed for both of us. Almost there.

And then with an explosion of undergrowth Cullen burst from his hide and hurled his javelin.

No!

The half-breed leaped, no frozen moment, no fight-or-flight hesitation from her, just instant kinetic motion. Upwards, a short beat of her wings giving her extra height, her head brushing the canopy above her, where she hovered as Cullen's javelin hissed harmlessly beneath her.

Cullen was already running at her, his sword grating from its scabbard.

The half-breed drew back her spear-arm.

He's too far away, she's going to skewer him like a charging boar.

Drem crashed out of his hide, to the half-breed's left, making far more noise than he ever had before. Intentionally.

Her head turned towards him, a snarl twisting her features as she recognized him. Her wings moved, shifting her in the air, and in a heartbeat her spear was hurtling at him instead of Cullen, the half-breed bursting into flight behind it, straight at him.

Drem dived to his right. The forest litter was thick and spongy with fallen pine needles, the spring in it helping him to roll to his knees as the half-breed's spear slammed into a tree trunk that had been immediately behind him.

Drem hurled his javelin, the half-breed throwing herself to the side, swerving but not breaking her flying charge at him. Drem's weapon pierced a leathery wing but passed through it with no apparent effect, other than a small tattered hole in the wing.

Drem grabbed for the hilt of his seax, and then she was slamming into him, her shoulder punching into his belly, lifting him bodily from the ground, both of them flying through the air. Drem crunched into a tree, stars exploding in his vision, air expelled from his lungs, hot lines of pain opening up across his back as the claw wounds from the Feral burst open. The half-breed wrapped a fist around his throat, holding him upright, squeezing.

Drem's vision swam, his hand fumbling for his seax, finding

the bone hilt, drawing and slashing in the same move, cutting across the half-breed's vest, slicing through leather and the fur lining beneath, through the linen under-tunic, and into flesh.

The half-breed flung herself backwards, a grunt of pain, a long diagonal line welling blood across her chest.

A whistle of air and she was ducking, turning as Cullen's sword slashed through air, grazing her wing.

She reeled away, backhanded Cullen in the mouth, sending him staggering to one knee, and she stepped forwards, punched him in the temple, knocked him sprawling to the ground.

Drem pushed away from the tree and slashed at her again, drawing red across her back, cut the base where one wing met her back muscle. She cried out, stumbling forwards, regained her balance and ran, wings snapping wide; a beat, and she was lifting from the ground.

Drem chased after her.

The half-breed rose, swaying in the air, lost altitude, her feet grazing the ground, still running, wings trying to lift her again.

I've damaged her wing.

Drem increased his speed. He was tall, muscular and strong, but he had long legs and was unusually fast for someone so heavy. He gained on the wounded half-breed. She flew low to the ground, hindered by the low branches of the pine trees. Drem's legs and arms pumping, drawing closer, thirty paces behind her, twenty, ten. And then she burst out from the trees into open air, the river wide and foaming white, shingle slopes rising on the river's far side.

Drem exploded from the trees onto a grassy verge, sloping down to the silt and reeds of the riverbank.

The half-breed was rising, swaying erratically in the air, lurching towards the river. Drem skidded to a halt, breathing great blasts of mist into the cold air as he watched the half-breed fly ever higher into the grey sky, hoping that her injured wing would fail her and she would plummet back down to the ground.

She flew beyond the bank, out over the river.

Footsteps drumming behind him and Cullen staggered out from the trees, ran on past Drem, down the slope towards the river. Drem saw Cullen's hand fumble at his belt, unclipping a folded net, a lead-weighted ball stitched to each corner. The half-breed was at least twenty paces out and up from him as Cullen reached the water's edge. She saw the warrior, gave him a hate-filled snarl, then saw him raise the net over his head, swinging it in looping circles, the lead balls humming through the air.

The half-breed's expression changed, a twisted flash of fear and she turned in the air, wings beating harder, a grunt of pain.

Cullen threw the net.

It whistled through the air, rising up, fast and high, reached the apex of its flight and the net opened, lead balls spreading, dragging it down, folding perfectly around the half-breed, the weights spinning around an ankle, a wrist, snaring her wings. She struggled for a weightless moment, then with a despairing cry she tumbled from the air, crashed into the river in an explosion of crystal-cold foam.

The creature disappeared, submerged. Drem, staring, saw her come up twenty or thirty paces downriver, carried by the fast-flowing current. She bobbed on the water, trussed and struggling.

Cullen strode into the water, but almost immediately it rose too deep. Drem ran to his side, splashing into the icy-cold.

The half-breed was carried along, sinking and rising, spluttering and gasping, bound tight in the net's grip, and then she was gone, the river sweeping her around a bend.

Cullen looked at Drem, blood dripping from his lip; he cuffed away more from a cut above his eye.

'Hope the bitch drowns,' Cullen said, and spat blood into the water.

CHAPTER THIRTEEN

FRITHA

Fritha looked up through a mesh of branches at the purpling sky, the sun a red line across the western peaks of the Bonefells as day relinquished its grip upon the world.

Where is Morn?

It was the third day since Fritha had fought the draig, since Drem and his companions had escaped her by leaping into a river.

Since Gunil found my egg.

A shiver of excitement at that thought, banishing for a few moments her unease about Morn's absence and her vexation at Drem's escape. It was quick to return.

She should be back by now. I warned her only to scout. To find Drem and then return to me, so that she could lead me to them. I thought Morn had learned her lesson, understood that she would not achieve her revenge alone, without my help.

'What should I do?' she whispered to herself. 'Stay and wait for Morn?'

But every day here is a day behind Drem, or a day away from the cause. Should I continue my pursuit of Drem?

She swore at the first stars that winked into life, then turned on her heel and marched back to her camp. Her leg ached, a wound across her thigh; ragged rather than a neat cut, it was most likely from the draig's claws.

Arn had cleaned and stitched it for her. A stab of worry at

the thought of him, knowing he was sat at vigil with Elise. Fritha quickened her pace. She felt the presence of a Feral close by, loping in the darkness.

Ah, my babies are protective of me. The thought gave her a warm feeling.

They had buried their dead and then moved a short way from the draig lair, carrying their injured far enough to escape the hideous stench of the draig dung. Fritha walked through the sentry line, glimpsed one of her people standing guard, his shadow merged with a tree. Deeper within the boundary of their camp, Fritha saw the outline of Gunil in the gloom, standing with the shadowed bulk that was Claw. He was tending to the bear's wounds. Fritha wasn't sure the animal would survive – some of its injuries were leaking pus and starting to smell bad.

It will be a grievous loss to the cause, if it dies, she thought. She shrugged and moved on, towards a flicker of flame.

They'd dug a fire-pit, a dozen men and women ringed around it, hands warming on bowls of broth, their breath a mist in the air.

A crude hide tent had been erected close to the fire-pit. Fritha nodded a greeting to those around the fire, then stepped into the tent.

She saw Arn kneeling beside a prone form, his dark hair shaved short, his silvering beard neat and braided, as always. He looked up at her as she entered, his eyes pleading.

'Any change?' Fritha asked him. She received a curt shake of his head in answer as she joined him and knelt beside Elise.

'Help her,' Arn said.

'I have tried,' Fritha muttered, feeling a twist of emotions in her belly. Fear, that she would lose her friend – and they were few and far between. Shame, that she was not skilled enough to work a healing; and annoyance, at Arn, at Elise, at herself, that this should bring her lack of ability so unpleasantly to light.

She stroked Elise's cheek, slick with sweat, remembering the time Arn and Elise had cared for her, when they had found her slumped on the blood-soaked ground, her dead baby in her lap.

I owe her.

Fritha began methodically checking over Elise's wounds. Her ribs had been manipulated back into position and a collection of broken bones had been splinted where possible – right arm broken above the elbow, both of her legs broken in multiple places.

Shattered is a more appropriate word. Even if I save her, I do not know if she will ever be able to walk again.

But it was the internal injuries that worried Fritha most. Elise was coughing blood and her breath was shallow and erratic. Probably from when the draig had struck her in the chest with its tail, snapping ribs and bruising her lungs. There were a number of other possibilities, all of them worse. Internal bleeding highest on the list.

'Look what you are capable of doing, what you have accomplished so far,' Arn whispered. 'The Ferals, Gulla, Revenants . . .' He stared at her, dark eyes desperate.

'I will try again,' Fritha murmured.

She unlaced a leather vambrace from her forearm, pulled the wool tunic back to bare her arm, and drew a knife from her belt. The blade hovered over her pale flesh and she closed her eyes . . .

She remembered a woman's face, severe, hard lines and scars. A fresh cut along one cheek, blood scabbing. A warrior, an empty scabbard at her hip, an iron cloak-brooch fashioned in the shape of a four-pointed star. She was sitting against a tree, chained to it, her hands bound in her lap. Fritha had stood before her.

'Tell me your secrets,' Fritha had said.

The woman had just returned her gaze, strength and defiance in her eyes.

'You will tell me everything,' Fritha had said, drawing a knife.

The same knife she held now.

'*Fola agus focail chumhachta, ceangail an fheoil seo, leigheas an cnámh seo*,' Fritha breathed now as she drew the knife across her forearm, blood welling in a dark line. '*Fola agus focail chumhachta, ceangail an fheoil seo, leigheas an cnámh seo*,' she repeated as she turned her arm and held it over Elise, raising her elbow so that the blood trickled down to her hand, gathering into a droplet on one fingertip, fat and heavy, and dripping into Elise's mouth, another drop on her lips, another, and another as Fritha breathed the words over and over. A sharp wind blew into the tent, swirled around them, sounding like whispered voices.

Elise sucked in a deep breath, her back arching, eyes bulging, and then a long, stuttered sigh, her body relaxing. Her breath seemed a little stronger, a little steadier.

Arn grabbed Fritha's hand.

'Thank you,' he said.

Fritha gave him a wan smile.

'It has helped, but I am not a healer,' she said. 'I wish now that I had questioned the Bright Star warrior more, and for longer. As it was, to learn this much I put her to the question for three days. But I was focused on other matters. I wanted to create things. But healing . . .' She shrugged. 'Let us see how she responds to this.'

'She will be well. I know she will,' Arn said, stroking his daughter's brow. He looked up at Fritha. 'What is your plan?'

'I am torn,' Fritha said. 'Drem and the others could be leagues away by now, so we may never catch them.'

'And is there any point, now?' Arn asked. 'The goal was to catch them quickly, before they could send word to Dun Seren.'

'Aye,' Fritha grunted.

'Their crow, it was not with them,' Arn said.

'I know,' Fritha snapped. 'Which means they've most likely sent it ahead of them, to warn that bitch, Byrne.'

'We should go back to Gulla, then,' Arn said.

Not a pleasant prospect. He doesn't react well to failure. I do have the draig egg, though . . .

'There are reasons to continue our pursuit,' Fritha said quietly. 'Drem shouted a name during the fight, before the draig appeared.'

'I heard,' Arn said. 'Cullen.'

'Aye. Who would have thought that cocky child was Corban's descendant? A prize indeed, if we took him prisoner.'

Arn shrugged. 'If we can find them again, if we can catch up with them, if we can take him alive. A lot of *ifs*.'

Yes, but the glory and honour of returning with Corban's descendant. It would be worth the risk.

'And the huntsman,' Fritha continued. 'Did you hear him speaking the Old Tongue, using the earth power? He turned his blood to fire.'

An indrawn breath from Arn.

'I would like very much to take him alive and put him to the question,' Fritha said. 'We both know how few of the Order are taught the old ways of blood and bone.' She looked at Elise, glanced quickly at Arn. 'He could be skilled at healing. The Order value that.'

She could almost hear Arn's mind focusing on that word, *healing*, and clinging to that shred of hope.

'Perhaps we should continue our pursuit, then,' Arn said. 'But what of Morn? We need her. And she is Gulla's daughter.'

He left the rest unsaid. Fritha knew if Morn was lost, Gulla's wrath would be great indeed. She breathed deep, straightening her shoulders. She knew what she had to do, just did not want to admit it.

'I hope that Morn returns to us. But if she is not here by the time we have broken our fast on the morrow, then we must move on. I will need to speak with Gulla.'

'He will not be happy,' Arn said.

'*I* am not happy,' Fritha snapped. She calmed herself. 'Death smiles at us all,' she said.

'All that we can do is smile back,' Arn replied, repeating their mantra, something they had said a thousand times to each other since the day they had first met. The day the Ben-Elim had come.

Fritha nodded, her thoughts already elsewhere. She squeezed Elise's hand and made her way to the back of the tent, lifted up a fur hide to reveal what lay beneath.

The draig egg.

Fritha crouched beside it, stroked it gently with her palm.

I can feel you stirring, my baby, she thought.

Soon.

She rose and left.

Fritha shared a bowl of broth with her warriors around the fire. A pile of bones, teeth and claws were heaped close to the fire, and the draig's skin was staked out where it had been scraped of flesh and fat.

It will make a score of cloaks and boots.

Then Fritha stood and paced into the shadows, finding a handful of her Ferals gathered together in a huddle, a weave of limbs and fur, the glint of teeth in the dappled starlight. The others had been sent out as guardians, their noses, ears and eyes making them far better than any human sentry. Some were sleeping, but they stirred and looked up at Fritha as she approached.

'Don't get up, my children,' she crooned as she reached them, crouching and stroking the jutting brow of one. He looked at her and whined.

'We'll find them soon,' Fritha said, knowing that the Ferals did not really care; they were guided by much baser instincts: hunger, thirst, a pack mentality. But they were faithful and true to her; if she wanted something done, so did they.

Fritha lay down with them, felt them shift to curl around

her, their warmth seeping into her, a barrier that sent the winter's chill fleeing. The smell wasn't too good, Fritha had to admit, musty, damp fur and sweat, but it was a fair bargain for being warm and feeling safe, protected. Even loved, and that was a feeling that Fritha hadn't known for a very long time.

She closed her eyes.

Fritha raised her hand, calling a halt.

She was standing on the slope of a hill, looking east onto the great plain of the Desolation that opened up before her, jagged and scarred. Snow had softened the fissured landscape, giving it an endless, undulating appearance. It was late in the day, Fritha having set her pace by the injured bear and those carrying the wounded on stretchers.

Here and there on the plain she saw pinpricks of light marking isolated holds. Her eyes fixed on the closest one, roughly two or three leagues from her position.

That will do.

With a gesture, she started her small column moving, picking a way down the slope, through wind-blasted pines in the failing light as dusk settled around them.

Morn had not come, and so Fritha had made the decision to move out. Waiting was achieving nothing, only allowing Drem to widen the gap between them. She had made her decision, knew that she wanted to catch them; she could not turn her back and walk away from the lure of the huntsman's knowledge and power and the prize that was the young Cullen. But she could not build rafts and follow them down the river; they could not fashion a raft big enough to safely take Gunil's bear, so Fritha made the decision to travel by land, which meant back-tracking on their route and attempting to find new paths through the Bonefells that would lead them back to the river.

She was concerned about Morn but knew that if the half-breed was alive and found her way back to the draig lair, she would have no great difficulties in tracking Fritha.

It had taken her most of the day to lead her dwindling, bat-tered survivors to the ravine where Drem and his companions had fooled them and changed their course, but since then they had made better time, the sharp gullies and ravines of the Bonefells shifting to the foothills that bordered the mountains.

Fritha was deeply aware that she was losing time, that each moment was allowing Drem to widen the gap between them, but there was nothing that she could do about that right now, and as annoyed and vexed as she was about it, she was ever the pragmatist.

And besides, there is something else that I must do.

I need to communicate with Gulla, and for that I require certain . . . ingredients.

Fritha crept through the snow, slow and steady, minimizing the crunch of each frozen step, until she reached the post-and-rail fence of a paddock, marking the boundary of the hold.

Silent as smoke, she slipped between the rails and moved into the paddock, Arn a shadow behind her, a deeper darkness behind him that was Gunil. Fritha knew that her people were doing the same all around the hold, edging closer, like wolven stalking an unsuspecting elk. Fritha had commanded her Ferals to stay further out in a loose circle around the hold.

She needed people taken alive.

A building loomed and Fritha pressed tight against it, took a few moments to listen. From the smell and sounds, it was a stable. She leaned out from the shadows, saw two ponies and a thick-boned plough-horse. Beyond the stable was a courtyard, snow glistening like crystals in the starlight. It was bordered by outbuildings – a barn, a chicken coop, a pig-pen. A few goats roamed free. At the courtyard's head was a small feast-hall, snow thick on the turf-covered roof. Light glimmered through shuttered windows, and Fritha heard the murmur of conver-sation.

There was a small gap between the stable and the feast-hall,

Fritha slipping across, climbing the few steps that raised the feast-hall from the ground, Arn behind her, Gunil remaining in the darkness of the stable.

A shadow on the porch before the hall's doors shifted, and then a hound was standing, growling and barking.

Arn stepped around Fritha, took half a dozen steps and put his spear in its chest; growls turned to a high-pitched whine, cut short.

The doors flew open, a dark silhouette with a tangle of beard, standing in a moment's frozen shock. Arn tugged on his spear, trying to turn, but the blade was snagged in the dog's corpse.

Shouts and footsteps came from inside the hall.

The silhouette threw himself at Arn, the two of them stumbling over the hound's body and going down in a snarl of limbs.

Another figure burst from the hall, a woman, lean and wiry. Fritha slammed her spear-butt into the woman's head. She dropped sprawling to the ground and didn't move. Arn and his attacker rolled down the steps to the courtyard, but before Fritha could reach them she was attacked by another figure rushing from the hall, a gangly youth swinging a wood-axe at her. She blocked and retreated, blocked and retreated, resisting the opportunities to stab into his throat or belly.

Then Gunil was there, a fist clubbing the lad across his shoulders, and he was on the ground, too.

Arn was stood over his assailant, who was kneeling on slush-churned ground, a handful of Fritha's crew around him, spears levelled.

'Bind them,' Fritha said.

She strode into the hall, saw a fire-pit with a pot hanging over it, a few stools and chairs around it. An old woman was sitting in one. She held out a knife as Fritha approached.

'I'll not stand and knife-fight you as I would have once,' the woman said, 'but I'll give you a cut or two 'fore you take me.'

'I'm sure you would, grandmother,' Fritha said, dipping her

head respectfully, 'but it would be better for me, and for your kin, if you just drop the knife. I don't want to hurt them, just need the use of your hall for the night.' She stood in front of the old lady, out of knife range, and rested her spear-butt on the ground. Fritha knew she could just skewer the old woman where she sat.

Behind Fritha her crew were entering the hall, dragging their captives.

'No harm will come to them?' the woman said.

'They will all live through this night, you have my oath,' Fritha said.

The woman nodded and dropped the blade.

'A wise choice,' Fritha said. She turned to Arn. 'Take them to the barn, light a fire for them so they don't freeze.'

Arn nodded and left, the captives herded with them.

'What about my mother?' the one who had attacked Arn called, a thickset man with a heavy beard.

'She and I have things to talk about,' Fritha said. She felt sympathy for these people, knew that they had likely come north into the Desolation to escape the rule of the Ben-Elim. They were not the enemy.

But these are hard times, and hard decisions must oft be made.

'Take them away,' Fritha said with a wave of her hand. She inspected the contents of the pot: mutton stew, by the smell of it. She gave it a stir with a ladle, offered some to the old woman, who shook her head, and then scooped herself a bowl-ful. She sat on a stool and shuffled closer to the old woman.

'A hard life for you, here in the Desolation,' Fritha said.

'Hard times all round,' the old woman said suspiciously. 'Just different kinds of hard. The Desolation isn't so bad.'

'Aye,' grunted Fritha, sipping from the bowl. It was greasy and watery but tasted as fine a meal as Fritha could remember right now. 'Freedom's worth much,' she said, watching the grandmother.

'True enough.'

'The Ben-Elim?' Fritha said.

After a long hard stare, the old woman nodded.

'I've heard talk of the Ben-Elim's flesh tithe,' Fritha said. 'They wanted your grandson?'

A long sigh. 'Aye, they did. We were not of a mind to give him up, like coin in some kind of tax.' The old woman spat into the fire.

Fritha nodded, understanding. She wished she had time, knew that the Desolation was filling with people like this, with grudges against the Ben-Elim. But time was no longer a luxury that she and Gulla had. Not with Drem likely only a ten-night away from Dun Seren, and his cursed talking crow closer than that.

Still, she felt that she had to try.

'They'll come here, too,' Fritha said.

'Maybe, maybe not,' the woman said.

'They will,' Fritha said. 'And soon. You could stand against them, fight them. You and your kin.'

'Fight the Ben-Elim and their White-Wings?' The woman snorted. 'Hah. I am no coward, but I am no fool, either. That way's a quick path to an iron-edged death.'

'There are others that would fight the Ben-Elim. You could join them.'

'Who?' the woman said, eyes narrowing suspiciously.

'The Kadoshim,' Fritha said.

'Are you a mad woman?' the grandmother said. 'They are worse than the Ben-Elim. Why fight for them?'

'I'll wager all that you've ever heard of the Kadoshim has come from the mouth or quill of the Ben-Elim. Who has ever spoken highly of their enemy?' Fritha shook her head. 'The Kadoshim are not the monsters that the Ben-Elim make them out to be. They would not be the masters of the Banished Lands, it is just the defeat of the Ben-Elim that they strive for. When the war is won they will share their power, and they will remember those who help them achieve that goal.'

'You're insane,' the woman hissed. 'You would have me trade one tyrant for another. No, better to come here, to leave them to their scrapping and start a new life. A hard life, aye, but a free one.'

'Free today, but for how long?' Fritha said. 'You think the Ben-Elim will not come here? Of course they will, maybe not this moon, nor the next, but soon. Before your grandson is a man, is my guess.'

The old woman scowled at her.

'Why do *you* fight for them, then?'

Fritha looked at the old woman, saw a genuine question in her eyes.

'Because the Ben-Elim killed my baby,' Fritha whispered, choosing to tell the truth.

Footsteps. Fritha knew from the way the floorboards shook that it was Gunil.

The way the grandmother's eyes widened as she looked over Fritha's shoulder also gave Fritha the same answer.

'What monsters have you brought into my hold?' The old woman spat out a curse.

'War makes monsters of us all,' Fritha said. 'And the trouble with war is that it follows you. Sometimes there's no escaping it. Sometimes the only choice is to choose which side you stand on.'

'My son and his wife, my grandson,' the grandmother said, eyes fixed on Gunil, who was towering over Fritha now, as he examined the contents of the pot over the fire-pit. 'You swore they would live.'

'They will,' Fritha said. 'I can't just leave them here, though. They will come with me and choose a side. You, though, grandmother, you are not up to the journey. And I did not swear to keep you safe.'

Fritha shook her head, leaning forward and patting the old woman's hand. She felt a wave of sympathy for this woman, a sadness at what she had to do.

'I am sorry,' Fritha said, 'but I need your face.' And, faster than a blink, she drew her knife and stabbed the old woman in the throat.

Fritha sliced her knife across her palm and squeezed her hand into a fist, letting the blood flow and drip into a small iron bowl she'd set on a table. Beyond it was a wooden frame she'd quickly crafted, four hooks in each corner. Attached to these hooks was the skinned face of the old woman she'd just killed, stretched out across the frame, hanging loose like an empty sail. Globs of fat and blood still dripped from it. The dead woman's body lay cast upon the ground. Out of the corner of her eye Fritha saw a rat scurry from the shadows and start nibbling at the meat exposed beneath the hastily skinned face. She ignored it.

'*Glacaim liom anois, Gulla, aingeal dubh, agus tríd an fhuil,*' Fritha chanted as she dripped her blood into the bowl. It rippled as if some hidden wyrm were uncoiling within it.

'*Glacaim liom anois, Gulla, aingeal dubh, agus tríd an fhuil,*' she repeated, louder. The skin stretched upon the frame twitched and spasmed. Although the doors had been closed and barred, the windows tightly shuttered, a cold wind blew through the room, sending the flames in the fire-pit dancing and hissing, making shadows dance. Behind her, Fritha heard Gunil grunt.

'*Glacaim liom anois, Gulla, aingeal dubh, agus tríd an fhuil,*' Fritha said for the third time, and the skin on the frame shifted, filling as if a breeze moved it, then more violently, the mouth jerking, opening, the cheeks filling, changing shape, and the eyes sparking to red life.

'Fritha,' a voice rasped from the animated skin, Gulla's voice. 'What do you want? I am busy.'

Fritha drew in a deep breath.

Little point worrying about a thing. Best just to say it.

'Morn is missing, and Drem and his companions are likely

going to reach Dun Seren. Even if we catch them, the crow that took your eye is no longer with them. I think it likely they've sent it on ahead to take word of you to Byrne.'

'What!' The face snarled, grating like iron scraping over a cairn-stone. A smell of decay wafted from the mouth of the skinned visage.

Fritha repeated her words. 'I am sorry, Lord,' she added.

'Gunil?' Gulla's voice asked.

'I am here,' the giant said. He was looking at the rat, still feasting upon the dead woman's skinless face.

'Report,' Gulla ordered.

'Things have not gone well.' Gunil shrugged. 'My Claw has been wounded.'

Is that all he cares about? Fritha scowled.

'By a draig,' Fritha added. 'We have sustained casualties. Drem and the two Order warriors escaped by leaping into a river while we fought the draig.'

'And my daughter?' Gulla growled.

'She went out scouting four days ago and has not returned.'

The skinned face scowled, not a pleasant expression. Fritha controlled the urge to shudder.

Gunil raised a foot and stamped on the rat. Bones crunched.

'The Order are likely to hear of our presence at the Starstone Lake,' Fritha said. 'Of the sword, of you . . .'

'I understand the implications,' Gulla snapped. 'I am not ready yet, have more to do.' A silence. The red eyes shifted and flickered. 'We will have to speed up the plan. There is nothing else we can do. I shall send forth the Seven.'

'You are able to do that?'

'Aye. We have turned half a thousand already, from Kergard and the surrounding holds. I wanted more before I sent out my Seven, but . . .' The face twitched, a movement like wind blowing across a sail.

'I will send them into the Land of the Faithful,' he said. A fierce shifting of his mouth, a ghastly parody of a smile.

'What of our allies in the south?' Fritha asked.

'I will send word to the Shekam also, but this may be too soon for them.' A snarl rippled across the skinned face. 'A hundred years in the planning, and now there is no time. Because of a talking crow.'

Plans are wonderful things until they go wrong, Fritha thought. *Which they always do.* She held her tongue, though, and remained silent as the parody of Gulla's features twisted in rage.

'Your numbers,' Gulla eventually said, 'and, where are you?'

'Thirty of us,' Fritha said. 'We are at a hold at the southern tip of the Bonefells; likely thirty leagues from Dun Seren.'

Another silence, the jaws of the animated skin opening and closing, as if Gulla were gnashing his teeth.

'You must return to me. You carry the Starstone Sword and you're too close to Dun Seren. We cannot risk it falling into the hands of the Order of the Bright Star.'

Fritha hated to fail at a task, and she longed to take Drem and his companions prisoner, just so that she could drag them back to Gulla and cast them at his feet.

She muttered a curse to herself.

'What?' Gulla's voice said.

'There are reasons to continue the pursuit,' Fritha said. 'One of them, the huntsman, knows the earth power. He spoke the old words, melted the faces from a handful of my people. And the young one, he is Cullen, descendant of Corban.'

The skinned face creased as Gulla frowned. 'Two valuable prizes.' The lips moved, a sibilant hiss. 'One with the closely guarded secrets of the Order, the other a trophy to crush their spirit and raise our own. I remember that Corban.' Gulla spat the words like a poison. 'The worm that dared stand against our king.'

'He slew Calidus, Asroth's chosen commander, the legends tell,' Fritha said, intrigued to hear a Kadoshim speak of those days.

'Aye,' Gulla grunted, 'through trickery. Calidus was a fool.'

'To capture his grandchild would be a great triumph, my Lord. One that you could proclaim to your kin. Something to set against the blow of being forced to move sooner than planned.'

Gulla's face twitched and snarled.

'Hunt them a little longer,' he breathed.

'As you command, my Lord,' Fritha said.

'Good. Do not fail me.' With a long, exhaled sigh like the rattle before death, the skinned face deflated, sagging in its framework.

Fritha set to taking it apart, packing it away into a small wooden chest she'd found in the hall. She folded the skinned face and wrapped it in a piece of linen, putting it into the chest on top of the frame and iron bowl.

A fist pounded on the door and Fritha turned, swept up her spear.

Gunil strode to the doors and lifted off the bar he'd set across it. Arn was there, his arm around a figure half-slumped against him.

It was Morn.

She was wet and bedraggled, ice glistening in the hair on her stubbled head, and one of her wings drooped at an odd angle. Something was draped about her, a tattered net snared in one wing and arm, wrapped around her leg.

Arn half led her, half dragged her into the hall, Gunil taking the half-breed in his thick arms.

Morn lifted her head and looked at Fritha.

'I've found them,' the half-breed said.

CHAPTER FOURTEEN

DREM

'Some help here,' Cullen said, pointing to a pot hanging over a small fire. They were sitting within their rough-made tent, a screen of hide blankets and cloaks stitched together and tied to coppiced branches, a fire-pit scraped into the hard earth.

Drem stood, wincing as the knife-cut along his waistline rubbed, scabs cracking, and the stitches in his back and arm pulled.

I hope she drowned, Drem thought, echoing Cullen's words at the riverside. Three days had passed since the half-breed had fallen into the river, and there had been no sight or sound of her or Fritha's acolytes. So the likelihood was she had drowned.

And good riddance.

The knowledge that they needed to move seeped through Drem, making him anxious and fidgety. But he also knew they could not leave. Keld was in the grip of a fever, and Hammer was slumped outside, unable or refusing to walk.

Our only option is to leave them, which I won't do. I hope that Rab has reached Dun Seren.

Cullen passed a branch through the handle of the pot and they both lifted it, carrying it away from the fire. Dappled starlight lit their way as they walked a dozen paces beneath the shelter of pine trees towards the prostrate form of Hammer. The bear lifted her heavy head from her paws and looked at them, a morose growl rumbling in her belly.

'Here you go, girl,' Cullen said as they placed the pot in front of the bear. She sniffed it and looked away.

'That won't do,' Cullen said, squatting before her and using a ladle as a spoon, scooping a thick, porridge-like substance from the pot and lifting it to the bear's lips.

'She usually loves *brot*,' Cullen whispered over his shoulder to Drem, his voice heavy with worry. 'Can't get enough of the stuff.'

Drem checked the numerous bandages about the bear, applied more honey and compresses to the bear's many injuries, a multitude of claw marks and puncture wounds. None smelled bad or leaked pus, which was something, though Drem feared that the bear would never walk properly again. He'd checked the bones in her shoulder where he'd seen the giant strike her with his great war-hammer, and from what he could tell nothing seemed broken, but since Hammer had pulled and clawed her way out of the river and onto this riverbank, she had taken her weight for only a few score seconds or so. Rising briefly to stagger across the shingle bank, up higher onto a grassy slope and into the cover of these towering pine trees, and then a little further to collapse against a granite boulder. She had not stood since then, even during the half-breed's attack, despite every effort to encourage her from Cullen and Drem.

Cullen managed to spoon a few ladles of *brot* into Hammer's mouth, and Drem stroked her neck, felt her swallow once. They persevered, tried to give her more, but Hammer just lay her head down on her paws and gave out what sounded like a long, rumbling groan, almost like a sigh.

Has she given up? Pining for Sig, and now her injuries and exhaustion on top of that grief.

'That'll have to do for now,' Cullen said dejectedly. He rubbed Hammer's furry cheek and stood. They made their way back to their shelter and hung the pot back over the fire,

Cullen stirring its contents. When it started to bubble again he filled two bowls and passed one to Drem.

'Eat it while it's still warm,' Cullen said. 'And trust me when I say it doesn't get to taste any better when it's cold.'

Drem sniffed it.

The *brot* was as thick as porridge, though it tasted more of earth and bark than hot oats. After his first taste Drem had declined, but Cullen had insisted, claiming it was made by giants and would fill and sustain him far longer than any other meal.

Starving hunger had eventually convinced Drem to eat it. Cullen had been right: Drem had felt strengthened and fortified, the effects lasting far longer than he would have expected, though he'd been tempted to add some of their small supply of honey to help it go down better, but they were saving that for the treatment of the many wounds they seemed to be collecting.

Keld lay within their shelter, eyes closed, his chest rising and falling in what looked like sleep. He was thick with sweat, his skin mottled and patchy, a lump the size of an egg on the back of his head, his chest criss-crossed with claw marks from the Feral that had felled him. Drem and Cullen had cleaned the wounds, but on the second day they had turned angry and inflamed, by the third day had started weeping thick yellow pus. On the fourth day Drem had thought Keld was going to die, but then something had turned in him, and by the fifth day the fluid leaking from Keld's wounds was clear. His fever had lessened, though it was not beaten yet. Keld's head cast about and he murmured something, a word breathed from cracked lips.

'Fen.'

Drem felt a deep guilt at leaving the wolven-hound behind. Cullen had slung the unconscious form of Keld over his shoulder and run for the river, Hammer limping and lumbering after him, and Drem had run to the hound, a pile of fur at the base of a tree where the draig had thrown it. Fen was breathing, but Drem could not get the animal to stand. He'd tried to lift the wolven-hound and had managed to raise him into his arms, a prodigious feat, as the animal weighed the rough equivalent of a pony. Fen had snapped at him, whined with the pain. Drem was no weakling, in fact men had picked fights with him because of his size and freakish strength, but a score of paces and Drem's back and legs were crumpling. He'd been unable to go on, had tried calling to Cullen and Hammer, but they were out of earshot and couldn't hear him over the din of the draig and giant bear anyway, and there was no time to get them and come back for the wolven-hound, so he'd veered into the trees and laid Fen down behind a fallen rotted tree. A rib-bone was protruding through the wolven-hound's side. Drem put one hand on the bone, another on the hound's side, and pushed, trying to manipulate the bone back into place. He'd got a snapping growl and a half-hearted bite for it, but with a click the bone slotted back into place.

'I'm sorry, lad,' Drem said, 'but I can't carry you.' He heaped a mound of litter over the wolven-hound, then ran for the river and Cullen.

The guilt of it lay heavily upon him.

Cullen checked Keld, wiped his brow tenderly with a damp cloth, his eyes creased with worry.

'Come back to me, Keld,' Drem heard Cullen whisper. 'I cannot lose you, too.' A teardrop dripped from the young warrior's nose and he sniffed and cuffed more tears away.

'Can you not do . . . something?' Drem asked, thinking of how Keld had revealed the runes upon his seax. And of how his father Olin had forged the Starstone Sword, chanting words of power.

'What do you mean?' Cullen said, frowning. 'I've done all I can think of.'

'I mean, the earth power. Keld made the runes appear on my seax. Can you not help Keld's healing?'

'The Order does not spoon out the earth power like *brot*, more's the pity,' Cullen said glumly. 'Only a few are invited to learn. *It is a great honour, a privilege, and we must be sure you can handle the responsibility of that power*,' he added in a high-pitched voice, as if he mimicked someone else's speech. 'Apparently, I am not deemed *responsible*, yet,' Cullen muttered.

Drem spooned *brot* into his mouth, forcing himself to swallow.

'There are worse ways to stay alive.' Cullen grinned at him as he ate his own bowl of steaming *brot* with apparent gusto. Shockingly, and remarkably, Cullen had escaped the fight at the draig den almost completely unscathed. A few scratches, a bruise on his shoulder, but nothing more serious. Drem had needed stitching on the cut Fritha had given him on his forearm, as well as the deep gouges across his back from a Feral's claws. The knife-cut from the half-breed along his waist was the shallowest, but also the one that hurt the most, almost every movement pulling and rubbing at the scabbing wound.

We should leave here soon. Should have left days ago. But how can we, with Keld still unable to walk? Cullen and I could build a litter and carry him, but we would be so slow, Fritha and her beasts would be upon us in no time. It's amazing that they haven't found us already. We need Hammer to carry Keld out of here, if only she would try and stand. It seems that she's lost the will to live.

'I can't leave Keld or Hammer behind,' Cullen said fiercely, as if reading Drem's thoughts. 'I've known them all my life, spent most of my days in their company. They're close to me as kin.'

'I'd not ask you to,' Drem said. 'Some things are more important than breathing a little longer.' His thoughts drifted to his da, Olin, the only constant he had ever known in his life – a stab of pain in his belly, grief, like a leviathan stirring. All of his life Drem could only remember his father, and that had been enough for him. He had loved the brief mentions of his mam, longed to hear more of her, and in the last year he had become more and more agitated at his father's reticence to tell Drem of his past. In the end Olin had, and Drem understood now why it had been such a closely guarded secret. He wished that he'd had more time to spend with Olin after he had heard the truth from his father's lips. If anything, it had made them closer, Drem hearing how Olin's whole life had been dedicated to keeping Drem safe.

He blinked, banishing tears that threatened to rise.

He looked at Cullen, so young, only eighteen summers old, and yet he had seen so much, was so skilled with a blade.

Though that is hardly surprising, given his lineage. Cullen was the great-grandson of Corban, greatest hero of the Banished Lands.

'Do you remember my mam and da?' Drem asked Cullen.

'Ach, no,' Cullen said. 'I was barely two summers old when the Battle of Varan's Fall and all that happened with the Ben-Elim occurred.' He shrugged. 'I felt as if I knew them, though, for all the tales that are told about them. Fine warriors, the both of them, but your mam, she was a terror, if Sig spoke true – and Sig always spoke true, even when the truth would cut like a blade.' He smiled, a weight of memory behind the expression.

'I only know what anyone at the Order knows,' Cullen continued. 'That the Ben-Elim wanted you as a ward, because your mam was sister to Byrne, our high captain. Olin stole you away from the Order, both to save you and to prevent a war between the Order and the Ben-Elim. A brave man, your da, that's what Sig said.'

'He was.' Drem sighed, thinking of how Olin had kept him safe, moving, living a solitary life.

Da wasn't just my kin, he was my only friend.

'What of Byrne, my aunt?' Drem asked. It felt strange saying that out loud. For all of his life Drem had not known of any kin related to him beyond his father and his dead mother. And Byrne was High Captain of the Order of the Bright Star, descended from Cywen, Corban's sister.

'Ah, now there's a warrior. Not to look at, not like Sig, where you just *knew* crossing blades with her would end badly. Byrne, though, she looks . . .' He paused and thought, tapping a tooth. '*Ordinary*. She's not, though. I've had more bruises from Byrne in the weapons-field than from anyone else, including Sig. Byrne's adder-fast, and she uses this.' He tapped his forehead. 'She's got a sharp tongue on her as well, doesn't suffer fools gladly.' Cullen grimaced, and Drem could tell there was a weight of memory and experience behind that expression, too.

Beyond their shelter, Hammer growled.

In a heartbeat Cullen was on his feet and striding out of their shelter into the night, sword hissing into his fist. Drem was a moment behind him, ignoring the pain from his complaining wounds. He drew his seax and stood next to Cullen, staring into the night-black, silvered by starlight.

Hammer's head was up and she was snuffling the air in great snorts.

'Hold your breath, Hammer, I'm trying to listen,' Cullen muttered, eyes scanning the darkness.

Drem moved away from the shelter and the soft fire-glow that leaked from the hide entrance, slipping into the tree-dark. He looked up, knew that their shelter was shielded from eyes above by the combination of thick canopy and hide tent. He'd reconnoitred all three of the paths that led away from this spot, knew that only one of them twisted roughly north, in the direction of their last encounter with Fritha.

If they've found us, that will be where they come from.

Drem had set a few traps, more as a chance of early warning than in any hope of defeating Fritha and her horrific crew. But as he listened to the coal-black woods he heard nothing.

Then . . .

More a whisper of sound, the hint of a footfall. He strained, trying to hear, to cut through the darkness with eyes and ears. Nothing, and then there it was, again but louder, like a shuffling gait. His eyes snapped towards the sound. A deeper darkness in the gloom formed, the suggestion of movement. Growing larger, closer.

Drem crouched, Seax held ready, and Cullen took a step into the darkness, sword gilded in starlight.

A whine.

Then Cullen was running forwards and Fen the wolven-hound was limping out of the murk.

Drem was only a footstep behind as Cullen dropped to his knees and hugged the wolven-hound, wrapping his arms around the beast's thick neck.

Drem felt such a sense of relief that a grin split his face, the weight of their circumstances leaving him for a while.

'Ah, but you're a tough one,' Cullen was saying, laughing and crying. 'I saw you jump at that draig, you lunatic.'

Fen gave Cullen a rasping lick on the cheek, but then he was pushing through Cullen's embrace, shaking him off and limping forwards, towards their shelter. Cullen let the wolven-hound go, eyes shining.

Drem followed Fen as he limped his way into the shelter. The hound stopped then, took a long sniff of the air, head weaving, eyes fastening upon Keld lying beyond the fire-pit. A quickening of his pace and he was beside the huntsman, nudging him, licking him, whining. Keld stirred, muttered something incomprehensible, but did not wake.

Fen turned in a circle and lay down tight to the uncon-scious huntsman; with a very human-like sigh he rested his head on the huntsman's hand, and in a handful of heartbeats the wolven-hound was asleep, his deep chest rising and falling.

'Ach, with friends like this, how can we ever lose?' Cullen grinned at Drem.

Drem smiled back, overwhelmed to see the wolven-hound, the guilt he had felt at leaving him lifting from his mind.

That hound has a will of iron. Drem remembered how bad his condition had been.

He has had a long hard road to find us.

They settled down for the night, Drem taking first watch. He stepped outside their rudimentary shelter and found a pine tree to lean against, pulled tight the bearskin cloak about his shoulders and looked out into the darkness. He rested a hand upon the seax at his belt, loosened the blade in its scabbard, something that was becoming a habit with him. The cold would make the blade stick, and the last thing he wanted was to need his blade and not be able to draw it.

Something was telling him that he might be needing a blade in his hand, all too soon.

Because if Fen could find us, then so can other things.

Drem woke to the sound of Fen the wolven-hound urinating up the side of their shelter.

I've had better starts to a day.

He rolled over and saw Cullen was banking the fire and setting a pot to bubbling.

Drem slipped out from under his blanket as Fen pushed his way through the stitched cloaks that acted as a tent flap and padded over to Keld. He set to licking the huntsman's face, nibbling at his beard as if he were grooming Keld.

'Ach, get off,' Keld said, a hand reaching up to attempt a feeble shove. Fen *yipped* and leaped in a circle, his wagging tail threatening to bring down the tent, began pawing at Keld, crouching and barking, pawing again.

'Keld!' Cullen cried, rushing to the huntsman's side.

Drem grinned.

Keld sat up, rubbing his head.

'I'm *starving*,' he said.

'Ah, but it's good to have you back with us,' Cullen said to Keld.

Keld nodded, said something incomprehensible through a mouthful of *brot*.

Drem was starting to feel a little worried about the

JOHN GWYNNE

huntsman. He knew that half a bowl of the foul-tasting gruel had filled him to bursting and made him feel as if he'd had a stomach full of lead for the next day and a half. Keld was on his *third* bowl.

He's going to eat himself to death.

Drem handed Keld a spit of squirrel meat that had been turning over the fire. He was a trapper, after all, and had been sitting in this camp for six days. He'd had to do something, so their food bags were full, and *brot*, thankfully, was no longer a necessity. Keld looked up from his bowl and took the squirrel meat, tore off a chunk.

'It's hot, you might want to take it slo—'

Keld swallowed the chunk of meat, hardly chewing it, and ripped off another slab of meat.

'Never mind.'

'So, what trouble are we in?' Keld asked, wiping grease from his mouth and beard.

'Remarkably, none that I can report on,' Cullen said good-naturedly. 'I thought Fritha and her arsewipes would have sniffed us out by now.' He patted his sword hilt. 'But thus far, no such luck.' He gave his mad grin, the one that Drem was starting to associate with Cullen's desire for against-all-odds danger.

They'd told Keld of how the battle had ended, of the draig and their mad scramble for the river, of tying Keld to Hammer's back and leaping into the ice floe.

'After a day in the river Hammer dragged us onto the riverbank, managed to heave herself this far, and then collapsed. Since then we've been thawing our toes out by the fire, waiting for you to wake up . . .' Cullen grinned.

'You should have left me, made for Dun Seren,' Keld said, frowning. 'Byrne must know of what is happening in the north.'

'I wasn't going to be leaving you anywhere, not while there was breath in your body.'

Keld swallowed the chunk of meat, hardly chewing it, and

'This is too importan—' Keld started to say, but Cullen held up a hand.

'"We leave no one behind," remember,' Cullen said, a surly expression twisting his mouth. 'It's part of my oath, so if you think I've done wrong, you can take it up with Byrne when we get back to Dun Seren.' He stood and took their bowls. 'I'm going to wash these out.' He paused at the tent flap. 'Maybe I should have left you, but Hammer's refused to move for six days, too. Hasn't even stood up since we got here. And Rab's gone to Dun Seren. Byrne will hear of Gulla whether we make it back or no.' He turned and stomped off before Keld had a chance to speak.

The huntsman looked at Drem and gave him a wink.

'He's a good lad, our Cullen,' Keld said, 'but he needs a bit of encouragement to use this sometimes.' He tapped his temple with a finger.

'I think he was right,' Drem said with a shrug. 'Rab should have reached Dun Seren by now.' He paused, looking at Keld. 'Would you have done any different? I don't think you would.'

'Ah, maybe you're right, lad,' Keld said, sighing. 'This knock to my head, and running away from half-breeds and traitors.' He shook his head. 'Makes me angry.' He stood slowly, stretched, Fen rising from his spot by the fire.

'Best go and see Hammer, then, see if we can convince her to join us in a walk.'

Keld limped out of the tent, still carrying the remains of his squirrel breakfast. Drem tried to support him, but the huntsman gave Drem a dark look.

'If I can't walk out of a tent without help then I might as well throw myself back into the river,' he growled.

Cullen returned from the riverbank and followed as they made for Hammer. Fen padded ahead of them. Drem could see the wolven-hound was favouring his right foreleg, limping a little, but his ribs seemed to have set well enough, which he was relieved about.

'Hello, lass,' Keld said gently, as he drew near to Hammer. The bear was sleeping, snoring loudly enough to shake pine cones from boughs in the trees around her. She roused at his voice, raised her head and gave out a rumbling sound that wasn't quite a growl.

Keld crouched down beside the bear and wrapped a fist in the thick fur of her cheek.

'It's good to see you, lass,' Keld said. He leaned into the bear, pressing his forehead against her long muzzle. Hammer dwarfed him, her head roughly the size of Keld's crouching body, but as Drem stared at them he thought there was something almost vulnerable about the bear. She made snuffling noises as she sniffed Keld.

'I miss Sig, too,' Keld said, and more rumbling echoed from the bear's deep chest. 'She was the best of us, and no denying. And I can see you've had a hard time of it.' He stroked one hand along scabbed cuts that scarred Hammer's muzzle, then ran his hand down to her shoulder, his fingers probing as he did so. She didn't complain, which Drem thought was a good sign.

'Some squirrel?' Keld said, offering Hammer the remains of his spitted breakfast.

Hammer took the food, hardly more than a morsel for her vast maw. Keld gestured with a hand, and Drem ran to their tent, fetched a whole squirrel and hurried back, giving it to Keld.

'You've had a hard time of it, lass, I've been beaten up, too,' Keld was saying to the bear.

Fen rubbed his body against Hammer's side, whined and licked her mouth.

'And Fen, too,' Keld said.

'Here you go,' Keld said, pulling more pieces of meat off the skewer, bones and all. 'We're in a bit of a mess, you, me and Fen,' Keld continued, 'but we can't just give up, now, can we? What would Sig think?'

More squirrel went into Hammer's mouth, bones crunching.

Keld stood up.

'Come on, girl, let's go home,' he said, and gave a tug on the fur of her cheek. 'Let's do it for Sig. Make her proud.'

Hammer raised her head, looking at him with her small, bright, intelligent eyes, then looked at Fen. The wolven-hound barked at her.

A rumbling sound deep in Hammer's belly, then a slow shifting, like a whale rising out of the sea, and then Hammer was standing, her wounded leg shaking, her shoulder quivering.

Drem looked at them, Keld, Fen and Hammer, the three of them battered and scarred, but not beaten. He felt a lump in his throat.

'Ah, see, she's just been waiting for Fen to join her and old Keld to wake up,' Keld said over his shoulder to Drem and Cullen. 'Now, be right quick and break camp.'

Drem took the rearguard position as they walked away from their campsite. Cullen was in the lead, Fen scouting a little ahead of him, Keld and Hammer in between. Keld had refused to even try and sit on Hammer's back, saying it would be too much for the bear, and Drem thought he was probably right. Hammer was upright and steadier than Drem had dared hope, but she was clearly weak on her left side; walking would be enough of a trial for her. They'd stripped all of her tack, bridle and saddlebags that had been strapped to her, and tried to share them out between each other. Anything they didn't class as essential had been left behind, but there was still a lot of extra weight on Drem's back. It didn't help that he had given himself extra baggage, deeming himself bigger and stronger than Cullen.

Besides, if we end up in a fight, Cullen's the one who's most likely to save us with his swordcraft. He'll need his blade in his fist quick, and not have to be worrying about extricating himself from a mountain of packs.

He can be the fighter, I'll be the packhorse.

Drem looked back at their old camp as they walked deeper into the pinewoods and smiled. If Fritha ever did catch up with them, he'd left a little surprise for her. He'd had six days to fill, after all, and there was only so much trapping he could do.

He set his face to the trail ahead and followed Hammer's gigantic furry backside.

They were climbing slowly upwards, curling through a sea of pine, following a path that Drem had tracked a little way during the last few days. Not really a path, more just about the only route that wasn't blocked by boulders, sheer cliffs or snow. It took them roughly south and east, which Drem judged was the way to Dun Seren.

If we ever find a way out of the Bonefells.

They were in uncharted territory, deep within the hills and mountains of the Bonefells, a western region that Olin had never taken Drem into before. From the tales in Kergard, no one else had tried, either. It had a bad reputation, with all manner of wild stories putting off sensible trappers.

And now I know why.

If we manage to stay ahead of Fritha and her followers, we must have come through the worst of it. There can't be anything worse than draigs in these mountains and hills.

CHAPTER FIFTEEN

RIV

Riv stood in the shadows of one of the alcoves carved into the walls of Drassil's great keep. The walls curved in a vertiginous dome around the colossal tree trunk that the entire fortress of Drassil was built around. Riv was high above the ground, gazing down into the Great Hall where, far below her, people were gathering, flowing in through the wide gates and sitting upon the tiered stone steps of the Great Hall. Even from her lofty vantage point she could see almost every detail of those who came in. That was something else that had changed about her: her vision sharper and keener since she had grown her wings.

Riv saw Bleda enter, felt something shift in her chest at the sight of him. She remembered him calling to her, that night on the road as they had been journeying back to Drassil. She knew he wanted her to explain why she was behaving like this, to tell him what was happening. She'd wanted nothing more than to fly back down to him and tell him everything. He must have heard Aphra's revelation at the cabin, that Kol was her father. Just the thought of it filled her with shame. She had wanted to tell Bleda of all that had happened in the cabin, that she had made a deal with him, sworn an oath, but only to protect Bleda and her friends. But something inside her would not, *could not*, tell him.

How could she tell him that she had made a deal with Kol!

The man who had killed Bleda's brother and sister! Hard enough for Bleda to learn that Kol was her father. She still could not grasp it fully herself, and she felt a shame deep as her bones about it. There was a logical part of her that knew the shame she felt was ridiculous, that it was out of her control, that it was as deranged as feeling shame if you'd been born male or female, or in this town instead of that one but, nevertheless, that shame was there, like a worm in her veins. And, to be honest, the logical side of her never usually came out on top.

Bleda walked straight-backed, with a touch of the rolling gait that hinted at the master-horseman that Riv knew him to be. His face was set, his cold-face in place, eyes scanning the room, taking everything in. This was the Bleda she had seen over the last six or seven years, but now she knew what she saw was merely the tip of the iceberg above water. There were great depths to him hidden beneath the surface.

Ellac and a few of his honour guard were ranged about Bleda, all stony-faced, as Riv would expect of the Sirak, and with them came Jin, Princess of the Cheren Clan and Bleda's betrothed. Riv felt her lips twist at the sight of the young woman. Not only had she entirely forgotten that Jin and Bleda had been betrothed as some kind of political union to bring the Clans of the Sirak and Cheren under the protective wing and control of the Ben-Elim, but she had also forgotten the depth of her dislike for Jin. She could not stand her arrogance, the way she spoke to Riv, or even looked at her. Or the way she looked at Bleda. Jin sat next to Bleda on the tiered steps, shuffled closer to him, leaned closer still and whispered something in his ear.

Riv felt an almost overwhelming desire to fly down there, grab Jin by her hair and hoist her into the air. With a shuddering breath she fought the urge and forced herself to look away.

A host of Ben-Elim were spread amongst the ever-growing crowd, thousands of them, more than Riv had ever seen before. Many Ben-Elim existed in the Banished Lands, three thousand, four thousand of them, maybe, scattered throughout the Land of the Faithful. There were over two thousand of them in the Great Hall right now.

White-Wings, the elite warriors of the Ben-Elim, numbered in the region of ten thousand swords, most of them garrisoned along the borders of the Land of the Faithful. Between one and two thousand usually remained within Drassil's walls, guardians of the statues of Asroth and Meical, as well as a reserve force to deal with outbreaks of rebellion or the discovery of a Kadoshim nest. Far more than two thousand White-Wings were filing into the Great Hall. Ben-Elim and White-Wings – they had all returned from the four corners of the Land of the Faithful at Kol's summons, at the news of Israfil's death. At least two or three score more Ben-Elim flew in lazy circles around the enormous expanse that towered over the hall, Riv recognizing them as some of Kol's most trusted men.

On the ground, Kol sat upon a carved chair; the other chairs either side of him that were usually filled by Ben-Elim or giants were all empty. Behind him, though, were ranks of loyal Ben-Elim, three, four hundred at least, their chainmail bright, and on either flank were units of White-Wings, leather and steel polished and gleaming. On Kol's right stood Aphra with her hundred, Vald and Jost standing amongst their ranks, and on Kol's left Lorina with her hundred.

Further still behind Kol, the iron-coated figures of Asroth and Meical stood upon a wide dais, frozen and locked in their perpetual conflict. Meical, once High Captain of the Ben-Elim, was upon his knees, grasping at Asroth, the Lord of the Fallen. Asroth's leathery wings were spread, held in mid-flight, Meical pulling him back. One of Asroth's hands gripped Meical's throat; the other arm was pulled back as if to strike at him, except that now there was only a stump where Asroth's fist had been.

Bleda was here when the Kadoshim and their acolytes attacked

Drassil and carved Asroth's right hand from his arm. He said he saw Asroth blink.

Something changed in the hall below her, the murmured hum of a crowd settling. Kol had stood from his seat.

Riv sucked in a deep breath, knowing what was to come.

Hating what was to come.

'Greetings, people of the Land of the Faithful,' Kol said. By some ingenious effect of the curved architecture of the hall, his voice echoed around the chamber, effortlessly filling the huge room. 'Both humankind and Ben-Elim, I am grateful that you have come so quickly at such a dark time.'

He stepped forwards, everything about him assured and confident.

'Our high captain, Israfil, is dead, slain by a dread conspiracy amongst our own.' He hung his head. 'It has been the greatest of tragedies.'

Murmurs rippled amongst the crowd.

A Ben-Elim stepped out from the crowd, tall and finely handsome, dark hair pulled tight to his head and tied at the nape. He wore a cuirass of polished leather, embossed upon it a serpent, body coiling in a circle, at its apex two heads meeting, fangs bared. About his neck was a silver torc of twisted silver, the same two serpents' heads meeting. Riv recognized him as Sariel, a captain of the Ben-Elim rarely seen at Drassil. He led the legions who guarded the south-eastern border. The crowd hushed.

'Who?' he said.

Kol met Sariel's eye and waited for the hall to become utterly silent.

'Adonai,' Kol said.

Gasps and outraged shouts rippled around the chamber.

The Ben-Elim Adonai had been one of Kol's closest friends, one of his inner circle. He was also the father of Fia's baby. Israfil the Lord Protector had put Adonai on trial in this very room, found him guilty of consorting with a White-Wing.

Israfil had drawn a sword and dealt out the punishment himself, hacking Adonai's wings from his back and exiling him from the Banished Lands.

Kol was telling the truth when he said it was Adonai who had slain Israfil. Riv had seen it with her own eyes. But Kol wasn't telling the whole truth. He did not say that when Adonai plunged a sword into Israfil's chest the Lord Protector was on his knees, Kol standing behind him with his knife to Israfil's throat.

And who is to say different of Adonai now. He is dead, slain by Bleda because Adonai was trying to kill me.

'Adonai did not accomplish this dark deed alone,' Kol said to Sariel, though his voice filled the chamber. 'He had help; there were traitors within our own. Garidas, captain of a White-Wing hundred, aided him.'

Riv snorted a shocked laugh. Even though Kol had told her all that he was going to say, hearing him saying it out loud to all of Drassil made her feel physically sick.

I liked Garidas. It is not right that he is blamed for this.

But what can I do to defend him? I am in this too deep now, cannot see a path out of this dark place. There is nothing I can do without breaking my oath to Kol and sentencing Bleda to death.

She realized her fists were clenched, knuckles white and popping.

'These are dark days, and filled with mourning,' Kol continued. 'But the Banished Lands are not safe, the Kadoshim are stirring and we must be ever vigilant, must fulfil our sacred calling to protect mankind. We need to elect a new Lord Protector, and soon. Someone strong enough and wise enough to lead us through this war and claim the victory that has eluded us for so long.' He looked away from Sariel now, eyes slowly taking in the vast crowd that filled the hall.

'As his chosen second in command, I nominate myself for the task,' Kol said, spreading his arms and wings wide.

A total silence.

Sariel's wings stirred, somehow commanding attention.

'The appointment of a new Lord Protector is a matter for the Ben-Elim to decide,' he said. 'In council.'

'I grieve Israfil's loss as much as anyone,' Kol continued, voice raised for the crowd, ignoring Sariel. 'But we must think of the future. The Land of the Faithful is not home to just us Ben-Elim; the races of men and giants dwell here. They should have a say.'

Murmuring spreading through the crowd, scattered shouts and cheers from many, especially large groups of White-Wings, but not them alone. Many of the free folk of Drassil, too – traders, smiths, farmers, all manner of people.

Sariel frowned. Riv noticed many of the Ben-Elim amidst the crowd shifting uncomfortably.

'This is a new world, a new age, and we should change with it, not keep it leashed,' Kol said. 'I propose a new order, where Ben-Elim and mankind rule together. Israfil was a great leader, but he had one foot still in the Otherworld, was clinging to a way of life that we left behind over a hundred years ago.'

'You should be silent,' Sariel said furiously. 'This should be discussed in the Ben-Elim's council.'

Some jeers from the crowd, spreading. Riv knew who had started them: White-Wings allied to Kol set the task before this meeting had been convened.

'Why not speak freely, now?' Kol said. 'I have nothing to hide. Do you, Sariel?'

All eyes in the chamber turned upon the dark-haired Ben-Elim, whose face twitched.

'Of course not,' Sariel said.

Kol is cunning, and a master of misdirection.

'And we are the Ben-Elim, protectors of these people, not their rulers. That is why we need to elect a new Lord *Protector.*'

Sariel stared at Kol, eyes wide with shock. They slowly narrowed.

'Stop this,' Sariel said.

'These are not mere words,' Kol said, continuing to ignore Sariel. 'I am proposing a new order, one that embraces these Banished Lands and the people who dwell within it, a land and people that we have come to value, to respect, to love.'

Love! Does Kol even know what that word means? He talks well, though, but then, he always has.

'And here is a symbol of my commitment to forge this new world.' Kol looked up at Riv.

Riv took a deep breath.

She had kept herself hidden since her return to Drassil, Kol flying her in during the dead of night, and hiding her away in the tower above the keep, once Israfil's chambers, but now taken by Kol.

Others were following Kol's gaze, looking upwards into the heights of the domed chamber.

Riv hesitated in the shadows of the alcove, knew that her world was about to change again.

How am I here? How have I let myself become so ensnared in this mess, in Kol's scheming? But whatever I do, wherever I go, I will be reviled and hunted. This is a chance to change that. A very slim chance, granted.

Deep down she knew there was more to her choices than self-preservation. Her eyes searched out Aphra, saw her staring up at her, then she looked to Bleda, felt the anger and hardness within her soften, just for a moment.

She stepped out of the alcove and dropped into the huge expanse of the chamber, arms open wide, and let herself fall.

People in the chamber gasped, pointed, a scream here and there.

And then Riv spread her wings.

A pulse of her wings checked her fall and for a moment she hovered high above the crowd, then tucked her wings in tight, dropping into a dive. A grin split her face, for despite everything, she *loved* to fly. People leaped away as she sped towards the ground, at the last moment spreading her wings wide to swoop low over the crowd, spinning in the air, spiralling up and looping so that she was behind and above Kol, where she hovered for long moments with slow, powerful beats of her wings, letting all see the colour of her wings, the shape of her body, taking in the fact that she was not a Ben-Elim. That she was a woman and a half-breed. But a half-breed with feathered wings, not the skin and leather that the Kadoshim spawned.

And she was wearing a black cuirass with two white wings embossed upon it, and a short-sword at her hip, the uniform of the White-Wings, Drassil's elite troops.

Then she touched down, wings folding behind her shoulders, and she stood next to Kol.

Things looked a lot different now that she was upon the ground. Her distance had given her a certain objectivity and detachment from the proceedings. Now she could see the looks on people's faces, hear their individual mutterings, smell their fear. It felt overwhelming.

A deep breath to keep the anger at bay.

Remember the plan.

'What is *this*?' Sariel said, revulsion twisting his face. He strode forwards, his hand going to the sword at his hip.

Riv forced herself to remain still and calm, which was a lot harder to do than it had sounded when she and Kol had spoken of this moment, of how she must react. Especially when a Ben-Elim was coming at her, murder in his eyes. Her fingers twitched for her sword, but she kept her arm rigid at her side.

As one, the Ben-Elim behind Kol took a step forwards, the White-Wings to either side of him also moving, shields snapping up with an echoing *crack*. And suddenly Ben-Elim were circling above them, Kol's followers dropping lower.

Sariel paused, looking about and up.

'What are you doing, Kol?' His eyes were drawn back to Riv. 'This *thing* is an *abomination*,' Sariel hissed; voices in the crowd called out their agreement.

Cries calling for Riv's execution rang out, her head snapping in the direction of the voices, searching for them. A white-haired Ben-Elim, about him a dozen White-Wings, men and women who had journeyed to Drassil with Sariel. She glared at them, tried to breathe deep and slow, knowing full well what would happen if she let her anger overwhelm her.

Rage.

Pain.

The executioner's block.

'Many of you know me,' Riv said, a tremor in her voice, part rage, all emotion. She looked around, saw thousands of faces staring back at her, shouts drowning her out.

'LET HER SPEAK,' Kol bellowed, and silence settled. 'Listen to her, before you judge,' Kol said, calmer.

Riv took a deep breath, gulped. 'Many of you know me,' she repeated. 'I have lived here, at Drassil, my *whole* life. I have dreamed of becoming a White-Wing, of standing in the shield wall, of serving the Land of the Faithful, protecting its people, fighting against the evil that is the Kadoshim in our Great War. That is who I am, in here.' She put a fist to her heart.

'Who is your father?' Sariel snapped. 'Who committed this obscenity?'

'She does not know,' Kol said, stepping forwards. 'And it does not matter. Many here know Riven, have grown up with her, taught her or trained beside her in the weapons-field. Marched on campaigns with her.' He stopped, looking around at nodding heads.

'She is an abomination, evidence of a great sin,' Sariel said. He was staring at Riv with disgust, eyes wide, drawn to her wings.

'Aye, she is evidence of the sins of her father, mayhap,' Kol said before Riv had a chance to say anything. 'But she is not guilty of that sin herself. How can she be held accountable for the crime that another has committed, long before she was even born?'

Riv's eyes scanned the crowd, saw expressions shifting, thoughtful, even a few nodding heads.

This is hopeful, she thought.

She looked at Sariel, who was staring death at her.

Not so hopeful.

'She has *wings*,' Sariel snarled.

'So, she has wings now.' Kol shrugged. 'She is the same person that we have all known for seventeen *years*. She was not evil before; she has not become evil overnight. If there is any sin, it lies with her parentage, not her. She is innocent, guiltless. How can any one of us be held accountable for our parents' deeds? If that were so, every wrongdoing that has a judgement meted out would be inflicted upon the children of the wrong-doer. If a man commits murder and goes to the gallows for it, do we hang his sons and daughters, too? If a woman steals, do we cut off the right hands of her children?' Kol paused, allowing the implications of his words to sink into the crowd.

'I have marched on a hundred campaigns with my sister's hundred,' Riv said. 'Wished only to serve Elyon. I am one of the Faithful. I am a White-Wing, but with real wings.' Riv grinned at Sariel, allowed her anger that small pleasure.

Sariel returned her stare, pinpricks of colour flushing his cheeks.

'Sariel, we Ben-Elim are Elyon's representatives on the earth,' Kol continued calmly, sounding like the voice of reason, his voice inflected with hints of friendship, as if he were an arbitrator in a dispute, 'and Elyon is just and fair. He would not condemn the innocent.' He raised his arms to the crowd. 'He would not condemn Riv for a crime she has not committed, or any others like her. And neither will I.' He looked at Sariel. 'Would you?'

'Yes,' Sariel said without pause or thought.

People in the crowd gasped, some jeered him.

Kol shook his head sadly, playing every inch the disappointed moral high ground. 'Let the people decide,' Kol said.

'And, also let them decide who is to be their Lord Protector.' He unfurled his wings, beat them and rose into the air, hovering above Sariel. 'Today you have the chance to choose your own future,' he shouted to the host that filled the Great Hall. 'Today you make your own history.

'Would you condemn Riv to death for the sins of her father? Whoever he is.'

A silence, growing longer, Riv feeling she was standing on the brink of an abyss, one foot hovering over it, unsteady.

'Let her live,' a voice cried out. Riv's head snapped towards it, and she was looking straight at Bleda. He returned her gaze and said it again – shouted it this time – and Ellac joined his voice to Bleda's, some of his guards, too.

Then others in the crowd were shouting it out: Ben-Elim who followed Kol scattered amongst the crowd, but others as well, White-Wings whom Riv had trained with, market stall holders whom she had bought food from, haggled with, blacksmiths she had laughed with, and then it felt as if the entire crowd was roaring, 'LIVE, LIVE, LIVE.'

Riv blew out a breath she hadn't realized she'd been holding. A smile spread across her face.

Kol smiled at Riv, and then at Sariel, who looked as if he'd just swallowed a bucketful of angry wasps.

The crowd quietened.

'And who would you choose to lead you?' Kol called out. 'Who would you trust not only to lead you against the Kadoshim, but to take us into a new age of peace and harmony? Him?'

Kol pointed at Sariel.

'Stand for him, now, if you wish him to lead you.'

'Kol. This is not the way,' Sariel was hissing, but people were already standing, some shouting Sariel's name. It was mostly Ben-Elim in the crowd who stood – more than two hundred, fewer than three hundred. White-Wings joined them – again, hundreds, not thousands, and a sprinkling of others.

'Or me?' Kol cried out as Sariel's followers sat.

It seemed to Riv that the entire host stood as one, though of course they did not. The end was the same, though, the balance so obviously, overwhelmingly, in Kol's favour. Ben-Elim and White-Wings in the crowd roared Kol's name, until Riv fought the urge to clasp her hands over her ears.

'This is not over,' Sariel said quietly to Kol. Only Riv heard over the din of the crowd. 'The Ben-Elim council will meet. This means nothing, and you know it.'

'It *is* over, Sariel. Look about you.' Kol gestured at the cheering crowd, smiling his beautiful smile. 'This is everything.'

Sariel looked about the chamber, listening to the horde roaring Kol's name. He turned to leave, other Ben-Elim stepping from the crowd, some White-Wings with them, waiting for Sariel.

Sariel looked at Riv. 'She is an abomination,' he said again, quietly, shaking his head.

'No,' Kol said. 'She is the future.'

CHAPTER SIXTEEN

FRITHA

Fritha crept through the trees, Morn walking beside her, a dozen of her Red Right Hand spread either side of them both, Gunil and her Ferals further back. Gunil was walking alongside Claw, who had made a sudden recovery from her wounds, the inflammation and infections peaking and then fading. The forest was still and quiet, only the sound of the wind soughing in the trees, the dripping of snow as it melted from boughs. Another sound filtered into her senses, soft as a sigh at first, growing as she stole through the trees. Constant.

The river. I can hear the river. We must be close.

Morn stopped and held up a hand, palm splayed, facing down. She pointed through the trees.

Fritha stared, could only see trees, what looked like a granite boulder in the distance.

Morn walked on, but Fritha put a hand on her shoulder, stopping her, at the same time signalling for two of her followers to go on ahead.

Morn scowled at Fritha, but she obeyed.

How long will that last, I wonder? Until her wing heals?

Morn had all but collapsed when Arn had carried her into the hold's feast-hall. Fritha had tended to her, spoken words of power over the wound in Morn's wing, a deep cut where the muscle and cartilage that supported her wing-arch met

155

the muscle and tendons in her back. It was healing, but not fully recovered yet.

Fritha had left Arn with Elise and five of her Red Right Hand to act as guards for the prisoners at the hold. It left Fritha with ten of her acolytes, plus thirteen of her surviving Ferals. Not the greatest warband in the world, but Morn had told Fritha that she had only fought against two men, Drem and the younger warrior, the red-haired fire-cracker, Cullen. Though she had seen a figure inside their tent, which must have been the huntsman, the fact he had not joined the fight against Morn suggested he was wounded.

Wounded, I hope. Dead he's no use to me.

Twenty-six of us. We are enough to take two healthy men and one wounded. Gulla will be pleased when I return with Drem and two warriors of the Order; success will erase my failure to stop word of us reaching Dun Seren.

They were close to the boulder now, her two men scouting ahead, flitting shadows between the trees.

Morn stopped again, frowning.

'What is it?' Fritha whispered.

'Their tent is gone,' the half-breed whispered.

There was the sound of snapping branches, a thud, followed by a scream.

Fritha put her fingers to her lips and whistled, heard an answering howl behind her and then she was rushing forwards, past Morn, her spear levelled, eyes searching everywhere. Screams echoed through the trees.

One of the two scouts was standing before a hole in the ground. Fritha reached him and looked down, saw a pit filled with stakes, the other scout skewered through the belly, shoulder and thigh, eyes glazing – then still.

This is Drem's work.

Fritha turned in a slow circle, scanning the area, trees spread wide, though the canopy was dense above. The Ferals

156

appeared out of the gloom, the bulk of Gunil and his bear not far behind them.

'*Cuardaigh*,' Fritha ordered, and the Ferals dropped to all fours, began sniffing and snuffling through the area.

The ground vibrated as Gunil joined her, his bear a score of paces behind. He stared around the empty space, saw the marks in the ground where a tent had stood.

'They're gone,' the giant said, then he looked down into the stake pit. 'He's dead.'

Fritha gave Gunil a dark look.

'Search the area, with care,' she called out.

'Their tent was here,' Morn said, pointing at the ground just beyond the pit. She stretched, arching her back and extending her wings, a tentative flexing.

'It feels good,' Morn said, rolling one shoulder.

'Be carefu—' But Morn was already jumping into the air and beating her wings. They took her weight, and she hovered there a few moments, then rose slowly in a wide spiral.

'I will see things differently from up here,' she called down.

One of Fritha's Ferals was snorting at the base of a huge boulder. Then it stood on two legs, sniffed the air and trotted off, away from the sound of the river.

Fritha followed.

It led her along a wide path that sloped gently upwards. Abruptly the Feral stopped, looking down at its foot. A length of twine had snagged around it.

'NO,' Fritha shouted as the Feral gave a tug, snapping the twine.

A whistling sound, a thud, something cutting through air and then the Feral was battered from his feet and hurled a dozen paces, slamming into a tree. It slid to the ground, blood leaking from nose and mouth, bones protruding from its smashed ribcage.

A felled tree trunk hung suspended across the path, creaking as it swung back and forth.

Fritha ran to her fallen Feral, saw it was already too late. She crouched beside it, stroked its misshapen jaws, then she raised her head to the trees and screeched her fury.

She blinked away tears and saw Morn standing over her.

'Come, my spear-sister,' Morn said, holding out a hand to Fritha. 'We will hunt them together.'

Fritha looked at Morn's proffered hand a few moments, then reached out and took it, rising to her feet.

'We have found their tracks,' Morn said. 'That way.' She pointed south-east, into dense woodland.

Fritha nodded, and without a word she was moving, along the path Morn had pointed to.

A beating of wings and Morn was in the air, while the Ferals and Red Right Hand fell into place around Fritha. It made her feel strong.

Drem, I will hunt you to the ends of the earth, and make you pay for what you have done.

CHAPTER SEVENTEEN

DREM

Fen stopped in front of Drem, the wolven-hound's ears pricked forwards, a low snarl and his hackles raised in a ridge between his shoulders. Drem pulled to a sudden halt, swaying with the weight of the packs upon his back.

They were standing close to the ridge of a long, shallow incline that they'd been steadily climbing the whole day, pine still thick about them, for which Drem was grateful. He had a compulsion to check the skies continually for leathery wings. Without thinking, he found himself looking skywards again, although most of it was obscured by layered boughs of pine. Here and there a gleam of light broke through, a few snow-flakes drifting down like white leaves.

Does it snow eternally in the Bonefells?

'What is it?' Keld said, joining Drem. The huntsman was sweating and pale but had managed to keep walking from sunset to sundown for the last four days. Keld ate like a starving man each evening and morning, and slept like the dead each night. Drem thought he saw a slight improvement in the huntsman each day.

Drem pointed to Fen, who was alert, totally focused on something he could sense or hear.

Drem couldn't hear anything.

'What's the hold up?' Cullen breathed, striding up from behind Hammer.

'Whisht,' Keld said, holding up a hand and cocking his head to one side.

Cullen was silent for long moments. The gentle snowfall had a muting effect on the pinewoods, as if the world were holding its breath.

'I can't hear anyth—'

Then they all heard it. A distant roar.

Behind them Hammer rumbled, deep in her belly.

Drem looked at Keld.

'It sounds like . . . a bear,' Drem said. He put his hand to his throat, found his pulse.

'Aye,' Keld agreed.

They heard it again, clearer. Beyond the ridge, almost dead south.

'Think we should go around,' Drem said, thinking of Fritha's giant and his bear.

'Good idea,' Keld said.

'Be quicker to go straight on,' Cullen said. 'Kill it, whatever it is, if we have to.'

'Do you never get tired of fighting, lad?' Keld snapped.

'No,' Cullen said without hesitation, looking at Keld as if he were mad.

Another roar, sounding louder, closer. There was an odd note in it. Drem had heard a lot of roaring from bears lately, challenging, fighting. This wasn't quite like that. Still . . .

'We'll go around,' Keld said firmly.

Hammer snorted behind them, dug a gout of forest litter with a paw and broke into a lumbering run, surging past them, limping a little, but showing more energy than at any point since she'd leaped into the river.

'What's got under her skin?' Keld frowned.

'Don't know, but whatever it is, we can't let her face it alone,' Cullen said, hefting the pack on his back and breaking into a laboured run.

A TIME OF BLOOD

Keld scowled. 'Damn it.' And then he was running, too, Fen keeping pace with him.

Drem sighed and followed.

Cresting the ridge, a gentle downward slope running away from him, Drem glimpsed to his right the sharp rise of a cliff face running parallel to his course, probably a few hundred paces away. To his left was a sea of trees.

Another roar, louder, that same odd edge to it that struck Drem as unusual. Then it dawned on him what it was.

Fear.

No; terror.

He caught up with Keld, the pack on Drem's back actually increasing his speed as he ran downhill. He saw the bulk of Hammer ahead, and close behind her Cullen, legs pumping away like a racing hare as he tried to catch up with the bear.

Drem glanced at Keld, saw that he was sweating and blowing a little, but looking as if he had it all under control.

The pinewoods were opening up, huge boulders scattered around them, looking like the long-buried skulls of giants poking from the forest floor. Snow was thicker on the ground as the density of the treetop canopy lessened.

An ear-splitting roar, very close now, and then Hammer was slowing. Drem heard an answering roar from her. Cullen finally caught up with her and skidded to a halt beside the bear.

Thirty paces from them, Drem's breath and pounding heart was all he could hear. He saw Cullen shoulder off his pack, draw his sword.

Never a good sign.

Drem drew his seax and a hand-axe in preparation. There were the two bears roaring, the sound of timber splintering, and something else, a sound beneath the clangour, constant, though ebbing and flowing – a *hissing*, like steam.

And then Drem was there, running around Hammer, almost colliding with Cullen.

For long moments he could not understand what was happening in front of them.

Struggling in the centre of a glade, there was a giant white bear.

Drem's breath caught in his throat as his hand went to the bear claw around his neck.

Is it my bear? The one that nearly killed me and Da?

He tried to check if it was missing a claw on its right paw, but it was impossible to tell, because the bear was fighting for its life.

Bone-white *things*, like huge coils of pearly rope, were looped and twisted around the bear – around its torso, its neck, its legs. For a moment Drem thought the bear must have become caught in some giant kind of net, with rope as thick as Drem's chest, except that the rope around the white bear had *teeth*. More than one set of teeth.

And they were ripping the bear to shreds.

Keld skidded to a halt beside Drem.

'Wyrms!' he hissed.

Fen crouched and growled, baring his teeth in a savage snarl.

Have I stepped out of the real into a world of faery tales?

The tales told of an ancient creature, bred thousands of years ago by giants and used in the War of Treasures; giant wyrms, snake-like, but bigger, much, much bigger, and the wyrms in front of Drem were a thousand times bigger than any adder he'd ever seen. For once, the tales didn't seem to have exaggerated.

They were huge, red-eyed sinuous lengths of scale and muscle, their jaws flat-muzzled and rowed with teeth. Drem counted at least four sets of eyes and teeth, though it was hard to understand where one wyrm ended and another began, not helped by the way the white bear was lurching around the glade, trying to break free of the coiled loops that were binding and constricting his movement.

The white bear was huge, at least a head taller and wider than Hammer, but it was obvious that it was losing this fight. Blood stained its white fur, oozing from dozens of puncture wounds, and the coils of the wyrms were wrapping ever-tighter about its torso, as well as seeking to tether the bear's legs. Its jaws were wide, clamping onto scales. The bear's teeth sank deep and it shook its head savagely, blood and scales spraying, but the wyrm just hissed and bared its fangs, twisting and bucking in muscular spasms to break free.

The white bear slashed with a paw, scouring red lines across the wyrm's body, and Drem saw for a clear moment that one claw was missing from the bear's paw.

It is my bear, then.

His instinct was to go and help this bear, though a voice whispered in his head that he was *mad* to think of such a thing.

It is the wild, nature's way, the voice said. *The strong kill and eat the weak. You have done it a thousand times yourself.*

And yet . . .

It was *his* white bear, and he felt a sympathy for it, some kind of bond. The first time he'd encountered it, the bear had tried to kill him and his da. *Not the best beginning,* he acknowledged. They had only just escaped, Drem cutting a claw from its paw, which he had worn around his neck ever since. It had not been long after that corpses had started turning up in the forests north of Kergard, torn and mauled with tooth and claw. Old Bodil, Calder the smith, Hask, Fritha's grandfather. Even the death of Olin, Drem's da, had been attributed to the white bear. But Drem had discovered the truth of it, that the true murderers were Fritha and her giant's bear.

The white bear had been hunted by the people of Kergard, trapped and caught, dragged back to the town and caged as a trophy. It had been close to a bear-baiting from the town's huntsmen and their hounds.

Drem had set the bear free.

Even now he didn't quite understand why he had done so,

only that he had felt a huge sympathy for it, this magnificent creature of the wild, blamed and about to be murdered for acts it had not committed.

The white bear roared, rage, pain, terror, all rolled into one, and Drem took a step towards it.

Don't be a fool. Walk on – you must reach Dun Seren, a voice in his head said. *Those wyrms will kill you all. And besides, why try and save a bear that would be as likely to eat you as to thank you?*

Despite the voice in his head, he took another step forwards, felt Keld's grip on his wrist, looked at the huntsman, saw Cullen staring at him as well.

And then Hammer was moving, roaring, throwing herself at the wyrms wrapped around the white bear.

Cullen shrugged, grinned and charged.

So did Drem.

He heard Keld swear behind him, then the sound of the huntsman and Fen following in his wake.

Snow on the ground had been churned to pink sludge. Drem's boots slipped as he chopped with his hand-axe at a twist of wyrm-coil that was looped around the white bear's foreleg. The axe pierced scales, but it was tough, and the blade did not sink deep. He stabbed with his seax, this time piercing flesh, his blade sinking to the hilt, dark, glutinous blood thick as porridge leaking from the wound, but Drem wasn't sure what real damage he had inflicted. The wyrm was not responding, as if it hadn't even felt his blows.

To his right he glimpsed Hammer sink her teeth into wyrm flesh, puncturing deep, and in a heartbeat a wyrm head was rearing, loosening a coil about the white bear, hissing, its malevolent red eyes fixing on Hammer.

It felt that, Drem thought.

The wyrm's jaws opened unnaturally wide, full of too many teeth, as its head drew back and struck at Hammer. She jerked away, but the wyrm was so swift, its teeth clamping onto her neck. Hammer shook violently, but the wyrm's bite held fast. A flash of steel, and Cullen was there, screaming, chopping at the wyrm's neck, Hammer retreating, tugging the wyrm with her, dragging its coiled length away from the white bear.

The wyrm did not seem to want to let go its grip on either bear, tail coiled around the white bear, fangs sunk deep into Hammer.

Gouts of flesh and viscous blood flew through the air as Cullen struck and hacked.

Drem left his seax and hand-axe in the wyrm he'd attacked, pivoted and drew his father's sword. Raising it high overhead, he rushed over to Cullen and Hammer, bringing his blade down diagonally – *lightning strike*, his father's voice whispered in his head – slicing deep into the wyrm flesh, the treacle-like blood seeping out. He raised and cut again, and then again, deeper into the great rent in the wyrm's torso, until a white fluid started mixing with the dark red of its blood. Cullen stood the other side of the wyrm, his blade rising and falling in a frenzy, more butcher than sword master.

Drem glimpsed bone through the carnage of his blows, felt his sword grate on vertebrae. The wyrm, finally relinquishing its grip on Hammer, twisted to look unsteadily at Drem and Cullen, much of its supportive muscle and sinew severed. It bared its fangs at them, snapping at Cullen, but Hammer's paw swatted it to the ground, the two men still hacking frenziedly, until, with a final blow from Drem, the severed head fell. Its lower body and tail twitched and spasmed, and then was still.

Hammer gave out a victory roar, stamped on the wyrm's head for good measure, and then leaped forwards, swiping at another wyrm wrapped around the white bear.

'Some help!' Keld cried out. Drem turned to see the huntsman clinging to the back of another wyrm, just below its head, legs and one arm wrapped around the wyrm, his hand-axe rising and falling as he slashed and hacked. This wyrm had detached itself from the white bear and was giving all of its attention to Keld. Fen was leaping in, biting, ripping out chunks of flesh, then jumping away as the tail whipped at him.

Drem and Cullen ran to Keld, began their butcher's work again.

A tail-strike caught Cullen, sent him spinning through the air.

The wyrm's head came for Drem, darting forwards, quick as thought.

Drem stabbed his sword up, by immense luck more than skill connected his sword-point with the wyrm's lower jaw, a burst of instinctive terror adding a wild strength to his blow, punching on up into its head, pinning the jaws together. It flopped to the ground, dragging Drem with it, Keld rolling away, the wyrm's head shaking frenziedly. Finding purchase with his feet, Drem pushed, driving his sword deeper, felt it scrape on the top of the wyrm's skull. He twisted his sword. A ripple of spasms through the wyrm's body as it died.

Drem stood, heaved his blade free.

Then he was flying through the air, lost his grip on his sword and rolled a dozen paces. Scrambling to his knees, he saw a wyrm speeding towards him, jaws open, fangs dripping. He lurched to one side as the head stabbed at him, fast as a spear-strike. As he staggered to his feet, the tail wrapped around his ankles. His natural inclination was to run, but as his ankles were crushed tight together, all he managed to do was fall over. Another coil looped around him. He started to panic, searched for a weapon – his belt empty, his sword out of reach – resorted to punching ineffectually at the thick coils as they constricted around him. Another ripple of muscle and another few loops curled around him, pinning one arm to his side, covering his stomach and lower chest.

He screamed. Regretted that when another constriction squeezed his breath out of him, made it difficult for him to inhale.

The wyrm's head reared in front of him, a malignant hiss, a tongue flickering, filled with the stench of rotting meat.

Cullen appeared, sword stabbing into the wyrm's mouth, the wyrm rearing away, its coils loosening around Drem. He sucked in air greedily and squirmed free. Keld offered him a hand and helped him rise. Cullen followed the wyrm, slashed up, left to right in a diagonal cut, like a scabbard-draw, opened a great rent in the wyrm's torso. Its head lunged at him, even as he stabbed straight into its belly, its jaws opening, vomiting blood as Cullen's blade sank deep, and two-handed he ripped it upwards, opening its guts as if he were filleting a giant fish.

The wyrm's jaws closed around Cullen's head and shoulders, but it was dying, its strength deserting it, the power in its jaws fading. Teeth locked around Cullen, scraping on his skin, but not piercing much deeper than that. The wyrm collapsed in an explosion of blood and slime, dragging Cullen down, burying him in a mountain of its entrails.

An earth-shaking roaring grabbed their attention, Drem looking to see Hammer and the white bear clamping jaws into another wyrm, both of them shaking their muscled necks, tugging the wyrm in two directions. There was a tearing sound as they chewed and tore the creature in half.

The last surviving wyrm uncoiled itself from the white bear's neck and wove unsteadily from the glade, disappearing through foliage into the cover of woodland in half a heartbeat.

The white bear lifted its head and roared, spittle flying, the ground quaking. It took a staggering step after its fleeing attacker, then a shudder rippled through its body and its front legs collapsed. It toppled onto its side, its chest rising and falling in short, shallow gasps.

'Help . . . me,' a muffled voice called.

Cullen!

Drem and Keld ran to the pile of dead wyrm, heaved its lifeless bulk away to reveal Cullen buried in a heap of offal, slime and putrescence.

Cullen sat up, looked at Drem, wiped wyrm slime from his face. Spat more of it up. Retched. There was no grin from him now.

'Drem, a question.' Cullen spat out more slime. 'Why the hell would you choose to live out here?'

Drem stared at Cullen, started to chuckle, looked at Keld, who laughed, too, and then Drem was throwing his head back and laughing from the pit of his stomach. He hadn't laughed in a long while, and especially not like this, a deep, uncontrolled laughter that shook his core, rattled his bones and made his jaw ache.

'Well,' he said, cuffing tears away when he could finally draw breath. 'At least things can't get any worse.'

'Can they not?' Cullen said, eyes drifting up.

Drem followed his gaze, and saw a black silhouette high above them, framed against the luminous glow of snow clouds.

A black silhouette with wide, bat-like wings.

CHAPTER EIGHTEEN

RIV

Kol poured Riv a cup of wine.

I hate it here.

They were sitting in Kol's chambers, situated in a tower high above Drassil's Great Hall. Not too long ago it had been Israfil's chambers, and Riv could still see the bloodstains upon the flagstoned floor.

It is a constant reminder of why I hate Kol. My mo–, no, my grandmother Dalmae died in these chambers. And Kol insists that I stay here, still, when all I want is to return to my siste–, no, my mother's barracks.

Her head was still spinning with the changes in her life. Kol and his deeds were ever-present in her head and heart, a constant test of her self-control. Because her anger was still there, a swirling tornado in the pit of her belly that threatened to drag her into its violent grip.

She knew where that always ended.

Blood and violence.

And she could not allow that to happen, for Vald and Jost's sake.

For Bleda's sake.

And Kol is my father. She stared at him, a mixture of revulsion and fascination shifting through her.

A tall, high-arched window let in gusts of cold air, though

a Ben-Elim stood before it, jet-black hair braided and tied at
the neck.

*Ben-Elim do not only guard doors. An attack is just as likely to
come through a window as through a door.*

'I think that went quite well,' Kol said, pouring wine for
Aphra and Lorina as well. He was talking about the meeting
yesterday in the Great Hall, as this was the first time they had
all met since then.

'Before we drink,' Kol said, 'we need something to toast.'

Other than me being still alive, Riv thought.

'I remember my friends and reward loyalty,' Kol said. 'And
as I'm in the mood for making changes, you two are now pro-
moted.' He raised his cup to Aphra and Lorina. 'You are now
my two high captains of the White-Wings. Five hundred
swords for each of you.'

Riv blinked at that. The White-Wings numbered in total
around ten thousand strong. They had never had high captains,
had always been divided into hundreds. Riv had never thought
twice of it before, but now she found herself questioning
everything, and in hindsight considered the demarcation of the
White-Wings into comparatively small groups of a hundred as
another way that the Ben-Elim had maintained their control.
Drassil's garrison was traditionally a thousand White-Wings,
and now Kol was giving them all over to Aphra and Lorina, the
two captains who had supported his coup.

Aphra frowned, but said nothing, and Lorina smiled, the
act not much changing her dark, severe features.

'So, to my new high captains, and to a new order. Cheers,'
Kol said, raising his own cup. Aphra and Lorina also raised
theirs and drank. Kol stared at Riv, arching an eyebrow.

Riv did not feel much like celebrating, still remembering
Sariel's look of revulsion as he had called her an abomination.

*But I am still alive, and it looks as if I will not be put to death
in the immediate future. That's something, I suppose.*

She sipped red wine from her cup, discovered that she liked the taste.

'That's the spirit,' Kol said.

Riv found his endless joviality irritating.

A day had passed since Kol's revelation in the Great Hall, during which Riv had kept herself hidden away in these chambers. She was greatly encouraged by the response of Drassil's residents to her, after Kol had worked a little of his oratory magic, and a large dose of manipulation.

But alive is alive.

'So, now the Ben-Elim and Drassil's residents are reconciled to . . . *you* –' Kol looked at Riv – 'thus paving the way to a more relaxed, intimate relationship between Ben-Elim and mankind.' He drank from his cup, smiled.

'It just leaves Ethlinn and her giants to win over,' Aphra said.

'They will be far easier to pacify than Sariel and his Ben-Elim,' Lorina murmured.

'I should hope so.' Kol sighed. 'Though I doubt we have heard the last of Sariel.' He shrugged. 'The first and hardest step has been made. As for the giants, I think once the situation is on firm ground here, that I should take my new . . . *figurehead* to go and see Ethlinn and her giants.'

Figurehead! Riv didn't like that.

'Where is Ethlinn?' Riv asked.

'Dun Seren.' Kol sighed again. 'I suppose I may as well deal with *them* as well as the giants and get this all over and done with.'

'The Order of the Bright Star?' Riv said.

'Aye. A den of stiff-necked fools, but stiff-necked fools that we need, at least until the Kadoshim are annihilated.' He smiled.

Kol's going to take me to the Order of the Bright Star! Riv felt a thrill run through her at that thought. As she grew up with the White-Wings, the warriors of the Bright Star were always considered allies, but also competition. The issue of who was better was an oft-asked question.

We are.

She had seen a small group of the Order before. A scouting party sent to give information to Aphra on a suspected Kadoshim nest. There had been a giant upon one of their great bears – Riv was used to giants and bears, so that hadn't overly impressed her – as well as a huntsman with a brace of wolven-hounds and two more warriors. They had seemed to lack the discipline and uniformity that the White-Wings prided themselves upon, but they had all displayed a certain grace, an air of self-assurance and fluidity around them. And even when they were just *standing,* they exuded a confidence, a deep-seated knowledge and security in their abilities that set them apart as masters of their art.

Because war is an art. Just a deadly one.

It will be interesting to finally see them train. Maybe spar with a few of them.

'The Order of the Bright Star are none too fond of me,' Kol said. 'I have had . . . disagreements with them in the past.'

Sound like sensible people. She felt a smile twitch her mouth at the thought.

He shrugged and poured himself some more wine. 'The joys of ruling.'

There was a surge of wind through the high-arched window, a turbulence as a Ben-Elim hovered in the air beyond. The guard standing there shifted to block entry, hefting his spear.

'I bear a message from Sariel,' the Ben-Elim beyond the window called out.

'Let him in, Hadran,' Kol said with a gesture, and the Ben-Elim in the window stepped back, raising his spear-point, though Riv noted that Hadran still held it ready.

A Ben-Elim flew into the room, great white wings furling as he touched down gently and approached Kol. He was tall, his hair so fair it was almost white, and classically handsome in the Ben-Elim way, with chiselled features and sharp, intelligent eyes.

He held out a rolled parchment, proffering it to Kol.

'What does it say, Kamael?'

'That you are summoned to the Moot, to answer for your deviation from the Way. It meets two days from now.'

'I see.' Kol sighed.

He seems to be doing a lot of that, lately.

'Anything else?' Kol asked.

'Aye. We will decide on who will become the new Lord Protector,' Kamael said.

In a heartbeat Kol was on his feet, face a handspan from Kamael. To his credit, Kamael stood his ground, did not recoil or flinch.

'That is already decided,' Kol said. 'The people have spoken.'

'Sariel says differently,' Kamael said. 'We Ben-Elim have not decided, and we both know that is all that matters.'

He dismisses us like we are worthless insects. Riv realized she still considered herself human, not Ben-Elim, despite the obvious reminder of her mixed heritage that was sprouting from her back.

'We shall see,' Kol said.

'Yes,' Kamael agreed. 'Will you attend the Moot?'

'Of course,' Kol said, and waved his hand in dismissal, turning away and returning to his seat.

Kamael stood and stared at him, then disdainfully threw the rolled-up parchment onto the table and walked away. He did not glance at the Ben-Elim guard as he stepped from the high tower window. A beat of his wings and he was gone.

Hadran looked out of the window, watching Kamael's departure.

Kol took the parchment and broke the seal, unrolled and read it. Sneered and tossed it over his shoulder.

'Sariel is determined to be a thorn in my flesh,' he snarled.

'You have the people's vote,' Lorina said. 'Most of Drassil is behind you.'

'It is the Ben-Elim I must contend with,' Kol said. 'They have to support my claim if my rule is to last.'

'You have over a thousand Ben-Elim who have pledged their allegiance to you,' Aphra said.

'Aye. But there are more than three thousand of my brothers in these Banished Lands. I need a majority.'

'Who else could rule, if not you?' Lorina said.

Kol pulled a face, which Riv thought meant *no one.*

He has always been arrogant, but that is a Ben-Elim trait, not confined to Kol.

'Sariel is my only real threat. He has governed the south of the Lands of the Faithful for half a hundred years, has fought campaigns there, exterminating the Vin Thalun pirates, stamping on all opposition to the yoke of the Ben-Elim. He has many supporters from that region, both Ben-Elim and White-Wings.'

'We have come this far, are so close,' Lorina said. 'Sariel will not stop us now.'

'I hope you are right,' Kol muttered, tapping his teeth with a thumbnail. He sipped his wine, brooding darkly.

'I want to go back to Aphra's barracks,' Riv said into the growing silence.

Kol looked at her and frowned. Riv saw a gentle smile touch Aphra's face.

'I am sick of being hidden away,' Riv said.

Sick of being around you every waking breath, Kol.

'I am concerned for your safety,' Kol said.

'My safety?' Riv snorted, glancing at the scar on her shoulder.

'That was before I knew you were my daughter,' Kol said.

Riv stared at him.

'I have much resting upon you, Riven ap Kol,' Kol said, humour in his eyes.

'But you would not call me your daughter in public,' she snapped.

Not that I want you to.

'Of course not. It's better that your parentage remains nameless. You are a symbol of past crimes, a symbol of forgiveness, and of hope for the future. Best to leave it at that.'

Because you would not be so popular if everyone knew you were the father who committed the sin.

'I still want to go back to Aphra's barracks,' Riv said.

'Perhaps it would help your cause against Sariel?' Aphra said.

Kol raised an eyebrow.

'What you said in the hall,' Aphra said, 'stirred people's blood, won their sympathy, but they were just words. If people saw those words in action – Riv bridging that gap between Ben-Elim and us . . . then it would only cement the step you have made.'

'Yes, your point is well made,' Kol said. 'But what if harm were to come to her?'

'Guards?' Lorina said.

'A few, in the shadows. Not so many that she looks like a prisoner,' Aphra said.

They are talking about me as if I am not a person.

Riv ground her teeth.

'Very well,' Kol said. 'You may go back to Aphra's barracks and be free to roam Drassil, within reason. Train in the weapons-field, if you will. With guards. I'll set some of my Ben-Elim to watch over you. And Aphra, some White-Wings, please.'

'Of course,' Aphra said.

Kol looked at Riv's wings, furled behind her. 'You may even train with us Ben-Elim, soon. I'll teach you how better to use those.' He nodded to Riv's wings.

I know how to use them.
'My thanks,' Riv grunted. She rose to leave.
'One thing,' Kol said as she walked to the door.
'What?' Riv said, looking back.
'Don't lose your temper.'

CHAPTER NINETEEN

DREM

Drem looked up at the sky again, searching for any sign of the Kadoshim half-breed. She had wheeled above them as the fight with the wyrms had ended, but now she was nowhere to be seen.

And that worries me more. I'd rather know where she is. We need to move, and move fast.

Cullen had found a stream to wash the wyrm slime and muck from his body, while Drem and Keld checked Hammer and Fen over for wounds.

The white bear still lay upon its side. Its breathing was steadier, though, but it appeared to be unconscious. Hammer rumbled over to the fallen beast, sniffed a wound and licked it with her rasping tongue. The white bear didn't so much as stir.

Without thinking, Drem approached the prone bear, carefully, with one hand on his seax.

Its fur was stained pink, a tapestry of long red lacerations and puncture wounds covering its body. Tentatively, Drem reached out and put his hand upon the bear's chest, felt its ribs flex as it breathed. Hammer nudged the bear with her muzzle, pushed into it none too gently, rumbled a sound deep in her belly, not quite a growl. The white bear rocked back a little, then rolled back.

Most of the wounds Drem checked were superficial, but then he found an injury high on the shoulder of its left foreleg that was leaking a lot of blood. He bent down and lifted its paw, grunting with the weight. He looked at the point where its claw had been severed, a hand reaching to his throat and touching the claw tied around his neck. A flash of memory, his da throwing himself upon Drem, the two of them rolling out of the bear's way, Drem lashing out with his seax and slicing the claw. And then followed by another memory, the bear standing over him, sniffing him as he set it free from its cage of iron bars before the walls of Kergard.

It let me live.

He looked at Keld, who was standing back, staring at the bear.

'We need to leave,' Keld said. 'Cullen,' he called out.

'Be with you soon,' Cullen called back, 'but I can still taste and smell wyrm.'

'I've met this bear before,' Drem said, raising the bear claw around his neck and pointing to the bear's front paw, with its missing claw.

Keld and Cullen shared a look, Keld nodded. 'Just until Cullen is ready,' the huntsman said, and Drem hurried to his pack, unbuckled it and pulled out a smaller kit bag. He threw a wad of linen bandages to Keld and the two of them set to patching up the white bear as best they could, cleaning and packing the wounds with honey, comfrey and yarrow, and then binding them with strips of linen.

Footsteps behind them and Cullen ran into the clearing. His red hair had grown back about a knuckle's length, and it glistened with icy water.

'Think my stones have frozen and fallen off in that stream.' Cullen shivered. He looked at them both, then at the white bear and its bandages. 'Are you both moon-mad?' he asked them. 'That thing will eat you for its supper.'

'Best be gone before it wakes up, then,' Keld said, hefting his pack onto his back.

Drem threw Cullen his pack.

Cullen slipped it onto his back. He was standing beside one of the dead wyrms. He looked down at it, his mouth twisting in disgust. Drawing his hand-axe, he crouched and chopped at one of its long fangs, hacking it free. He tossed it to Drem.

'Something to add to that bear claw around your neck,' he said with a grin. He chopped the other fang free and threw it to Keld, then strode to another wyrm and took a fang for himself.

'Keepsakes.' Cullen grinned. 'To remind us never, ever to come to the Bonefells again.'

'It's not so bad,' Drem said, feeling protective of this place that had been home to him and his da. As dangerous as it was, it felt like his home, and there was something safe and reassuring about that.

Cullen snorted a laugh and just shook his head.

A rumble issued from the white bear, and its legs jerked.

They all took an involuntary step away from the beast.

The white bear raised its huge head and looked at them. It took a few great sniffs, let out a growl, though to Drem it seemed more confused than aggressive.

Fen padded in front of Keld and bared his fangs at the bear.

The white bear rumbled another growl at Fen.

Now, that one was *aggressive.*

The white bear rolled onto its belly, managed to get its legs beneath it and heave itself upright, swaying, head lowered with the effort. Spittle drooled from its open mouth as it breathed heavily with the exertion.

Fen growled again, hackles a ridge on his back.

'Easy,' Keld said, resting a palm on the wolven-hound's side.

The bear took a step towards them, lips curling in a snarl at Fen.

'Here we go again.' Cullen sighed and drew his sword.

Hammer stepped between them and the white bear. She

roared at the bear, making its fur ripple as if in a strong wind, and it froze, regarding her.

Drem's hand dropped to the hilt of his seax and he held his breath, balanced on his toes, waiting for the violence to explode.

The white bear stepped forwards and licked Hammer's nose.

Fen took a step, snapping and snarling, and the white bear's head switched onto him, another deep growl from the bear.

Hammer raised a paw and slapped the white bear across the muzzle.

To Drem it looked more like a reprimand than an attack.

The white bear took a step back, its head swivelling onto Hammer, a small growl and a curled lip at her, but nothing else.

Hammer growled back.

The white bear took a step forwards and licked Hammer's muzzle again.

'I think he likes her,' Cullen whispered, a smile twitching his mouth. 'What should we do?'

'Well, as bonny as this all is, we are being hunted by a Kadoshim half-breed, Feral beasts and a giant, so we should probably leave,' Keld answered.

'Agreed,' Cullen said.

Fen growled again at the white bear.

'That's enough of that,' Keld scolded, and Fen's ears dropped, tail tucking between his legs. 'You're looking after me, I know, but you can be a bit over-protective sometimes, and right now you're going to start a fight, lad.' He ruffled the wolven-hound's head.

They backed away, Fen following them. As they reached the edge of the clearing and stepped into the cover of the pine trees, Keld looked back to call Hammer. She was still standing before the white bear, the two of them sniffing and snorting at each other.

'Come on, girl,' Keld called.

Hammer looked around at Keld, then back at the white bear. She shook her body, fur rippling as if she'd emerged from water, and then lumbered after them.

The white bear stood and stared at Hammer's considerable rump as it walked away from him, then gave out a rumbling snort and shambled after her, limping.

Keld raised an eyebrow and looked at Cullen and Drem.

Drem shrugged.

They turned and walked on, the two bears following behind them.

Drem stepped out from a thinning stand of pine; snow-covered meadows opened up before him.

The foothills of the Bonefells rose behind them, framed by the looming bulk of mountains, but before Drem and his companions was a long, undulating slope that led down to a vast plain, broken by clusters of jagged crags, knots of woodland and notched ravines.

Drem knew that Keld and Cullen were glad to be leaving the Bonefells.

Because it means we are that much closer to Dun Seren, which is good. But the ground is more open, so we will be much easier to find, especially from above.

'Dun Seren is less than a ten-night that way,' Cullen said, pointing to the south, with his other hand scratching at the red hair on his head that was growing longer now.

'A while before I have my warrior braid back,' Cullen muttered ruefully.

Drem looked up at the sky, searching for bat wings, subconsciously put a finger to his throat and counted the beats of his heart.

'Waiting's not going to make it any easier,' Keld said and walked out from the cover of trees, choosing a path that hugged boulders and wind-blasted stands of hawthorn.

Some cover, at least.

Fen padded alongside the huntsman, both of them seeming fully recovered now from their injuries.

The Order of the Bright Star breeds them tough.

Drem absently scratched at the scab on his waistline, checked the sky again and then followed, picking his way down the slope. After a short while there was a scraping and creaking of trees and Drem looked back to see Hammer emerge from the pine trees. A few score paces behind her was the white bear, still limping. He had followed Hammer for two days now, keeping his distance, disappearing at night when Drem and the others stopped and made camp, but reappearing each morning to snort and snuffle around Hammer. Hammer did not seem to dislike the attention. After another scolding from Keld, Fen had taken to pretending the white bear was not there.

Keld led them through shadowed paths, though Drem was certain that even if they were hidden from eyes in the sky, Hammer and the white bear were not.

Another glance upwards and Drem saw a flicker of movement, a dark smudge silhouetted by pale cloud.

'Ware,' he called to his companions, and they all melted into the shadows of an overhanging crag. As Drem watched the silhouette above, he realized it was too small for the half-breed Kadoshim.

Just a crow, then.

As Drem looked at it, the bird banked to the left, flying in a wide-looping arc.

Then Cullen was stepping out from the shadows and waving his hands in the air.

The bird above them started cawing, flying in a tighter spiralling loop down to them. As it drew closer, the squawks started to resemble words.

'*Cullen, Cullen, Cullen,*' the crow squawked, and Cullen held his arm out, the crow alighting on his shoulder. It was huge for a crow, far bigger than Rab, its feathers neat and glossy.

'Ach, but it's good to see you, Flick,' Cullen said, scratching the bird's chest.

'*Flick happy see Cullen*,' the bird croaked. '*And Keld and Fen.*' Flick regarded Drem with one shiny eye, his head cocked to one side. '*Well met, Drem ben Olin*,' he said, bobbing his head.

'Well met,' Drem said, a little taken aback.

'Flick is the politest bird in Crow Tower,' Cullen said, grinning.

'Flick, what news?' Keld said.

'*Rab told us all. Gulla in north. Sig dead.*' Flick shook his head mournfully. '*Byrne ANGRY*,' he squawked loudly, flapping his wings for emphasis. '*Byrne called the muster, Byrne want to KILL GULLA.*' Flick shrieked. '*All of Order summoned to Dun Seren. Byrne sent lots of huntsmen to find you. Stepor closest.*'

Hammer lumbered up behind them.

'*Well met, Hammer*,' Flick croaked. The bear rumbled at the crow. Then Flick jumped into the air with a flap of wings when he saw the white bear appear behind Hammer.

'Hammer has an admirer,' Cullen said, with a roll of his eyes.

Flick landed back on Cullen's shoulder.

'Stepor? Good,' Keld said. 'How far away is he?'

'*Two, three days*,' Flick croaked, shrugging his wings. '*Follow Flick.*' With a beat of his wings the crow leaped into the air.

CHAPTER TWENTY

RIV

Riv stepped out of the tower into Drassil's Great Hall. It was almost empty, apart from the ring of guards around the statues of Asroth and Meical. Usually giants held that vigil, but all the giants of Drassil had gone with Ethlinn to Dun Seren, so it was White-Wings that circled the frozen statues now.

Riv felt their gaze upon her as she strode through the hall, her footsteps echoing. She looked at them, a glare at first, then one nodded to her. She hesitated a moment, then nodded back. Walking out into the winter sunlight, she blinked, heard the whisper of wings above her and her hand went instinctively to the hilt of her short-sword.

A Ben-Elim drifted down and alighted beside her, Hadran, the guard from Kol's chamber.

'I am to guard you,' he said, his face as unreadable as Ble-da's. She felt a pang at the thought of her friend, a deep sense of loneliness cutting through her. She had wanted to go to Bleda, to speak with him, but shame had held her back, the fact that Kol was her father, the man who had slain Bleda's brother and sister. And she had made a deal with Kol.

Does Bleda hate me? Despise me for the blood that runs in my veins? And would he hate me for the deal I have made? He would feel ashamed that I have turned away from what is right, and he would hate that I have done it for him.

She burned to go and ask him; not knowing was driving her

mad, itching away inside her head like ants on her skin. She had eventually overcome her shame and tried to speak to him, searched him out, but every time, Jin had been there. At his side.

Riv saw Hadran frown at her and realized she was grinding her teeth.

'Guard me, then,' she muttered and strode down the stone steps into the courtyard before the great keep. He lingered, walking a dozen or so steps behind her, then she felt the shifting of air as he took to the sky, until his presence was just a shadow on the flagstones around her.

Finding herself free of Kol's chambers, Riv was abruptly aware that she did not quite know what to do with herself, and her footsteps faltered. She walked on, aware that people were looking at her, or more accurately, at her wings. Instinctively, she tried to furl them tighter, which of course didn't make them disappear, and then when she realized what she was doing she purposely and slowly unfurled them, spreading them wide.

Because I am not ashamed of who I am.

She heard some gasps, whispered comments, and looked around. Some eyes looked away, discomfited, but a few stood and met her gaze. A group of children stared unashamedly at her. Riv gave a fast pulse of her wings, making them crack like a whip, and one of the children screamed. Others laughed.

Riv grinned at them and walked on.

She passed through the wide streets of Drassil, a host of different reactions happening around her. Some hurried out of her way, others stopped and gawped, some that she knew raised a hand in greeting or offered a nod.

Then she heard footsteps running up behind her and she twisted, hand on her hilt, but it was only one of the children who had been staring at her. A red-haired boy, no more than six summers. She knew him – Tam, son of a wool trader. She used to pass his stall on her way home from training in the weapons-field, and Tam would more often than not stick his tongue out and wave a stick carved as a sword at her, and she'd often get on her knees and let him swat at her in mock combat. Sometimes she'd even let him win.

'Is that really you, Riv?' the lad asked her.

She got down onto her knees. 'Aye, Tam,' she said. 'It is.'

'I like your wings,' he said, looking at them with wide eyes.

'I like them, too,' she said.

'Can I touch them?' he asked.

'Of course you can,' she said, and smiled.

She curled a wing tip in towards him, and he reached out tentatively, fingertips brushing a feather.

'It's soft,' Tam breathed.

With a pulse of her wings, Riv rose from her knees and hovered a handspan off the ground, just for a few heartbeats. Tam gasped, and there were 'ooohhs' around her. Riv alighted gently on the earth.

'Walk with me,' Riv said, holding her hand out to the little lad. Without hesitation he did, and together they strolled down the street.

People came and spoke to her now, walking along beside her for a while, asking her a hesitant question or two, saying they stood for her in the Great Hall. She told them she was grateful.

And then, before she had a chance to realize where her feet had taken her, she stood before the entrance to the weapons-field.

'Wow,' Tam said, who was still holding her hand. His eyes were wide.

Riv stood and stared at it a while: a huge, open expanse within the southern boundary of Drassil's walls. Sounds drifted out to her, the *clack, clack, clack* of practice blades, the shout of '*SHIELD WALL*' followed by a reverberating thud as units of White-Wings drilled their formations, the drum of hooves further away as riders cantered and then galloped at targets, leaving spears shivering in their enemies' straw bellies. And behind it all the whirring *thrum* of the archery range.

For a long, timeless moment Riv closed her eyes and just let the sounds and smells wash over her. For as long as Riv had memories, Drassil had been her home, but of all the parts that she associated with that notion of *home* – her barracks, the feast-hall, her dormitory – this weapons-field was the place that felt most precious to her.

Probably because I have spent more of my time here than anywhere else in all the world.

Her eyes fixed on the portion of the field that was given to archery practice, with its ranges and straw targets. She saw a few score men and women with their bows of yew and ash, people who belonged to the scouting and hunting units, but there were also others there, in woollen deels of grey and blue, heads shaved apart from long, thick warrior braids.

The Sirak and Cheren. The honour guards of Bleda and Jin.

She saw Bleda immediately, her sharp, new-found vision picking him out amongst the crowd. He was sitting upon a horse at the end of a range, arms folded, Old Ellac beside him as well as a handful more of his guards, and he was watching Jin as she stared down the range at a target over a hundred paces distant. A recurved bow was held loosely in one of her hands.

Then Jin moved.

In one fluid motion she reached into the quiver at her belt, grabbed a handful of arrows, three at least, holding them in the hand she used to grip the bow, and then she was sighting, nocking, loosing.

Three arrows were in the air before the first one hit the target, and then with a sound like hailstone drumming on clay tiles they thumped into the target, two in the straw man's chest, one in his head, roughly where Riv imagined his eye would be located.

Riv's first reaction was a moment of respect for Jin's skill, a warrior's gut reaction at seeing skills so precise, an action that she knew was difficult made to look so easy and effortless. That moment was rapidly followed by a rush of anger.

The hot blood-rush flooded her veins, and something distant in her recognized the warning signals, attempting to calm them, remembering Kol's words to her.

Don't lose your temper.

Riv was also a little surprised at the depth of her feeling.

I must really hate her.

Hate? Maybe not. Perhaps it is just loathing. Extreme loathing. And a touch of jealousy.

The distant, sensible side of her whispered a question.

Jealous of what?

Of her skill with a bow, of course, the red mist snapped back.

I must get better with a bow, she resolved.

Riv took a step into the field, felt a tug on her hand and she looked down, realized that little Tam was still there. Others were behind her, a crowd thirty or forty strong that had gathered as she'd walked through Drassil's streets. Some were children, but many were adults, intrigued by this strange new being amongst them.

'It's forbidden,' Tam said nervously. 'I'm not allowed in the training field yet.'

'Haven't you heard?' Riv said. 'Times are changing,' and she hoisted him into her arms, setting him on her shoulders, his legs dangling. Then she walked into the weapons-field.

Tam didn't complain.

No one else followed, but Riv noticed that most of them stayed at the gates, just watching her.

Riv walked past the duelling square, where one-to-one combat was practised, from wrestling to weapons work. Racks of wooden weapons edged the square, all manner of types and sizes, because it was not just men and women that trained in the field, but giants as well.

Ert, one of Drassil's many sword masters, took his eyes

from a pair of duelling White-Wings to watch Riv as she strode by. He was bald and wore his warrior braid in his white beard. He limped from an old wound, but all counted themselves lucky if they had the good fortune to be trained by him. Riv met his gaze, resisted the urge to look away, fearful of what she would see in his eyes. She respected Ert, and it would hurt if he thought less of her now.

Ert dipped his head to her, a curt movement, like when Riv scored a touch against him when sparring. She felt a grin stretch her mouth wide.

Behind Ert a White-Wing stared at her, revulsion etched on his face.

Riv walked on, past the White-Wings in shield wall training, saw some of Aphra's hundred there, caught a glimpse of bull-necked Vald and the top of Jost's unruly hair. Even when it was cropped short in the White-Wing style, it still managed to stick out in all directions. For a moment she wished that she was there in the shield wall with them, that all of this had just been a bad dream. She stumbled to a stop, suddenly realizing that she would never stand in the shield wall again. How could she, with wings? Ben-Elim were not built for the wall.

It was like a punch to the gut.

She had loved the shield wall, the claustrophobic camaraderie and exhilaration, the feeling of strength, of belonging, of brothers and sisters either side, trusting you with their lives, and knowing that you trusted them.

All gone now.

Her wings gave an agitated ripple, an extension of how she felt.

But I can fly, now. That is better than any shield wall. Though lonelier.

She sighed.

'You all right, Riv?' Tam asked from above her.

I don't think I'll ever be all right again.

'Aye,' Riv grunted. She turned to walk on, almost collided

with someone. A White-Wing, young, the feather carved into his leather vambrace indicating he had not long passed his warrior trial and moved from Fledgling to White-Wing. Riv knew him – Sorch, almost as big and muscular as Vald, but where Vald was only an arrogant idiot when he'd drunk too much wine, Sorch was an arrogant idiot *all* of the time. Riv had never liked him much, even less after she'd seen him lead a dozen of his comrades into giving Bleda a beating.

'You don't belong here,' Sorch said. His cheeks were red, fists clenched and knuckles white.

Don't lose your temper.

'Get out of my way, arsewipe,' Riv said.

She could feel the tendrils of her anger creeping through her blood, twisting through her body, making her heart beat faster, her muscles tense.

'You're an abomination,' Sorch said. 'You deserve to die, should be executed.' Voices behind him added their agreement. Others were gathering in his wake, some of his own hundred, plus older White-Wings, men and women whom Riv didn't recognize. Ten, twelve others joining them.

'You disgust me,' Sorch sneered.

Breathe. Calm. Jost is always saying I need a sense of humour.

'Now you know how I feel every time I see you eat in the feast-hall,' Riv said. She wasn't lying. Sorch seemed to lack the ability to eat without half the contents of his mouth spilling out and sounding like someone was slurping on offal.

By the look on Sorch's face, her attempt at humour to defuse the tension hadn't worked, though one of Sorch's companions chuckled.

Sorch didn't seem to like that, either.

He spat in Riv's face.

She felt the dam on her anger crack, begin to leak.

Very slowly, Riv wiped spittle from her eye. She flicked it away. Then, just as slowly, she reached up and took hold of

Tam, lifted him gently from her shoulders and set him on the ground.

'Move away, Tam,' she said.

Then she punched Sorch in the face.

Riv had always been strong. A lifetime spent in the weapons-field, living in a barracks with a White-Wing hundred or out on campaign and attending to the myriad duties that entailed had honed her musculature and sharpened her reflexes, but since she had come into her wings, that strength, speed and fitness had seemed to increase immeasurably.

Her punch lifted Sorch from the ground and hurled him back into his comrades, scattering them like chaff.

A moment's shock and silence, like an indrawn breath, as Riv saw Sorch sprawled atop half a dozen others, those still standing behind him dumbfounded. As if in slow motion she saw their expressions change, from shock, to outrage, to action. Fists were clenched, sparring weapons raised as they came at her. Distantly, Riv was aware of shouting, figures moving in her peripheral vision, running, of Tam's eyes wide in something that wasn't fear, more resembling . . . *awe.*

A shadow on the ground cast from high above moving, growing larger.

Riv knew that all of them would be too late.

She bent her legs and leaped at the onrushing crowd, pulsed her wings and gave her leap added speed and power. She hit them like a battering ram, sent bodies hurtling in all directions, landed with feet spread and a fierce smile on her face. It felt so good to just give in, to allow so much suppressed rage finally to run free.

A White-Wing from her left, a veteran, practice sword-swinging in a diagonal arc for her head. She swayed, felt the air of its passing across her face, grabbed his wrist, twisted, smiled at the *crack* and scream that followed, cast him to the ground, kicked him in the head as he tried to rise. He didn't try to get up again.

A blow across her back, a pain in her shoulder-blade and the arch of her wing, and she spun around, backhanded a female White-Wing across the jaw, dropped her to the floor, unconscious before she hit the ground.

And then all was constant motion, Riv ducking, swaying, punching, kicking, using her wings to give bursts of speed, to turn tighter and faster than was humanly possible, and all who came against her fell away in bloody heaps. Dimly she became aware that she was not the only one with wings in the melee, glimpsed Hadran her guard dragging a White-Wing off her, casting him aside, and behind him other figures came into focus, Vald and Jost, Ert the sword master, all of them locked in combat against other White-Wings, fighting for her, trying to defend her.

Then a crack across her head, exploding like a drum inside her skull, and she was dropping to her knees. She punched a knee, heard a scream, kicked out at an ankle, saw someone fall, but more blows were raining down upon her.

A rumbling thunder, growing rapidly louder, the ground shaking, and suddenly she was being grabbed by the neck of her leather jerkin, heaved up, into the air, weightless, and then she was swinging onto the back of a horse as it rode away and her arms were wrapping around Bleda's waist.

Half a dozen heartbeats and he drew his horse into a canter, then a halt.

Bleda twisted in his saddle, his bow in his hand, and drew it, aimed at the first White-Wing that was running after them.

It was Sorch.

Bleda loosed, and his arrow sank deep into the ground at Sorch's feet. He skidded to a halt, blood running from his pulped lips and nose, looked from the arrow to Riv, took another step.

'I can kill you, if you wish,' Bleda said calmly, another arrow nocked and drawn in a heartbeat.

Something in Bleda's voice drew Sorch up where Riv's violence had not.

'I would *like* to kill you,' Bleda said. 'Give me the excuse.'

Sorch took a step back, raised his hands.

'Shame,' muttered Riv.

'You're bleeding,' Bleda said to her.

She licked blood from her lip, felt the red mist still coursing through her, but retreating now, not gone, but a lull.

'Pulling you out of fights is becoming a habit,' Bleda said to Riv. His horse danced on the spot, excited.

'I'll try and return the favour one day,' she said.

Riv looked around, saw her conflict had spread into a brawl hundreds of people strong, some still fighting on. She saw Vald and Jost standing back to back, practice shields and swords still in their fists, a handful of her old White-Wing comrades with them, as well as Ert. Amongst the various warriors of the field involved in the melee, Riv saw others, not warriors at all, and realized with a jolt of shock that they were from the crowd that had gathered about her and followed her through the streets of Drassil.

They have rushed the field to help me.

Some were still fighting. Hadran the Ben-Elim was trading blows with a trio of White-Wings, as well as two Ben-Elim. Even as she watched, she saw Hadran fall.

Voices were raised behind Riv, a glance showing Aphra running into the field, more White-Wings with her, these with real shields and drawn swords. And Ben-Elim in the air behind her – Kol and his guards, other Ben-Elim swooping in from different directions.

Ach, Kol will not be happy. All this, she thought, looking at the bodies strewn across the ground, rising, groaning. *Because of Sorch.*

With a *snap* she spread her wings and took to the air, Bleda calling out after her. She rose briefly, then tucked her wings in and dropped into a dive, a flexing of her wings to adjust her angle, and she was speeding along parallel to the ground.

Straight at Sorch.

He saw her coming, saw the look in her eyes, and then he was turning, breaking into a stumbling run.

Far too slow. Riv caught him in moments, grabbing his leather training vest, her wings beating hard as she dragged him from his feet, sweeping him up and along in her momentum.

Sorch screamed.

Riv laughed.

She flew low, just above the heads of those who had been involved in the melee, Sorch's feet smacking heads, then she dived down again, barrelling a Ben-Elim out of her way and reaching down, grabbing at an arm, her fist closing around a wrist, and then she was veering up, wings straining as she dragged two bodies up into the air above the weapons-field.

Sorch continued to scream, rising in pitch. As they climbed higher it became a whimper.

The other body was Hadran, battered, a cut above his eye leaking blood over his face.

He was stunned, eyes glazed and fluttering for a few moments, but his senses returned to him quickly enough and he stared at Riv.

'What are you doing?' he asked.

'You watched my back, I'm just watching yours,' she said.

Hadran realized he was in the air and extended his wings, flexed them once or twice.

Riv let go and he flew away, but not far, spiralled around her, a strange look on his face.

Riv gave Sorch her attention.

He had his eyes squeezed tightly shut, was whimpering and shaking.

The words Sorch had said to her came back in a rush.

You're an abomination. You deserve to die.

Anger flooded Riv's mind, red dots dappling her vision. She put a hand around his throat and squeezed. Sorch croaked a scream, his face turning red, then purple. He swatted at Riv, feebly. She was dimly aware of Hadran shouting at her, flying closer.

You are an abomination. You deserve to die.

She squeezed harder.

A spasm from Sorch and he shrieked, hard and loud, and jerked his leg. Riv glanced down, saw an arrow protruding from his calf, blood leaking from the wound, raining down upon the field. She blinked, felt the red mist of her rage retreat and looked down to the weapons-field far below her.

Bleda was standing in his stirrups, his bow in his hand. Another arrow flew from his bow, whistling past Sorch's head. Instinctively, Riv jerked him away, felt herself coming back to her senses. She released her grip around Sorch's throat and held him by his training vest.

'Open your eyes. Look down,' Riv said, hovering with great, slow beats of her wings.

He didn't, so Riv shook him, like a cat with a mouse.

He screamed, Riv was impressed with the strength of his lungs.

'If you don't open your eyes I'm going to drop you,' she said.

He didn't open his eyes.

Riv let go of one arm and let him dangle a little.

More yelling as his eyes snapped open.

'P-please,' he begged. 'Please, please, please.' Tears streamed from his eyes, snot from his nose.

'Look down,' she growled at him.

Slowly, inch by inch, his head shifted and he looked down. He whimpered again, a pitiful sound. Riv had only flown about the equivalent of a hundred or so paces straight up, but it was still high enough to splatter Sorch over a wide area if she dropped him. The ground seemed a very long way away, everyone on the field frozen, staring up at them.

'Remember this,' Riv snarled at him. 'Remember that I have your life in my hands, could kill you if I wished.' She paused. 'Do you realize that?'

He opened his mouth but nothing came out.

'I can't hear you,' she said.

'Yes,' Sorch squeaked.

'Good.' Riv nodded. 'Now, you are a worm, but you are still one of Elyon's creations, and so have the right to live. Just like I do.'

She stared into his eyes.

'Do you understand what I'm saying to you?'

He nodded frantically.

'Tell me.'

'Th-th-th-that you are not an abomination,' he stuttered. 'Th-th-th-that you should live, do not deserve to be e-e-executed.'

'That's right,' Riv said. She narrowed her eyes. 'But do I believe you? If I take you back to the ground, see you safe down there, will you just do this again, or worse?'

'N-n-n-n-n-no,' Sorch said. 'You can trust me, I swear. Live and let l-l-live, that's what I say.'

'Because I could still drop you. It would be easier that way. No need to worry about whether you can be trusted, then.'

Riv glimpsed Ben-Elim swooping towards her, Kol amongst them. She glanced over Sorch's shoulder and saw Hadran. He was close, but just observing, making no attempt to interfere.

Then Riv heard a sound, distant, a horn blowing, far away, beyond the walls of Drassil.

An answering horn blast from Drassil's towers.

What's that?

Riv beat her wings and rose higher. Sorch let out a yelp and shut his eyes tight again, his arms flailing, reaching out and grabbing Riv. He pulled himself tight against her body. She could feel his trembling.

The horn calls resounded again and Riv climbed higher, level with Drassil's towering walls, then higher still, until she could see the sea of green that was Forn Forest, stretching in all directions for endless leagues. Hadran flew close to her.

A column of horses was spilling onto the plain that surrounded Drassil, coming from the east road. Easily two to three hundred, with still more appearing. Riv squinted, the figures not much more than pinpricks, but she glimpsed a banner, stared a few moments longer and made out a white horse on a green field.

I recognize that sigil.

Kol and a score of Ben-Elim reached her then, but they were not giving Riv any attention, all of them staring out at the riders on the plain. With a beat of his wings and a shouted command Kol sped forwards, towards the riders.

Then Riv was descending, by the shrieks and yelps that escaped Sorch, a little too fast for his liking. When she was about the height of three horses from the ground she extended her wings wide, checking her speed, and touched down with a whisper of feet. Sorch collapsed in a heap on the floor, hugging and kissing the ground, quivering and shaking.

Riv ignored him, ignored the cheers and shouts from the crowd that were all staring at her, instead turning to Bleda, who was still sitting upon his horse where she had left him. Ellac and Bleda's guards were about him now, as was Jin and a few of her honour guard. She was looking at Riv with that superior expression, as always. Riv ignored her.

'Bleda, there are Sirak riding onto the plain. I think your mother has come to Drassil.'

CHAPTER TWENTY-ONE

FRITHA

Fritha stepped into a clearing and stopped for a long moment, unsure of what she was looking at. It was a large space, thirty or forty paces wide, edged in boulders, shrubs and trees. Churned snow on the ground was melting to slush, and there had been no fresh snowfalls since Fritha had reached Drem's abandoned camp by the river. The weather was shifting as winter retreated before spring's tentative advance. Much of the ground was stained pink, with scattered pools of almost black blood. But that was not what Fritha's eyes were drawn to.

Two of her Ferals were standing at her shoulder, sniffing and snapping and snarling, scared and vicious at the same time as they all stared at heaped mounds of dead flesh.

Some of us are at our most dangerous when we are scared. They do not recognize what scent they are smelling, but they don't like it.

Fritha had been sceptical about Morn's tale of giant wyrms and *two* bears, one of them white, fighting alongside Drem and his companions. But these piles of coiled scales suggested that Morn was right.

Fritha hefted her spear and pointed it at the closest heap, took a few steps into the clearing.

A shadow skimmed across her, Morn descending in a whirl of wings.

'Are you sure they are dead?' Fritha muttered.

'I saw them slain by the Order and two bears,' Morn answered.

Fritha noticed that Morn was still levelling her spear at the nearest coiled body, though.

They smell dead to me.

Ferals and her warriors emerged from the bushes and trees around the clearing to join Fritha, all of them edging closer with sharp steel glinting, a noosed circle growing tighter.

As Fritha drew closer, details became clearer amidst the coiled heap: a red wound, tattered skin, darkening flesh and the glint of vertebrae where its head should be.

Wyrms, Morn was right, Fritha realized, a tremor of awe passing through her. She had heard tales of these fabled beasts, but never dreamed of seeing one. Each coil of the creature's torso was thicker than her waist.

The wyrm's head was on the ground nearby, as big as a hound. Its skin hung torn and ragged, eye sockets pecked empty. Fritha prodded the severed head with her spear and it rolled over, maggots squirming out of the empty sockets and spilling from its nostrils and mouth. Fritha crouched for a closer look and saw that its two fangs had been hacked from its gums. She wrinkled her nose at the smell.

One of her Ferals leaned close and took a sniff of the heaped coils that had been the wyrm's body.

'Eat it, if you wish,' Fritha said, looking at lengths of gnawed flesh hanging in strips. 'You're not the first to try.'

There were two more dead wyrms in the clearing. One lay amidst a pile of its own entrails, whilst the other had been literally torn in two.

The ground was a trampled mess, sections of it showing the prints of a massive snake's rippling movement. There were half-visible boot-prints in the melting snow, wolven-hound paw-prints and bear-prints, many of them, and of different sizes.

Morn was right about two bears, as well.

'There were two bears,' Morn said beside her, as if reading her mind.

Morn had returned to them close to three days ago, bursting with excitement as she'd told Fritha of her sighting, and of the wyrms and white bear. Fritha had been excited at the ground they had gained, but sceptical about wyrms and white bears. She resolved not to doubt Morn's eyesight again.

'Where did they go?' Fritha asked.

'That way,' Morn said, pointing with her spear. The two of them padded to the clearing's edge, following the prints that led away from the battle. Boot-prints, bear-prints, wolven-prints. They followed them a way into a stand of pine trees, stooping.

'Have they met someone from the Order of the Bright Star?' Fritha wondered. 'Another giant and their bear?' She felt a stab of anger and frustration at that thought, to be so close and for Drem to escape her. Another bear and giant would probably be too much for her depleted numbers.

'I saw no one else,' Morn said. 'But I was high, did not get too close, as you asked.' The half-breed's lips curled; Fritha realized it was her attempt at a smile.

Since Morn's return, when Fritha nursed her back from the edge of death and spoke words of power into her, Morn had changed, not softened, exactly, but there was something less aloof and abrasive in Morn's demeanour towards Fritha.

Perhaps the fact that I saved her life has broken through her shell of pride and rage.

'Good,' Fritha said. 'I would not lose you, and those nets they have are deadly.'

'Aye, curse them.' Morn spat. She reached a hand to her belt, where the patched net that had almost killed her was neatly folded.

Behind them, Gunil's bear let out a rumbling growl and crashed into the trees at the edge of the clearing, disappearing. Gunil gave chase, a handful of Ferals bounding after them.

Fritha and Morn shared a look, and then Gunil was shouting, the snap and snarl of Fritha's Ferals, the growling of Claw, and Fritha turned and ran. She heard Gunil's voice, booming through the trees. He was yelling commands.

'Get back! Hold!' he was yelling.

Fritha ran faster, Morn running and leaping into the air, gliding ahead. She sprinted through the clearing, past the dead wyrms where some of her Ferals were feasting, on through a thicket of hawthorn to catch up with some of her warriors, who were doing the same as her, running towards the sounds echoing about her.

And then she saw Gunil and Claw, a handful of Fritha's Red Right Hand around them, Ferals standing in a half-circle, growling like hounds with hackles raised. Gunil had his war-hammer in his fist and was dragging on the reins of his bear, which was rearing and growling, trying to reach something beyond Gunil. The giant heaved on the reins, forcing Claw down, and gave the bear a mighty cuff with the back of his hand.

'Hold, now,' Gunil yelled at the bear.

'What's going on?' Fritha shouted as she ran up; with a beating of wings Morn touched down to her right.

'He doesn't like it, wants to kill it,' Gunil grunted, cuffing his bear again. Claw was more composed now, giving Gunil what Fritha thought was a sulky look.

Fritha pushed through her warriors and Ferals, who were ringed around something, spears and all manner of sharp iron pointing.

Then she saw what the bear wanted to kill.

It was a wyrm, long and sinuous, coiled in the shadows of a boulder. Fritha could not guess at its size, probably the length of one of the pines that towered around them, but its body was thick, as thick as the pine's trunk, with pale, pearl-like scales coating its wide girth. It was injured, that was plain to see, with open wounds raking its torso. The creature was having trouble even lifting its head, though it managed to bear its fangs and hiss at Gunil's bear.

More than injured, it looks close to death.

Even as Fritha watched, its head sank to the ground, the effort too much for it, and it gave out a long, rattling hiss.

Fritha just stared at the wyrm, lost for long moments in its magnificence; even on the brink of death its power and deadliness were clear. Fritha respected that.

'Morn, your net,' Fritha said, holding out a hand.

Morn put a hand protectively on the net at her belt.

'I have plans for it,' the half-breed muttered.

'You'll get it back,' Fritha said, hand still extended.

Morn unclipped it from her belt and gave it to Fritha, who shook it out, spun it around her head and cast it at the wyrm.

The net fell over the wyrm's head and neck. It hissed and raised its head, a feeble motion, the weight of the lead balls on the net almost too much for it to lift. Fritha stepped forwards and staked one corner of the net into the ground with her spear, then gestured for another spear. Morn saw what Fritha was doing and staked another corner with her own weapon.

Fritha stepped away from the head and prodded the snake's torso with her toe. It hissed, but nothing more. She kicked it, hard, and its head twitched, more hissing, but it lacked the strength to fight free of the net.

Fritha knelt down beside it, running a hand along its scales. It was cool to the touch, the scales smooth. The sense of muscle and malice that emanated from the creature almost took her breath away. She touched one of the wounds, flesh red and raw, then shuffled closer to the wyrm's wide head. She stroked it, ran a finger across its jaw line, tracing one long fang. It regarded her with a reptilian eye, a twitch of its mouth, but nothing more.

'It's as if Drem is leaving me gifts, to make up for all of the difficulties he is causing me. First the draig egg, and now you.'

Fritha smiled.

She reached to her belt and drew her knife. She opened her palm, saw the scabbing cut from the hold, when she had communicated with Gulla. Gritting her teeth, she drew her knife across the half-healed wound, fresh blood welling, and she squeezed a fist, let her blood drip into the wyrm's wounds, across its body, finally onto its fangs and into its mouth.

'*Fola agus focail chumhachta,*' Fritha whispered, '*ceangail an fheoil seo, leigheas an cnámh seo.*' She smiled as she did it. 'I will save you, my beauty,' she whispered, and intoned her spell of power again, and again, until the wyrm shuddered and lay its head down, sleeping.

'Gunil, build me a cage,' she called over her shoulder.

CHAPTER TWENTY-TWO

BLEDA

Bleda's heart was pounding. He was riding through the wide streets of Drassil, his horse's hooves sparking on the flagstones of the road, dimly aware of Ellac and his guard urging their mounts after him. People were jumping out of his way, and a shadow flitted across the road, a glimpse showing the silhouette of Riv above him.

So much had happened in the weapons-field, a brawl turning into a riot. Bleda had thought for a few heart-wrenching moments when he saw Riv fall beneath an abundance of foes that she was going to be beaten to death. He hardly remembered galloping across the field, people leaping out of his way as he leaned out of his saddle, grabbing Riv and hauling her onto his horse.

And then, when he thought the worst was over and all was returning to calm, Riv had flown down and said those six words that had set him to riding through the streets.

Your mother has come to Drassil.

He felt excited, scared, thrilled, worried.

And then he was bursting into the great courtyard of Drassil, its huge gates and tower rising like a small keep ahead of him. The courtyard itself was large enough to hold a small host, a thousand warriors on horseback could probably fit into it.

Bleda touched his reins and gave a quick squeeze with his

knees, his mount responding beautifully, slowing to a trot, to a walk and then to a standstill. Ellac and his guards, a dozen men and women, formed up perfectly to either side of him. Tuld, Ruga and Mirim were closest. They seemed to have been permanently at his side since their return to Drassil and had taken great pride in telling Bleda's guard that had remained in the fortress of their Prince's exploits against the Ben-Elim. Bleda had been relieved to discover that his honour guard who had remained in Drassil when he'd fled with Riv had not been harmed, merely detained and watched closely. They had shown unusual joy when he had returned to them, and upon hearing of his actions, seemed to hold Bleda in higher esteem than before.

'What did she say to you?' Ellac asked him.

'Huh?' Bleda grunted, then realized Ellac was referring to Riv.

'My Queen and mother is here.' Bleda kept his face emotionless. 'She is riding towards Drassil's gates,' he said, and saw a brief lapse of Ellac's cold-face, a ripple of surprise and pleasure before the control came back.

Bleda's other guards heard, and instantly all were checking their deels and weapons, straightening arrows in their belt quivers, sitting taller in their saddles.

The gates of Drassil were open. Horn blasts rang out and, through the gateway, Bleda glimpsed movement on the plain.

Others started arriving in the courtyard – Jin and a score of her honour guard. She looked at Bleda with a quizzical expression, but Bleda avoided her gaze.

Bleda had felt awkward with Jin since his return to Drassil. He was betrothed to her, knew that their marriage had been arranged to secure the bonds between the Sirak and Cheren Clans and to put their old grievances into the past. And Bleda liked Jin. She had been his closest companion for the last five years, his only friend in the fortress.

Until Riv.

He knew that it was his duty to wed Jin, that he was honour-bound for the sake of his Clan, and it was not the worst thing he could imagine. She was intelligent, strong and skilled, and not unpleasant to look at. With her sharp features, quick reactions and wit she reminded Bleda of the hawk that was the Cheren sigil.

But then why is it that every time I close my eyes, the only face I see is Riv's?

Bleda searched the courtyard and the skies above, and although there were many Ben-Elim in the skies overhead, he could not see her distinctive wings and silhouette anywhere.

Aphra and her White-Wings marched into the courtyard, not her full hundred, but enough to form an imposing shield wall, even if their shields were slung across their backs, with other units of White-Wings hastily gathering behind them. More Ben-Elim arrived, wheeling in the sky above, some flying on out beyond Drassil's walls.

And then more horns were blowing and riders were thundering through the gate tunnel and pouring into the courtyard. Bleda's heart soared to see his kin, a wave of mounted men and women in their deels of grey, heads shaved and long warrior braids flowing. Each rider carried short curved swords strapped across their backs, recurved bows in leather cases and quivers of arrows buckled to their saddles, and at their head rode Erdene, Bleda's mother, Queen of the Sirak.

She rode straight-backed and proud into the courtyard, a long surcoat of lamellar armour over a grey deel tunic, a fox-fur cloak slung across her shoulder, and her boots trimmed with ermine. A silver ring was wrapped around her arm, two horse-heads facing each other. She reined in a score of paces from Bleda, a whispered word and her horse was rearing, hooves punching the air.

Bleda fought to hold back the grin of joy that threatened to spill all over his face.

Hundreds of Sirak slipped into neat lines behind her, the

thunder of hooves abruptly silent. Erdene's horse, a magnificent piebald, shook its head, its mane rippling, and whickered.

Bleda clicked his horse on and walked out into the open space between them. A double-click of his tongue and pressure from one knee, and his horse stretched one foreleg forwards, bent the other, for all the world seeming as if it were bowing to Erdene.

She looked at Bleda, then gave him a curt nod for his display of horsemanship, and another for his mark of respect to her.

And then there was a maelstrom of wings descending upon them, Ben-Elim falling from the sky. Kol alighted in the space between Bleda and Erdene, bright and gleaming in a shirt and breeches of white wool and polished leather tunic, studded with iron. A few score Ben-Elim stood behind him, forming a line between Bleda and his kin, and many others circled low over the courtyard, the cold sun gleaming off their spear-points.

Other Ben-Elim spiralled in from a different direction, a mass of them in the air like a flock of white eagles. Bleda saw Sariel touching down on his right flank. Kol saw him, too, and with a gesture of his hand many of his Ben-Elim landed before Sariel, swelling Kol's ranks and blocking Sariel's approach to Erdene. At the same time Aphra's White-Wings were moving, filling the empty spaces of the courtyard around Sariel's Ben-Elim. There were no angry words, no weapons drawn, but tension filled the area. Sariel was glaring at Kol, then casting his dark look upon the Ben-Elim and White-Wings blocking his way.

Bleda could tell he was caught in that moment of indecision, whether to act or hold, and he saw his mother's eyes taking it all in.

'Welcome to Drassil, Queen Erdene of the Sirak,' Kol said loudly and formally as he took a step towards Erdene.

Bleda saw Sariel say something to his Ben-Elim behind

him, then take a step back, folding his arms and staring coldly at Kol and Erdene.

'An unexpected pleasure,' Kol said to Erdene. Kol's voice was polite, but Bleda could see a tension in the Ben-Elim, though well hidden, a stiffness across his shoulders, a clenching in his jaw. Being a student of the cold-face, Bleda was a master of analysing all of the tell-tale signs a body could give away.

He did not know that my mother was coming, and he is ready for violence.

The sound of many footsteps behind him, a glance showing more White-Wings entering the courtyard – Lorina leading over a hundred warriors. They slipped silently into a loose shield wall formation behind Aphra and her group.

'I bring you what you asked for,' Erdene said, and with a flick of her reins her horse was sidestepping, the rows of Sirak behind her parting, their mounts moving to the flanks of the courtyard to reveal yet more riders. But these were not warriors, they were children, their heads as yet unshaved. Boys and girls, lots of children, a hundred, perhaps more.

'I give you your flesh tithe,' Erdene said.

Bleda walked into a large chamber, Ellac and Ruga either side of him, as befitted his rank. A fire-pit in the centre of the room crackled with hungry flames, spreading a welcome warmth through the stone room. It was part of a building large enough to pass for a keep at any other fortress, but here at Drassil it was just one of many buildings built by giants so long ago which still stood empty. Kol had given it to Erdene as quarters for her and her retainers for the duration of her stay in the fortress.

Erdene was seated in a high-backed chair close to the fire, her first-sword Yul behind her, a table at her side with jug and cups.

Kol was standing before Erdene, Lorina at one shoulder, Riv at the other. Bleda's step faltered at the sight of her.

Riv looked at Bleda as he approached, her face mottled with bruises and cuts from her fight in the weapons-field.

She smiled on seeing him.

He felt something shift in his belly at that, like the fluttering of a moth's wings, and at the same time he was painfully aware of his mother's gaze upon him. With an effort he kept his face emotionless, saw Riv's smile wither and fade.

He stopped a few paces from his mother and dropped to one knee before her, his head bowed. He heard the scuff of Ellac and Ruga's knees scraping the stone floor behind him.

A silence.

'Rise,' his mother grunted, and the three of them stood before her. She looked older, deep lines in her brown-weathered face, a white scar standing stark across her shaved head. Her warrior braid was curled across one shoulder like an iron-grey serpent.

She studied Bleda with her dark eyes, then stood and held her arm out, offering him the warrior grip.

He stood as still as stone, frozen with surprise, then reached out and took the offered embrace, felt the corded muscle of her arm through her wool deel. Inside, his heart was soaring.

She recognizes me as a warrior, no longer a child. He wanted to laugh and dance, to lift his mother up and spin and squeeze her.

Instead he stared at her, his face an emotionless mask.

Erdene released his arm and nodded a greeting to Ellac.

'The moons since I last laid eyes upon you have treated you well,' Erdene said, looking Bleda up and down. She prodded his belly. 'Though a little too well, perhaps.'

Bleda blinked at that. He prided himself on his fitness. He trained with his honour guard each morning, where Ellac put him through his paces, and through his pouring sweat and pounding heart Bleda had regularly cursed the old man for having no heart or compassion. And then after a meal break and his lessons Bleda trained in the weapons-field each afternoon, learning Drassil's many varied military disciplines. He didn't think there was an ounce of fat on his body, but he wasn't going to point that out to his mother.

He looked down at her bony finger poking his belly, felt it digging into the washboard-hard ridges of his abdominal muscles.

A moment's thought. *Is my mother making a joke?*

'I will watch you train in the weapons-field, and make sure that life here is not too soft for a Sirak prince,' Erdene said.

Kol smiled. 'You will not be disappointed,' he said. 'Bleda excels in the field at most disciplines. His body and mind are strong. Honed. As is his aim.' Kol didn't smile at the last remark.

'I will be the judge of that,' Erdene said. 'So –' she looked at Kol – 'much has changed here, since my last visit.' Her gaze moved pointedly to Riv.

'Aye, betrayal and tragedy has struck us, with the death of Israfil,' Kol said. 'But the light behind the clouds is that we are moving into a new age. A more tolerant age, which should bode well for all peoples in the Banished Lands, the Sirak included.'

Erdene looked at Riv, her thick musculature, her wings, her bruises and scars.

'Tolerant? I suppose she is still breathing,' Erdene said. 'Your Lore spoke of abomination and execution where half-breeds are concerned, I am told.'

'Riv is no abomination,' a voice said. When Bleda saw that all were staring at him he realized it had been his voice.

A flicker of something across his mother's face, too fast to read.

'I am *not* an abomination,' Riv growled, 'and any who wish to execute me –' she looked at them all, slowly, one by one, then gave a shrug of her muscled shoulders – 'I say, let them try.'

So fierce. So much against her, and yet she would fight the world, if she had to.

'It looks like some have already tried,' Erdene said.

'Aye, they have. And yet here I stand,' Riv said, a vicious smile cutting her face.

Kol threw his head back and laughed.

'Riv is a fierce one, and no denying,' Kol said, still chuckling. He reached for the jug on the table and poured them all a cup of wine, taking a long draught from his own cup, draining it and then pouring himself another.

'But these are fierce times, and fierce is what I need; the Kadoshim are moving throughout the Banished Lands, have attacked Drassil itself, though they were taught the error of that.'

Bleda remembered that all too well: the Kadoshim attacking the Great Hall, attempting to free Asroth from his gaol of iron. Bleda had even played a part in fighting them off, had slain some of their Feral beast-men. It had showed him that no matter what he thought of the Ben-Elim, the Kadoshim were worse. An evil that could not be negotiated with.

'We must talk of strategy,' Kol said, 'of how to work together to best defeat their scheming.'

'Aye,' Erdene said. 'I have heard much of the Kadoshim. Of bonfire signals, of human sacrifice, entire towns slaughtered. But, is it not the Lord Protector with whom I should be talking about this matter?'

'I am the Lord Protector,' Kol said. 'To all intents. It is just a formality to proclaim me.'

'Really?' Erdene said. 'I have heard that Sariel sees things differently.'

A flicker of malice twisted Kol's face, replaced in a heartbeat with his sardonic smile.

'Trust me, Sariel is of no matter,' he replied, taking another long sip from his cup. 'Now, enough of abominations and executions and fighting to the death, and on to happier matters. Your arrival was timely – and I thank you for your tithe of flesh. We are lacking in range troops at an elite level, and your contribution will be perfect to redress that balance, along with Uldin's tithe of flesh from the Cheren Clan.' He paused for another drink.

'I had already sent messengers to bid you join us at Drassil,' Kol continued, 'and Uldin of the Cheren. My messengers must have reached Arcona by now and delivered the message to him. But I was not requesting you to speed your tithe to us here at Drassil, I was asking you to join us for altogether another reason.' Kol's smile drifted to Bleda, giving him a bad feeling in his belly.

'I see no reason to delay our plans for unifying the peoples of this Land of the Faithful. Bleda and Jin will be married upon Midsummer's Day.'

Bleda strode along Drassil's streets. It was cold and dark, torch-light flickering from shuttered windows around him. He was walking from the meeting with Kol and his mother, where he had spent as long as it took for a candle to burn from wick to stump as he had listened to the myriad details that went into planning his own handbinding.

Planning how I will be packaged and sold to seal a covenant between my people and the Ben-Elim, as if I were a prize bull at market.

He sucked in a long breath and blew it out slowly, trying to control his sense of unease about it all.

It is my duty to serve my Clan, to protect them. Wedding Jin will put generations of blood-feud behind the Sirak and Cheren.

'Life is complicated,' he breathed, to himself or Ruga, he was not sure.

Ruga strode along half a step behind him. She wore a cloak against the cold, though she'd pushed the hood back, her eyes always moving.

'For you, Lord,' she agreed. 'Not for me. I serve my Queen, my Prince, my Clan. I eat, sleep, fight.' She shrugged.

Bleda wanted to smile at that, felt jealous of the simplicity of her life.

A muffled shout drifted down to them from above, and in a second Ruga had her bow in her hand, an arrow nocked. Bleda rested his hand on his bow in its case, staring up into the darkness.

Clouds masked the stars, the moon a silver sheen that gave little light. Either side of Bleda, buildings towered, most of them empty, here and there the flicker of firelight behind shuttered windows. They were in a section of the fortress used as barracks for new arrivals to Drassil, which was why Bleda was here – his mother was housed in the same quarter.

Another shout, almost directly above, a stirring of air, more like turbulence than wind. Unnatural, somehow.

Something dropped from the sky, a clang as it bounced and sparked on flagstones. Bleda ran to the object and picked it up. It was round, glinting in the wan light. A silver torc with two serpents' heads. Parts of it were coated in something black and sticky. Bleda touched it.

'Blood,' he whispered to Ruga, who was scanning the coal-black above.

There were no more sounds, no sense of any kind of presence. Bleda slipped the torc into his cloak, both of them still looking up. Then something materialized out of the darkness, pale and floating. A large white feather drifted down between them and landed at Bleda's feet.

It had blood on it.

CHAPTER TWENTY-THREE

DREM

Drem blinked sweat from his eyes and stumbled over a rock. He was trying to keep Flick in sight, without breaking his ankle or neck on the loose terrain.

And that crow sets quite a pace.

They had followed Flick south and east into the Desolation, four days of almost constant movement, ever using the gullies and ravines that twisted through the land like the desiccated veins of a corpse.

Flick was swooping back to them, low over their heads.

'*Wait here, wait here,*' the huge crow squawked, '*Flick find Stepor.*'

Drem turned to watch Flick pass over them all, the white bear far to the rear of their column raising its head and rumbling at the crow. Flick ignored it and banked into a half-circle, disappearing up and over the edge of the ravine they had been following since dawn.

Drem looked to the north-west, eyes searching the skies. There was still no sign of Morn's bat-like silhouette. Drem had seen no evidence of the half-breed since the day they had fought the wyrms, almost a ten-night ago.

Doesn't mean she's not up there, though, Drem thought. He felt more vulnerable now that Flick was gone, especially down here in a ravine, no way of knowing if enemies prowled above them, just beyond the ravine's edge.

A bad spot for an ambush.

In the distance, the white-topped peaks of the Bonefells reared like jagged teeth along the horizon, making Drem realize how far south they had come. The weather had changed, the snow clouds disappearing, the ground underfoot free from snow, and the temperature had risen.

A handful of days had passed since Drem had woken and not had to crack ice from his beard.

We are leaving winter behind us.

He twisted his head, squinting into the distance as something drew his eye. A flicker of movement, a speck in the sky. Drem blinked, straining to see better, but whatever it was had gone, if there had been anything there. Absently, his hand reached to take his pulse.

'Stepor must be close, then,' Cullen said.

'Must be,' Keld said. The huntsman seemed to have fully recovered from his injuries, though Fen still walked with a limping gait at Keld's side. Drem suspected that would never leave the wolven-hound.

'Good old Rab,' Cullen said. 'I knew he wouldn't let us down.'

'He's a good bird,' Keld nodded.

Drem walked back to Hammer and checked on her injuries, the bear lowering her head to give him an affectionate nudge with her muzzle. He was pleased to see she was mending well, all her wounds healing, scabs thick, some of them already peeling to reveal white scars underneath.

Her fur will never grow back there, Drem thought. 'A record of your courage and loyalty,' Drem murmured as he stroked a scar along Hammer's muzzle.

He looked at the white bear. It was thirty or forty paces behind Hammer and had sat down with a rumbling sigh. It was still following them, or following Hammer, seeming quite happy to shamble along with them, though sometimes it would fall behind as it paused to rest. Its wounds had taken their toll.

They were far worse than Hammer's, and each night Drem, Keld and Cullen had tried to change its dressings. They had not been entirely successful, the bear growling, curling his lip to reveal teeth as long as Drem's seax. At one point Hammer had intervened and swatted the white bear with a paw, and although the white bear was significantly bigger than Hammer, he had acquiesced to her reprimand, bowing his head and rumbling quietly in his belly.

But then Drem had discovered the trick to approaching the white bear safely. He reached into his pack and pulled out a clay jar, un-stoppering it and pouring some of its contents into his hand.

Honey.

'Here you go, lad,' Drem said as he approached the white bear, holding his hand out.

The white bear lifted his head and took a great sniff, then heaved his bulk from the ground and ambled towards Drem, who waited patiently.

The bear licked Drem's hand with a huge, sandpaper-rough tongue, lapping the honey from his palm and all the while making contented snuffling, grumbling sounds. With his other hand Drem patted the bear's cheek and dug deep into the animal's thick fur to scratch his neck.

When the bear had licked every last fraction of honey from Drem's hand, leaving it drenched and dripping with saliva, Drem flicked globs of spittle from his hand and scooped some more honey from his jar, spreading it over a rock.

The bear set to licking that clean and Drem checked on his wounds, used his water skin to wash them out, then applied fresh poultices of yarrow and comfrey. They were improving but were not yet as healed as Hammer's.

'We are all slaves to our bellies,' Cullen said from behind Drem. He was leaning against a boulder with his arms folded across his chest.

'Speak for yourself,' Keld grunted as he clambered up onto

the boulder, allowing him to see a little further into the distance.

Two specks were in the sky, a black smudge and a pale one, growing quickly larger, swooping down into the ravine.

'*Stepor coming*,' Flick squawked, over and over.

'Rab!' Cullen called out happily as the white smudge materialized into their friend and spiralled down to them.

'*Friends, friends, friends*,' Rab cawed as he alighted upon Cullen's outstretched arm.

Flick landed on the boulder beside Keld and set to grooming his feathers on one wing, all the while a beady eye watching Rab.

'You did it, Rab,' Cullen said. 'You brought help.'

'*Rab did, Rab did*,' the white crow squawked, hopping up and down from one claw to the other in his excitement. '*Told Byrne Rab's friends need help.*'

'Ah, but you're a good friend to us, Rab, and no denying,' Cullen said, grinning as he scratched the bird's chest.

'*Flick found you*,' Flick reminded them from his boulder, shaking to ruffle his feathers up.

Do crows sulk? Drem wondered.

'*Flick clever, Flick brave*,' Rab cawed, bobbing his head.

'And we're grateful to you, Flick,' Cullen said.

'*Welcome*,' Flick croaked.

Fen stood and sniffed the air, eyes fixed on the shadows in the ravine.

And then there were shapes appearing, two four-legged shadows flitting amongst boulders and twisted hawthorn, another figure forming behind them. A dark-haired man dressed simply in leather and fur, the only hint of ornamentation the silver-starred brooch that pinned his cloak. He had a scarred, honest face above a snarl of black beard as thick and wild as the hawthorns in the ravine, his body lean, like Keld's, honed by the wilderness.

The huntsmen of Dun Seren all look like trappers. But with more weapons.

Axes and knives bristled from various belts strapped around his body, more hilts poking from his boots.

'Well met, Keld,' the dark-haired man said as Keld climbed from his perch atop the boulder and strode to him.

'Well met, Stepor,' Keld said, gripping Stepor's forearm in the warrior grip.

'What took you?' Cullen said as he strolled over.

'The Desolation's a big place,' Stepor grunted at Cullen, giving him a dark look from beneath bushy brows, but he took the young warrior's arm all the same.

'Well, better late than never,' Cullen said, grinning.

'Late! Well, if you hadn't gone and got yourself lost in the arse-end of the world, in winter . . .'

'I'm only jesting with you.' Cullen grinned, holding his hands up. 'Ach, but it's good to see a slice of home, is it not, Keld?'

'Aye, that it is,' Keld said. He was crouching, two enormous wolven-hounds sniffing and licking him. One was crow-black with a splash of white on one paw, the other was as red as rust. With a growl, Fen pushed in, reminding them who Keld belonged to.

'No need for jealousy, lad. You know Grack and Ralla, and we're all on the same side here,' Keld said, tugging on one of Fen's ears.

'And you must be Drem,' Stepor said.

'Aye,' Drem said.

Stepor strode to him, offering an arm. 'Well met.'

Drem took Stepor's arm. 'Well met,' he said.

Stepor looked Drem up and down. He was shorter than Drem, most men were, but Drem still felt like a child being inspected. He resisted the urge to look away and forced himself to meet Stepor's gaze. He'd never liked to be stared at, but his father had told him it was important to meet another man's eye, and so Drem had trained himself to do it.

'I can see your mother in you,' Stepor said.

My mother.

It felt strange that others had known her, when Drem remembered so little of her. Her voice, her laugh, but so much else had faded.

'Hope you can fight like her, too, if half of what Rab's told us is true,' Stepor said.

'*Rab tell truth,*' the white crow squawked.

'Gulla in the north, acolytes, Feral men. Revenants,' Stepor said, part statement, part question.

'Aye, it's all true, and more,' Keld said. 'It's the time we've been waiting for. And Gunil stood with Gulla.'

Stepor blew out a long whistle. 'That's not going to go down well with old One-Eye.'

'It's a long walk from Drassil to the Desolation,' Keld said.

'Aye, it would be, if Balur One-Eye was at Drassil,' Stepor said. 'But he's not. He's about half a league to the south, helping us look for you.'

'Balur One-Eye,' breathed Drem. It was as if heroes of myth were coming to life. Warriors of the Bright Star, giants . . .

'You'll meet him soon enough,' Stepor said, glancing up at the sky and the sun. 'If we ever stop talking and start walking.' He looked at Hammer. 'Sig,' he said, looking from Keld to Cullen, grief washing all of their faces. 'I grieve for your loss,' he said to them all. 'For all our loss, but you were her crew, were closer to her than any other, except maybe Byrne. Sig was one of the greatest amongst us. Gave me more than a few bruises in her time, but each one taught me something.'

'Aye. Move faster, duck quicker, or better still, just drop your weapon and walk away from Sig,' Cullen said, a faint smile on his face, a tear in his eye.

'Ha,' Stepor barked a laugh. 'True enough. Not that you

ever walked away, young Cullen. I've seen some of the lessons that Sig taught you.' He winked at Keld.

'Never have learned to walk away,' Cullen admitted.

'There's much to talk on,' Stepor said, 'including your new travelling companion.' He raised an eyebrow and nodded at the white bear. 'But let's move out and set you on the path for home.'

Home? Dun Seren. I was born there, and yet I barely remember it.

Drem drew in a deep breath and shouldered his pack.

'Flick, watch our backs while Rab leads us home,' Stepor said, and with that they were moving out. Rab and Flick flapped into the sky, Fen, Grack and Ralla loping ahead and slipping into the shadows, Stepor setting a brisk pace, with Hammer and the white bear shambling after them.

Going home? If Dun Seren is my home, it is only because some-thing of my mother and father abides there, Drem thought. And, he reminded himself, looking over his shoulder at the sky behind:

We are not safe yet.

CHAPTER TWENTY-FOUR

RIV

Riv ducked a sword-swing, felt the air of it whistle over her head, stepped under Kol's arm and inside his guard, close enough to smell his sweat, and stabbed at his belly.

With a burst of speed she would not have thought possible, he somehow moved, twisting out of the way of her strike, swirling around her in a blur of white wings, and then his sword was resting on the back of her neck.

'You're dead,' he said calmly.

Riv snarled, a spasm of frustration racking her body. It was not the first time she'd heard that phrase today.

Kol stepped away, a smirk edging his lips; other Ben-Elim were behind him. Amongst them Riv saw Hadran, who had become her permanent guard. A dark bruise stained his eye and forehead from the fight in the field.

Riv took a few paces and deep breaths to calm her simmering anger. They were back in the weapons-field. It looked different from the last time she'd seen it, with bodies wrapped in combat, or sprawled across the ground. Looking back on it, much seemed to have changed since then, when so many had stood for her, even crowds of traders and other ordinary citizens rushing in from beyond the field to defend her.

Or maybe they all just like a good scrap.

Even if there was some truth in that, Riv knew there was more to it. Ever since then, people had treated her differently, walking and talking with her in the street, sitting and eating with her in the feast-hall, treating her more like a wonder than a monstrosity.

There were still the dark looks, the glares and twisted mouths, but they seemed to be in the minority, and Riv found herself caring less.

Aphra had said to her that it was because she had not killed Sorch.

'*You showed mercy*,' Aphra had said.

'Think,' Kol was saying. 'You have a new weapon now, you must learn to use it.'

He was talking about Riv's wings. That was what this whole training session was about, helping Riv to adjust to her wings, and to learn how to use them in combat. She thought she had, but sparring against Kol made her realize how much more there was to learn.

'There are strengths and weaknesses to having wings,' Kol continued, pacing around Riv. 'The main weakness is that we are a bigger target; there is more of us to hit, and therefore injure. Also, our wings are vulnerable, they cannot be armoured or protected, so you must always be mindful of that. And for you, you must remember that you will not fit through spaces as you used to, that your wings are wider and taller than you, and you are wide enough already.'

Riv was already learning that, had discovered that sitting in chairs was difficult, and that some doorways were not wide enough for her, though fortunately Drassil had been built by giants for giants, so that was rare.

'The great strengths of wings in combat is speed and directional change,' Kol continued.

I think you just demonstrated that, Riv thought glumly.

'I can see you are judging my capabilities by your own ability, your own concept of speed and movement, and that of humankind,' Kol said. 'You stabbed where you expected me to be. You must make allowances for that, and in time it will become automatic. You know most combat is too fast for thought, it is set reactions, drilled into us. So, you must drill hard, because the Kadoshim are as fast as us Ben-Elim, and you are going to be fighting Kadoshim.'

'Best way to learn is to do,' Riv growled, and attacked Kol, pulsing her wings to speed her cut at Kol's chest, a diagonal sweep that caught his hip as he swayed right. Riv grinned and followed with a stab and slash at his belly and thigh, Kol stumbling backwards, but just when Riv thought she had him, Kol was gone, the grass swirling from the beating of his wings and his feet disappearing over Riv's head. She stabbed up and missed, glimpsed Kol looping over her, alighting behind her.

With a snarl, Riv leaped into the air, her wings powering her up, out of Kol's range, twisting to turn and face him, slashing down at his head. Kol blocked the blow and then he was in the air, too, both of them spiralling higher, swirling around each other, the crack of their practice swords a rapid discordant beat.

Riv swept in close, stabbed at Kol's chest. His wings folded in tight and he just seemed to drop from the sky, her blade stabbing fresh air, then his wings were extending and he was cutting at her legs, striking her ankle and calf, rising up behind her to stab her in the back.

Riv resisted the urge to leap at him, cling onto him and batter him with her fists. Instead she took a shuddering breath and flew a few wingbeats out of range, calming herself, thinking about the technical lessons being taught here.

It's about fluid motion, about speed, and using that speed to attack the flanks, striking from unexpected angles. The unseen blow is what ends the fight.

She gritted her teeth for another attack.

'Enough,' Kol said, raising a hand. He was hovering in the air, wings beating lazily as he looked down at the weapons-field. Riv followed his gaze and saw that Erdene had ridden into the field with a large entourage behind her, making for the archery range. She saw Bleda riding at Erdene's side. He was staring up at her, and for a moment Riv remembered how she had smiled at him when he had arrived at the meeting with Erdene. She had felt like a fool, and something else, as if some bright, fragile thing within her had withered when she got no response from him.

But he spoke out for me, when Erdene said I am an abomination.

She rolled her shoulders to ease the ache from hovering in the sky as emotions broiled in her gut.

'I must talk with Erdene,' Kol said. 'Do not stray far, I must have you at my side in the Ben-Elim Moot.'

'Huh,' Riv grunted at Kol's back as he tucked his wings in and dived down towards Erdene.

Riv was not looking forward to the Ben-Elim gathering, where once again she would be the topic of discussion. Although Kol clearly had a large proportion of Ben-Elim loyal to him, it was mostly other Ben-Elim that seemed to be struggling with her existence.

She scanned the field, saw Aphra drilling her shield wall, five hundred strong now. They were being broken up into five units of a hundred each, then training on the manoeuvres to merge and then split again.

I miss the shield wall. Having wings is . . . lonely.

Riv's eyes drifted back to Kol. He was standing beside Erdene now, though she seemed far more intent on watching Bleda ride the archery range. He was trotting onto the greensward, a gauntlet of land flanked on either side by two rows of straw targets. This was a new addition to the weapons-field, designed and erected after Bleda and Jin's honour guards had arrived, specifically for them to train and drill in their traditional ways. Riv had been stunned by their skill, both as horsemen and archers.

Bleda sat relaxed and easy upon his horse, moving fluidly from a trot into a canter and then a gallop, guiding his mount with his knees while he pulled a fistful of arrows from his quiver. He held them in his left hand that gripped his bow, leaning into his high-fronted saddle, and in a blur he was drawing and loosing, straw men jolting and shuddering with the impact of his arrows.

Riv glided down, wings spread wide, watching as Bleda reached the end of the gauntlet, her admiration for his skill temporarily outweighing her shifting emotions. As Bleda left the range and curled round to return to his mother, two more riders entered the greensward, a man and woman, and in heartbeats their mounts were galloping, both of them leaning and loosing arrows, one to each side of the gauntlet. One target spun and pitched to the ground, the twine tying it to its pole snapping with the power of the shot.

Riv flew down to Bleda, who was trotting now, and she matched her speed to his. Kol and Erdene were about a hundred paces away, deep in conversation.

'Fine shooting,' she said.

Bleda shrugged, an acknowledgement.

'I saw you sparring in the sky,' Bleda said.

'Kol is teaching me how to use my wings,' Riv answered.

'You use them well enough,' Bleda said. 'Back in the glade, you put Kol down.'

I wish we were back there still, that we could leave all of this behind. I felt . . . happy there, with you.

That is not real, now, Riv scolded herself. *Live in the now, not the what-might-have-been.*

'Aye,' Riv nodded, 'but I didn't win.'

'True enough.'

'And most of that was blind rage and luck.'

'Rage, yes.' Bleda nodded. 'Luck, no.'

'I had good people at my side, watching my back.'

'Yes,' Bleda agreed again, 'but you fought Kol alone.' He looked up at Riv and met her gaze, his dark eyes sad and full of emotion, even though his face did not shift or change even a fraction. For a moment Riv felt the world fade and she was sitting back on the roadside in Forn with Bleda, laughing and giving him a flower of mountain thyme.

Bleda reined in his horse.

Riv alighted beside him.

'Why are we here?' Bleda said, quietly. He looked around, eyes settling on Kol.

Because it was the only way to stop Kol from executing you. The only way for us to live without spending our lives – most likely our very short lives – being hunted to the ends of the earth.

'It was the wise thing to do,' Riv said.

'Wise? You are a lot of things, Riv, but I would not have counted wise as one of them.' Bleda's mouth twitched, a moment of shock and humour before his cold-face locked back into place.

Riv grinned at him. 'I can be wise, sometimes.'

'Betrothed,' a voice called out.

'See what your wisdom has done to me,' Bleda whispered.

Riv looked up to see Jin walking to the archery range, a score of her honour guard at her shoulders. She started to veer towards Bleda, but Queen Erdene called to her.

With a sigh, Bleda clicked his horse on and Riv walked beside him.

'Why did you try to kill Sorch?' Riv asked him.

'Ah. I did not try to kill him.'

'Are you telling me you *aimed* for his leg?' That thought had not crossed Riv's mind.

'Of course! You think I would miss if I wanted to kill him?' Riv shrugged. 'It was a hard shot.'

'I do not miss.' Bleda snorted. 'If I had wanted to kill him, he would be dead.'

Riv remembered watching Bleda a few moments ago, at the gallop and still putting his arrows in hearts and eyes.

'So why did you shoot him in the leg?'

'To distract you. You were strangling him. I thought you were going to choke the life from him, right there in the sky, in front of a whole field of people. It would hardly have ingratiated you to the folk of Drassil.'

'So, you tried to distract me by shooting Sorch in the leg?'

'Yes.'

Riv roared her laughter, wiped tears from her eyes when she regained some control. 'That was thoughtful of you.' She chuckled.

'I must confess, I may have enjoyed it a little,' Bleda said, which set Riv to laughing again.

Jin stared at them with cold eyes, though Erdene was talking to her.

'This fighting in the sky,' Bleda said, 'it strikes me that you are limited. You still have to be close to kill. You are missing a great opportunity.'

'What's that?' Riv asked.

'You should wield ranged weapons. The bow, javelins. You would be death from above. And you should carry a shield.'

'Why?'

'In case Jin wanted to shoot you from the sky.'

That was a sobering thought. Riv had seen Jin's skill with a bow, and also the way the Cheren Princess looked at her.

'I'm not good enough with a bow,' Riv said. It was her worst weapon. Sword, spear, knife she felt she could match most people, but with a bow . . .

'You could get better,' Bleda said. 'And you haven't used the right bow. You couldn't take one of those logs in the air with you.' He nodded towards some of Drassil's huntsmen and scouts practising on the range. 'You would need a Sirak bow, they are more suited to motion, to fighting whilst moving. They are smaller, easier to draw and with a greater range.' He halted his horse again and lifted his bow from its case at his hip, his touch loving. He paused a moment, then offered it to Riv.

She was used to it, had looked after Bleda's bow secretly for over five years, and had regularly tended to it, but somehow, with Bleda offering the bow to her now, it felt different. She reached out and took it, almost reverently. The bow was light, much lighter than the bows of yew and ash and elm that Drassil's huntsmen used, and it was balanced differently. She turned it in her hand, saw the layers of wood and horn and sinew.

How do you ever make something like this?

Riv took the bowstring and began to draw.

'No,' Bleda said, shaking his head. 'Never draw without an arrow nocked.'

Riv just shrugged and released the string.

What Bleda was saying did make sense. Of course, there was a great advantage to being airborne in battle, but how much greater would that advantage be if you could strike at your enemy but they could not strike at you.

And the Kadoshim – it could be used against them, too.

'Where would I get one of these?' Riv asked.

Bleda shrugged. 'I'll see what I can do.'

They were approaching Erdene and Kol now, Jin talking with them, too.

Bleda slipped gracefully from his saddle, one of his honour guard stepping forwards to take his reins – a dark-haired woman with a limp. Riv recognized her as one of Bleda's guards who had been at the cabin, so she nodded a greeting.

The warrior nodded in return, her eyes drifting to Bleda's bow in Riv's hand.

'Come, try it now,' Bleda said, leading Riv to the toe-mark for a target on the range. A straw man about seventy or eighty paces away.

'Nice and close to start with,' Bleda said.

Riv snorted, thinking he was joking, then saw from his face that he was not.

'Here,' Bleda said, offering her arrows from his belted quiver.

Riv took one.

'No, three or four, like this,' Bleda said, grabbing a fistful and threading them through his fingers, showing Riv how to hold them and the bow at the same time. 'Time is the key to success, so why waste time reaching to draw one arrow at a time?'

Fair point.

Clumsily, Riv took one from her left hand and nocked it, started to draw.

'Wait,' Bleda said. 'See your target first. Imagine your arrow sinking deep. Think about the range, the poundage of the bow, the wind, balance it all in your mind first. Never take your eye from the target, even as you draw, and *aim* as you draw. Do not pause at the end of the draw. One motion, draw and release. Draw and release.'

Riv took a moment to think about all of that.

It's like the draw-attack from a scabbard, she thought. *So many elements in one move, yet all of them made to look effortless.* She took a deep breath, then nocked, drew and released, aiming a little high and to the right of her straw man's heart.

It hit him in the shoulder. Better than she would have done with a yew bow. The bow was remarkably smooth to draw, feeling much easier than one of Drassil's solid wood bows, and yet she had felt the power in the arrow as it had left the string, a rich *thrum*, and she'd known it would sink much deeper than from the bows she was used to using.

'Again,' Bleda said, 'but this time, draw and loose a second arrow without waiting to see where the first one lands.'

Riv did. A deep, calming breath, then nock, draw, release, a slight fumble to nock the next arrow, then draw and release. She lowered the bow, saw the third arrow sink deep into the straw man's thigh. The second was buried in its belly.

'It is a start,' Bleda said, 'from which you can only get better.'

For the first time she could remember, Riv was glad of Bleda's cold-face, knowing that he was probably disgusted with her efforts, but secretly Riv was just pleased to have not missed with any of the three arrows.

'I will teach you,' Bleda declared.

'A big auroch like her cannot master the skills of a Cheren bow,' a voice behind them said. Riv wheeled around to see Jin standing behind her.

'It's a Sirak bow,' Riv growled.

'Cheren, Sirak, we will be one Clan, soon,' Jin said with a shrug. 'Isn't that right, my betrothed.' Her eyes stayed fixed on Riv.

Bleda grunted something unintelligible.

'Bleda, I have good news. Kol has just told me that my father is less than a ten-night from Drassil, come with much of my kin to celebrate our handbinding.'

'But Midsummer's Day is moons from now,' Bleda said, a hint of emotion in his voice.

Panic? Riv wanted it to be panic.

'There is much to organize,' Jin said, her eyes still on Riv. And then Jin smiled at her, an expression that looked wholly alien on Jin's normally stony face.

'Riv,' a voice called, and Kol beat his wings and took to the air, hovering above them. 'Come, Riv, it is time for the Moot,' Kol called down to her.

Riv handed Bleda back his bow, then bent her legs and leaped into the air. She angled her wings and beat them harder than necessary to channel a blast of air at Jin, making her stumble back a step. Riv couldn't keep the grin from her face as she climbed into the sky, looking back once to see that Jin was talking animatedly to Bleda. Then Riv noticed someone staring at her, a fixed gaze that followed Riv through the sky as she flew after Kol.

It was Erdene, Queen of the Sirak.

CHAPTER TWENTY-FIVE

FRITHA

Fritha stood watching the two crows descend into the ravine. She was hiding in a stand of alder and beech that stood on a plateau above the ravine, Morn at one shoulder, Gunil at the other, her Ferals and Red Right Hand spread out behind her.

Fritha muttered a curse.

Crows most likely meant the Order of the Bright Star were not far behind. She was tempted to rush them, knowing that Drem and his bedraggled companions were so close and unsuspecting of her presence.

'We should strike now,' Morn whispered. 'They are so near.'

Morn had found them two days ago, returning to guide Fritha, but because of the wyrm, Fritha had not been able to move as fast as she'd have liked. Gunil had built the wyrm a cage, and two saplings had been cut down to make poles and a litter that they had tied to the girth and saddle of Gunil's bear, a makeshift travois that allowed them to continue tracking Drem and his companions. The weight of the sickly wyrm and its cage was not a problem to Claw, but the terrain was. Fritha had had to scout a way that would not shake the cage to pieces, and so they were slower than Fritha had liked. She had thought about leaving the wyrm in its cage under guard, but it was so close to death that she had needed to spill her blood and chant her words of power twice since they had found the wyrm. If she left it, she knew it would die.

It would not take us long to reach that ravine; one burst of speed and we could be on them.

But it was open ground between this stand of trees and the ravine. If the Order of the Bright Star were close, she would be vulnerable. She knew her ability and that of her crew, knew they were deadly and dangerous.

But so are the warriors of the Order. I am no fool to risk a battle I might lose.

And although Morn had been far wiser and not flown close, she had still been able to see and report to Fritha that even without any new additions from the Order of the Bright Star, there were still three men, the wolven-hound, and another bear down in the ravine.

Where in the Otherworld did that come from? It must be one of the Order's battle bears, but where is its giant?

Do I rush them?

Her palm rested on the hilt of her short-sword. She was not afraid to use it, not afraid to fight. But she was afraid to lose, and to see her crew cut down.

Eleven Ferals. Ten of my Red Right Hand. Gunil and his bear, against three men, two bears and a wolven-hound. The odds are not so clear now, and that is without any of the Order of the Bright Star arriving. They must be close for their crows to be here. They could already be in the ravine with Drem.

Claw rumbled a growl in the trees behind them.

'Keep him quiet,' Fritha snapped as she balanced on the knife-edge of indecision. The bear growled again and Gunil strode back to him. She heard the giant swear.

Fritha shifted on her feet, felt her muscles tense and she gripped her sword hilt, ready to draw it.

And then the two crows flapped out of the ravine, the white one heading south-east, away from them, while the black one rose higher into the sky, circling towards Fritha and her stand of trees.

'Still,' Fritha called to her people.

Claw growled again, somehow sounding different from his usual one.

I will go back there myself and kill that bear if it does not shut up.

'Fritha,' Gunil called to her.

Swearing under her breath, Fritha twisted on her heel and crept back into the stand of trees, a hundred or so paces and she saw the bulk of Claw. The wyrm cage was set behind him, unstrapped from its litter for the time being. The wyrm lay coiled and still within its bars.

'What is it?' Fritha hissed.

Gunil just looked at the ground.

He'd unstrapped a large panier from Claw and laid it on the ground, opened the lid. Inside was a chest, the draig egg packed carefully within it, tight with straw.

The egg was moving.

A draig is hatching.

Fritha froze for a moment, excitement and fear and wonder sweeping through her, washing all else away. She forgot about Drem and the others, about the crow somewhere in the sky above her, about the Great War, about the Banished Lands.

And then she was on her knees, gently lifting the egg from the chest, straw falling away, and she was placing it on the ground, building up a bank of woodland litter around it to keep it from tipping over.

The side of the shell moved, like when she had seen her baby stir in her belly, the imprint of a hand or foot.

A crackling sound, and a line appeared in the rippling hues of the egg, as fine as a hair, growing, branching into tendrils, like the veins of a leaf. A shape pushed out from the egg, a pinprick hole materializing, growing rapidly bigger and thick, mucus-like fluid leaked from the hole.

A series of *cracks*, as if Fritha had stood on a cluster of snails, and suddenly a shard of the egg was splintering away, something dark pushing it out. An eye blinked at Fritha.

She tentatively reached out and pulled the splintered part away, gripped another piece, gently working it loose, her hands slippery with jelly-like slime.

A flat muzzle appeared, the creature within the egg squirming and wriggling, its first sight and breath filled with Fritha. Fritha worked harder at the shell, her excitement almost frantic, the creature within thrusting its snout through the hole, in moments its head free, then stuck at its broad shoulders, twisting and snapping as it tried to break out.

'Patience, my love,' Fritha crooned, hands slick with slime as she snapped another piece of shell, and then there was a concussive popping sound, cracks cobwebbing through the whole egg and it exploded, showering Fritha and Gunil's feet in shell and slime.

A creature stood before Fritha on squat legs with a broad skull and flat muzzle. Wide, heavily muscled shoulders and a scaly torso tapered into a thick tail. From snout to tail-tip the baby draig was about the length of Fritha's arm. It opened its jaw, revealing rows of needle-like teeth, and let out a croaking dog-like bark, then it sniffed the air, snapping its jaws.

It's hungry.

Fritha lifted a portion of slime-covered eggshell and the draig sniffed it, a long red tongue appearing, licking the mucus, and then it was crunching into the shell, devouring it in a series of rapid gulps. It looked at Fritha, wanting more.

Fritha laughed and fed it more of the eggshell; in a few moments all of it gone into the draig's belly. It stared at Fritha again, thick tendrils of jelly hanging from its jaws, its tail twitching.

Still hungry.

'Gunil, some wyrm meat.'

They had stripped the wyrm carcasses of meat once her

Ferals had had their fill – not that there had been much left after the feeding frenzy of eleven Ferals and Gunil's bear. Gunil had cooked it and packed it with salt. Fritha had found it surprisingly tasty.

Gunil opened a barrel strapped to his bear and passed Fritha a filleted section of wyrm. She waved it in front of the draig, its snout following the meat, sniffing it, and then its head was lunging forwards, chomping into the meat, a head-shake like a terrier with a rat, and it tore a chunk, chewed and gulped, then immediately attacked the remaining meat. It swallowed the last portion, belched, then turned in a circle, scratched at the forest litter and lay down. Within heartbeats its belly was rising and falling in sleep.

Fritha stroked its broad head, scales still slick with glutinous slime. She looked over her shoulder, up at Gunil, and grinned. He did not look so happy as her, a slight twist of disgust on his lips.

It is life, new life. There is nothing but beauty in that.

'Gunil, we might need another cage.'

A rustling of branches above and behind Fritha, a bird squawking, and she jumped to her feet, turning, sword hissing into her hand.

It was Morn, descending through the treetop canopy, something in her arms. She alighted before Fritha and held out a shifting, squirming bundle. It took Fritha a moment to realize what it was.

The net Morn had been snared in, and within it, a big black crow.

Fritha smiled at Morn.

'*Let Flick go,*' the crow squawked.

Fritha clapped her hands in delight.

'Thank you, Drem,' she said to the sky. 'One of Dun Seren's talking crows. Your gifts just keep on coming.'

CHAPTER TWENTY-SIX

RIV

Riv stood in a huge chamber, a half-circle of tiered stone seats leading down to a dais about a hundred paces wide. Ben-Elim thronged the room, a real sense of awe filling Riv at the sight of so many of the winged warriors in the same place.

Is this all of them?

She had lived her whole life at Drassil and so was used to seeing many Ben-Elim, and she had been on numerous campaigns as support to her sister's hundred, but never had she seen this many Ben-Elim gathered together.

There must be three thousand of them in here.

Riv had been made to stand on the dais before the gathered Ben-Elim. She had received more than a few harsh looks, but to her surprise she also saw many faces that regarded her with something that resembled interest more than hate.

Or perhaps it's wishful thinking.

Kol stood up. He was seated in the lowest tier, on the far edge of its arc, so that as he stood he could angle himself to look up at all of the gathered Ben-Elim, and still be facing Riv.

'We must vote,' he said. 'The day is almost done.'

Beams of light through huge unshuttered windows cut into the room, low as the sun dipped into the horizon. Riv had been standing in front of the gathered Ben-Elim long enough for her feet to ache. It had not been the most pleasant time of her life, bearing the brunt of three thousand judging pairs of eyes.

'Not all are here yet,' a voice called out – Kamael with his fair hair, standing on the far side of the room, a dozen tiers up from the ground.

'You mean, *Sariel* is not here yet,' Kol said.

'Aye. Sariel is leader of the southern garrison, a respected elder. We cannot proceed without him.'

'If Sariel cannot find the time to come to our Moot, the first that has been called for over half a century, then perhaps he is not worth waiting for,' Kol said. 'This is a sacred meeting and should be respected as such.'

Voices called out their agreement.

A Ben-Elim flew in through one of the large windows, gliding to Kamael's side. A few whispered words, Kamael frowning.

'Well,' Kol said. 'Will Sariel be gracing us with his presence?'

'He . . . cannot be found,' Kamael said.

'Perhaps he has returned to Ripa,' Kol offered.

'No. This is not characteristic of Sariel. We should search for him,' Kamael said.

'Break off the Moot to find one straggler?' Kol snapped, waving his arms. 'Ridiculous. I say we cast our votes for the new Lord Protector now.'

Kol, you are so clever. Riv eyed Kol suspiciously, wondering if he had played any part in Sariel's lack of appearance at the Moot.

It would not surprise me. She felt a sense of discomfort at that thought, another reminder of how far Kol was from Riv's moral code.

Am I becoming like him, by ignoring his myriad dark deeds? Is this how Aphra felt? Each small step taken for a greater good, and then before you know it, you have walked a thousand leagues from where you used to be. And how do you return to that place, return to the person you were? Or if you cannot do that, how do you become the person that you wish to be?

Kamael scowled at Kol. 'Where is Sariel?'

'I am not his keeper,' Kol said, his expression flat and cold.

'Nothing would keep Sariel from this Moot.' Kamael took a step closer to Kol. 'Something, or someone, must have stopped him.'

Kol returned his gaze. 'Are you making an accusation? If you are, you must present your evidence, else you are spouting conjecture and fancy. That is not becoming of the Ben-Elim.'

He is daring Kamael.

Kamael glared at Kol a moment, his wings trembling.

'I have no evidence yet. But this Moot should be postponed until Sariel is found, or until we have answers for his absence.'

'The fate of the Banished Lands should be postponed, with the Kadoshim stirring, because Sariel is late to a Moot?'

'We should wait,' Kamael maintained.

'It is not your decision to make,' Kol said.

'And neither is it yours,' Kamael answered. 'You are not our Lord Protector.'

'Very well, let us vote on whether we should vote, then,' Kol said, rolling his eyes. 'Or does that not meet with your approval either, Kamael? Would you be dictator to us all?'

Calls for a vote rang out.

A long silence, Kol and Kamael staring at each other as if the world around them was gone.

'Of course, let us vote,' Kamael eventually said, though the twitching of his wings gave away his feelings on the matter.

It did not take long, the vast majority of the gathering stood to show their desire to vote.

'I propose Kol be inducted as our new Lord Protector,' a voice called out: Hadran, who remained on his seat even as the host who had stood were sitting back down. The bruises on his pale face from his fight in the weapons-field stood out like a smudge on pale parchment.

'First, we should discuss . . . *this*,' Kamael said, waving a hand at Riv.

'There is nothing to discuss,' Kol said. 'Riv was voted on

before the whole of Drassil. To disregard that would be to disregard the people.'

'*We* rule here,' Kamael said.

Riv just stared at the white-haired Ben-Elim. He was not the same as Sariel, did not seem to have his strength or force of presence. As much as she had despised what Sariel had said, his presence had been commanding. When he spoke, it felt natural to listen.

'We will *not* punish the innocent for the sins of their fathers, or mothers,' Kol said. 'That has been decided, agreed by the people. To go back on that would risk much, would even risk their faith in us, I fear. And let us not forget, when all of us are gathered together, there are little more than three thousand of us, whereas the mortals of these Banished Lands number in the hundreds of thousands. We rule because they allow us to rule.'

'You speak nonsense.' Kamael snorted.

'Do I?' Kol replied. 'Our authority was accepted because we entered this world as the saviours of humankind, vanquishing the Kadoshim. But that was over a hundred years ago. Those grateful people are all long dead and in the ground. This new generation must accept us for what we do now, and they have already spoken on this matter. To overrule them now . . .' Kol left the consequences of that hanging.

Rebellion? Riv thought.

Which is why you made your stand in front of the people, Kol. To put these Ben-Elim in a position that they could not withdraw from gracefully.

'Who was your father?' Kamael said, ignoring Kol's words. He lifted into the air from his seat and glided down to the dais, landing a few paces before Riv. His eyes bore into her.

'I don't know,' Riv said, returning his stare with matched intensity.

'Who was he?' Kamael asked again, lips curling in a snarl.

'I. Don't. Know,' Riv said, quietly, anger pulsing with the beat of her heart, a drumbeat in her skull.

'Your mother?'

'Dalmae,' Riv said. 'Once a captain of a White-Wing hundred.'

'And where is she?'

'She was slain,' Riv said. 'The night Israfil died.'

'She fought in Israfil's defence,' Kol said, loudly, for all to hear.

No. She fought in my *defence. Against you, Kol.*

'Against traitors. Dalmae is a hero.'

Murderer, Riv thought, straining to keep her anger at Kol leashed, her focus directed at Kamael.

'This is all so convenient,' Kamael said. 'Your father unknown; your mother dead.'

'Convenient?' Riv said. 'Convenient that my mother is dead?' She felt her fingers twitch, the memory of Dalmae's lifeless eyes staring at her. Mother, grandmother, it did not matter to Riv. Dalmae had raised Riv as her own, a lifetime of caring, teaching, loving. Just the memory of her stirred grief in Riv deep as her bones.

'I *loved* my mother,' Riv snarled. 'Her death was a tragedy, not a convenience.' The thought of wrapping her fingers around Kamael's throat was growing ever more appealing.

And then, without warning, Kamael was moving, drawing a knife, stabbing, wings beating to close the gap between them.

Riv saw the blade coming at her chest, its tip glinting in the last rays of the sun. She threw herself backwards, her wings snapping out and beating to break her fall, holding her bent almost parallel to the ground. Kamael's knife passed above Riv, slicing only air, and then Riv was grabbing Kamael's wrist, a twist of her hips and a beat of her wings and she was turning in the air, rolling around his arm, spinning him, too, snapping his wrist and taking his feet from the floor. She slammed him into the ground, standing over him, fists clenched, nostrils flaring.

Her hand reached to the short-sword at her hip.

Then Kol was there. Kamael tried to rise and Kol kicked him back down, put a foot on his chest.

'Riv is the future,' Kol said, leaning over him.

'She is an affront to Elyon's Lore,' Kamael spluttered.

'There is no Elyon's Lore,' Kol snarled back. 'You know this. You know that *we* wrote it.'

'What?' Riv said, stunned.

Kol froze, staring at Riv. A silence settled around them, like a held breath.

'Elyon's Lore was written by the Ben-Elim,' Kol said finally. 'It did not come from Elyon the Maker, it was, is only what we thought his will would be.'

Elyon's Lore, a lie.

All those countless hours listening to the Lore, learning, praying, obeying. The guilt of any wrongdoing.

And it is a lie.

Her world was continually shifting, like standing on a sheet of ice that flowed upon a river. Riv tried hard to keep her emotions from her face, the sense that she should not have heard this revelation heavy upon her.

I must not give the Ben-Elim another reason to want me dead.

'But we are not Elyon, we are not divine,' Kol said, staring up at the thousands of Ben-Elim gazing down at him. 'We wrote the Lore intending it to be a guide for mankind, and a way of pleasing our Maker, when he returns. But perhaps on this one Lore, we were wrong. I ask you all, is it worth ruining our relationship with Elyon's creation, worth division with them, perhaps even a war with them? I ask you, is it worth losing all else we have gained in this land of flesh? Let this one Lore go, and let us move on with mankind. Let me lead you, name me your Lord Protector and I shall lead us through this. A new order for a new world. It will make us stronger; it will make us more able to destroy the Kadoshim, our eternal foe.'

A silence, then one Ben-Elim stood.

And then another, and another, and then the whole

chamber seemed to shift, a wave of mail and wings as thousands of Ben-Elim rose to their feet.

Kol leaned over and gripped Kamael's hand, helping him to his feet.

'Be my friend, Kamael,' Kol whispered, low enough that only Riv could hear, 'or you shall be my enemy.'

Kamael cradled his broken wrist, looking at Riv and then around the chamber. He slowly nodded. 'The Moot has spoken,' he said, then spread his wings and flew back to the tiers.

'Well, I'm glad that's over with,' Kol whispered to Riv through a beatific smile, even as he raised a hand in thanks, cheers of acclamation echoing from the Ben-Elim. 'Now we must fly for Dun Seren. Time to tell the good news to Ethlinn, Balur One-Eye and the damned Order of the Bright Star.'

CHAPTER TWENTY-SEVEN

DREM

Drem stood open-mouthed and looked up.

'Well met, One-Eye,' Keld said to the giant, who towered over them.

They had just crossed the ridge of a shallow slope and stood on a plateau that abruptly gave way to a sheer drop, the sound of a river far below. Balur was leaning against the wall of a wide bridge that spanned the drop. Beside him another giant sat upon the ground, passing a whetstone across the edge of a long-hafted axe. This giant was black-haired, the sides of his head shaved to stubble, the hair on the top of his head long and woven into a thick warrior braid. Another axe, like the one across his lap, was slung over his shoulder. But Drem's eyes were irresistibly drawn to Balur One-Eye.

Balur One-Eye.

Thousands of years old, the tales tell, one of those that drank from the Starstone Cup, giving them long life and strength. Not that he looks as if he needed any more strength. Though he does look old.

Balur's face was a map of scars and ridges, skin puckered around one empty socket, his hair white as milk and tied into a thick warrior braid. His long, drooping moustache was bound with leather cord. But Drem could see the knots and slabs of muscle that bunched beneath Balur's clothes. Even beneath layers of wool, leather and fur, Balur's musculature was formidable. His legs were wider than some trees Drem had seen.

Tattoos of thorn and vine coiled around his thick forearms, disappearing beneath leather vambraces and fur-edged sleeves of linen. A war-hammer was slung over the giant's shoulder.

'Stepor found you, then,' Balur One-Eye rumbled.

'*Flick found them*,' Rab the crow squawked. He was perched on Cullen's shoulder.

'Aye, that's the truth of it,' Stepor said.

'Well met, Balur One-Eye,' Cullen said, swaggering up to the giant.

'Well met, little Cullen,' Balur replied, the edge of a smile touching his lips. 'I am glad to see your hubris has not put you in a cairn yet.'

'No one out there capable of doing that,' Cullen replied with a grin.

Balur looked at the dark-haired giant. 'You see what I mean?'

'Aye,' grunted the giant, not breaking a stroke of his axe-sharpening.

Hammer crested the ridge behind them, and the dark-haired giant rose, slinging his axe across his back and calling out to her.

'Ach, it is a sore sight, seeing that bear's back riderless. Sig, how could you fall?' Balur's face twisted in grief, shifting to a glowering anger. 'Sig, I will avenge you,' he growled.

Then the white bear appeared behind Hammer. He saw the giants and stopped, though Hammer lumbered down to them, the dark-haired giant striding to her and wrapping one of his thick-muscled arms around her neck, laying his head against the bear and murmuring quietly.

Balur looked at the white bear, then at Stepor and Keld, and raised an eyebrow.

'Don't look at me,' Stepor said. 'This lot have been making friends in the wilderness.'

'Found him being set upon by a brood of white wyrms,'

Keld said. 'We helped him out a little, and since then he's taken a liking to us.'

'Taken a liking to Hammer's rump, is more like it,' Cullen said.

'Ha.' The dark-haired giant barked a laugh.

'Though the white bear likes Drem well enough as well,' Stepor said. 'Or at least, he likes the honey Drem gives him.'

'So,' Balur rumbled, pushing away from the stone wall and taking a pace closer to Drem, glowering down at him with his one eye. 'You are Neve and Olin's boy, then.'

'I am,' Drem said nervously.

'Byrne tells me we are in your debt, for the warning you bring us.'

Drem didn't know what to say to that, so he didn't say anything at all, just shrugged.

'It may not sound like it,' the black-haired giant said, lifting his head from Hammer's thick fur, 'but Balur is saying thank you.'

'I do not need an interpreter, Alcyon,' Balur said, and continued to glower down at Drem.

'Dun Seren had to know of Gulla and all that he is doing,' Drem said.

'Aye,' Balur agreed. He looked up, into the expanse of the Desolation. It was close to dusk, and lights were winking into existence, marking the scattered holds that dotted the landscape. 'Best be getting you back to Dun Seren and see if Byrne's mustered enough swords yet, to go and take Gulla's head.'

'Ah, Dun Seren,' Cullen said with glee. 'You'll be spending some time in the weapons-field whilst you're there, then, One-Eye?'

'I will.' Balur shrugged.

'Good. I'll look forward to teaching you a thing or two with a blade, then.'

Balur looked down at Cullen a long while, and much to

Drem's respect, Cullen returned the look, and even managed to maintain his infuriating smile.

'Out of respect for your great-grandfather, I will not squash you where you stand, little Cullen,' Balur rumbled.

'Stop calling me that,' Cullen muttered.

Balur frowned. 'And why did you cut all of your hair off? It makes you look like a bairn.'

'Ach, don't say that,' Cullen said. 'The ladies loved my long locks.'

'Let's move on,' Stepor said. 'I want to make Dalgarth soon.' He looked at Drem, Keld and Cullen. 'Once we are at the traders' town I'll feel you are safe.'

'I'm safe wherever I am,' Cullen said, patting the hilt of his sword. 'Safety is my middle name.'

Alcyon barked a laugh.

Balur shook his head and sighed, then shouldered a pack and hefted a long spear that was leaning against the bridge.

'Rab, go and spread the word that we've found our friends,' Stepor said. 'Tell them to turn back for Dun Seren.' Stepor looked up at the sky, searching the clear blue.

'Where's Flick?' he said to himself.

CHAPTER TWENTY-EIGHT

RIV

Riv sat on the edge of her cot, her head in her hands. She felt in turmoil.

So many lies. My parentage, Elyon's Lore, when will it end?

Footsteps on the stairwell, and Riv looked up as the door creaked open. Aphra walked into their dormitory, beds rowed on either side of a long chamber.

She looks tired, Riv thought, and not just physically. Aphra's head was bowed, her face pale, and new wrinkled lines were etched upon her forehead and around her mouth.

I am not the only one that these dark days are taking their toll upon.

At seeing Riv Aphra paused. Then she came and sat beside her. A hand reached up, hovered a moment, then stroked Riv's fair hair.

'It is getting long,' Aphra said gently. 'Would you like me to cut it for you?'

For as long as Riv could remember, Aphra had always cut her hair, cropping it short in the uniform style of the White-Wings. Just another small part of how Riv had been fashioned and moulded from birth to be part of the Ben-Elim's war-machine, instilling that desire and belief that she was destined to become a White-Wing.

'No,' Riv snapped. 'I am *not* a White-Wing and can never be one. I wear my wings upon my back, not my chest. Why would I cut my hair like one of you, when I can never stand in a shield wall again?'

Aphra sighed and continued stroking Riv's hair.

'You are still Riv,' Aphra said into the silence, 'in here –' a finger tapping Riv's chest – 'the fierce, loyal, kind, too-honest and oft-times too-angry little warrior that you have always been.'

'Am I?' Riv said, looking at Aphra now. She felt hot tears fill her eyes. 'I do not look the same.' A ripple shivered through her wings. 'Or feel the same, inside.' She put her fingers to her temples and rubbed. 'This blood in my veins makes me part human, part Ben-Elim, but not fully one or the other.' She sucked in a shuddering breath. 'That, I can deal with. It's not all bad. I like flying. *Love* flying. And wings make me a better fighter.' She shrugged, enjoying just being honest. 'Getting to sleep was a bit difficult at first, uncomfortable, but I've worked it out now.'

Aphra snorted a laugh.

'It's not those changes that hurt,' Riv said. 'It's the *lies*. They are tearing at me like hounds at a stag. Kol murdered Israfil, his Lord. He is a traitor. But he's also my *father*. And now I find out that Elyon's Lore is *made up*, by the Ben-Elim.'

Aphra paused stroking and turned Riv to face her. 'They are not evil, the Ben-Elim. They strive to be good, like their Maker, Elyon, but they are *so* focused on their goal, to destroy the Kadoshim, that they cannot see the wrong they have done in the chasing of that end. And they are flesh and blood now, and so are part of all that comes with that. Its desires and temptations. Its weaknesses. They are fallible, though most of them would not like to admit to that.'

'Pride,' Riv said. 'Elyon's Lore has much to say about that. Or should I say, the Ben-Elim have much to say about that.'

'That they have,' Aphra agreed, both humour and resignation in her voice.

'And then there is you, of course,' Riv said. 'You, my sister, but no, you're really my mother. And Dalmae, whom I thought of all my life as my mother, she was my grandmother.' She shook her head, saw the look of pain that swept Aphra. 'I am starting to understand. You made mistakes, and then you were forced to make choices, when there was no clear choice to make.'

'I did make mistakes,' Aphra said. 'Or more accurately, one mistake, and that was Kol. But after that you are wrong. The choice was always clear. The choice was you, Riv, always and ever only you. I love you, Riven ap Aphra, my beautiful daughter.' She blew out a long breath. 'Ah, how I have longed to say that out loud to you.'

Riv blinked away tears. 'I love you, too,' she whispered, and put her head on Aphra's shoulder.

A silence settled between them, Aphra continuing to stroke Riv's long hair.

'I hate living like this,' Riv said. 'Feeling what's right, in here . . .' she put a palm to her chest, '. . . but not able to do it.'

'Life is harsh, and complicated,' Aphra said. 'To survive each day and be with the ones you love, that is becoming enough for me.'

'I want *more*,' Riv said. 'I want justice, for Dalmae. Kol should pay for what he's done, for what he's doing.'

'Kol is your father,' Aphra said. 'No matter what else he is, he is still that. And remember, we have the Kadoshim to fight. No matter how terrible you think the Ben-Elim, the Kadoshim are worse.'

Riv took a deep breath, trying to control the frustration boiling away inside her.

I would like to kill some Kadoshim. Finally, a focus for my anger.

'There is much in life that is beyond our control, events that sweep us up and along, actions that wrap us tight in their consequences. Stop raging about the things you cannot change. Just be true to yourself and do what you can do. Love those worth loving, and to the Otherworld with the rest of it. That is all any of us can do.'

Riv stared at Aphra, feeling the words sink into her. It felt . . . profound.

There is truth in that.

'What do you want, Riv, that you can actually do something about?'

'I want . . .'

A face materialized in her mind, dark-skinned, almond-eyed.

Riv stood and walked to a shuttered window, undid the clasp and opened it.

'Where are you going?' Aphra asked her.

'To clear my head,' Riv said, and stepped out into the night sky.

First she flew up, through the night-black, until she was high over the fortress, close enough to touch the branches of the great tree that spread its branches over Drassil like protective arms. She scrambled onto a branch as thick as a bridge and sat, gazing about her. A pale line touched the eastern horizon; dawn was seeping across the land, pushing back the darkness.

That is what the Ben-Elim think they are, the light of the world, burning away all darkness before them. But they are not so perfect. Sometimes they burn what they touch.

The creeping march of the sun had not touched Drassil yet. Torches small as pinpricks guttered below Riv, marking the towers and walls of the fortress.

She felt better, somehow, for talking to Aphra, as if a weight had been lifted.

Be true to yourself, and do what you can do, that is what she said. I will steer my own path, somehow. Stay true to what I am. But what is that? What do I want to do, and what can I do?

So many thoughts rushed through her mind, great deeds of

courage and justice. Setting wrongs right. But one thing kept on rising to the top of her mind, above all else.

A face.

She slipped off the branch and fell, enjoying the rush of wind in her face, dragging her hair like a banner behind her, and then she snapped her wings out, whooping for the joy of it as she sped through the air, diving and looping ever closer to Drassil. In heartbeats she was level with towers, weaving amongst them, until she reached her destination, hovering for a few moments as she caught her breath, and her courage.

And then she tapped quietly on a shuttered window.

Silence, then a groan, a bed creaking, the sound of flint and crackle of kindling as a torch was struck, then soft footfalls and the shutter was opening.

Bleda stood there, blinking, his hair sticking out at all angles, a blanket wrapped around his waist.

'Riv,' he said.

'Well spotted,' Riv said. Then, more hesitantly, 'I wanted to talk with you.'

Bleda stepped back from the window, ushering her in.

She flew in, folding her wings tight and standing in his chamber. It was sparsely decorated, a bed, a desk and chairs, a chest.

'What is it? What's wrong?' Bleda said to her.

'I am leaving Drassil today,' she said.

'Why?' Bleda asked her.

'I am flying with Kol to Dun Seren, home of the Order of the Bright Star,' Riv told him. 'Kol wishes to speak with Queen Ethlinn and Balur One-Eye, about the death of Israfil, about Kol's succession as Lord Protector.'

'How much of the actual truth will be involved in that?' Bleda asked her.

Riv felt her face twist at that, a rush of shame and anger mixed.

'Very little, I imagine. The truth has felt like a fading,

distant light to me lately,' Riv admitted. 'So much is happening, is out of my control, and it is twisting me. I feel it is breaking me.'

'You mustn't let it,' Bleda said fiercely. 'You are strong, Riv, strong and good.'

Riv smiled at him, then. 'You really believe that, don't you?'

'I do,' Bleda said. 'You are like the sun, burning the darkness away.'

Will I burn what I touch, too? Like the Ben-Elim.

'You are good, too,' Riv said, and she saw emotion twitch his face. They stood there long moments, locked in each other's gaze. 'I will . . . miss you, Bleda, while I am away,' Riv eventually said.

'I will miss you, too,' Bleda answered. The flickering torchlight painted the muscles of his naked torso in light and shadow.

Do what you can do, Aphra's words rang in her mind. *Love those worth loving.*

Riv reached out and squeezed Bleda's hand, then leaned and brushed her lips against his cheek. Bleda froze, not even blinking, but she could hear the beat of his heart, a drum in his chest. Riv leaned away and smiled at him, stroked his cheek.

'You are worth loving,' she whispered and then she leaned in again, kissed him on his lips this time.

Bleda didn't push her away, or resist. Quite the opposite. After a shocked moment he pulled her into him harder, his hands rising to her waist.

She folded her wings about him.

CHAPTER TWENTY-NINE

DREM

Drem crested a hill and stared at the view before him. A town lay sprawled before them, little more than a league away. It was much larger than Kergard, and Kergard was the largest town Drem could remember. He could smell it from here. Absently, a hand went to the pulse in his neck.

'Dalgarth,' Stepor said from beside him. It's a market town, first and biggest of the Desolation. And just beyond . . .' Stepor pointed into the distance, where Drem saw the dark curl of a wide river, a bridge arching over it, and beyond that a hill with a fortress built upon its summit, buildings and walls cascading down from it.

Dun Seren.

'And that,' Stepor said, pointing to the east, towards a dark stain that seemed to cover the whole world east of Dun Seren, 'is Forn Forest.'

It seemed as if faery tales were coming to life for Drem. He had seen beautiful, breath-taking sights in the north, the Desolation cold and harsh, but also full of beauty. But these places he was seeing now, Dun Seren and Forn Forest, were steeped in the histories, myths and legends of the Banished Lands. He had heard so many tales of these places that he felt he almost knew them already.

'Keep moving,' Balur said as he strode up behind them, 'and never stop on the ridge of a hill, little Drem.'

Little Drem. I have not been called that before.

'Why not?' Drem called out as he stumbled on.

'Because your silhouette can be seen for leagues around,' Alcyon said as he strode up behind Balur, his two axes hung diagonally over his shoulders like wings of wood and steel. 'Not the wisest place to stop if you're being hunted.'

They wound their way down the hill, Stepor pausing periodically to stare at the sky, searching for the crow, Flick. They were all concerned that the crow was nowhere to be seen.

Hammer and the white bear brought up the rear of their company, while blurred shadows of red, black and slate flitted either side of them through patches of gorse and banks of fern, the three wolven-hounds guarding their flanks.

As the ground levelled, the white bear started growling, a low rumbling in its belly, sounding more as if it had gut-ache than that it was being aggressive. Dalgarth was looming tall ahead of them, now, thick palisaded walls circling the town, columns of smoke rising into the air from countless fire-pits. There was a hum of sound emanating from the place: voices, hammers, cattle, wheels turning, blacksmiths, street traders, children shrieking, dogs barking, all melding into an undefined cacophony of noise.

The white bear growled louder. Drem looked back over his shoulder to see it lagging fifty or so paces behind Hammer, and it was waving its head from side to side, nostrils wide and flaring. Then it sat on its haunches.

Drem strode back to it, shrugging off his pack and delving inside, pulled out the honey jar Alcyon had given him. He unstopped the cork and scooped out a handful, waiting for the white bear to invite him closer.

It is a wild animal, after all, not like Hammer and used to people all of her life.

The bear sniffed the air, then waved its paw.

Drem approached the bear, holding his hand out, and the bear licked it.

'Come on, lad,' Drem said, filling his other hand with the thick white fur and scratching the bear's cheek. It seemed to like it. 'I don't like towns either. Too loud, too crowded, and they smell bad. But we've got to go through. For once, it's more dangerous to stay out here, in the wild.'

The bear stopped its licking and looked at him with bright, intelligent eyes, then went back to scraping Drem's glove clean.

Drem took a step away from the bear, took his last honey jar from his pack and opened it, wafted it in front of the bear's nose. Took a few steps backwards.

The bear rose onto all fours and took a hesitant step after him, then stopped and stared at him. It looked from the honey jar to Drem, and then over Drem's shoulder at Hammer and the town beyond.

It sat down again.

'All right, then, lad,' Drem said. 'But know this, I'll miss you.' He scooped the jar clean and pooled the honey on a rock for the bear, then turned and walked away. Hammer gave a rumbling, mournful sound, but the white bear stayed where he was and Drem rejoined the rest of his party.

Dalgarth's gates were open and Balur One-Eye led them through. Drem paused to look back at the white bear and saw that it was gone. With a sigh he turned and walked into the town.

People in the packed streets of the town cleared a path before Balur and Alcyon, some stopping and staring, a gang of excited children running along beside them, every now and then a brave one darting in to tread close to Balur or Alcyon. The giants ignored them, until Alcyon jumped round and growled at them, sending the children bolting and shrieking, mostly with laughter.

Drem tried to take long, slow breaths, as Olin had taught, to help calm himself. It wasn't working. The smell was repulsive, rotting food, sweat, urine and excrement, and people everywhere, closing in on him. He hawked and spat, feeling a pressure in his chest building, as if he were too long under-water, not walking through a town. No matter how hard he tried to control his breathing, he found he was slipping towards short, shallow breaths.

It is too big. Kergard I could cope with, but this . . .

He hoped to be through it as soon as possible.

Stepor stepped away from them, slipping into the crowds, but Balur led them ever onwards.

And then they were through the town, exiting through wide gates and following a road that wound towards a river, its waters so dark they looked black.

Running feet behind them and Drem looked back to see Stepor emerge from the gates, jogging to catch up with them.

'What news?' Keld said, looking at the sour twist of Stepor's face.

'Plague,' Stepor said. 'Or at least, some are calling it that. A wasting disease, sudden and deadly. Thirty dead of it in the last two days.'

Drem looked back at the town. The smell of it made it easy for Drem to imagine disease running amok. He felt unclean just walking through the town.

As they put some distance between them and the town Drem's breathing eased, the road they were on leading them on towards Dun Seren.

Drem looked up at the fortress as they reached the bridge, which crossed a wide, languorous river. A host of boats were moored on both banks, along with a multitude of piers, jetties and boatyards. Timber trunks floated in great swathes, banging and thumping together as water lapped. Balur One-Eye's spear marked time as they crossed the bridge, the spear-butt cracking on stone with every long stride of the giant.

Dun Seren rose tall before Drem. If he had thought Dalgarth was big, then Dun Seren was monstrous. He felt that shortness of breath return, a tightness in his chest, like when the white wyrm had wrapped its coils around him and began to constrict.

Stone walls circled the base of the hill, rooftops visible in tiered rows led up towards a fortress comprised of a dark keep upon the hill's summit, one grey-stoned tower rising from it.

The bridge forked into two roads, east and west, circling the fortress, with gates in the northern wall that faced the river. Balur didn't lead them that way, as Drem had expected, but instead took them along the western road that soon circled south, following the arc of Dun Seren's walls. They climbed a shallow slope and then crested onto more level ground, huge meadows opening up before them, an undulating landscape rolling south.

And then they were curling east again, following a road that led up towards a gateway in an outer wall, then on, climbing the hill towards a higher wall and towering arched gateway, flanked by grey gate-towers. Banners snapped from the walls, a white, four-pointed star set upon a black field.

Keld, Cullen and Stepor had stopped for a moment to gaze at the huge fortress.

'We shall never forget,' Drem heard them murmur, and then their column was moving on, through the outer wall. Horns rang out, proclaiming their arrival, voices calling greetings, grim, hard-looking men and women regarding Drem, scores of giants standing amongst them.

They wound their way through narrow streets lined with buildings of timber and sod, a constant bustle and thrum of activity around them. Blacksmiths' hammers rang out a discordant song, the hiss and stink of steam and hot iron, in the distance a fainter sound, but familiar – the *clack, clack, clack* of practice weapons. Drem felt something as he passed through the busy streets, a nervous energy in the air that set the hairs on his neck on end.

They are preparing for something, but more than that. It is as if they are . . . excited.

And then they were passing through the high-arched gate of Dun Seren's inner wall and spilling into a courtyard before the grey keep. Balur's iron-shod boots clattered on flagstones, Hammer's claws scraping, the three wolven-hounds loping wide on the group's flanks. Warriors lined the walls, men, women, giants; horn blasts and cheers welcomed Balur and the company. Cullen grinned, raising his arms and turning in circles, like the returning hero, as if no one else was there but him.

He deserves a warm welcome, after all he has been through, thought Drem. *As does Keld.* But the huntsman gave only a brief look at the crowd gathered for them, a curt nod of acknow-ledgement here and there. In his hand he held a bundle of grey wool.

In the centre of the courtyard a statue towered. It was huge, two or three times the height of Balur and Alcyon, two figures carved from dark stone. One a warrior, serious-faced, clothed in mail and surcoat, a round shield slung across his back and a drawn sword in his fist, the tip resting upon the ground. The sword's pommel bore the shape of a wolven's head, raised and howling.

The warrior's other arm rested about the neck of a wolven, as tall as the warrior's chest, broad and muscular. Its long canines were bared in a snarl, and Drem could see that its coat was latticed in scars.

'My great-grandfather, Corban, and his wolven, Storm,' Cullen said to Drem, waving a hand at the statue. 'He is the founder of our Order, and the greatest hero in the Banished Lands.' He leaned close to Drem. 'And his blood runs in our veins. Mine more than yours, of course, which means I'm more of the hero than you, but yours as well.' He winked at Drem.

They marched beneath the statue towards the keep, wide stone steps leading up to its oak-and-iron doors.

Three figures stood at the top of the steps. Two of them giants, one a woman, regal and dark, a spear in her hand, the other male, slimmer than Balur and Alcyon, with a tangled mess of hair. But Drem's eyes were drawn to the figure between them. A stern-faced woman, her dark hair tied back to her nape, dressed in simple leathers, the bright star embossed upon her surcoat. A curved sword arched across her back.

Balur halted at the bottom of the steps, the others spreading either side of him, except for Keld, who strode up the steps and stopped before the dark-haired woman.

'Byrne, High Captain of the Order of the Bright Star,' Keld greeted her. 'I report the fall of our sword-sister, Sig, of the Jotun Clan.' He looked from Byrne to the crowd gathered in the courtyard and on the walls. 'She fought bravely,' Keld called out, his voice cracking, 'and gave her life that we might live.'

A memory flashed into Drem's mind, of Sig ordering Keld and Cullen to tie her to a post because her legs were failing her and she wished to fight on to her last breath, buying them precious moments to escape into the night. Emotion swelled in his chest. He had not known Sig long, but somehow he had felt a bond to her, and that was a rare thing for him. Perhaps it was because of their shared love of Drem's father, Olin, and the scattered, faint memories Drem had of Sig, from when he had lived at Dun Seren.

Keld bowed his head and handed Byrne the folded bundle in his hand. She took it, unwrapping it carefully, to reveal Sig's cloak-brooch, a silver four-pointed star.

'Sig will be sorely missed,' Byrne said, holding the star up high for all to see. 'She will be grieved, and she *shall* be avenged.'

Drem felt a shiver run through his body at Byrne's words, and he believed her, completely and utterly.

'We shall never forget,' Byrne called out, and the crowd echoed her, Drem instinctively adding his voice to theirs. A silence fell over the courtyard, just the snap and ripple of banners in a cold wind.

'Change and eat,' Byrne said to Keld, reaching out and

squeezing his wrist, 'and then report to me.' She walked past Keld, down the stone steps, nodding to Stepor and Cullen, but her eyes were fixed on Drem. She stood before him, looking up at him, and slowly a gentle smile spread across her face, softening her stern features.

'Drem ben Olin, my sister's son, welcome to Dun Seren,' Byrne said, and then wrapped her arms around him and pulled him into a tight embrace.

CHAPTER THIRTY

BLEDA

Bleda sat at a desk in his chamber, scratching a quill across parchment. Mirim, Tuld and Ruga stood before him.

'This one is for you,' Bleda said, waving a parchment strip at Mirim. She took it and read aloud.

'Maple wood. Tendons from the leg of an auroch. Auroch horn.'

Bleda tore another strip, wrote on it and passed it to Ruga.

'Fish glue, made from sturgeon. A bone from a stallion,' she read.

'And for you,' Bleda said as he passed the last strip to Tuld.

'Oak and felt,' Tuld read, raising an eyebrow. They all knew what these ingredients were for.

I am going to make a Sirak bow.

'May I build you the conditioning box as well, my Prince?' Tuld asked. 'My father is renowned for his skill at building these boxes, and he taught me the art.'

'You may,' Bleda said.

They stood before him, all wanting to ask why he was making a bow, or who for, but their deference to his rank forbade them such informality.

'Go on, then, away with you all,' Bleda said, 'and remember, only the ingredients I've asked for. Tell the traders the Prince of the Sirak requests it, and nothing else will do. Fish glue, from a sturgeon.' He wagged a finger at Ruga. 'Not hide glue. And only the tendons from the lower leg of an auroch, nowhere else,' he said to Mirim.

'Of course, my Prince,' Ruga and Mirim nodded together.

'Well then, what are you all waiting for?'

'You will be left unguarded,' Tuld said.

'Unguarded, in my own chamber, with two score of my honour guard in the feast-hall below, and Old Ellac lurking in the shadows in the corridor outside?'

Tuld nodded, a little begrudgingly, Bleda thought, but he turned and left the room, Ruga and Mirim following him.

Bleda leaned back in his chair and let out a long sigh. Then he smiled, a small expression of the depth of joy that he felt inside. He closed his eyes, could almost still feel Riv's lips upon his own.

He missed her already, had begun to miss her as he'd watched her fly away from his window.

He had not been good with words, he felt, never had been, and he wanted to do something to show her how strongly he felt for her, to show how much he cared for her.

So, he was going to make her a Sirak bow.

He had helped his brother Altan make his own bow, the one that rested in its leather case leaning against his cot, along with a quiver full of arrows. Bleda had only been nine summers old at the time, but the memory of it was so imprinted upon his mind that he was certain he could do it again.

Riv needs a bow. But there was so much more to it than that. Making Riv a Sirak bow was a symbol of how close he had taken her to his heart. As close as kin and Clan. Closer.

There was a knock on his door.

'Yes,' Bleda said.

Ellac opened it and dipped his head inside.

'The Princess Jin of the Cheren wishes to speak with you,' Ellac said.

'Oh, get out of my way,' Jin said behind him, trying to elbow her way past Ellac.

Bleda gave a quick shake of his head to Ellac as he saw the old warrior about to step in front of Jin, so Ellac allowed her to pass him. But he was not so lenient with the warrior who stood in the corridor behind Jin, a dour, sharp-faced man who attempted to follow the Cheren Princess. Ellac stepped in front of him and, although not a word was said for a moment, there was a cold tension in the air.

'Gerel, keep Old Ellac company and wait for me in the corridor,' Jin said with a wave of her hand.

'But, my Princess –' Gerel began, but Jin interrupted him.

'I am *betrothed* to Bleda,' she said. 'He will soon be King of the Cheren, as I will be Queen of the Sirak. He is hardly going to cut my throat.' She looked at Bleda, then back to Gerel. 'He would not dare.'

'As you wish, my Princess,' Gerel said, 'I'll be ri—' the rest of what he was saying became too muffled to hear as Ellac closed the door.

Jin stood in the middle of the room, looking at Bleda. Her face was calm, but in her eyes emotions flickered. There was a hesitancy, a suggestion of vulnerability and uncertainty, of indecision, like someone standing at a crossroad and not knowing which way to go.

'Please, sit,' Bleda said, gesturing to a chair on the other side of his desk. Jin walked to it, picked it up and carried it around the desk, placed it beside him and sat down.

'We are betrothed,' Jin said. 'And yet I hardly see you.'

Bleda felt a squirm of nausea in his belly. After seeing Riv only a short while ago, this was not the way he'd hoped to spend his morning. Being reminded of his impending doom.

I cannot do it. I cannot wed her.

He mumbled something about being so busy, about too much to do and too little time.

'I know,' Jin said. 'Much has changed, and there is much more to do now. Israfil dead, the new Lord Protector is . . . different from his predecessor, and your mother is here.' She shrugged. 'Much of the change is for the better. My father will be here soon, we are to be wed, and yet . . .' Jin put her hand over Bleda's, giving it a squeeze. 'Sometimes I wish that we could go back to how we were, before . . .'

Bleda resisted the urge to pull his hand away.

'Before?' he said.

'Yes. When it was just you and me, together against the world, it felt like. We used to spend our days together, training, learning –' a glint of humour in her eyes – 'complaining about the Ben-Elim and White-Wings and their foolish, barbaric ways. I miss those days. You were my friend, my only friend.'

It was true. For five years they had spent most of their waking hours in each other's company, and on the whole Jin was not unpleasant to be around, though Bleda had often thought that her devotion to her Clan and her disapproval of all else was too plainly writ in her. She thought of the Cheren as superior, and the Ben-Elim as inferior fools. Bleda knew that was too simplistic, and that the Ben-Elim were to be respected, no matter whether they were friend or foe.

'But that is not all that has changed,' Jin said. '*You* have changed.'

She looked at Bleda then, a penetrating, unblinking gaze.

What does she know? A sensation in his belly, like a stone being dropped.

'Things have happened,' Bleda said, thinking of all that had occurred since Riv had given him his bow. He had fought the Kadoshim, slain Feral beast-men, and even Ben-Elim. 'Events change us.'

'You have changed since *she* came along,' Jin said. She gave Bleda that long look again, as if trying to delve through his eyes and into his head, trying to read his thoughts. Bleda had no doubts about who the *she* was that Jin was referring to.

'Since Riv gave you your old bow.'

'My brother made it for me,' Bleda said carefully. 'It was a great gift to me.'

'And yet she kept it for five years,' Jin snapped.

'Aye, she did. But then she gave it to me, and for that I am grateful.'

'Be grateful,' Jin said. 'But not too grateful. I see you watching her.' She stopped, a silence growing between them. A deep breath. 'I am your betrothed. We have a great destiny to fulfil, and together we can accomplish much.' She hesitated again. 'Do not throw that away. Have your *friends*, if you must, but . . .' Now Jin's hand squeezed Bleda's, much harder than before, an iron strength in it. 'Do not shame me. I will *not* be shamed.'

Bleda felt an overwhelming urge to tell her the truth. His eyes glanced to his bed, the sheets still crumpled where they had lain. But he also felt a wave of sympathy for Jin. She seemed always so strong, so in control. Self-certain and judging. And yet Bleda could feel the frailty and pride within her. She was a Cheren princess, plucked from her kin and home and dragged away to a foreign land, raised amongst strange people who bore her no love. He understood, because it had happened to him. He knew that she could not be made to appear weak or ridiculed. Strength was all to the Horse Clans of Arcona.

But Riv has my heart.

He breathed in deep, vowing to find a way through this, to find an answer, before it was too late.

'I will not shame you,' he said.

How is it that I have changed so much, and she has not? He remembered the night the Kadoshim came, when he and Jin had run to Drassil's courtyard and seen the Kadoshim for the first time. Bleda had been frozen, stunned by the Kadoshim's malice. In the face of their evil he had felt compelled to do something, to try and fight them, but Jin had been happy to sit back and watch them and the Ben-Elim slay one another. A sole memory stood out from that night, when the acolyte had severed the iron-coated hand of Asroth the demon-king. For one terrible moment Bleda had seen the iron encasing Asroth's body ripple and shift, and worse still, a malevolent light had flared in the demon's eye, bright and sharp with intelligence and a deep malice that had chilled Bleda's blood.

Their threat is real.

Ever since that night, Bleda had felt himself drifting from the person he had once been.

'Good,' Jin said, blowing out a long breath. There was even a twitch of a smile at the edges of her lips, 'because I would hate to have to kill you.'

Bleda blinked and she smiled wider, what must have been a conscious decision to allow her emotions onto her face. As Bleda had told Riv, the Sirak and Cheren were not cold-hearted, emotionless monsters. They kept their emotions hidden, under guard, and revealed them like a gift to those they trusted and cherished. Jin was telling Bleda she trusted him and allowing herself to be vulnerable, even if only for these few moments. Her smile changed her face.

She will kill me, he realized, *if my relationship with Riv becomes . . . public.*

He felt that he should return her smile, knew that it was appropriate, in his culture, but he did not *feel* the desire to smile. Quite the opposite. He sat looking at her, feeling sympathy for her, edged with guilt.

I will hurt her, if I do not return her smile. I will hurt her more, when the truth comes out. It will; better now than allow this to fester. It will only grow harder if it is left. I must call off our betrothal. But what of Mother? She wants this for our people, the seal upon our new peace with the Cheren.

He thought of Riv, hovering beyond his window, looking so beautiful in the starlight, remembered her lips upon his.

I love her.

He opened his mouth to tell Jin.

Horns blew in the distance, both of them looking out of Bleda's window.

Ellac opened the door.

'That is a Cheren horn,' he said.

Bleda stood in the courtyard before Drassil's gates, waiting, much as he had done for his mother's arrival. This time he was not mounted, but stood alongside Queen Erdene, their honour guards about them both, and close by stood Jin, her guardians arrayed behind her. She wore her face cold and flat, but Bleda could imagine the emotions roiling within her.

A Cheren horn. Her father, King Uldin, is come.

Many Ben-Elim and White-Wings were gathered in the courtyard, too. The White-Wings were in their neat, disciplined lines, a score of Ben-Elim before them, more of the winged warriors circling in the sky above.

Standing at the head of the Ben-Elim in the courtyard was Hadran, the dark-haired warrior who had fought for Riv in the weapons-field. For that reason alone, Bleda found himself liking this Ben-Elim more than most of his kind. The remnant of a bruise was still on his face.

He must be Kol's captain and representative, for Kol is gone with Riv.

Bleda had stood on Drassil's battlements, just after dawn, and watched them sweep over the field of cairns and then the endless green of Forn Forest, the rising sun glinting on feathers and mail.

The blaring of horns and thunder of hooves snapped him back to the present, and then riders were racing through the gate tunnel of Drassil, hooves cracking on stone as they spilt into the courtyard.

Something was wrong – that was immediately clear. They were Cheren riders with their shaved heads and long warrior braids, the banners of their stooping hawk snapping, but they did not enter the courtyard with the fluid grace and skill that Bleda expected, nothing like the disciplined horsemanship of Erdene's entrance.

Many of them were injured, garments bloodstained.

An older man rode at their head, King Uldin, streaks of iron-grey in his braid and beard. He was swaying in his saddle, blood crusted on his head, blood-soaked rents in his felt deel and wolf-skin cloak.

CHAPTER THIRTY-ONE

DREM

Drem stepped into Byrne's chambers, Keld, Cullen and Stepor with him. He was suddenly exhausted; the realization that he was safe, that the running and fighting and constant checking of the skies was over, at least for the time being, was finally sinking into him. The only thing keeping him upright was the wonder of this place. Dun Seren was staggeringly immense, an abundance of people and giants, horses, bears, wolven-hounds, all manner of trades and disciplines taking place in some kind of organized whirlwind of activity. It was a marvel to him, although it was also profoundly exhausting. He found that his hand reaching to take his pulse was becoming a semi-permanent position.

'Please, Drem, all of you, sit,' Byrne said to them, gesturing to seats.

Byrne's chambers were sparse, a large desk and chairs scattered around the room, huge windows opening out on views to the north and east. The slim, scruffy-haired giant with a tangle of black beard was leaning against the window. A large black crow was perched upon his shoulder. The crow looked old, many of his feathers missing; the ones he had left were sticking out at odd angles. And he was staring at Drem with far-too-intelligent eyes.

'*Who are you?*' the crow squawked.

'Craf, this is my sister's son, Drem ben Olin,' Byrne said.

'Drem, allow me to introduce you to Craf, progenitor of the Dun Seren crows.'

'You're Rab's sire?' Drem said.

'*Rab Craf's fledgling*,' Craf cawed.

'Rab saved us,' Drem said.

'*Rab good boy*,' Craf agreed.

Drem and the others sat in chairs before Byrne's desk.

Byrne was not alone. Balur One-Eye was there, sitting in a chair clearly made for giants, and next to him sat the giantess Drem had seen on the steps beside Byrne.

'And Drem, let me introduce you to my other companions. Craf's perch is Tain Crow Master.'

'Crow slave, more like,' Tain said, dipping his head to Drem.

'Balur One-Eye you know, and this is Ethlinn, Queen of the giants.'

'Well met, Queen Ethlinn,' Drem said, standing and giving an awkward bow, remembering the manners his da had drilled into him.

'Well met, Drem ben Olin,' Ethlinn said with a ghost of a smile, gesturing for him to sit, her gaze uncomfortably penetrating as she regarded him. 'So, you are the bairn Olin stole away,' she murmured.

'Aye, so I've been told,' Drem nodded.

It felt strange to Drem, hearing himself spoken of like this. It was only recently that his da had told him of his past, of how the Ben-Elim had insisted on Drem being given to them as a ward, because of a supposed crime committed by his mother, Neve.

Byrne had refused to hand Drem over, and the Ben-Elim had threatened to take him by force. So, Olin had sneaked Drem away in the night, both to save Drem and to avert a war. Drem had been five years old, and ever since then his life had been a solitary, nomadic existence with his father.

Until we dug up that lump of starstone and started finding muti-
lated bodies in the forest.

'Drem is my kin, my sister's son,' Byrne said.

'Aye, the lad you almost went to war with the Ben-Elim
over.'

'Yes,' Byrne said simply. She looked at Drem. 'I grieve for
Olin. He was a good man. A great man, and while I wish dearly
that he had not left with you, I respect him for it. He put his
son first, but also the Order, walking away from all that he had
known, both to save you and to save us from a war that would
have damaged all who fought in it.'

'He was my father.' Drem shrugged. 'The greatest man I've
known.' He felt a swell of emotion at his words, taking him by
surprise, and he took a long, measured breath to contain them.

'I know it will hurt you, but tell me how your father died,'
Byrne asked, a sadness in her eyes. 'Olin was a member of the
Order of the Bright Star, and his life and death must be
remembered, written down.'

'He was slain by Fritha and the giant, Gunil, and his bear.'

'Gunil,' Ethlinn said, a hint of ice in her voice.

'*Rab told you Gunil there,*' Craf squawked.

'It is a shock to us all, Craf,' Byrne said. 'We thought that
Gunil fell at the Battle of Varan's Fall.'

'I never did like him,' Balur said, knuckles popping as he
made a fist. 'Always whining, complaining of some slight to his
vanity. But Varan loved him, always spoke for him.'

'Sig loved him, too,' Ethlinn said quietly.

'The heart cannot be ruled, but it can be fooled,' Byrne
said. She fixed her eyes back on Drem. 'How did this happen,
Drem?'

A pause as Drem thought on it.

'Because I did not listen to him. Because I was enamoured
of Fritha and wanted to find her. Olin is dead because of me.'

A lump in his chest, then, sudden and violent, stealing his

breath and bringing hot tears to his eyes. He waited a moment, blinked the tears away.

'This is hard for you, Drem Olin's-son,' Ethlinn said, 'but these are momentous times, and I feel much of what you know is of great importance to us, and to the war against the Kadoshim.'

'*Rab already told you,*' Craf squawked.

'Aye, he has, which we are grateful for,' Tain said patiently, scratching Craf's chest. 'But we all need to hear the tale again. Everyone sees something different, Craf, and we need all of the information we can get. This is Gulla, High Captain of the Kadoshim that we are talking about. These details could mean victory or defeat.'

'*Craf trust Rab,*' the crow muttered, ruffling what feathers he had left and tucking his beak into his wing.

'Please, Drem, if it is not too painful, tell us what you can,' Byrne said.

So Drem took a deep breath and told them all he could remember. He started with the finding of the starstone rock in his elk pit, going on to talk about the beacons and those they found dead, that Drem now knew had been sacrificed; told them about Olin's forging of the Starstone Sword, of his plan to slay Asroth with the sword, of his da finally telling him who he was, about the Order of the Bright Star, and then of how Olin had died, in the woods as they had searched for Fritha.

'They took the Starstone Sword,' Drem said. 'I tracked them back to the mine at Starstone Lake and sneaked in.' He paused, remembering the bloodstained table and cages. 'I found . . . terrible things. Experiments on people and beasts.'

'Feral men,' Cullen said. 'We fought them, too. I slew many, of course.'

'Let Drem tell his tale,' Byrne said quietly.

'I escaped, tried to warn the town, but they wouldn't listen. They thought I was mad. So I went home, to my hold. I knew they would be coming for me. I thought about running here, but it's a long walk from Kergard to Dun Seren, and I thought they'd catch me in the wild. Better to fight them there, at my home, where I knew the ground, and could . . . prepare.'

Keld snorted. 'Prepare is an understatement,' he said.

Byrne looked at him, raised an eyebrow.

'He dug an elk pit, in the grip of winter, and then sank a dozen spears into it. And that wasn't all. A nail trap, a bear trap, a mini-stampede, and he blew up a barn. On purpose.' Keld smiled, like a proud, maniacal father.

'Impressive,' Byrne said with a small smile.

'I like this Drem ben Olin,' Balur rumbled to Ethlinn.

Was that supposed to be a whisper?

'And then?' Byrne asked. Drem looked to Keld.

'That's when we found him,' Keld said, 'a rope around his neck, legs kicking as he hung from a tree. We slew the few Drem had left for us.' Keld continued the recounting of the tale. He spoke of their decision to spy out the mine, discovering Gulla and his half-breed children, Fritha as some kind of witch priestess and the dread ceremony where Asroth's severed hand was used to transform Gulla into a Revenant. Their attempt to sneak away and the betrayal by Ulf of Kergard, and the ensuing battle.

'Sig was mortally wounded, a blow from the Starstone Sword severing the artery in her groin,' Keld said. Cullen was sitting with his head bowed, knuckles white in his lap. 'She was bleeding out, nothing that any of us could do. She ordered us to strap her to a post so that she could guard our retreat.'

A silence fell over the room. Drem saw the respect and love that all there held for Sig. Tears were rolling down Tain's cheeks.

'*Poor Sig*,' Craf croaked.

'We shall never forget,' Byrne said quietly, Keld, Stepor and Cullen whispering the words.

'I'll have Gunil's head on a spike for this,' Balur growled.

'And Fritha's,' Drem said.

Another silence settled amongst them. Byrne let out a long, slow breath.

'What now, then?' Cullen asked.

'*Muster, kill Gulla,*' Craf squawked.

'That is the short of it,' Byrne said. 'Word has gone out to every outpost. The full strength of the Order of the Bright Star is gathering here. As soon as we are ready, we shall ride out for the Starstone Lake and put an end to this.' She looked to Ethlinn. 'What are your plans in all of this?' Byrne asked her.

'I will march with you,' Ethlinn said. 'We have been searching for Gulla's nest for a hundred years. I will not miss this now. It could be the end of this war, the culmination of all that Corban and Cywen built your Order to achieve.'

'It could,' Byrne said, a cold ferocity in her voice.

'What of the Ben-Elim?' Stepor asked.

'We have had no word from Drassil for close to two moons. I fear something is amiss, there.' Byrne shrugged. 'We do not need the Ben-Elim or their White-Wings for this. Tain will send a crow to tell them of Gulla, and what we are doing. They may wish to join us. If so, they can ask politely.'

'Talking of crows,' Stepor said, 'I'm worried about Flick. He was our rearguard, and I've not seen him for a ten-night. It's not right. I've a bad feeling about it.'

'*Craf's Flick is missing!*' Craf squawked, flapping his wings and arching his back.

'Most of your crows are out in the Desolation,' Tain said soothingly. 'If Flick is not back by the time they've returned to us, we shall let them all search for him.'

'*Craf go search,*' the black crow squawked, flexing his wings. A feather floated down to the ground.

'Craf, you can't fly far these days. Let your strong children do it.'

Craf sighed. '*Craf worried,*' he said, his head bobbing.

'I am, too,' Tain said, staring out of one of the large windows, looking onto the Desolation.

'How long,' Balur said to Byrne, 'until you are ready to ride?'

'At best, half a moon, perhaps longer,' Byrne said. 'We cannot linger, but it would be foolish to ride out at half-strength.'

'Agreed,' Ethlinn said.

'Then we will train hard while we can.' Balur shrugged, a ripple of muscle. 'I shall let little Cullen show me some of his swordcraft.'

'You sure you're not too old and slow?' Cullen said. 'I would not wish to hurt you.'

'I'll show you how old and slow I am, you yapping pup,' Balur growled.

Cullen grinned.

Byrne dismissed them then, telling Drem she would lead him to his new chambers.

He followed her through high-arched corridors and down spiral stairwells, torches flickering, until finally she stopped at an oak door.

'This was Olin and Neve's chamber,' Byrne said, opening the door. 'It has remained empty ever since Olin took you from Dun Seren.' She gave a wan smile. 'Though I ordered it cleaned when Rab told me you were on your way here. Apparently, there were some spiders who did not wish to give up their cob-webs.'

Drem stepped into the room, a large bed with clean linen neatly folded, a chest, a fire crackling in a hearth. A smaller bed against one wall. Drem walked to a shuttered window and opened it, saw a view of rolling meadows and the dark smear of Forn Forest in the distance.

'You must be exhausted,' Byrne said. 'Rest, sleep. The feast-hall is always open, night or day. As is my door, to you.' She paused, looking solemnly at Drem. 'Ah, but you have your mother's look about you.' She reached out a hand, tentatively, and took his, gave it a gentle squeeze. 'We have much to catch up on, you and I. Fifteen years of catching up, but we are together now. You may feel alone, but I am your kin, your aunt, and we are together again.' She looked around the room. 'I thought you would like to be here. You probably don't remember it, but that is where you slept.' She pointed to the small bed. 'You were all happy here: you, Neve and Olin. They adored you, and adored each other.' A tremor ran through Byrne's voice then, so out of place with the strong, stern figure she seemed to be.

They stood looking at each other a few long moments.

'My thanks,' Drem said.

Byrne shut the door.

Drem sat on the bed, running a hand over the white linen sheets.

We lived here, the three of us, together.

Byrne's words echoed in his mind. *You were all happy here.*

A tightness in his chest, a burning in his eyes.

You were all happy here.

And then great, racking sobs were bursting from him, the building wave of emotion in his chest impossible to contain any longer, erupting out of him, an outpouring of what felt like years of suppression. A flood of memories, all the half-conversations about his mother, the empty longing, and then the death of his father, lying in Drem's arms, blood speckling his father's lips. It all came out of him, his vision a blur as he cried and sobbed, hands twisting fists of linen sheets as he rocked on his bed.

The sound of his door opening and closing. Drem strained to see who it was, a blurred figure, dark-haired, then Byrne's voice. He didn't know what she was saying, he was too busy trying to control his weeping, and there was a roaring in his ears. He felt Byrne's hands on his shoulders, her arms enfolding him, but he didn't want that, felt embarrassed and claustrophobic and tried to push her away, but she was strong, her grip immovable as she pulled him into a tight embrace. At first he struggled through his sobbing, but slowly, incrementally, he allowed himself to sink into Byrne's embrace, lay his head on her shoulder and wrapped his arms around her, all the while Byrne rocking him gently and stroking his hair while she whispered comforts to him.

CHAPTER THIRTY-TWO

BLEDA

Bleda rose from his chair as Uldin, King of the Cheren, strode into a high-vaulted chamber. For a man of the Horse Clans he was taller and broader than most, a stern-faced warrior with streaks of iron-grey in his thick warrior braid and beard. His wounds had been cleaned and tended to, a row of stitches running across his forehead, but apart from that only a slight limp betrayed that he had recently seen battle and been injured. He looked far more a king now than when Bleda had seen him ride through Drassil's gates. A wolf-skin cloak was pulled tight over his sky-blue deel, edged in fine-gold embroidery. His curved sword he wore at his hip, hanging from a soft tooled belt twined with gold chain.

Two warriors walked a step behind him, a man and woman, his honour guard, both of them blooded with fresh cuts. One carried a sack slung over one shoulder.

'Well met,' Uldin of the Cheren said to the two Ben-Elim that stood in place of Kol. One was Hadran, Kol's second. The other Ben-Elim had hair as pale as silver, and his right wrist was bound and splinted. He introduced himself to Uldin as Kamael.

'Welcome to Drassil, King Uldin,' Hadran said, Uldin grunting a response.

'I am glad to be here,' Uldin said. 'My daughter is soon to

be married, so all the wild horses of Arcona would not keep me away.'

I wish people would stop talking about my wedding, Bleda thought.

Uldin put a hand to the wound on his forehead. 'Though some have tried.'

'Tell us what has befallen you on your journey,' Hadran said.

'First, let an old father greet his daughter.' Uldin stood before Jin and looked her up and down. 'Well met, daughter,' he said, offering her his arm. Bleda knew the honour Uldin was giving Jin, knew how she must have felt inside at her father's gesture of approval, recognizing her as a warrior of the Cheren. Despite that, Jin kept her face perfectly still, clasping her father's forearm in the warrior grip.

'And I would not have the Sirak say I am rude in my dotage,' Uldin said, moving to Erdene. 'Well met, Queen of the Sirak.' He offered her his arm. She also took it in the warrior grip. 'It would have been a better journey for your company,' Uldin said to Erdene, 'and safer, I don't doubt, with the might of the Sirak at my side.'

'I brought the Ben-Elim their tithe of flesh from my Clan,' Erdene said, 'and knew that you Cheren had not gathered your offering yet. I felt it would have been discourteous to have hurried you in that task.'

Uldin dipped his head. 'The flesh tithe of the Cheren will be here soon. I left when I received word from Kol, but the tithe was close to being gathered.' Then he moved to Bleda.

'You mean, the Lord Protector,' Hadran said, correcting Uldin.

'What?' Uldin said.

'Kol is now the Lord Protector of the Land of the Faithful,' the fair-haired Ben-Elim, Kamael, said.

'Ah, that is well. Kol is a strong leader, and these are dark times, as I have just learned.' Uldin moved from Erdene to stand in front of Bleda.

'Ah, so, my future son stands before me,' Uldin said. He looked Bleda in the eye and Bleda returned the gaze unflinchingly.

I have looked Asroth in the eye, what is Uldin of the Cheren to that?

'Are you worthy of my daughter, child of the Sirak?' Uldin asked him.

A silence lengthened, Bleda knowing that he should give a fitting response. But the words choked in his throat. Riv's face hovered in his mind's eye. He felt his mother's gaze, and that of the two Ben-Elim, and most of all, Jin's eyes burning into him.

'You must be the judge of that,' he finally said.

'Oh, I will be,' Uldin said.

'His arm is strong and his aim is true,' Erdene said. Bleda felt a swell of pride at his mother's words.

'That is good to hear,' Uldin said. 'Because, as I said, these are dark days.'

'Your news?' Hadran asked Uldin.

'Aye, so to it,' Uldin said. 'It has been a long, hard journey from Arcona to Drassil. There is much fear in your realm, much talk of the Kadoshim and their blood rites. But worse than that, there is plague.'

'What?' hissed Kamael, the pale-haired Ben-Elim.

'A ten-night ago we stopped at a town for rest and found the place almost empty,' Uldin said. 'Those that still lived spoke of a wasting disease, sudden and violent, two, three days until death. We remounted and rode on, only to find all of the other towns and villages telling a similar tale. We camped and slept on the road, thinking it would be safer.' He paused, looked at them all, one by one. 'It was not. Half a ten-night's hard riding from here we were attacked, at dusk, a warband swarming from the darkness of Forn.'

'Who were they?' Hadran asked.

'I saw Kadoshim flying above us like great bats.'

Kamael spat a curse when the Kadoshim were mentioned.

'They were not alone; there were men and women with them, shaven-haired fanatics, but there were other . . . *things* . . . as well. Part man, part beast, that killed with claw and fang, not sword and spear.'

Bleda remembered the Feral beast-men that had attacked Drassil. He remembered putting arrows into one, seeing it fall and rise again, ripping arrows from its body, charging at him in a snarling, berserker rage.

He shivered.

'And there were other things with them. Human in form but, believe me, human they were not.'

'What do you mean? Speak clearer,' Kamael the Ben-Elim said.

'They are difficult to describe, unless you see them, but perhaps this is clear enough for you,' Uldin said, nodding to his honour guard with the sack. The warrior stepped forwards and emptied its contents on the ground.

A severed head rolled across the stones, strips of skin, flesh and gristle draping from its neck. It was a woman, Bleda thought, though it was hard to tell. Her face looked malformed, eyes sunken, the skin stretched too tight, its mouth misshapen. Her lips were fixed in a savage rictus of a snarl, revealing a mouth that looked too big for the face it was set within, and either side of its elongated canines were rows of sharp, needle-like teeth.

Bleda resisted the urge to take a step away from the severed head.

'What is that?' Hadran said, moving closer and leaning in for a better look.

'I do not know, but they are hard to kill,' Uldin said. 'A dozen arrows, a spear in its belly, but only when I took this one's head did it stop trying to sink its teeth into me.'

Erdene stood and nudged it with her toe, sending it rolling in an arc across the stones.

'This is intolerable,' Kamael said. 'Kadoshim and their followers so close to Drassil. We must send out the White-Wings.' He looked to Hadran, and Bleda realized that Kamael did not have the authority to order such a campaign.

'Yes,' Hadran said. 'We shall muster the White-Wings and fly out with them.'

'White-Wings, on foot?' Uldin said. 'Better to send your giants on their bears. White-Wings would take a moon to walk the journey we have ridden since we were attacked.'

'Ethlinn and Balur One-Eye are not here,' Hadran said. 'They are at Dun Seren.'

'Send for them,' Kamael said.

'Dun Seren is the opposite direction,' Hadran said. 'Word must be sent to Kol, but it is too far for Ethlinn and her bear-riders to reach us and then march on this new threat. Might as well send out the White-Wings as wait for the giants to arrive.'

'But we cannot do nothing,' Kamael said. 'The Kadoshim, so close.'

'We will fly out,' Hadran said. 'There are more Ben-Elim gathered at Drassil now than there have been for fifty years.'

'But Forn is a mask from above. Remember Varan's Fall, the ambush in the trees. We need eyes and swords on the ground,' Kamael said.

'I cannot conjure what does not exist,' Hadran snapped. 'The choice is fly quick or march slow with the White-Wings.'

Bleda looked at his mother. 'I have seen the Kadoshim, fought their Feral beasts. They are an evil that must be stopped.'

Erdene looked at Bleda a long moment.

'I will lead the Sirak out,' Erdene said. 'I have half a thousand riders here. We shall ride out and meet this threat. We shall be your swords and eyes on the ground.'

'I shall ride with you,' Uldin said.

'You are recently wounded,' Hadran pointed out.

'I will ride with Erdene,' Uldin said. 'We are to be one Clan, soon, I know, but I would not have the Sirak steal the battle glory from us. The Cheren will ride to battle.' He touched the stitched wound across his forehead. 'Besides, I have a score to settle.'

CHAPTER THIRTY-THREE

DREM

Drem stepped out onto Dun Seren's weapons-field and paused, blinking at the enormity of it. It was only a little past dawn, the sun pale and fresh, painting the field in long shadows and hues of amber.

People were everywhere. Thousands, it felt like – more people than Drem had ever seen in any one place in all of his life. It was overwhelming. He raised a hand to find the pulse in his neck.

'Come on,' Cullen called back to him, the red-haired warrior strutting onto the field, looking for all the world as if it belonged to him. Cullen glanced back at Drem, saw him hovering at the entrance to the field, and walked back to him.

'You've fought draigs, wyrms, Feral beasts. And a mad witch. This is nothing,' Cullen said, wrapping an arm around Drem's shoulders and steering him onto the field. Drem allowed himself to be led, though he wasn't sure he agreed.

I feel more comfortable in the wild.

Cullen steered Drem through a knot of giants sparring with wooden hammers and axes, the ground shaking as they crashed into each other, and then beyond them towards where the main mass of people were gathered, more joining them with every moment.

Byrne stood at their head, with two others beside her, a squat and muscular man and a tall, dark-skinned woman.

Byrne looked very different from the kindly aunt who had comforted him only a day ago, dressed now in simple working leathers, her hair tied back severely to show her sharp-angled face. The other two were dressed similarly. The tall woman looked at Drem as he followed Cullen.

'Who are they?' Drem whispered to Cullen.

'Those with Byrne, they're Kill and Cure,' Cullen said.

'Eh?' Drem frowned.

'Byrne's two captains,' Cullen said. 'A quick history lesson is needed, I think, else you'll go embarrassing yourself, and that will make me look bad.' He grinned at Drem's confused expression. 'This Order was founded in remembrance of two people, Brina and Gar, Corban's dearest friends. They fell in the battle on the Day of Wrath, and Corban swore to honour and remember them.' Cullen gestured at Dun Seren. 'This is how he did it, by building this place. Not just the walls and towers, but the people you see around you. Gar was a warrior, Corban's teacher, and Brina was a healer. So here at Dun Seren Corban founded an order dedicated to both arts. How to kill, and how to cure. We learn both here, and so there are two captains – one to oversee each discipline. Kill and Cure.' Cullen pointed at the man and woman with Byrne.

'Ah, so those aren't their real names, then?' Drem asked.

'Ha, no, but they might as well be. No one calls them by anything else, now.'

'So . . .' Drem began.

'More questions later,' Cullen said as he took a place in the lines, beckoning Drem to stand beside him. 'No more time now.'

'What are we doing?'

'This is the Order of the Bright Star, how else do you think we'd start the day? Not too close, now,' Cullen said, 'else you'll end up slicing someone's body parts off.'

'Eh?' Drem said.

Then he saw Byrne draw the curved sword from her back, holding it loosely.

Drem realized what they were doing.

The sword dance.

'Stooping falcon,' Byrne called out, raising her sword two-handed over her head.

Drem drew his father's sword, *his* sword now, set his feet and raised the blade high.

'Lightning strike,' Byrne called out and over a thousand swords slashed down, diagonally, right to left, the sound of it like a high wind passing through the gullies of the Bonefells. It was exhilarating.

They held the pose for long moments, sweat dappling Drem's brow, steaming in the morning's chill air.

'Boar's tusk,' Byrne cried out, all those gathered on the field taking a step and stabbing forwards, low to high, legs bent, arms extended. Holding the pose again, muscles beginning to burn in thigh and back, shoulder and wrist.

'Iron gate,' Byrne cried. Drem took a step back, bringing his sword across his body, a diagonal defence.

'Scorpion's tail,' called Byrne, and Drem dropped into a squatting stance, one hand in front for balance, his blade above his head and behind, parallel to the ground, like a scorpion's tail about to strike.

All around him men and women were doing the same, and as Byrne called the forms Drem heard his father's voice and imagined his mother and father working through the sword dance, on this very field, just as he was now.

There was a comfort in that, something warm and satisfying.

Before he realized, it was over, people all around him were sheathing their blades, Cullen stepping over to slap him on the shoulder.

'Come on, don't let the sweat dry,' Cullen said. He laughed

as Drem fumbled sheathing his sword and then led Drem away from the centre ground, towards racks of wooden weapons.

All around the field groups gathered in different disciplines. Some stood in a loose-ordered line, four ranks deep, with the Order's round shields on their arm. A command was shouted and the ranks closed up, shields coming together with a loud snap, forming a wall of wood and iron.

Beyond them riders galloped, swords slicing at fruit on stands. Elsewhere a warrior ran alongside a cantering horse, grabbed its saddle and leaped into the air, swinging himself up onto the horse's back, grabbing reins and urging the horse to a gallop.

'The running mount,' Cullen said.

'That's amazing,' Drem told him.

'Part of every warrior's training here. Fail that and you fail your warrior trial.'

'You can do that?' Drem asked Cullen.

'Oh aye, of course I can.' Cullen grinned.

Drem shook his head, continued looking around. He saw giants on bears, archers loosing at straw targets, another group of warriors practising with the lead-weighted nets Drem had seen Cullen use on the Kadoshim half-breed.

Everywhere, the art of killing was being rehearsed.

Cullen hefted a few wooden swords, then put them back, finally settling on one for himself and for Drem.

'Sword belt off,' Cullen said as he unbuckled his own weapons-belt and lay it alongside a rack of other scabbarded swords. 'It's wood for sparring, not steel.' He threw Drem a wooden practice sword. Drem caught it, to his surprise found it was heavier than his sword. He questioned Cullen about it.

'These wooden blades are drilled out, hollowed, and then lead poured inside,' Cullen said. 'Train hard, fight easy.' He smiled. 'After a moon in the field with this you'll feel as if you're wielding a feather when you use your blades of steel. And you'll have wrists and arms of iron.'

And then Cullen came at Drem, using the forms they'd just practised in the sword dance, pausing between almost every strike, talking to Drem about his stance, his footwork, describing how he should blend it all into defence and attack.

Cullen started slowly, explaining the theory of every strike and defence after he executed them, but as time went on his attacks became faster, then combinations of blows, and Drem found himself sweating, managing to defend a few blows, but always the end was the same, Cullen's sword giving him a bruise, or a touch to neck, heart or groin.

Cullen stabbed at Drem's shoulder; as Drem swept his sword to block the blow, Cullen twisted his wrist, dropped his sword below Drem's parry and stabbed him in the belly.

I am dead a hundred times already.

As they sparred Drem became aware of people gathering around them, of eyes on him.

'The power in a strike does not come from your arms alone,' Cullen said to Drem. 'It's more legs and hips exploding up, into and through your arms. And little steps,' Cullen added. 'Never over-extend. Lose your balance, lose your head.' He grinned again, luring Drem into a lunge that ended with Cullen's sword on the back of Drem's neck.

'Drem, try fighting him with these,' a voice called out, and Drem turned, saw Keld throwing objects at him. Instinctively he caught the first, dropped his sword and caught the second. Looking in his hands he had wooden versions of a short-sword and axe.

'Closest thing I could find to the seax Olin forged for you,' Keld said. 'Now put Cullen on his arse.'

Drem nodded his thanks. He didn't really know what was expected of these weapons, had not learned any forms with them. But he was used to them, familiar through over a decade of use, even if it was only through trapping and hunting. And he had used them against Fritha and her Ferals.

Not that that turned out too well.

He glimpsed giants in the crowd around him, Balur and Alcyon there with Tain the crow master, all watching him and Cullen, and amongst them, Byrne, arms folded across her chest, face set in stern lines. A handful of women were all staring at Cullen, who was blowing them a kiss.

Drem set his feet, short-sword in his right hand, axe in his left.

Cullen grinned at him, circling, Drem shifting to face him.

Cullen lunged in, sword snaking out, cutting at Drem's shoulder. Drem's axe swept the blow wide, but somehow Cullen twisted his wrist, his sword suddenly below Drem's axe and it was cutting in at his ribs. Drem threw himself backwards, narrowly avoiding the blow. Cullen was grinning, ear to ear, and striding at him. Drem retreated, a flurry of *clacks* as he managed to block a torrent of blows.

He didn't know how long it went on for, only that his lungs were burning as he instinctively tried to stay alive a few heartbeats longer. The fact that Cullen was pausing for a heartbeat here and there to lavish a smile on someone in the crowd, or to wink at some female, gave him a few moments of recovery. Thoughts began to filter into his mind – Drem's logic analysing how he was being manoeuvred and out-skilled.

He is dictating this, while all I do is defend.

'Get in close,' a voice called out, Keld, Drem thought.

He's right, Cullen has the advantage of reach with his sword. If I am to score a hit, I must get closer to him.

And then Cullen was stepping in, a stab at Drem's shoulder. Drem made to block it, recognized the feint Cullen had used on him when he had been using his practice sword. He parried with his axe, at the last moment dropping the angle, catching and hooking Cullen's blade as it made to sweep under his arm.

There was a moment's surprise on Cullen's face, his grin wavering as Drem dragged him off balance. Drem stepped in and then his short-sword was at Cullen's throat.

'Ha, Cullen's dead,' a voice called out, Stepor, perhaps.

Cullen was standing frozen still, just staring at Drem, a shocked expression on the young warrior's face. Then he was moving back, holding his hands in the air.

'Well, aren't I the arsewipe,' Cullen said, a smile splitting his face. He looked at the crowd gathered about them. 'That'll teach me to underestimate a foe.' He looked at Keld and Stepor, who were laughing hard. 'Thought I'd say that before you two did,' Cullen said to them, which made them laugh all the harder.

Drem looked around the crowd, saw Byrne staring at him. She gave him a small, almost imperceptible nod. A ghost of a smile, then she was moving on, talking to another pair who were sparring, checking and adjusting their stances.

'Come on, Drem, my lad,' Cullen said. 'Let's see how you get on with a shield in your hand.'

I wish he'd stop calling me lad.

A noise drew Drem's attention; people were stopping in their training and pausing to stare towards the entrance field. Drem looked, too, and saw a group of men and women walking onto the field, a hundred of them at least.

They walked with the self-assured confidence of warriors, a harnessed grace about them, an air of violence. All were clothed in dark breeches and shirts of mail beneath hard-boiled leather cuirasses.

They were clearly warriors of the Order, as all of them wore the bright star emblazoned upon their cuirasses, but to Drem they looked startlingly different to the other warriors in the field. They were dark-skinned, all with long, jet-black hair tied at the nape, and all wore curved, two-handed swords across their backs.

Like Byrne's.

Cheers rang out to welcome these newcomers.

A man led them, dressed the same, with a hooked nose that reminded Drem of a hawk. His dark hair was streaked with grey and silver, but something about him set him apart from the others. Perhaps it was the way he was smiling, nodding and raising a hand to the greetings echoing out. Or maybe it was the way he seemed to all but glide across the ground, his movements fluid and contained.

'Who are they?' Drem asked Cullen.

'That's Utul and his crew, answering the call to muster, I'd guess,' Cullen said. 'Not bad in a scrap, is Utul. Not as handy to have around as me, of course, but not bad. He's captain of the Order's garrison in Balara.'

'Balara?' Drem asked, the name vaguely familiar to him.

'Aye. An old giant fortress far to the south, on the coast of the Tethys Sea.'

That's a long way from here, if my lessons were taught right, Drem thought.

Close by, the giant Tain looked up, shielding his eyes to stare. A shape was approaching in the northern sky, a pale pinprick that grew, squawking and croaking as it descended down to the weapons-field.

Rab alighted on Tain's outstretched arm.

'What news, Rab?' Byrne asked as she approached, Kill and Cure either side of her.

'*Death in the north,*' the crow squawked. '*People running, hunted by Twisted men.*'

Drem felt his back stiffen. That was the name Rab had given the Ferals.

'*They need help,*' Rab squawked.

Byrne looked to Keld and Stepor.

'Let's go get them,' Cullen said.

CHAPTER THIRTY-FOUR

FRITHA

Fritha tapped heels against her stolen horse, urging it into a canter as she turned a corner in the road and saw Starstone Lake appear before her, its dark waters glittering in the bright sunlight. In a cluster upon its northern bank squatted the mine, the sight of it setting off an abundance of memories for Fritha.

This is where it all began. My creations. Making new life. Absently she put a hand to her belly, for a heartbeat could almost remember what it had been like to hold a new life within her, to feel it growing, changing.

The most wonderful feeling in the world.

And the Ben-Elim tainted that for me.

To her left, woodland spread as far as her eye could see, sweeping up to the foothills of the Bonefells. The last time she had been here the landscape was snowbound, but now spring was asserting its grip upon the land. Snow still clung stubbornly to the trees, but it was melting, boughs creaking as the weight upon them shifted, new streams of snowmelt winding their way into the lake.

The gates to the mine opened as she approached; Fritha rode through first, nodding a greeting to the men and women manning the gates, part of her Red Right Hand that she had left behind.

A shadow skimmed the ground and Fritha looked up and

saw Morn sweeping low over the mine, circling down towards the central square, where Fritha's table was set.

Fritha led her column through the complex towards its centre, where the cave-riddled boulder of granite reared. Shaven-haired men and women greeted Fritha, acolytes she recognized, and others she did not.

More that have answered Gulla's call.

As she rode on she saw people everywhere, a frenetic energy in the air.

Something is happening.

Elsewhere were groups of men and women, standing in huddled masses. Fritha's eye was drawn to them. Hair matted and unkempt, clothes lank, torn, arms hanging limp at their sides. They were standing perfectly, unnaturally still. The acolytes seemed to avoid these groups, swirling past them like water parting for rocks in a stream.

Space opened around Fritha as she rode her horse into the clearing before the boulder, a gesture ordering her column to halt in the shadows of a street. Her bloodstained table dominated the open space, wide and deep, iron hooks and chains littered upon its surface, and beyond it was Gulla, High Captain of the Kadoshim.

He stood tall and broad, leathery wings folded and arching behind each shoulder, his face all sharp angles and tight skin, the gaping socket where the white crow had taken his eye a dark, skin-puckered hole. When he moved there was a shimmer of darkness around him, a black nimbus.

A figure stood behind him, unnaturally still. It took a moment to recognize him as Ulf the tanner of Kergard.

No, no longer Ulf the tanner. Now he is Ulf the Revenant, one of the Seven.

He was thinner than Fritha remembered, his face gaunt, features chiselled, with deep pools of shadow around his eyes and cheeks. A smear of something dark and crusted ran from his lip to his chin.

Gulla strode around the table and stood before Fritha as she reined in and dismounted, one of her Red Right Hand hurrying over to take her reins and lead her horse away.

Morn swept down from the sky, landing beside Fritha, and together they dropped to one knee, bowing their heads before Gulla.

'Greetings, my daughter,' Gulla said, and Fritha heard Morn stand.

'Father,' said Morn. An embrace.

'Priestess, where are those I sent you out to capture?' Gulla said, his voice sounding as if it hissed and scratched inside Fritha's skull.

'Forgive me, Lord,' Fritha said. She paused, struggling with the words she was about to say. Knew she had to say. 'I have failed you.'

Fritha left a silence as Gulla stared at her.

'The huntsman, versed in the earth power, and Cullen, descendant of Corban, both slipped through your fingers,' Gulla said quietly, dangerously.

Fritha gulped. 'But I have brought you gifts,' she said.

'Gifts,' Gulla said. 'They must be great indeed to make your failure fade.' A brush of his fingertips upon her shoulder bidding her to rise.

Fritha felt her blood burn at his words as she stood.

Failure.

'Behold,' Fritha said, gesturing behind her and turning.

A shouted command, the crack of a whip and her column rolled into the space.

First came a dozen of her Red Right Hand, all on stolen mounts, and swirling at their flanks were her Ferals, loping, some on two legs, others using their extended arms as extra legs. They all filed left or right, making way for Gunil upon his giant bear, dipping his head to Gulla as he reined in. Claw was pulling a travois with a cage upon it, sheets of stitched hide covering its contents. Fritha heard a sibilant hissing from within the cage and smiled. Her wyrm was still alive, stronger than it had been.

Behind the bear and the cage a wain was being pulled by a harnessed bull auroch, its chest as broad as the wain. Its head reared up as Arn touched its flanks with a whip and it let out a mournful bellow. On the bench seat beside Arn stood another cage, far smaller than the one that contained the wyrm. The crow from Dun Seren sat upon a perch, head bowed, feathers ruffled and shoulders hunched as its intelligent eyes swivelled back and forth, taking in all it could see of the mine.

He is a nosy bird, perfect for being a spy of the Order.

The crow's eyes touched on Gulla and froze, staring.

In the back of the wain lay Elise, pale and sweat-stained, and beside her one last cage, this one larger than the crow's cage, smaller than the wyrm's, and in it was Fritha's draig. She could hear it snoring as the cart rolled to a halt before her.

All he does is sleep and eat, thought Fritha affectionately.

Another wain rumbled along behind Arn's, this one full with people they had taken on their journey back to the mine. Some were from the hold Fritha had taken to contact Gulla, the rest from holds they'd encountered during their return journey.

Another gift for Gulla, to appease him for my failure.

Behind this vehicle the last of her Red Right Hand rode. The stolen mounts and wains had speeded their journey back to the mine considerably. That and the fact that they could cut straight across the Desolation, instead of following the pro- tracted route through the Bonefells that they had taken in pursuit of Drem and his companions.

Fritha approached the cage harnessed to Gunil's bear. She undid the knots that tied the hide covering to the cage's bars, then grabbed a fistful of the hide and pulled it free.

The white wyrm reared on its coils, head weaving. It was still not healed, some of its wounds leaking a stinking pus, but it had returned from the shade of death. A rattling hiss emanated from its throat as it bared long fangs at Fritha.

'A wyrm, survivor of the breed created by the giants in their War of Treasures,' Fritha said. 'We thought them long dead, but I bring you one, my Lord.' She bowed.

'Impressive,' Gulla said, leaning close to the bars.

The wyrm's head darted forward, as big as a shield, then froze, its tongue darting out, tasting the air. A ripple as it slithered away, pressed its bulk against the bars at the back of the cage, away from Gulla.

'It fears you, my Lord,' Fritha said. 'As is only right.'

Gulla smiled.

'And I bring you this,' Fritha said, walking away from the wyrm's cage, towards Arn's wain. The draig was awake in its cage now, grown already, roughly the size of a war-hound, though lower to the ground, but broader across the chest and shoulders. It scuttled over to Fritha as she approached the bars, mouth open, and she reached into a bucket and pulled out a still-dripping liver, cut from an elk that her Ferals had tracked and brought down that morning. She threw it into the cage and the draig set to ripping it apart, swallowing great chunks of it.

Gulla drew near and it stopped its feasting, one taloned foot on its food, and growled at Gulla. A deep rumbling in its belly, like gravel sliding down a slope.

'It has more courage than your wyrm,' Gulla observed. 'Or less intelligence.'

He stepped closer to Fritha and the draig threw itself at the bars, crunching into them, wood bending, cracking, jaws and claws reaching for Gulla, but the cage held.

'I don't think he likes you,' Gunil observed from the back of his bear.

Fritha shot Gunil a dark look.

'The draig has bonded to me, my Lord. He has an acute sense of loyalty.'

'Not a fault,' Gulla said. 'I like it. Use it well.'

'And my last gift to you, my Lord,' Fritha said, gesturing to the crow in its cage beside Arn.

Gulla looked at Fritha, an eyebrow raised.

'A crow?' he said.

'Look closer,' Fritha said.

Gulla leaned in, peering at the crow, which shuffled on its perch, ruffling its feathers.

'*Kadoshim, bad man,*' the crow muttered.

Gulla smiled.

'This is Flick, a crow of Dun Seren,' Fritha said.

'I think you must have much to tell me, Flick of Dun Seren,' Gulla said.

Flick hopped on his perch.

'*Tell bad man nothing,*' Flick croaked.

'We shall see.' Gulla smiled, then looked to Fritha. 'You have done well, Priestess. Maybe not redeemed yourself, quite. But well enough.' His look darkened. 'Dun Seren will know of us by now. They will march on us.'

'They will, my Lord.'

'We must be ready,' Gulla growled. 'A hundred and thirty years of war in these Banished Lands, coming down to these few last moons.' He looked at Fritha, long and appraising. Then at the wains and beasts in their cages.

'And these?' he said, waving his hand at the score of prisoners.

'Recruits.' Fritha shrugged. 'Acolytes, or perhaps to feed your new thirst. Or that of the Seven.'

'The Seven I have sent out,' Gulla said. 'All but Ulf, who has a purpose here.'

Fritha looked beyond Gulla to Ulf, standing perfectly still, like a carven statue behind her table.

'I thank you for these gifts you bring to me, and yet I see the light in your eyes, Priestess,' Gulla said. 'I see your greed.'

'They are for you, to help you win this war. But if I worked with them a little, made them into something new, I am certain they would be of greater use . . .'

'Very well, then,' Gulla said. 'Work your magic with them.'

CHAPTER THIRTY-FIVE

DREM

Hooves clattered on stone as Drem rode across the bridge that led away from Dun Seren and back into the Desolation. Beside him was Keld, sitting easily on a dappled mare, Fen loping ahead with Stepor's wolven-hounds, Grack and Ralla.

'Thank you,' Drem said to the huntsman.

'What for?' Keld frowned.

'Speaking for me.'

When Drem had heard Rab's news of people being hunted by Ferals he had instinctively volunteered to ride out with Keld. The huntsman had been given the task of putting together a scouting party to try and find them before it was too late. Drem didn't like the thought of riding into battle and violence, but he knew better than most what the Ferals were capable of and the devastation they could cause.

Byrne had pursed her lips, not happy at Drem riding back into the Desolation.

'*You have been here little more than a day,*' she had said.

'*Drem'd be welcome in my crew,*' Keld had replied. '*He's as fine a huntsman as you'll find.*'

Byrne had given Keld a stern look but she had not refused him.

'Meant what I said,' Keld replied. 'You are a fine huntsman. But more than that, I trust you with my back.'

Cullen's laugh rose up behind them, and Drem twisted in his saddle to look back.

The red-haired warrior was riding alongside two of the warriors from Balara in the south, Utul, their captain, and a woman named Shar. Cullen and Utul were laughing about something, the woman stern-faced and unamused. Behind them were five more riders – the man named Cure with four more healers. They were riding to Dalgarth, the traders' town, as the plague there was rumoured to be worsening.

Last of all, two giants towered at the rear of their small party, Alcyon with his twin axes slung behind his shoulders and Tain the crow master striding beside him.

Drem looked at the bulk of Dun Seren rearing behind them and breathed a sigh of relief to be out in the open again. While he already felt a fond sentiment for the fortress because of his parents and now Byrne, the sheer numbers of those living within its walls were not the easiest thing for him to deal with. Almost all of his life he had lived alone, just his da and the wilderness for company, so Dun Seren was overwhelming.

He turned and set his face to the north, to the rolling terrain and wide blue sky.

'We'll be leaving you now,' Cure said as Dalgarth came into view. He was a squat, muscled man who looked more suited to the pugil ring than healing, but there was a steady kindness in his gaze that had Drem trusting him almost instantly.

'Ride wide around the town,' Cure said to Keld and Stepor. 'Take no risks. I'd not have you on a sickbed when there's fighting to be done.'

'Nothing out there that'll keep me from a fight,' Cullen said.

Cure shook his head at Cullen with a wry grin. 'Stay safe, Cullen.'

Cullen twisted his face as if Cure had insulted him, or he had caught a bad smell.

'Safe!'

Cure rolled his eyes, then with a click he urged his horse into a canter towards the plague-ridden town, his four healers riding with him.

'Stay safe yourself,' Cullen called out after them.

Cure just raised a hand in farewell.

'So, let's go find these Ferals, then,' Cullen said, grinning at them all.

'*This way, this way*,' Rab squawked, flapping into the bright blue.

Moonlight silvered their camp as Cullen leaned forwards and offered Drem a strip of salted pork. He took it and chewed, pulling his cloak tighter about his shoulders. Keld had forbidden a fire because Rab had told them they were close, the crow spying strange movements in the scrubland and ravines only a few leagues ahead.

They had made camp in a sheltered gully beside a stream. Keld and Fen were out standing guard somewhere in the darkness while the rest of them ate or tried to sleep. There was not much of that going round, though, except for Stepor and his two wolven-hounds. All three of them lay curled tightly together, and all of them were snoring.

Alcyon the giant sat with one of his axes across his lap, sharpening it with a whetstone. Drem thought it was more habit than necessity, as Alcyon had performed the same routine every time they had made camp during the journey back to Dun Seren.

Tain was sitting silently beside him, looking up at the sky. It was a cloudless night, moon and stars a shimmering tapestry hanging above them.

Drem's gaze shifted to Utul and Shar, who were also tending to weapons, swords and knives on their laps being oiled and scoured.

'You both look different from other warriors of the Order,' Drem said to them.

Shar looked sharply at him, making him blink.

Did I say that wrong? Da was always telling me I could be too straightforward. It's so hard to know without him here to tell me. Drem felt a twist in his gut, a twinge of the always-present grief lurking deep in his bones.

'Well, our skin is darker than you northerners,' Shar said. She looked at him stonily.

'I don't mean that,' Drem said, trying to explain. 'There is just *something* about you. All of you . . .' He could not put into words the quiet confidence that exuded from the warriors or the graceful way they moved.

'We *are* different,' Utul said. 'We are *better*.' He smiled at Cullen.

'You'll have to prove that on the weapons-field when we get back,' Cullen told him.

'It will be my pleasure.' Utul grinned.

'And mine,' Shar said, though with less humour.

'Utul and his crew are different,' Alcyon grated. 'You have good eyes to notice, little Drem.'

Little! Lad! Why do these warriors in the Order keep calling me these names?

'How so?' Drem asked.

'They are descended from Gar and the Jehar, and they take their lineage very seriously,' Alcyon said, not breaking time in the rasp and grind of his whetstone.

'The Jehar?' Drem asked.

'You've not heard of the Jehar?' Shar said, eyes widening.

'No.'

Shar tutted.

'The Jehar were the guardians of the Bright Star, of Corban,' Alcyon said. 'Gar watched over Corban from when he was a bairn, protected him and taught him his swordcraft, and much more besides.' Alcyon paused in his axe-sharpening, eyes distant.

'You knew them?' Drem breathed.

'I did,' Alcyon said. 'They were both great men.'

'So, what were the Jehar, exactly?' Drem asked.

'The greatest of warriors,' Shar said flatly. 'Swordcraft, horsecraft, there was no one to equal them.'

Alcyon grunted and shrugged. 'Give or take a warrior or two,' he rumbled.

Shar snapped her eyes on the giant.

'Veradis. Maquin, Coralen,' Alcyon said, holding Shar's gaze.

Utul shrugged. 'Two or three, then,' he allowed.

'The Jehar came from the east,' Tain joined their conversation. 'They lived in a fabled fortress called Telassar, the white-walled. It was there that they trained for many generations, dedicating their lives in preparation for the coming of the Bright Star.'

'And they tested their swordcraft on the Shekam,' Shar added.

'The Shekam?' Drem asked.

'A giant Clan from the east,' Tain explained. 'They rode draigs into battle, like the Jotun ride bears.'

'Draigs!' Drem hissed, sharing a look with Cullen. 'We met one of those in the Bonefells.' He shook his head. 'I cannot imagine how it would feel to face a charge of them in battle.'

'I can,' Alcyon said, a smile twitching his moustache.

'You faced them?' Cullen asked, leaning forwards now.

'Aye. I stood in the shield wall with Veradis.' Alcyon nodded. 'We faced their charge.'

'What was it like?' Cullen asked eagerly.

He looks as if he wishes he was there!

Alcyon gazed down at his axe, took in a deep breath and sighed. 'Not something I would choose to do again.'

I am not surprised by that, Drem thought, remembering the

bone-shaking roar of the draig in the Bonefells. *And that was just one. A charge of many would be unspeakable.*

'Not much chance of that,' Tain said. 'The Shekam were wiped out.'

'No, not wiped out,' Alcyon breathed. 'Defeated, routed. But there were survivors. I watched them ride away on their draigs.'

'I did not know that,' Tain said. 'It should go in the histories.'

'It is not a part of my life that I wish to recall,' Alcyon grated. 'They were . . . dark days.'

'Does Mother know?'

Mother?

'Is Tain your son?' Drem asked Alcyon in his usual forthright way.

Alcyon nodded, smiled, ruffled Tain's already-scruffy black hair. Something about the action was endearing and made Drem miss his da for a sharp heartbeat all over again.

'Does Mother know?' Tain asked again.

'Raina knows.' Alcyon shrugged. 'Though it would not affect her. She is in the wilds of Arcona, not Tarbesh.'

'Tarbesh is a lot closer to Arcona than we are,' Tain said.

'Why is your mother in Arcona?' Drem asked.

'On a fool's errand.' Alcyon growled, looking back to his axe.

'She is searching for survivors of our old Clan, the Kurgan,' Tain said. 'She has been gone many years, now.'

'Too many,' Alcyon muttered.

'You could have gone,' Tain said quietly. 'Should have gone.'

Alcyon stared at his son, a dark look.

Wings flapped from above; Rab was descending to them.

'Any news?' Cullen asked the white crow.

'*Too dark*,' Rab squawked.

'Flick?' Tain asked.

Rab shook his head mournfully, then tucked his beak under a wing.

Abruptly, Stepor sat up and looked around at them all, then up at the moon. 'Time for Keld to have a nap, I'm thinking,' he said. He stood and clicked his tongue, his wolven-hounds' ears pricking.

'With me,' he said, and Grack and Ralla followed him into the night.

Screams in the distance, growing louder.

'*Faster, faster,*' Rab squawked at them as he winged low, then rose into the sky again, leading them onwards. Drem was riding up a shallow slope alongside Cullen and Keld, Stepor a little ahead of them. Utul and Shar rode wide on the right wing, and Alcyon and Tain were running at a startling pace on the left.

A riderless horse burst over the ridge of the slope they were climbing, white-eyed and sweat-stained. It galloped down towards them, veering just in time. Drem saw bloodied claw marks staining the animal's haunch.

Stepor reached the ridge, Grack and Ralla either side of him, and reined in. Within heartbeats Drem, Keld and Cullen were alongside, all of them pausing to take in the scene before them. On either side Utul and Alcyon crested the ridge a heart-beat behind them.

A shallow slope ran away from them, down onto an open plain. Figures moved, Drem instantly recognizing the unnat-ural gait of thick-muscled, long-limbed Ferals. They were circling and charging a handful of wains that were gathered in a loose half-circle, one of them overturned, one wheel slowly spinning. Figures were amongst the carts, some running, some standing, fighting. Terrible screams rang out, and Drem saw a woman burst from her cover, running hard for a slope.

A Feral appeared on the overturned wain, crouched for a moment, muscles bunching, then it leaped. It hit the ground a dozen paces behind the woman, a heartbeat later was slamming into her, both of them going down, the woman screaming, limbs flailing. The Feral's jaws opened unnaturally wide and bit down onto her face, more screams, higher in pitch, then a wet gurgling.

'Plan, boss?' Stepor said to Keld.

'Kill the bastards,' Keld growled and kicked his mount into a canter. Drem followed, the three of them hurtling down the slope, the three wolven-hounds ahead, growling and snarling.

Drem was on the plain in a dozen heartbeats, reaching a full gallop in a dozen more.

A flicker of movement in Drem's peripheral vision – Utul and Shar pulling ahead of them.

A handful of Ferals bounded to meet them, their jaws and claws dripping red. They saw Utul and Shar, howled and threw themselves at the two warriors.

Drem saw Utul draw his curved sword, heard him shout something.

'*LASAIR*,' and then Utul's sword burst into flame.

'TRUTH AND COURAGE,' Utul and Shar yelled as they rode at the Ferals. Utul sliced an arm from the first Feral, the stump going up in flames, the stench of burned fur and flesh sharp in the air, and then Drem was too close, dragging on his reins for his mount to turn. He pulled a hand-axe from his belt, hefted it, felt his weight shift in his saddle.

I'm not used to fighting on horseback.

Keld, Cullen and Stepor rode through the line of wains a few moments ahead of him, Fen leaping and snarling.

Drem made a snap decision, leaping from his saddle, hitting the ground in a stumbling run, drawing his seax with his other hand.

Within the wains all was chaos: men, women, children, all screaming, running, Ferals killing indiscriminately, small groups of survivors fighting back.

Glimpses of Keld, Stepor and Cullen working together, the three wolven-hounds throwing themselves at Feral beasts, savage snarling.

Drem ran towards them.

A Feral looked up from feasting, jaws crimson. Drem took half of its face off with his axe, heard it yowling as he skidded to a halt, turning and stabbing with his seax. It slashed long claws at him even as its legs gave way beneath it. The claws raked Drem's chest, slicing through leather and wool, opening red lines. Drem yelled as his axe rose and fell again and again as the Feral slumped, gnashing its teeth as it died.

He stood there, breathing hard, saw the Feral had torn open a young boy. He looked away.

There was a bellow to his left as Alcyon and Tain burst through the wains, Alcyon swinging his two axes and Tain stabbing with a long spear. A Feral's head spun through the air, its body running on. Tain skewered another beast with his spear, pinning it to the ground. It began to climb its way along the spear shaft towards Tain, then Alcyon's axe crunched into its head, an explosion of fur, bone and brain.

More screaming drew Drem's eyes. A horse – Utul's mount – was rearing, lashing out and crunching into a Feral's chest, bones snapping. Beside Utul, Shar was laying about her with her sword. A Feral's arm flew lazily through the air.

More Ferals slammed into Utul's horse, blood spurting, the horse neighing, screaming, toppling over.

Drem ran, as if in slow motion, as he saw the horse roll, pinning Utul's leg, a Feral's swipe opening the horse's belly, intestines spilling. Another Feral moving towards Utul. Shar was trying to reach him, but there were two Ferals leaping at her.

The Feral stood over Utul, a foot stamping on his sword arm, pinning it, jaws opening wide.

Drem crashed into the creature, both of them tumbling to the ground, rolling. Foul breath washed over him as teeth snapped a hair's breadth from his face. He raised his knee high, managed to lever the creature away and stab with his seax, deep into its waist.

The Feral roared, teeth snapping frenziedly. Drem twisted his blade, felt blood sluice over his hand, his grip slipping. He pushed, scrambled in the dirt, managed to slide away from the beast, rolled, came to one knee and hurled his hand-axe.

It crunched into the Feral's face. The beast collapsed backwards, spasming, then was finally still.

Drem staggered to his feet and wrenched his seax and axe free from the corpse.

Utul was still pinned; Shar reached him at the same time as Drem. He pushed and heaved at Utul's dead horse and Shar dragged Utul free.

'My thanks,' Utul said to Drem. He looked down at his mount and bent to lay his palm on the dead animal's side, Drem seeing tears blur the warrior's eyes.

'They shall pay for that,' Utul snarled. He swept up his sword, which was no longer flaming, and looked around.

Cullen was still mounted, laying about with his sword, Keld and Stepor fighting side by side close by.

Drem and the two Jehar ran to support the group, Utul limping but still bellowing a war-cry.

Drem chopped his axe into the spine of a Feral rolling with Fen and ripped it free. He slashed claws that were swiping at his face, swayed away from snapping teeth and stabbed his seax up into the jaw of a Feral, felt his blade cut through the soft tissue of its mouth, on, up into its brain. He kicked the dead beast away.

Then the two giants were there.

Drem was chopping into the chest of a fallen Feral, axe and seax windmilling, hacking and stabbing, blood and fragments of bone spraying. Blood in his face, clouding his vision, but he kept on stabbing. Something grabbed his shoulder, shook him. He snarled as he turned, raising his blades.

'It's over, laddie,' Alcyon said, Drem freezing, staring. He looked about, saw Alcyon was right. He glimpsed a Feral bounding away, but everywhere else the deformed creatures were still and twisted in death.

Drem looked at the ring of people they had aided. Tough men and women, the type Drem was familiar with from the Desolation, weathered and hard. All were bloodied, wide-eyed and breathing hard.

An old woman stepped out of the ring, grey hair matted, her face stained with blood and soot, clothes tattered and torn. She had a knife in one hand, a small axe in the other, like him.

'Drem, Drem, is that you?' she called out, eyes fixing on him.

'Hildith?' Drem said, taking a step towards her.

'Of course it's me,' she said, brushing back strands of her matted hair and smudging soot around her face.

'We should have believed you,' she told him grimly. 'When you came to the Assembly and warned us about the mine. You told us Olin was murdered.' She bowed her head. 'Kergard is destroyed, they rolled through it like a plague.' She looked up, mouth an angry, thin line. 'They burned down my mead-hall.'

'You're safe now,' Drem said, helping Hildith stand as she swayed and half fell onto him.

CHAPTER THIRTY-SIX

FRITHA

Fritha stepped into the cave mouth, Gulla at her side, Gunil behind them. It was wide and high enough for Gunil to walk comfortably without stooping.

On either side iron bars reflected torchlight, cages housing more of Fritha's Ferals. Some she could tell were obedient to her, by the way they whined and snuffled as she walked by, but others threw themselves into the bars, snapping and snarling and grasping with long talons or ruined hands.

They are not so tame.

They walked deeper into the tunnels that bored far beneath the ground, proof of their search for remnants of the starstone. They had found none, and yet fate had seen fit to give Fritha the Starstone Sword, ready-forged! It was a sign that she was following the right path, that if there was any such thing as a power looking down upon them, it was looking after her.

Torches set into the rock walls sent shadows dancing, and as they descended further Fritha saw pockets of people, huddled close together, still as statues.

Revenants.

Some were Gulla's brood, others were Ulf's.

Even though Fritha had played a part in creating them, she felt a sense of unease at the sight of them, eyes dark holes, skin stretched too tight across their bodies, revealing every line of muscle and tendon.

And then they were walking into a circular chamber, the path leading both ways, curling around a pit, roughly as deep as two giants.

Fritha leaned over and saw the floor of the pit was seething, a mass of furred limbs, of tooth and claw.

'You are to be commended, Priestess,' Gulla said. 'Your breeding programme has worked.'

Fritha smiled, feeling a deep warmth for her creations. Hundreds of Ferals, if not thousands, roamed the pit, an abundance of sizes, from cub-like bairns to full-grown adults. She had hoped that they would breed, had worked words of power into her newest creations, enhancing and accelerating their reproductive and growth systems, but she had never dared to imagine that it would work this well. A stench emanated from the pit, of fur and sweat, of blood and urine and excrement, but Fritha did not care. Here and there on the pit floor there were twisted carcasses, some little more than bones picked clean, but others were fresher, were distinguishable as various manifestations of her Ferals. She shrugged, sad to see some casualties, but it was for the survival of the strongest and the most robust. There was no room for the weak and feeble in her new order.

'There are a lot of them,' Gunil commented.

For once his declaration of the obvious did not annoy Fritha.

She smiled at Gulla and Gunil.

'Give me the Sword,' Gulla said to Fritha.

They were standing in Gulla's chambers, another cave that burrowed far into the ground, though this one was not so deep or so crowded as the labyrinth Fritha had housed her Ferals within. Gulla's chamber was luxuriant, furs and silks draping his bed and chairs. There was also a bolthole in this tunnel, a wisp of air filtering down from Gulla's escape route if the Ben-Elim or Order of the Bright Star discovered this lair.

They are too late now.

Fritha rested a hand protectively on the hilt of the Star-stone Sword. She did not want to give it up. It was her right. She had discovered it, schemed to steal it from Olin and Drem. It was she who had taken the risks and earned it.

But more than that, she *needed* it.

'It is mine,' Fritha said, daring to speak against Gulla, though his eyes bored into her. 'I was *chosen* for the task by the Covens.' She remembered that fateful day, six years ago, standing within the ruins of a giant fortress, the Kadoshim gathered together for the first time since the Battle of Varan's Fall. More than five hundred Kadoshim had cast their lot.

'They voted for me,' she repeated. 'I was given the greatest honour as a symbol of the Kadoshim's commitment to a new world, and to mankind. A covenant to build this world together, not like the Ben-Elim, as dictators, but you and your kin in harmony with mankind.'

'Nothing has changed,' Gulla said. 'You were chosen. You still are. But you have failed in your set task, allowed the Order to discover our existence and whereabouts. That cannot be over-looked. You must prove that our faith in you is warranted. Prove that you are worthy.'

This was what Fritha had feared: the possibility that all that she longed for and had fought so hard for would be taken from her.

I must accept his judgement. He is high captain, greatest amongst the Kadoshim until Asroth is awoken.

Fritha bowed her head, felt Gulla reach out a hand, long-taloned fingers caressing her shaven scalp.

'But this is not a punishment. I am setting you a new task. Accomplish it and you will still have the greatest honour. But you must fulfil your task *first*,' he growled. 'If you fail it, you will be dead.'

'What is this task, then?' Fritha asked.

'To destroy the Order of the Bright Star.'

'But we were to leave together, I must be at the great battle.'

'Now Dun Seren knows we are here they will send their scouts out, their damned crows and their sharp eyes. If the mine is still and silent and the land is empty, then the Order of the Bright Star will not march north.'

He cupped her chin, tilted her head up to hold her gaze.

'The Order *must* march north, must be occupied and led into the Desolation, else they will be a danger on my flank. If they did not know we were here, were unaware of our strength, then it would be different – you would be travelling at my side. But they know.'

He shrugged. 'You must stay here, or be seen somewhere in the Desolation.

Fritha acknowledged the logic and knew that she had played a part by allowing Drem and the others to escape.

But face the Order of the Bright Star? She felt a rush of fear, and also of excitement. The most difficult of tasks, yes, but what if she succeeded? Her battle fame would live on for a thousand years.

The Order marching north, into the Desolation, away from their high walls and defences, where they will be vulnerable. Not weak. Never weak. But vulnerable.

Did you plan this all along, Gulla?

'And you will have more than your Ferals at your side. I sent word south, and more acolytes have come to us, you saw many when you arrived. I will not take all of them with me. And most of all, I am leaving Ulf with you, and with him comes his brood of Revenants, all that he or his disciples have turned. His blood is spreading, infecting the Desolation.'

Fritha nodded, already thinking through strategies, terrain, deployment.

'It is dangerous, with no guarantee that you will succeed, and this is why you must give me the Sword,' Gulla said. 'If you are victorious and are at the appointed place on the appointed day, then the great honour will still be yours, and all the greater for your victory. But if you are not there . . .'

I will do this. I will lay the Order of the Bright Star low.

She unbuckled her weapons-belt and slipped the scabbarded sword from it, held it for a moment in her hands, turning it. The leather-bound hilt was simple, unadorned, the dark metal of the pommel and cross-guard almost coal black. She half-drew the blade, the steel dull as night, seeming to suck in the light around it, a dark cloud halo pulsing, emanating from the blade.

Then she slid the sword home and handed it to Gulla.

CHAPTER THIRTY-SEVEN

RIV

Riv felt a thrill of excitement as she saw the grey fortress of Dun Seren upon a hill in the distance, meadows of rich pasture rolling around it. It was past highsun, the sun dipping towards the horizon, silhouetting the tower and keep.

I have heard so much of the Order of the Bright Star but only seen a few of their huntsmen in the flesh. This will be an education.

She was high in the sky amidst tattered wisps of cloud, Kol and a score of Ben-Elim around her. Her arms were goose-fleshed with cold, and Riv resolved to make herself a fur-lined jerkin as soon as she possibly could. She had never flown so far or for such a prolonged time before. Five full days, from dusk until dawn, and now the muscles in her back were aching, dull and deep, but nevertheless it was glorious. She loved to fly, to feel free, all the cares of the world somehow left below her, insignificant as ants.

Only one memory from her life below had kept her company through the long days of flight, all else blurring.

Bleda.

If she closed her eyes, she could still feel the sensation of his lips pressed against hers, the tangle of their bodies. Just the thought of him sent moth wings fluttering in her belly. She wanted to see him, now.

A shout from her right, a glance to see Kol signalling, and they began their long, sweeping descent towards Dun Seren, clouds whipping past them, the fortress growing larger. Soon Riv was speeding over outlying paddocks, herds of horses beneath them.

There must be thousands.

Horns rang out from the fortress, deep and resonant, and then they were flying over Dun Seren's outer wall, a field opening up beneath them, filled with figures. Riv saw many giants scattered amongst them.

Is this their weapons-field? Riv was surprised to see it was close to the same size as the field at Drassil, even though Drassil as a whole dwarfed Dun Seren. And the numbers upon the field were a surprise to her, too – easily in the thousands.

Rarely will there be this many upon the weapons-field of Drassil at one time. They take their training seriously here.

They passed over the weapons-field, flying over sod and grey-tiled rooftops, a stream of figures hurrying along a wide road towards the keep and tower that dominated the hill of Dun Seren.

With a flurry of shifting wings they were above a courtyard and angling down, circling around a great statue of a warrior and wolven.

Is that Corban and his wolven, Storm?

Riv had heard tales of the founder of the Order of the Bright Star, that Corban had played some small part in the Day of Wrath, when the Ben-Elim had saved the Banished Lands from the hordes of Kadoshim that had broken out of the Otherworld.

Riv followed Kol and his Ben-Elim warriors as they swirled around the statue, wings adjusting, feet dropping, and then Riv was alighting in the courtyard, her wings folding into her back, Kol and his Ben-Elim around her, masking her from view.

A crowd was gathering in the courtyard, figures ranging upon the walls, more pouring in from the surrounding streets, but Riv's eyes were fixed on the stone keep before her, wide stone steps leading up to its open doors. Four figures stood at the top of the steps, three giants and a woman. Two of the giants Riv recognized: Balur One-Eye and Queen Ethlinn. The last giant was slimmer than most of his kin, a scraggly black crow perched upon his shoulder.

Is that one of Dun Seren's talking crows? Riv thought. She had met one once before, whilst in council with Israfil.

Flick, I think his name was.

Kol strode up the steps, Riv and his Ben-Elim following.

The woman with the giants stepped forwards. She was plain and stern-faced, dressed in simple training leathers. She moved with an economical grace, a certain way about her that Riv associated with the weapons-masters at Drassil like Ert. A confidence and control of their every movement. Riv saw streaks of grey in her black hair. A curved sword jutted over one shoulder.

Similar to the Sirak's, Riv thought, *although the hilt of this one is longer. A two-handed blade.*

'Welcome to Dun Seren, Kol,' the woman said.

'Greetings, Byrne,' Kol said, a dip of his head, a shifting of his shoulders, not quite a bow. He looked to Ethlinn and Balur One-Eye, nodded a greeting to them both.

'My apologies for arriving unannounced,' Kol said. 'But I bring momentous news from Drassil. The Lord Protector Israfil is dead.'

There were gasps around the courtyard, but Riv kept her eyes and attention focused on Byrne, Ethlinn and Balur. Of the three of them, Balur's expression changed the most, a deep frown creasing the slabbed bones of his face.

'How?' Ethlinn said.

'He was murdered. A conspiracy between Kadoshim and traitors. It went as deep as our own White-Wings. Garidas was chief amongst the traitors.'

Balur's frown deepened.

Riv had known how loyal Garidas was to Israfil, and if she had known, then Balur likely did, as well.

'This is shocking news,' Byrne said, no emotion showing on her face. 'I was concerned that all was not well at Drassil.'

'Aye, it is, which is why I have taken it upon myself to bring you the news myself. There is more you should know.'

'Go on,' Byrne said.

'I have been named the new Lord Protector.'

'My congratulations,' Byrne said.

'And one of my first acts has been to revoke the Lore against inter-relations between Ben-Elim and humankind. Riv, step forth,' Kol called.

The Ben-Elim about Riv parted and Riv stepped forwards. She felt the courtyard go silent, thousands of eyes upon her. She hated it, hated being this focal point of ideology and belief. But she was not one to bow her head and walk meekly, so she stood straight and tall and strode to stand beside Kol. Her eyes she kept fixed on Byrne, and when Riv reached Kol's side she snapped her wings open, made them beat, once, slowly, then furled them back in again.

The silence lengthened.

'Clearly, we need to talk,' Byrne said.

Riv followed Kol into a high-vaulted room, a fire-pit roaring, a table beyond it surrounded with high-backed chairs. Byrne led them to the table, gesturing for Kol and Riv to sit.

Balur and Ethlinn entered the room, the other giant with the crow upon his shoulder following them. They all took seats around the table, silent while Byrne poured warm mead for them all.

Byrne offered a cup to Riv.

'To warm your bones. It must be cold so high in the sky.'

'It is,' Riv said, surprised at Byrne's words. She had not expected . . . kindness. 'My thanks,' she added.

'What is your name, child?' Byrne said.

'Her name is Riv,' Balur said. Riv met Balur's eye, preparing herself for his disapproval or disgust, as she had done many times in the last moon. She was relieved to find an intrigued curiosity instead. 'Riv belongs to the White-Wings, she has the making of a fine warrior,' the giant rumbled.

Riv blinked at that, stunned at Balur's words. She had not thought for a moment that he had ever noticed her on the weapons-field. But more than that, it felt fine to not be defined by her wings, for once, but instead by her skill.

'I'm a White-Wing no more,' Riv said wryly. 'These don't fit so well in the shield wall.' She gave her wings a pulse.

Balur cracked a smile at that. 'No, I imagine not. The shield wall is not the only way to fight, though. Come see me on the field and we'll see what else you can do.'

Riv grinned at the honour.

Byrne moved on, poured her own cup and sat at the table. 'Israfil is dead, then,' she said.

'Aye,' Kol answered. He told them his version of events, much as he had the day Riv had watched him in the Great Hall at Drassil, using his oratory flair and charm. It did not seem to work so well on Byrne, Ethlinn and Balur as it had on the crowds at Drassil, though. They listened, asked questions, but at no point did Riv think they were ever swept up in Kol's rhetoric and glamour.

And then he spoke of Riv, explaining how he could not make the decision to execute her for the sins of those that had begotten her.

'I could not punish Riv, an innocent, for the sins of her father,' Kol said. 'I could not do it. And as I thought of the reasons behind that, I realized that it is time for things to change. That we Ben-Elim cannot be so rigid on all things. There must be compromise, a moving forward together. So, I am a new Lord Protector, with a new vision.'

Byrne just leaned back in her chair, fingers steepled as she listened to Kol speak of his vision for a new world and a new relationship between Ben-Elim and mankind.

When he had finished, a silence settled. Byrne spoke first.

'I welcome your new-found open-mindedness,' she said, something shifting across her face, behind her eyes. 'It is long overdue. As you well know, things are different here from life in Drassil, and Elyon's Lore has never been as . . . central to how we live our lives, or rigorously adhered to. We live our lives by Truth and Courage. Love and loyalty, friendship and honour are our guiding lights.'

Riv liked the ring of that, though by Kol's face he was not impressed that Byrne so easily dismissed the Lore of Elyon.

'But I, too, have news that you should hear, and I think it will affect both of our worlds significantly.' She paused a moment, studying Kol. 'We have found Gulla.'

'What?' Kol said, leaning forwards in his chair. The enigmatic, warm-hearted statesman of a few moments ago was gone, replaced with a cold hatred.

'Where is he?' Kol snarled.

'The Desolation,' Balur One-Eye said.

Kol snapped his fingers. 'You are mustering for a campaign,' he said. 'I saw all of the signs on our flight in. More warriors in Dun Seren than there have been for a hundred years, the forge fires burning, grain barns filling.'

'We are,' Byrne agreed.

'I should have been told.' Kol scowled. 'You cannot march without the Ben-Elim. The Kadoshim are my ancient foe. *Gulla* is my ancient foe.' He leaned back in his chair, a tremor running through him as he tried to master his emotions. 'You should have sent word. How long have you known?'

'Hints and rumours a little over a moon ago. It was only confirmed yesterday.'

'You have been mustering longer than one day,' Kol said.

'*Better to be ready than dead,*' the scruffy-looking crow croaked.

'Exactly, Craf,' Byrne said, the hint of a smile ghosting her lips. 'And I could not send word – all of my crows are scouting the Desolation. They will be back soon, and I planned on sending word then. Although we have heard nothing from Drassil, even though events that you describe as momentous have happened there. Israfil's death, three moons ago?'

'About that,' Riv said, nodding.

'And yet you did not think to send *us* word,' Byrne said quietly.

'I will send word to Drassil of Gulla's discovery now,' Kol said, ignoring Byrne. 'We will march out together, once my White-Wings are here.'

'We will march when *I* decide,' Byrne said. 'It will take over a moon for your White-Wings to march here from Drassil, and that may be too late.' She shrugged. 'I would welcome your White-Wings against our common foe, and we are mustering now, waiting for word from my scouts, so by all means send word if you wish, but know this: I will not hold back if the need to ride out before they arrive is necessary.'

'I know that it is new to you, but remember, I am the Lord Protector, now,' Kol said, a dangerous note in his voice.

'I do not answer to you,' Byrne said fiercely. 'Lord Protector or no, it means nothing to me. The Order of the Bright Star is your *ally*, not your subject.'

Kol stood up, leaned his fists on the table, staring at Byrne, white wings rippling behind him.

'You are as stiff-necked as your kin and founder of this Order, Corban,' he said. 'I knew your Corban, when the Day of Wrath was finished, saw him as my kin healed his wounds. He contributed *little* to our victory that day and was ever more a thorn in our flesh than a help against the Kadoshim. And they are *my* enemy. The Great War is *our* war. You and your kind are little more than witnesses to that.'

Byrne was on her feet, then, her face pale, lips a thin line.

'Tell that to the names on our Stone of Heroes,' she said bitterly. 'The thousands who have fought and bled and died against the Kadoshim. Because *you and your kin* schemed to bring them here. And if you ever talk about my great-uncle like that again—'

'You did not even know Corban,' Kol said, a wave of his hand. 'All you have is your inflated tales and your nostalgic sense of blood-ties.'

'*I* knew him,' Ethlinn said firmly. She did not stand, but her voice carried an authority that turned Kol's and Byrne's heads. 'And you *lie* when you say he did little. He turned the battle. He and his sister. Without them, Asroth would never have been chained, and the portal would still be open.'

'Pfah.' Kol spat.

'But more than that,' Ethlinn said, 'I *knew* him and am proud to say that he called me friend. You would do well not to speak ill of Corban the Bright Star, not in my hearing, and especially not when you are seated here, in these halls.'

'*Craf knew Corban, too. Corban good man. Corban best of friends,*' the crow squawked. He looked at Kol with a beady eye. '*Kol rude.*'

I have seen it all. A Ben-Elim admonished by a talking crow, thought Riv.

Kol stared a long moment at Ethlinn and then shifted his gaze to Byrne. He took a deep breath and sat down.

'My apologies, if I have offended you,' he said. 'For over a hundred years we Ben-Elim have been allied to your Order, have worked together with you to defeat our mutual enemy. I confess to feeling wounded that you have not told me sooner of your information about Gulla. And now this talk of marching without us.' He waved a hand. 'We Ben-Elim have been good to you.'

Byrne did not sit, but some of the tension leaked from her shoulders.

'You have had a long journey and must be tired,' she said. 'Rooms have been prepared for you. We shall talk more on the morrow, but for now, eat, rest, sleep.' And she walked away, her boots a soft slap on the flagstoned floor.

CHAPTER THIRTY-EIGHT

FRITHA

Fritha stood on the lakeshore, Morn and a few score of her Red Right Hand standing beside her, watching as teams of harnessed auroch dragged three huge cages on wains onto the piers that stood above the water of Starstone Lake. Timber posts and boards creaked under the strain as the wains rolled out over the lake, coming to a halt beside three fat-bellied ships moored and bobbing on the swell.

Orders were shouted, acolytes attaching straps and hooks, levers and pulleys, and then teams of men were using harbour cranes to winch the cages into the air. With a squeal of iron and wood, the cages were swung over the boats and lowered into the hulls of the moored vessels. Gunil manned one winch himself, stripped to the waist and sweating as he wound the pulley and treadmill.

'Farewell, my lovelies,' Fritha breathed, blowing a kiss to the cacophony of howls and growls that reverberated from the cages. Hundreds of her Ferals were contained within those cages, the ones she had determined were beyond obedience to her in the coming conflict.

But Gulla found a use for all of her creations, even the disobedient ones.

Crews of acolytes manned the boats, tightening leather straps about the cages and attaching them to an array of iron hooks sunk deep into timber decks.

Fritha looked to her left, where the prow of a ship emerged from one of the boat sheds, a sleeker vessel than the ones the Ferals had been loaded upon. A spume of water exploded into the air as the ship's prow cut into the lake, and Fritha saw more boats emerging from a row of boat sheds along the lakeshore, seven, eight, ten, more of them, all shallow-draughted, oars appearing and dipping into the water, rowing slowly towards the piers.

Gulla strode from the mine towards her, his wings folded and arched like a great cloak. Behind him a shadow-swarm followed, like a dark cloud, a multitude of shambling Revenants marching, their limbs strangely stiff and jerking, their skin pale and stretched, many of them gnashing their too-many teeth as they walked.

Gulla snapped a command and one of the Revenants peeled away from Gulla's side – Ulf, coming to stand close to Fritha. He did not look at her.

Gulla and his dark host passed Fritha in unsettling silence as they moved from the piers into the boats like a dark mist, filling the vessels with shadow.

Gulla took to flight, his wings snapping wide, rising high above the lake, and then he was gliding down to Fritha, alighting before her and Morn.

Gunil stomped his way back along a pier to join them.

'Farewell, my daughter,' Gulla said, reaching down and cupping Morn's face in his hands. He leaned forwards and kissed her brow.

She is consumed by the need to avenge her brother still.

Morn had begged to remain with Fritha once she had been told of the plan, knowing that Drem was sure to be found with the Order of the Bright Star.

'I will avenge your son,' Morn said.

Gulla turned to Fritha.

'Ulf is yours to command,' Gulla said to her.

She looked at Ulf, unsure that he even heard Gulla's words,

giving no sign that he had. She seriously doubted that he would acknowledge her existence, let alone follow her orders.

She raised an eyebrow.

'Give Ulf an order,' Gulla said.

Fritha shrugged. 'Tear out your left eye,' she said to the grey-skinned Revenant.

Without hesitation Ulf lifted a hand up to his face, a taloned finger reaching for his eyeball.

Fritha opened her mouth to yell *Stop*, but it was too late. With a sucking pop Ulf's eyeball flopped onto his cheek. He grabbed it in his fist and tore it free of its socket, then held it out on the flat of his palm for Fritha. She felt revulsion and shock, but also a thrill at such unwavering loyalty.

That is the loyalty I want.

'Much rests on your victory,' Gulla said to her. Fritha knew what was left unsaid.

Do not fail.

'I will see you on Midsummer's Day,' she said to Gulla.

He flashed a smile at her, not as charming as it had once been now that his mouth was filled with jagged rows of needle-sharp teeth.

'Gunil, watch over Fritha and my daughter, and let no harm come to Ulf.'

Gunil grunted a nod.

'Victory or death,' Gulla said to Fritha, and then he was leaping into the air, his wings driving him higher, into a climbing spiral, then swooping and dropping low over his ships.

'WE ARE FOR WAR,' he bellowed, his crew of acolytes answering with a cheer. Then Gulla's small fleet of Ferals and Revenants set sail. Fritha watched as they rowed east, sails unfurling as they headed towards the Grinding Sea.

'With me,' Fritha said and turned on her heel, crunching up the slope towards the mine.

Fritha marched through the tunnels, her followers gathering behind her, until she had over three hundred men in her wake. She strode into the clearing before the caves, saw all that she had ordered had been done, an array of cages set about her great table.

She turned to face her followers.

'Two days and we march. This is the beginning of the end for the Ben-Elim,' she called out. A rippling cheer.

'The beginning of our vengeance, when we shall make the world ours, and take what we are owed. Freedom and glory, vengeance and gold,' she cried, louder, which received a louder cheer.

Of those, vengeance and gold are the sharpest spurs.

'Two days,' she repeated. 'Until then, train hard, fight easy,' she said, dismissing them.

Fritha turned to look at the table.

The white wyrm sat coiled in its cage, watching her with a malignant eye. On the other side of the table her draig's cage had been placed, wooden bars exchanged for iron, and far bigger than the one Gunil had originally made, as the beast continued to grow in shocking spurts. It was already the size of a small pony.

Fritha dug a bucket into a barrel of fish guts, meat and offal and poured it into the cage. The draig began to eat with an abundance of repulsive slapping, tearing and slurping noises.

'Are you hungry, Flick?' Fritha said, waving the bucket close to the crow's cage, digging her hand in and showing him a pile of fish guts.

Flick glared up at her. He was hunched at the bottom of his cage, one wing hanging limp, feathers torn and bloody. Fritha felt a brief wave of sympathy for the creature, and a flicker of respect for how long the crow had held out against their questions.

This is war, and he has served my enemy, she reminded herself.

Flick looked at the pile of guts in Fritha's palm, but he said nothing.

'You're a brave bird,' Fritha said and dropped the contents into his cage.

A last supper for you, she thought.

'Arn, do it now,' Fritha called, and the warrior strode to the cages set in the cliff face, accompanied by four others. They entered a cage and emerged with one of the Bonefells' great bats, a chain about one of its claws. It was a bull-sire, its wing-span far wider than Morn's. They dragged the beast from the cage by a chain, hanging on as it lifted into the air and tried to fly for freedom, then jabbing with spears to keep it from attacking them.

They laboured across the clearing to the table. Arn swung the chain, dragging the bat down, his two comrades grabbing at its wings, and then they were slamming it onto the table, pulling its wings wide, hammering iron nails into it, pinning it to the timber. The bat screeched and hissed, head twisting frantically, jaws snapping in a frenzy.

Fritha nodded to herself.

'Gunil,' she commanded, and the giant slid the bolts on the draig's cage. The draig's muzzle came up, red tongue flickering, and then it was scuttling out of the cage, a shocking display of speed for so much bulk. It stood in the open ground, head swaying from side to side. Fritha stepped in front of it, still holding her bucket.

'Come to me, Wrath,' she said gently.

The draig's eyes fixed on her and it became perfectly still, then burst into motion, talons on its bowed legs raking the ground as it exploded towards her. It skidded to a halt, circling her and rubbing itself against her legs like an excited puppy. She reached out and patted its head, as high as her waist, now, and scratched its scaly neck.

Leaning down, she rested her head against its muzzle, felt its teeth pressing into her cheek.

'I will make you magnificent,' she whispered to the draig,

'your name and renown will live on forever.' Then she drew a razored knife from her belt and plunged it into the draig's neck.

A jet of dark arterial blood, the draig shuddering, as Fritha threw herself out of the reach of its snapping jaws.

'Gunil, now,' Fritha cried, and the giant stepped forwards, squatting and putting his arms beneath the belly of the draig as it began to slump, its strength failing as it bled out. Gunil heaved, veins bulging, legs straining, wobbling as he tried to stand with the draig.

'Help him,' Fritha shouted, a handful of her Red Right Hand running to Gunil's aid, taking the weight of the draig's tail, lifting, and with a great heave the dying beast was placed next to the pinned bat.

Fritha sped to the table, excitement jolting through her, and she reached for her tools, picking up a serrated-edged knife and a hammer.

'Morn, bring me the crow,' she said, and Morn opened Flick's cage, reaching in. Flick flapped away to the rear of the cage, fear giving him strength, but he could not evade Morn's grasping hand and it closed about the big bird, dragging him out.

'*Bad people, bad people,*' Flick squawked as he pecked at Morn's hand.

'No, not bad people,' Fritha said, 'but sometimes dark deeds must be done to accomplish great ends. I am sorry, Flick, you are brave and wise, but you have something I need.' She held up her knife and the bird squawked in fear.

'Your bloodline.'

Fritha drew the knife blade across her forearm, flesh parting and blood welling, though it was hard to differentiate her blood from the gore that coated her. But she knew her blood was joining that on the table, pooling and seeping into the concoction of her new creation.

'*Reiptílí, bás sciatháin, guth éan, ar cheann,*' Fritha chanted, her arms drenched in blood to her elbows. '*Reiptílí, bás sciatháin, guth éan, ar cheann,*' she breathed again, and again as she hunched over the mound of flesh spread upon her table.

Then she stepped back.

Body parts were scattered on the ground, parts of bat, crow and draig intermingled. Fritha's off-cuts.

Upon the table lay a huge mound of flesh and bone, still as death.

Fritha sucked in a deep shuddering breath.

She raised her arms.

'*Anáil agus beo,*' she yelled with all the strength of her lungs and stepped forwards, slamming her clenched fists onto the lifeless form on the table, her blow rippling through it.

A silence settled on the clearing as she and those around her watched.

A gasping tremor shifted through the thing before her, its chest rising and falling.

A thrill of excitement, the greatest, most wonderful feeling Fritha had ever known swept through her. The creature on the table raised its head.

Her draig, transformed.

Made new.

It rolled, flopped to the ground, and slowly took its weight upon its bowed legs.

'Wrath,' Fritha said, hoping.

Will he still love me, or will he remember our last moment, my knife across his throat? My blood is mixed with his now – that should bind him to me deeper than all things, should override any resentment of that one, fleeting moment of pain.

Its head weaved, side to side, then its small dark eyes filled with a new intelligence. They fixed upon her, and Fritha smiled.

The draig spread its wings wide, a ripple of muscle, testing its new limbs. A hesitant beat of air, then harder, and the draig's bulk shifted, its chest and forelegs lifting a handspan from the ground.

With a scraping growl its head swivelled, regarding its wings.

'Wrath,' Fritha said, taking a step towards the creature.

It regarded her for a long, timeless moment, then took an unsteady step towards her. It opened its jaws wide, saliva dripping.

'*Wrath hungry,*' the draig croaked.

CHAPTER THIRTY-NINE

BLEDA

Bleda passed sharkskin over the bow, sanding off the rough edges of glue and sinew. It was the full dark before dawn beyond the forge's doors, but Bleda knew that time was precious, and he could not leave this unfinished.

He put the sharkskin down, then ran his hand across the bow, slowly, feeling all the layers of maple, horn and sinew that had gone into fashioning it. In the centre of the bow's grip he felt the sliver of stallion bone he had placed there, to give a stallion's speed and strength to every arrow loosed.

'It will be a thing of beauty,' Mirim whispered, her eyes gleaming.

He looked at his guards and allowed himself a smile, both as a symbol of his trust in them, and because he *wanted* to smile. It was how he felt, an enormous sense of satisfaction welling inside him.

Tuld, Mirim and Ruga all smiled back at him, their joy at seeing and playing a part in the making of a Sirak bow shining in their eyes.

'The box,' Bleda said, and Tuld lifted a box made of oak and lined with felt. Bleda lifted his bow, tied and knotted still in extreme reflex, and he placed it in the box. They all stood and looked at it, then Tuld placed the lid on and buckled tight the leather straps.

'Good.' Bleda nodded.

'Now, let us make ready for war.'

They returned to Bleda's chambers, the first grey of dawn creeping into the air around them, and Bleda found Erdene and Ellac waiting for him. Ellac held a chest in his arms.

'Where have you been?' his mother asked him.

'Something I had to do,' Bleda said. She looked at him but did not ask more.

'We are riding to war,' Erdene said without any preamble, 'so you should look like a Sirak prince.'

Ellac opened the box, revealing a surcoat of lamellar armour, soft leather with a thousand iron plates painstakingly stitched into overlapping lines. Bleda hissed out a breath.

'It was your brother Altan's,' Erdene said, 'and your father's before that.' She looked him up and down. 'You are bigger than them, I think, but it should still fit.'

Tuld lifted out the surcoat, each iron plate gleaming and rippling in the light from the window like the scales of a fish.

'And there is something else,' Erdene said, looking into the box. A curved sword, the leather hilt wound with silver, horse-heads carved into the cross-guard. A laminated scabbard, again dressed in silver.

'My father's sword,' Bleda whispered.

'I will leave you to dress,' Erdene said. 'We leave before the second bell.' And then she was striding away.

Bleda stood there in something of a daze, and his guards moved around him, helping him dress in woollen breeches and deer-hide boots, under-tunics of linen and wool, then his grey deel, and over it all his surcoat of lamellar plate. It was heavy, an unfamiliar weight on his shoulders, but the sleeves ended above his elbows, leaving his arms unhindered for bow work. Once a belt was cinched tight about his waist, the weight upon his shoulders lessened, and then his new sword was strapped across his back. He tested the draw, Tuld adjusting the scabbard strap so that it did not snag the blade. A vambrace was slid onto his left forearm and tied tight, a rearing horse carved into the leather, and then his weapons-belt was buckled around his waist, with his bow-case and quiver upon it.

Bleda stood there when they were finished.

I feel like a god of war.

Ellac stood back, arms folded across his chest, and grunted his approval.

'Two more things you should know about your coat,' Ellac said. He tapped a plate on the bottom row of iron plates on the right leg. 'One plate, here, has been sharpened.'

Bleda looked at him, raised an eyebrow.

'In case you're in a tight spot and need it.' Ellac shrugged, then reached forwards, fumbled at the left half-sleeve with his stump and hand, muttered a curse.

'Help me,' he said. 'See, here,' he pointed to a row of the small, scale-like iron plates.

'What?' Bleda said, then realized that the stitching on them was different. They had been sewn as a row, rather than each one individually attached to the leather coat beneath, forming a flap over the sleeve that could be lifted.

'Look beneath it,' Ellac said.

Bleda lifted the iron plates and saw a hidden pocket, something protruding from it. He gripped it and pulled, revealing a needle-thin knife, the blade long and razor sharp.

'Just in case,' Ellac said, not managing to keep the twitch of a smile from his lips.

Bleda slid the knife back into its hidden pocket.

'Lead us out,' Ellac said.

Bleda strode from the room, feeling the extra weight in each step, along a corridor and down the spiral stairwell to the common room. He came to an abrupt halt on the last step. Gathered before him were his honour guard. Ninety Sirak warriors, men and women, clothed for battle. They let out a shout of acclaim as he appeared, and Bleda felt a swell of emotion.

'You men and women are pledged to me, to fight for me, protect me, to give your lives for me,' he said. 'But I am pledged to you, too. Oath-bound to respect your duty, to honour your faithfulness. I swear to you all, I *will not* let you down.'

He saw them straighten at his words, and as one they dropped to one knee before him.

'Come,' Bleda said, trying to hide the tremor of emotion in his voice. 'Let us make our Clan proud.'

Another shout and then they were parting before him and he was striding out into the street. Their mounts were all there, tethered and waiting at wooden rails. With practised ease Bleda vaulted onto the back of his horse, the new weight making no difference. It was something he had done for as long as he could remember. His honour guard mounted and then with a clatter of hooves they were trotting along the flagstoned streets of Drassil.

The courtyard was heaving with activity. Erdene, Queen of the Sirak, already there with five hundred riders about her. She saw Bleda and nodded to him, a glint of pride in her eyes making Bleda's chest swell.

And then more riders were cantering into the courtyard, Uldin in his war gear at the head of his warriors, another four or five hundred bows, hawk banners snapping above them, and Jin at his side. She was dressed in a leather jerkin over a long coat of mail that was split to cover both legs, still allowing her to ride. Her eyes sought out Bleda and she nodded to him, raising a fist.

She feels it, too, Bleda thought. There was an excitement flooding through him, and a faint fear as well, at the memory of the Kadoshim and their Feral beast-men. But right now, surrounded by the might of his Clan, he felt invincible.

Shadows skimmed over the courtyard and Bleda looked up, seeing rank upon rank of Ben-Elim take to the sky, hundreds of them, more, sunlight glinting upon steel and bright feathers. A handful of them swept down towards the courtyard, swooping low, Hadran alighting above the gate arch and facing them.

'Onwards,' he cried, 'death to the Kadoshim.' And he was

leaping back into the air, great beats of his wings lifting him higher. Horns blasted out, the gates of Drassil opened, and then Erdene led the Sirak out, Bleda riding at her side, a wave of horseflesh thundering through the gate tower and out onto the field of cairns beyond Drassil's walls.

Towards the Kadoshim.

CHAPTER FORTY

RIV

Riv beat her wings and flew. She climbed high, brushing the clouds, and then checked her wings, hovering as she watched the sun claw its way over the eastern rim of the world.

A few days had passed since she had arrived at Dun Seren. She'd been desperate to spend time in the weapons-field, to watch and see how her White-Wings surpassed these warriors of the Order of the Bright Star, but Kol had kept her by his side whilst he debated with Byrne about the best way to deal with the threat of Gulla and the Kadoshim. Riv had found it hard to concentrate, her mind dwelling on the first meeting between Kol and Byrne. It was troubling her, and she had decided that taking to the skies was the answer.

So much of what I have been raised to believe, so much of what I've considered the truth, is now just quicksand, sinking and shifting beneath my feet. All my life I've thought the Ben-Elim to be the heroes who saved us from the Kadoshim, but what Byrne and Ethlinn said . . . about the Ben-Elim scheming to bring the Kadoshim into this world, about Corban saving mankind from the Kadoshim, not the Ben-Elim. Is that the truth? Or is it as twisted and warped a version as Kol's?

Horn blasts brought her out of her reverie. Gazing around from her vantage point, she looked for some explanation for the horns blowing. Dun Seren spilt down a gentle hill, buildings lined in tiers within the inner wall. Beyond it were a snarl of wharves, barns, boathouses, piers and the river Vold, wide and languid in its last few leagues to the sea. A forest of masts sat upon the river, bobbing at their docks. A stone-arched bridge crossed the river, beyond it open plains, a road leading north. In the distance a smudge on the land hinted at a town.

There were figures on the bridge, twenty or thirty. Riv saw giants striding amongst them, the flitting movement of wolven-hounds, a mix of riders and wains.

A white crow flew above them.

Riv heard the hissing of air that heralded the beating of wings and looked around to see Kol flying towards her, a hand-ful of Ben-Elim with him.

'Another pleasant meeting with stiff-necked Byrne,' he said with a roll of his eyes as he drew level with her. 'She left because of these horns. What's happening?'

Riv pointed to the group. They had crossed the bridge and were making their way around a fork in the road that wound around Dun Seren's hill towards the gate tower and keep.

'Let's go and see what all the fuss is about,' Kol said, and they turned in the air and winged their way to the courtyard before the keep.

Crowds were gathering there, Byrne already waiting on the steps, Ethlinn at her side. Kol flew and landed beside her. Riv alighted further down the steps, and to the side.

The group from the bridge arrived, the white crow circling above them, calling out in a far-too-human voice, proclaim-ing the return of Dun Seren's huntsmen. Three men in hunting leathers passed through the gates, three wolven-hounds lop-ing around them. Behind the riders rolled two wains filled with the injured. Men, women, children. An old, grey-haired woman drove the first wain, a dark-haired warrior with a hawk nose and the bright star on his chest the second one. Two riders rode beside him, a young red-haired man and a stern, dour-faced woman. The red-haired man was smiling at everyone in the crowd, especially the women.

Last of all strode two giants, Riv recognizing one of them as Alcyon, who had spent much of his time in the service of Ethlinn at Drassil.

The white crow spiralled down from the sky, wings spreading, and it alighted upon the shoulder of Byrne.

'*Rab brought them home,*' the white crow squawked, '*told Keld and Stepor where to go.*'

'Well done, Rab,' Byrne said, scratching the crow's chest.

'*And Rab watch over Drem ben Olin, like Byrne ask. Drem brave, fight twisted men, save Utul.*'

Riv saw Kol look at the white crow, eyes narrowing, thoughtful.

The three men leading the party dismounted, stablehands running forwards to take their horses. All were dressed as huntsmen, all bearing various cuts and bruises, evidence of recent action. Two of them were dark-haired, the third one older, with iron in his beard. This one strode forward, up the steps to Byrne.

'My lady,' he said, dipping his head. 'We found them, though they were under attack when we reached them.'

'You have saved lives, Keld,' Byrne said, 'risked your own.' She nodded at the huntsman. 'Now, is there more news from the north? What of Dalga—'

'Drem?' Kol interrupted suddenly. 'I know that name. *Drem.*' He rolled it around his tongue, as if stirring up old memories. 'Olin?' Then his head snapped round to Byrne. 'Olin, husband of *Neve?*' Byrne returned his stare, said nothing.

Kol turned and marched down the steps, stopped a dozen paces from the two huntsmen. 'It cannot be you,' Kol said to one of them, a slim man with a thick black beard. 'You are too old.' Kol turned his eyes to the other.

This man was younger, only a stubbled beard on his chin. He was tall and broad at the shoulder, though he had a wiry musculature, not thick, like Vald's. His dark hair was tied back at the nape, loose strands hanging across his face. A sword and axe hung at his waist, and the biggest knife Riv had ever seen.

At first glance she mistook it for one of the White-Wing's short-swords.

He was covered in a lattice of cuts and bruises, looked as if he'd seen some recent action, wherever he'd come from.

'You are Drem ben Olin, son of Olin and Neve, warriors of the Bright Star?' Kol said.

The man was silent a moment, looking at the ground. Riv saw a hand move to his neck, fingers probing, as if searching for a pulse.

'Course he's Drem, Olin's boy,' the old lady driving the wain said. 'A fine man, Olin, may his soul rest in peace. What of it?'

Kol stood before Drem, prodded his shoulder with one finger, and Drem met Kol's eye. They were roughly of a height, which was unusual as Ben-Elim were taller than most men.

'I came here for you over fifteen years ago, because your mother murdered my friend. You are my ward, Drem ben Olin, the blood price for the unlawful slaying of Galzur of the Ben-Elim.' He put a hand on Drem's shoulder.

'Get away from him,' Byrne said flatly behind Kol. She was striding down the steps.

Ben-Elim were suddenly in the air, those close to Kol stepping up behind their leader, some hovering over the courtyard.

Drem reached up and gripped Kol's wrist, slowly and forcefully lifting Kol's hand from his shoulder.

'I am no one's ward,' Drem said. 'I am a *free* man.'

'You have never been free,' Kol said, 'and you are coming with me.'

'You'll have to fight me first,' a voice cried out, the red-haired warrior urging his horse forwards.

'And me,' Keld the huntsman called, striding back down the stairs.

Kol looked at them all contemptuously.

'I'll fight you all if you wish. I would have gone to war over this fifteen years ago, and I shall do the same now.'

'You won't have to fight any of them,' Byrne said, striding down to stand beside Kol. 'Stand down,' she ordered her warriors. They met her gaze at first, then slowly stepped away.

She needs the Ben-Elim in the war against Gulla and the Kadoshim, said as much the other night. It is the wise choice, to give up one man.

'The only one you need fight to claim Drem is *me*,' Byrne said calmly.

A silence settled over the courtyard.

'Don't be a fool,' Kol said with a snort of derision. 'We are allies, you *need* me in the coming war. Give up the boy.'

'Kol of the Ben-Elim,' Byrne called out loudly, 'I challenge you to the Court of Swords.'

'You would ruin everything for *him?* Risk the coming war?'

Byrne reached over her back, gripped the hilt of her sword and with a hiss drew it. 'Accept the challenge or forfeit your claim,' she told him.

Kol stared at Byrne, his wings twitching, then snorted.

'Have it your way.' He drew his sword. 'I accept.'

Riv could not believe what she was hearing. People crowded forwards, moving for a better view, but Riv flexed her wings and took to the air, and suddenly she had the best view of all. Other Ben-Elim circled above her, their expressions tense, hands on their weapons, but there was nothing they could do. Kol had flown here with only a score of warriors.

Kol strode forwards, his blade held contemptuously low.

Kol must surely win, Riv thought. *I have seen him fight, have fought him myself. He is too fast, too cunning. Would be nice to see him put on his arse, though.*

Byrne stood as still as stone, feet set, her sword held high in a two-handed grip.

Kol paced one way and then the other, his sword-tip grating on stone, eyes fixed on Byrne. Then he moved. A sudden lunge, a pulse of his wings adding to his speed.

A clang, echoing off the stone courtyard and statues.

Kol staggered away, off balance.

Byrne looked at him, resumed her stance.

Kol said something low, for only Byrne to hear as he strode to one side of her, then the other, his sword higher now, and he lunged again. Byrne sidestepped easily, chopping down as Kol stepped out of his lunge, cutting at her ribs. There was a crack of steel as their blades met and then both of them were fluid movement. Kol a swirling whirlwind, using his wings for speed, to check and turn, to leap and fly over Byrne, striking down at her, seemingly faster than human eyes could process; even Riv with her enhanced sight was finding it difficult to follow.

It must be impossible for these others to see what is happening.

Byrne parried and countered, all of her moves small, economical, always judging Kol's attacks perfectly, most of them hissing past her by little more than the width of a finger. And then Riv noticed something.

Byrne was smiling.

Not contemptuously, as Riv had seen Kol smile at her during sparring, not to elicit a response, as some kind of tactic. Byrne was smiling because she was in her element and loving it.

The battle joy.

Riv had felt it course through her before, and perhaps that was why she recognized it now in Byrne.

Another storm of blows, Byrne stepping and moving, never wasting her energy, parrying Kol's blurred attacks with impossible precision, almost as if she knew where the Ben-Elim's blade was going to be before he moved. A blistering combination from Kol as he swept in again, Byrne obscured from Riv's view for a dozen heartbeats.

Kol stepped away, his blade red.

Blood dripped from Byrne's cheek.

Gasps and mutters around the courtyard.

Kol smiled coldly.

Byrne's eyes flickered to the statues in the courtyard, of Corban and Storm. Riv saw her lips move.

And then Kol was moving again, leaping over her, twisting in the air, his sword a glittering arc, Byrne ducking, bunching her legs and leaping, stabbing at him.

There was a yell, blood and feathers sprinkling the ground and Kol was suddenly crashing to the stones. He slammed to the ground, a red wound across his shoulder, rolled on the cobbles as Byrne dropped, too, found her balance and came at him. His wings beat hard, powering him upright, but Byrne was already there, a flurry of chops, Kol parrying wildly, still off balance. His wings beat frantically, lifting his feet from the ground.

Byrne ducked a wild swing, crashed into him, grabbed onto Kol's leather jerkin and they were both rising into the air. Byrne headbutted Kol, once, twice and he was reeling in the air, falling back to the ground.

Byrne still held onto Kol as they hit the stones, then her pommel was crunching into Kol's head. His legs buckled and he was on his back, Byrne standing over him, one boot on his chest, her sword at his throat.

Riv stared, open-mouthed, part of her tempted to whoop in triumph.

A silence stretched, only Kol's ragged breaths heard.

'Do you yield?' Byrne asked.

Kol glared up at her. His hand searched for his sword hilt.

Byrne flicked her wrist and blood was leaking down Kol's neck.

'Do you yield?' Byrne snarled. 'I will *not* ask you a third time.'

'I yield,' Kol grunted.

Byrne stood there a long, lingering moment, still in the grip of the battle joy.

She's going to kill him!

Byrne blew out a deep breath, something shifting in the set of her shoulders.

'Then the matter is settled. Let us put it behind us,' Byrne said, taking her sword-tip from Kol's throat. She offered him her hand instead.

Kol looked up at her, then took her grip and climbed to his feet.

The crowd erupted in cheering.

Riv swept down out of a dive and landed in an open space before the weapons-field. A large stone dominated the clearing, twice as tall as Riv, and as wide as her with her wings spread.

It was the day after Kol and Byrne's duel, soon after dawn. A constant stream of people were walking past her, making their way into the weapons-field.

Finally, I will get to see Dun Seren's weapons-field and judge how they would fare against Drassil's White-Wings. I hope they don't all fight like Byrne.

Though I like her style.

Riv had risen early after a restless night. She'd thought after Kol's public defeat that he would have left Dun Seren immediately, but to his credit he had stayed. He told Riv later that night that he and Byrne had to agree on their tactics for the attack on Gulla, that there was nothing more important than that, even his pride. She had felt a brief moment of respect for him then.

A solitary figure was standing before the stone, staring at it. She knew him immediately. Drem, the man the duel had been over. His hand was reaching out, fingertips brushing the rock. Riv stepped closer, wondering what he was staring at. He started a little when he realized she was there, one hand going to his eye, rubbing it.

Is he crying?

Then she realized what Drem was looking at.

Names were carved into the stone, lit like gold as the rising sun bathed them in rosy light. Hundreds of names. A thousand. Maybe more.

This is the Stone of Heroes that Byrne spoke of.

She read the first names carved into the stone, high and faded by time and weather, but still clear.

'Garisan ben Tukul,' she whispered. 'Brina ap Fyrn.'

'Gar and Brina,' Drem said.

'What?' She frowned.

'They are Gar and Brina. Corban's two greatest friends, the people he dedicated Dun Seren and the Order of the Bright Star to. Brina was a healer, Gar a warrior.'

'Ah,' Riv said, though she had never heard the two names before. 'I thought I had learned all that needed to be known of our history,' she muttered, 'but it seems I was mistaken.'

Drem snorted a laugh. 'I can relate to that,' he said. He was serious-faced, almost a childlike innocence to the set of his features.

'Come on, Drem,' a voice called out, and they both turned to see a red-haired man, a broad grin on his face. It was one of the warriors who had tried to fight for Drem yesterday. 'Let's see how many new bruises we can earn today.'

Drem looked at Riv and touched his temple.

'I love Cullen like a brother,' he said. 'But he's totally mad. He doesn't just like fighting, which is bad enough – he likes getting hit.' He shook his head and walked off, following the red-haired warrior into the weapons-field.

Riv turned back to the stone, marvelling at the names. She looked where Drem had been standing and saw where he had reached out to, where he had touched the stone.

Two new names, freshly carved, dust still remaining from the stone mason's chiselling.

'Sig ap Tyr,' she whispered. 'Olin ben Adros.'

Stone crunched behind Riv, a tremor in the ground, and she turned to see Balur One-Eye striding past her, other giants with him. Alcyon was there, his hair shaven to stubble, apart from a thick wedge down the middle of his head, bound into a warrior braid that hung down his back. There were other giants about them that she didn't recognize, including the one who had been in the first meeting with Byrne. Craf was not upon his shoulder now.

'Come, lassie, and raise a sweat with us on this cold morning,' Balur said, blowing on his big slabs of hands. He didn't have to ask Riv twice. She followed them into the field.

Balur and a handful of giants stomped to a rack, full of all manner of weapons, some giant-size, some human. Riv saw that some of the other giants, Alcyon included, were joining most of the people in the field and gathering into a central square, forming loose columns. She saw Byrne standing at its head, the cut on her cheek from her duel a thin scabbed line. A dark-skinned woman stood beside her. As Riv watched, Byrne and the other woman drew their swords, Byrne holding hers two-handed over her head, just as she had begun the duel yesterday.

'Stooping falcon,' Byrne cried, and like a wave breaking, those gathered before her drew their blades and raised them in a mirror image of Byrne. Something about the sight of it stirred Riv's blood.

'What are they doing?' Riv asked.

'The sword dance,' Balur said, hefting a wooden war-hammer.

Byrne called out something else, and over a thousand blades flashed in the morning sun.

'I like it,' Riv said, feeling a grin split her face.

'It's a Jehar tradition,' Balur said. 'Gar taught it to Corban, so it's fitting that it starts each day at Dun Seren.'

'Does it work?' Riv asked, wondering if it would aid her swordcraft, or whether it just appeared to be impressive. She recognized variations of movements she'd learned during her training, but they had never been linked like this, forms and positions held until muscles burned. She could see sweat steaming as it dripped from noses, muscles quivering.

'Gar was one of the few that gave me *more* bruises than I gave him,' Balur said. 'Though I only knew him a few years.'

He paused, his craggy face softening a moment, lost in some distant memory. 'Yes, lass, I'd wager the sword dance works.'

'Why aren't you doing it, then?' she asked him.

'Because I'm an old man set in my ways. I was two thousand years old when I first saw the sword dance. And, besides, this is my weapon.' He hefted his wooden war-hammer. 'It's not made for their forms, but it still gets the job done. Speaking of which,' he said, 'choose your weapon.' He walked out into the sparring ground, turned and waited for her, tapping the shaft of his hammer in his fist.

Riv ran a hand across the wooden weapons in the racks, eventually settling on two short-swords that most resembled her White-Wing blade. She was used to fighting with sword and shield, but she knew she needed to adapt.

She grinned approaching Balur, spinning the blades in lazy circles. Her wings twitched in excited anticipation.

I am sparring with Balur One-Eye. Not all is bad with the world.

And then she was surging at him.

The rest became a blur for Riv, a glorious release of tension as she wove in and out of Balur's strikes and swings, hammer-head, butt and shaft all used as weapons by the wily giant.

Two thousand years! Two thousand years of weapons skill and learning. It's no wonder he's hard to kill.

And he was. As big a target as the giant was, as slow as she thought he would be, Riv struggled to touch her blades to any part of him. And she was not just using her feet, her wings lifted her from the ground over sweeps of his war-hammer, pulsing to give her speed as she drove at his chest, swirling her around and over Balur. Their blades clashed a thousand times, Riv deflecting Balur's strikes and sweeps, never taking the brunt of his blows, knowing that would shatter her bones, instead nudging, pushing, deflecting his attacks, attempting to push Balur off balance. Try as she might, she could not get close to him. A score of times the tips of her blades grazed his leather and fur jerkin, but no closer.

Her only consolation was that he couldn't touch his hammer to her, either, and to Riv's thinking, that was one of her greatest achievements.

They parted, both panting, chests heaving, sweat streaming from them, steaming in the cold air.

Riv became aware of a crowd around them, and the sound of cheering. Amongst those watching was Kol, both his eyes swollen and bruised purple. His Ben-Elim were about him.

Balur smiled at her.

'You've learned to use them quickly enough,' the giant said, nodding at her wings.

She beamed in return. It felt good to be treated as normal. As a warrior who just happened to have wings. She was more grateful to Balur for that than he would ever know.

A warrior stepped out of the crowd, the red-haired man she had seen earlier.

'Now you've warmed up, One-Eye, are you ready for a lesson or two?'

'Ha, you cheeky pup.' Balur grinned. Sparring obviously lifted his usual dour mood. He hefted his war-hammer.

Riv stepped back out of the ring, allowing the newcomer to face Balur. He had a wooden practice sword in one hand, a wooden knife in the other.

'Go easy on him, Cullen,' a voice called out, Alcyon the giant, Riv realized. 'Poor Balur is getting old.'

'Shall I let him win?' Cullen called back, smiling as he advanced.

'Don't break Cullen's bones,' someone else called out, the slim-built huntsman from yesterday with the dark hair and a tangle of black beard. Drem was standing with him and the older huntsman, who had fingers missing from one hand.

'Another with two weapons against my one,' Balur commented, before he had finished his sentence moving in a blur,

347

hammer swinging around his head, sweeping low. Cullen leaped over it and darted forwards, sword slashing, but somehow Balur was swaying out of the blade's reach, pivoting on his foot and bringing his hammer around again, forcing Cullen to jump away. He stumbled, controlled it and dropped into a roll, Balur striding after him.

As Riv watched, her respect for the red-haired warrior grew. At first, she had thought him a braggart who would end up on his arse quickly enough. Riv had seen Balur teach that lesson a hundred times. But this warrior was skilled, there was no doubt about that, balanced and light on his feet, and adder-fast. But so was Balur. The giant was like a wall, his defence almost impenetrable, his war-hammer seeming light as feathers in his fists, Balur using it as much like a staff as a hammer.

In time they separated, both breathing heavily.

'Are you holding back?' Cullen frowned.

Balur just shrugged.

'Because I have been,' Cullen said gleefully, springing back in at Balur.

They set at each other again, becoming a blur, time marked by the *clack* of their wooden weapons meeting.

Riv looked away, taking in the weapons-field around her.

The thud of shields coming together drew her eyes. It was a shield wall, sure enough, but not what she had expected. Where the White-Wings used rectangular shields, the warriors of the Order had big round shields on their arms.

There are gaps because of those shields, spaces that can be exploited in the curves, especially the lower legs. Not like the White-Wings' wall of shields, which is all but impenetrable.

She felt a smug sense of pride at that, a mark for the White-Wings in the tally of who were the greater warriors.

Then she heard a shouted command, saw the wall of shields open up into loose order, the second row stepping past the first, and they all had their hands raised over their heads, spinning something.

What is that?

Then they released, a score of nets rising up into the air, peaking and dropping, weighted balls giving them shape.

Nets. They are throwing weighted nets.

Riv knew immediately what it was for.

A winged foe. They are for the Kadoshim. Why have we never trained with these, when our whole purpose is to fight the Kadoshim? A cynical voice whispered in her ear. *Because those nets would be just as effective on Ben-Elim as they would Kadoshim.*

A mark for the Order in her tally.

Riv remembered her conversation with Bleda on the weapons-field at Drassil.

He is right. We need ranged weapons to fight the Kadoshim, or any winged enemy. I need a Sirak bow.

Elsewhere Riv saw warriors training on horseback, dark-haired men and women with white stars emblazoned upon dark leather cuirasses. She felt her breath catch in her chest as she watched them stabbing and chopping at targets with spear and sword, as well as practising the running mount, which amazed her. Riv trained with horses, considered herself an excellent rider, but the running mount was a specialized manoeuvre that was rarely practised amongst the White-Wings. Here it seemed to be part of their standard training.

Another mark for the Order in my tally.

Further away there was a pack of wolven-hounds chasing a giant wrapped in thick-padded wool and leather. A huntsman was whistling and shouting commands and the wolven-hounds were circling the giant, nipping at him, herding him, another whistle and then they were all leaping, bringing the giant down, the huntsman running forwards, calling them off.

There is much the same here as Drassil, but there are other things, too, more diverse. I think we would win the war of shields, but these other disciplines . . .

A grunt and a thud, cheers and shouts around Riv drew her back to Balur and Cullen.

The red-haired warrior was on his back, Balur standing over him, the butt of his war-hammer on Cullen's chest.

Cullen slashed at Balur's ankles with his sword, just missing.

Balur leaned on his war-hammer, just enough, Cullen wheezing out a flood of air, gasping.

Horns sounded, from the eastern wall. Heads turned to look.

Balur took his war-hammer from Cullen's chest.

'Ha, you're lucky the horns saved you, One-Eye,' Cullen said, trying to rise from the ground, grimacing and failing, but Balur was already walking away, following the sound of the horns.

Alcyon the giant stepped close and offered Cullen his hand.

'He tricked me,' Cullen complained of Balur as Alcyon heaved him upright.

'Aye,' Alcyon said with a grin, 'and in battle, you would be dead and Balur alive. Tricks are part of fighting, remember?' Alcyon leaned close to Cullen, wagging a thick finger at him. 'There's no complaining when you're dead.'

'I thought Balur always fought with honour,' Cullen muttered.

'Ach, the young are always too trusting,' Alcyon said. 'That's why you die quicker. Us old men; well, we are old for a reason.'

Beside Riv, Drem nodded, grunting, as if he'd heard those words before.

Riv saw fingers pointing skyward, and a new Ben-Elim was high in the sky above them, spiralling down to the weapons-field. He saw Kol and alighted before him, dropping to one knee.

'Rise,' Kol said, 'and tell me your news.'

'There is a warband of Kadoshim on the eastern road, moving towards Drassil,' the Ben-Elim said. 'They command men and Feral beasts and other things.'

Mutters rippled through the crowd in the field.

Kol looked at Byrne. 'I must leave immediately,' he said. 'Delay your march into the Desolation until you hear from me.'

'What measures has Hadran taken?' Kol asked the Ben-Elim messenger.

'He was mustering the White-Wings as I left and was sending out the Sirak. They are mounted and will move faster than the White-Wings.'

Kol nodded.

The Sirak? Has Bleda gone to war? Riv felt a worm of worry uncoil in her belly.

'With me,' Kol yelled and leaped into the air, wings beating, lifting him higher. His Ben-Elim followed, Riv lingering a moment, looking around the courtyard. She realized that she liked it here, felt some kind of kinship with those she had met. She looked up, at Kol.

But that is my father up there, no matter what else he may be, and he is flying to war, which is what I've been trained for, all my life.

She bent her knees and leaped, her dappled wings snapping open and powering her skywards. Soon she had caught up with Kol and they set their faces to the east, flying to war.

CHAPTER FORTY-ONE

FRITHA

Fritha stood before the bed where Elise still lay. The linen sheets were sweat-stained, her face pale, the skin pallid and stretched, looking as if it would tear with a touch. Her eyes fluttered open, sensing Fritha's presence.

Arn stood at Fritha's shoulder.

'There must be more,' he said. Fritha could hear the heartbreak and desperation in his voice. 'Something *else* you can do.'

'I have done all I know to heal her,' Fritha said. 'Her lungs have recovered, but the bones in her back and legs are shattered. She is broken, Arn; she will never walk again.' It hurt Fritha to say it, hurt her more to look at Elise's fractured, twisted frame. Elise had been a good friend to Fritha. More than a friend, closer than kin, saving Fritha from the dark abyss that she was plunging into when Arn and Elise had found her.

But the truth was the truth.

'Please,' Arn said. He reached out, his fingers brushing his daughter's cheek.

'There is only one thing left that I can do,' Fritha said into the silence. 'I can make her *new* . . .'

Arn froze, his fingers still on Elise's cheek.

'But, she would no longer be Elise,' he said.

'She would, but better, stronger,' Fritha said. 'This is not my decision. Or yours. Ask Elise what she would want.'

Arn stared at Fritha, then he leaned close to his daughter

and whispered in her ear. It seemed to Fritha that he spoke to Elise for a very long while. Then Arn straightened.

They stood together, watching Elise.

A tear fell from Elise's eye and rolled down her cheek. Then she nodded, a whisper escaping her lips.

'Death smiles at us all,' Elise breathed.

'All that we can do is smile back,' Fritha and Arn whispered in response.

'Do it,' Elise said, little more than a sigh.

'Gunil,' Fritha called, turning on her heel and striding out into daylight, 'carry Elise to my table.'

Fritha sat on the end of her cot, her head in her hands. She blew out a long breath and rubbed her stubbled head.

It is done. All is ready now. All the years of despair, of hatred, planning, preparations, the blood, sweat and tears, all coming down to this. The Great War is upon me. I must rise to the challenge.

She shifted her weight and leaned forwards, reaching underneath her cot and grabbing an iron handle. Her chest slid out, old nails scraping on timber, and for a while she just sat and stared at it. Finally, she unbolted it, paused to look at her hands. She had scrubbed them after Elise's surgery, scrubbed her friend's blood from her hands and arms, but there were still dark rims beneath her nails.

Blood always leaves a stain.

A knock on her door, but she didn't answer, too lost in the tangled weave of memories that her chest evoked. The door creaked open, footsteps, the rustle of leathery wings and Morn was standing before her.

'All is ready,' the half-breed said. She looked from Fritha to the chest. 'Are you?'

Am I ready?

Fritha sucked in a deep breath and threw open the lid of the chest. Inside was a short-sword, scabbarded in worn leather. It was wrapped in a weapons-belt. Fritha reached in and lifted the sword out, the grip smooth and cool, familiar as an old friend. She lay the sword to one side and looked at what lay beneath it in the chest.

A battered cuirass, a pair of white wings embossed upon its breast.

Memories flooded through her, a surge like the dam gates opening. Of training in Drassil's weapons-field, a nostalgic glow to the memories, of feeling accepted, whole, complete. Of passing her warrior trial and swearing the oath; obedience to Elyon and his Lore, obedience to the Ben-Elim, swearing to mete out destruction upon the Kadoshim and all enemies of the Faithful. And all the while she had felt his eyes upon her, his beautiful, beautiful eyes. Soon after, he had come to her, whispered soft, flattering words, a gentle caress, in time leading to a kiss, and then, more. And finally . . .

Her hand went to her belly as she remembered the fleeting sensation of life growing within her. Her baby. Her beautiful baby. And he had wanted her to kill it.

Tears blurred her eyes, then, running down her face to mix with blood that was not her own.

'It is fitting,' Morn said, 'that the warrior the Ben-Elim created will help to tear them down. Their hypocrisy and lies will come to an end soon.'

'I hate them,' Fritha breathed.

'They deserve to be hated,' Morn said, 'but why do you hate them so?'

A silence, Fritha's mind filled with images. Blood and tears.

'They told me to kill my baby,' Fritha whispered, 'said that I was privileged above all people to taste the love of a Ben-Elim, but that the world could not know. That the evidence must be destroyed, like a page ripped from a book and cast on the fire. I was a young, besotted fool, in love with the image of the Ben-Elim, with what I thought they were, but I found out at their heart they are rotten.'

Morn dropped to a knee, put a hand on Fritha's.

'The past is gone,' she said, her voice deep, like gravel.

'No, it is never gone. It is always here,' Fritha said, tapping her temple, hard. 'And here.' A prod to her chest.

'He told me to kill her,' Fritha said. 'Told me to ask the other White-Wings in their cabal what to do. I was instructed to go to a cabin deep in Forn Forest, to give birth to my baby, and then to *murder her*. To bury her beneath a pile of stones and walk away as if she'd never existed.'

She looked at Morn, felt more tears blur her eyes.

'I was not the first. It never entered my mind, but there were so many graves there, dug by infatuated, enamoured young women. You must understand, in that world, to be raised as a White-Wing, the Ben-Elim were like gods to us. Beautiful and wise, saviour, judge and jury all rolled into one. To be noticed was the greatest of honours.' Her hand brushed her belly. 'She would have been like you, a half-breed, but still beautiful. Her life meant something.' She reached out a hand and cupped Morn's cheek. The half-breed blinked at that, a stiffness in her shoulders, but she did not pull away. Fritha looked at Morn's wings. 'The Kadoshim raise their half-breed children, love them. Why could the Ben-Elim not do the same?'

'Their pride and arrogance,' Morn spat. 'They think they are superior to all others, that we are just food for worms, insignificant pawns in their grand plans.'

Fritha nodded, Morn's words stirring a thousand memories.

'What did you do?' Morn asked her.

'I ran. I told my mam and da, and they helped me. They ran with me, fast and far. Away from Drassil and the Ben-Elim, to start a new life.' She closed her eyes, could not stop the flood of memories, or the tears.

'And then?' Morn prompted her.

'For a while it worked,' Fritha sighed. 'A new life, and it was good, a hundred leagues from Drassil on the border of Ardain. I had my baby, my beautiful Anja.' She smiled through her tears. 'And then one day I returned home from market to see the flames. I ran, but I already *knew*, in here –' she jabbed a finger at her gut – 'that I was too late.' She chewed her lip, not trusting her voice. A deep, shuddering breath.

'Our home had been razed by the Ben-Elim, gone – just the timber frame smouldering when I arrived. I found my mam's body was a scorched ruin in the flames. My da I discovered outside, unburned, but a sword had hacked through his ribs and opened a lung. In his arms was Anja, my baby girl, blood on her lips.' She felt her grief like a rock of ice in her belly, turning her veins cold.

'That was where Arn and Elise found me,' she continued. 'They were brigands living rough in the Darkwood, victims of Ben-Elim Lore, Arn's wife hung from a tree for her supposed crimes.' Fritha snorted. 'They cared for me, brought me back from the brink, and turned my grief into a cold, relentless hatred.'

'Hatred is not so bad,' Morn said, a twist of her lips. 'Hatred keeps you strong.'

'It does,' Fritha agreed.

I hate them, the Ben-Elim. Hate them all, and all those who so blindly follow them. But most of all, I hate him.

She could remember his handsome features, blond hair and a scar through his face that somehow seemed to make him more beautiful, not less.

'Better revenge than grief,' Morn said.

'Yes,' Fritha agreed. 'I no longer believe in prayer, Morn, but if I did, there would only ever be one thing I would pray for. That I would be the one to put my sword through Kol of the Ben-Elim's heart. Oh, how I hate him.'

'That is good, Priestess. I will help you, as you will help me in my vengeance for my brother, Ulfang.' Morn turned her hand over, showed blue veins rigid on her palm. With one sharp-taloned finger she drew a cut across the vein. Held it out to Fritha.

Fritha drew her short-sword from her scabbard and tested the edge with her thumb. It was still sharp, a red line, a droplet of blood. She put the blade to her palm and drew her blade across it, blood welling. The pain felt good, a reminder of the life she had clung to. She stood and let the blood pool in her fist, then reached out and gripped Morn's offered hand, their blood mingling.

Their mixed blood dripped down onto her cuirass, a red stain upon the white wings.

'*O neamhchiontacht bán íon, fola dorcha le haghaidh díoltas,*' Fritha muttered, scrubbing their blood into the cracked white leather, seeing the stain spread, seeping through the leather like ink through parchment. The wings that were white became a dark, deep red.

'That is good,' Morn said, a smile cracking the flat plains of her face.

Fritha stood, and Morn helped her buckle the cuirass about her torso, holding the back-plate in place, Fritha buckling the chest-plate to it. Then Fritha wrapped her weapons-belt around her waist, added a sheathed knife and an axe ring. She stood there, then, feeling like the warrior she had once been.

She cuffed the tears from her face and nodded to Morn.

'My thanks,' she said, sweeping up her bearskin cloak from her bed and wrapping it around her shoulders, fastening the brooch-pin.

'Come, then, Priestess, and let us change the world,' Morn said, and together they walked out into the bright sunlight.

Gunil was waiting for her, sitting upon Claw with his war-hammer slung across his back. Behind him Fritha's Red Right Hand were gathered, all mounted on shaggy-haired horses, winter-hardened for the north. There were close to five hundred men and women before her. They were a mixture of those she had drawn about her since that fateful day when Arn and Elise had found her, when she had joined the resistance against the Ben-Elim, and the acolytes that had recently arrived at the mine.

It has been a long, hard road, but it has led me here. I now stand at the head of a fearsome warband.

'Release my Ferals,' Fritha said to Gunil. With a command, his bear lumbered into motion, turning and shambling towards the mine caves.

'WRATH,' Fritha bellowed, and there was an answering roar, the sound of earth scraping and a tremor in the ground as the draig scuttled around a corner, its new wings flapping, lifting it from the ground by a handspan or two, then dropping back to the earth.

He will learn, Fritha thought.

Horses whinnied and stamped as the draig drew close. Shouted commands rang out from riders to calm their mounts.

'*Food?*' Wrath growled as he reached her, saliva dripping from a long tooth.

'Soon,' Fritha said. 'We are going to battle, Wrath, where we will slay enough for you to feast on for half a year.'

'*Feast, good,*' Wrath rumbled.

Arn walked out before her, leading two horses by the reins. He held Fritha's mount steady for her as she swung into the saddle, then handed her a long spear.

'Elise?' Fritha said.

'She is . . . shy,' he said, 'still becoming acquainted with her new form. She will join us soon.'

'Good.' Fritha nodded. She raised her spear into the air.

'Better revenge than grief,' she cried out, knowing that Morn's words had struck a chord in her heart, and for that reason they would stir the blood of all of her Red Right Hand.

'Better revenge than grief,' they called back to her, Arn snarling the words, and then Fritha touched her heels to her horse and they were moving out. Fritha put her fingers to her lips, whistling high and keening.

'*LIOM,*' she cried out in the Old Tongue, answering howls

and barks echoing from behind her. Before she had reached the gates of the mine there was a swarm of Ferals sweeping around her flanks, like two great snarling wings. Over four hundred beast-men, beast-women and beast-children ran and loped through the streets and buildings of the mine, a wave of fur and muscle and teeth. Horses were wide-eyed, some rearing at the proximity of the Ferals.

They will calm when we are in the open, I will send my babies wider, into the woods and shadowed places.

They reached the gate. Something moved in the shadows, a deeper darkness, and then Elise was emerging, but not Elise. A creature of coil and fang, Elise's head, arms, torso, but the rest of her was the giant wyrm, slithering into the daylight on muscled coils. She wore an iron cap upon her head and a coat of chainmail upon her torso. Blood dripped down the scales of her coils, masking what Fritha knew was a raw, ragged scar where her flesh met and merged with the wyrm's scales. She had a sword strapped across her back and spear in her fist. The sight of her made Fritha's heart swell.

'You are *glorious*,' Fritha said to her and Elise replied with a hesitant, fanged smile.

They swept through the gates of the mine, Fritha at the head of her hybrid army, and onto the road that circled the northern rim of Starstone Lake and led to Kergard.

Not that there is anything left of Kergard.

Figures moved amongst the trees.

Ulf stepped out, pale and gaunt, dark pools for eyes, and behind him flowed a mass of bodies, pale, grey-skinned creatures with distended jaws and rows of razored teeth. Hundreds of them, more like a thousand, and Fritha had seen that more joined Ulf every day, trickling in from the Desolation, alone or in small groups, swelling his ranks.

An army of Revenants, and it is still growing.

His blood has swept the Desolation and turned all within it, those he has bitten himself in turn taking his strain of infection to any that they drink from. His influence spreads like the ripples from a rock thrown into a pool.

Fritha smiled at the genius of her own creation.

Ulf and his warband followed Fritha, keeping to the fringes of the forest, seeming to drag the shadow out from the woodland and drape it around them like a ragged cloak.

'TO WAR,' Fritha cried, the momentous joy of it all sweeping through her, and at her side Wrath scuttled forwards and spread his wings, beating them. A moment's weightlessness and then he was lifting from the ground. He hovered before Fritha a moment, then gave more powerful strokes and climbed higher, began to move in ever-widening circles above her, like a bairn learning to swim. He opened his jaws and let out a thunderous roar.

Fritha grinned, riding at the head of her mongrel army, Gunil upon Claw at one shoulder, Elise slithering upon her sinuous coils at the other, Morn and Wrath sweeping in looping circles above them. Behind her the land seethed with warriors and Ferals and Revenants.

And Fritha set her head towards Dun Seren.

We're coming for you, Order of the Bright Star. Time to learn what happens to those allied to the Ben-Elim.

CHAPTER FORTY-TWO

DREM

Drem knocked on Byrne's door.

'Enter,' Byrne called, and Drem opened the door and walked into Byrne's sparsely furnished chamber. She stood by a tall window, the shutters thrown wide, night spilling into the room. Drem walked forwards a few paces, shuffled to a stop. He still felt ashamed that Byrne had fought for him against Kol, the Ben-Elim. Not that he would have stood a chance against the winged warrior – that had been blatantly obvious from the first few moments of the duel.

But it still felt wrong, that someone else had done his fighting for him.

Byrne turned, the cut on her cheek from Kol's sword freshly stitched and scabbed. Another reminder of his shame.

'Thank you,' Byrne said.

'What for?' Drem frowned.

'For giving me the absolute joy of putting Kol on his arse.' She smiled, the stern high captain gone for a few moments. 'I have wanted to do that for a *very* long time.'

Drem shook his head, remembering how he had been wracked with the fear of losing Byrne, of someone else close to him dying. 'I thought he was going to kill you.'

'Kol? That bag of hot wind?' Byrne shook her head, saw Drem's expression and walked to him.

'That duel has been a long time coming. It should have

361

happened fifteen years ago. Olin begged me for the honour, but I forbade him. He said Neve would want it that way, that she would not want so much damage to come from her one moment of anger. But I feared you would be left an orphan. Olin was good, but not as good as me.' She said it matter-of-factly, no pride or arrogance in the statement. 'If I had challenged Kol then, when he came for you all those years ago, then Olin would have been shamed. In hindsight, I wish I had still done it. Olin's shame would have been better than losing you all these years, and Olin would not be dead.'

'He did what he felt he had to do, to protect me and the Order,' Drem said.

'Oh, I know that.' Byrne sighed. 'The fault was mine. But all is so much simpler when you look back on it.' She poured two cups from a jug, gave one to Drem. Spiced mead. Drem enjoyed the honey in his throat and the warmth filling his belly.

'So, the Desolation,' Byrne said. 'Keld has reported back to me on what happened. And Rab. He had a good view.'

Byrne looked Drem in the eye, held his gaze.

'You did well. Utul tells me he is in your debt. You saved his life.'

Drem just shrugged, not sure what to say.

'Moments like that, when you act when there is no room for thought, they show the truth of a person,' Byrne said.

Drem remained silent.

'But you left Dun Seren, volunteered to go back to the Desolation. Do you regret coming here?'

'No!' Drem said in a rush. 'I, it is . . . I do find it hard here. So many people, and walls everywhere.' He shrugged. 'I've lived in the Desolation for most of my life, in the company of one man, little else but trees, ice and sky for company.' He shrugged again.

Byrne nodded, thinking over his words.

'So, it is adjusting to this place, to us,' she said. 'It is not that you wish you had not come, or that now you've seen us you wish to leave? Better a hard truth than a kind lie.'

Drem liked that, because that was exactly how he felt.

He drew in a deep breath, thinking hard on it, because Byrne's honesty deserved it.

'I *want* to be here,' Drem said. 'I have not been here long, but as strange as it seems, it feels like home. Not the walls and towers, but because of . . . you. And Keld and Cullen. They are good men, and dear to me.' He blew out a long breath, felt he'd come close to expressing how he felt.

Byrne gazed at him a while longer. Then nodded.

'Good,' she said. 'Now that I have found you, I would not lose you again. I say that as your kin, but also as the high captain of this Order, because I see in you the makings of a fine warrior. We know that you can handle yourself in a fight. Keld and Cullen have told me in detail of the journey here from Kergard. And I've seen you put Cullen on his arse, which isn't the easiest of things to do.' Byrne smiled fondly. 'And Keld tells me you are as skilled as any of our huntsmen, more than most. Keld does not make high praise of anyone. Except Sig. So, I am hoping that you will stay, will join us, will take the Oath.'

'The Oath?' Drem asked.

'Aye. When those who have undergone the training have passed their warrior trials here, they take an oath and join the Order. Pledging their lives to our cause. To protect those who cannot protect themselves, to fight the Kadoshim or any other evil that threatens the people of the Banished Lands.'

Drem liked the sound of that. All his life he had lived with no direction or goal, other than to hunt and survive. It had not entered his mind, not seemed necessary at the time. His life had felt fulfilled, happy in the presence of his father. Now, though, so much had changed. He felt as if stones had been removed from his eyes and that he saw the world clearly for the first time.

And it was not a safe place.

Gulla, Ferals, Revenants. I cannot turn my back on the evil they do, will continue to do. Walking away is cowardice, allowing others to stand against it.

'I would like to take the Oath,' Drem said. He frowned. 'Though I have already made one of my own.'

'And what oath is that?' Byrne said.

'To kill Asroth.'

Byrne blinked at that, then chuckled. 'You are Neve and Olin's blood, and no denying. They would be so proud of you,' Byrne said.

I hope so.

'I think the two oaths are linked, so there would be no conflict there for you,' Byrne said.

'That's what I was thinking,' Drem said. He drew his seax, running a finger along the blade, smooth and pitted steel now, no sign of the runes Keld had revealed with his word of power.

'Do I need the Starstone Sword to kill Asroth, or will my seax do the job? My father forged this, and Keld showed me runes that he had carved into the blade.'

Byrne took the seax, turning it in her hand.

'It is heavy,' she remarked. Hefted it, testing its balance. 'A fine blade, well weighted. But Asroth is encased in starstone metal. To cut that you would need a blade forged from starstone.' She handed it back to him. 'You have Olin's sword, too.'

'I need to learn to use it. I feel more comfortable with this,' Drem said as he sheathed his seax.

'Olin's blade will be rune-marked as well. Rare weapons.'

'Doesn't every warrior of the Order have a rune-marked blade?' Drem asked.

'No.' Byrne shook her head. 'Only those who have learned of the earth power. And there are not many that do that.'

'Why?'

Byrne studied Drem for long moments.

'I am usually a good judge of character,' she said, turning on her heel and walking away. 'Come with me.'

Drem followed and they moved into an adjoining room. Byrne placed her hand against a stone wall and whispered something. There was a pulse of light, a glow leaving her fingertips and rippling through the stone, like veins, and then the outline of a door was visible. Byrne pulled it open and disappeared inside.

'Come on,' her voice echoed back out to him.

Drem stepped into a stairwell, flickering torches in sconces on the walls. Wide steps spiralled downwards.

'It is a great responsibility, the earth power,' Byrne said to him as he hurried to catch up with her. 'I do not choose lightly who I will give that power to.'

Drem remembered Cullen complaining that he was not considered responsible enough yet to learn the earth power.

'You pick who learns, then?' Drem asked, gazing around him as they wound deeper and deeper.

'The high captain of the Order chooses, yes,' Byrne said. 'Since Corban and Cywen, that has been the way, here.'

Drem nodded, thinking about that.

The staircase opened out onto a tunnel, wide and high, Byrne leading Drem on. It continued to slope downwards.

'What is this place?' Drem asked.

'A few things, but above all, a bolthole,' Byrne said. 'There are a number of entrances throughout Dun Seren that lead here. Corban planned for it. I have read in our secret histories that there are tunnels like this in the fortress where Corban grew up, Dun Carreg, far to the west. Maybe it reminded him of home.' She looked and smiled at him. 'It is a way of escape, if Dun Seren ever fell to attack. Eventually it leads to the river, though we will not go anywhere near as far.'

The tunnel spilt into a chamber, torches burning, sending shadows dancing. The ceiling was too high for the torchlight to penetrate.

In the middle of the chamber was a stone pedestal, a wide table and a dozen timber chairs. Byrne strode up to the pedestal and placed her hand on a thick, leather-bound book. She blew dust from it.

'This book was handed down to us from Brina, one of the two people the Order was dedicated to. It was written by giants, thousands of years ago.'

'What's in it?' Drem asked, his voice echoing around the chamber.

'History, to begin with. And then, the earth magic. There is much knowledge in here, and power.' Byrne stroked it.

'Why do you keep it down here?' Drem asked, gazing around the shadow-wreathed chamber.

'Because it is dangerous, and precious, and this is the safest place in Dun Seren. Down here rock walls are not the only guardian of this book.'

Drem looked around again, staring into the shadows.

'You are quite safe, while you are with me,' Byrne said at Drem's searching looks. 'The earth power is just a tool,' she continued, 'like a sword, or a plough. It can be used to save life, or to take it. Used for great good, or for great evil.'

'Why are you telling me this, showing me this place?' Drem asked.

'Because sometimes it is better to see a thing than to hear about it, Drem ben Olin, my sister's son. And because I see in you the potential for greatness. You do not crave power, or renown. You shun violence, and yet you will do what you must, for your friends, or to protect the innocent. One day, I would hope to bring you down here and teach you from this book.'

Drem stared between Byrne and the book, the leather cracked with age, the parchments within yellowed. He thought of his mam and da, of Gulla and Fritha, Sig and Keld and Cullen. The memory of Hildith falling into his arms in the Desolation just a few days ago, and how he had comforted her, telling her she was safe now.

But is she? Will she ever be? Not that she is defenceless, the tough old goat, but what is happening in this world, it is wrong, an

injustice, and I am being offered a chance to help. To make a differ-
ence, or if not a difference, at least the chance to stand against it.

'Drem, will you stay with me, learn the art of Kill and Cure, and stand with us against the darkness?'

'I will,' Drem breathed, not a moment's hesitation.

Byrne looked into his eyes and nodded.

'Then pledge it to me. Not the Oath. That is for another time, for your sword-brothers and sisters to hear, for you to declare to the world. But pledge to me, now, as kin, that you will stand with me, and fight the darkness until your last breath.'

'I swear it,' Drem whispered.

Byrne drew a knife from her belt and sliced it across her forearm. Blood welled. She offered the knife to Drem.

'Then seal it in blood,' she said.

He took the knife, looked at the bloodied blade, then pulled the sleeve of his woollen tunic up and cut a red line along his arm.

He offered his arm to Byrne and she grasped it in the warrior grip, blood on their forearms mingling.

When it was done, Byrne stepped away.

'We should go,' she said and returned to the tunnel that led back to her chamber.

Drem looked at his arm, a sense of weight upon him. He knew deep in his bones that he had committed to something for life, and it felt . . . good. He rolled down his sleeve, blood seeping into the linen, and followed Byrne. As he strode across the chamber he felt something above him, a turbulence in the air. He stopped and stared up, searching the shadows, but could see nothing, no sign of movement.

'What is it?' Byrne called back to him.

'I thought I felt something?' Drem said.

'There are strange draughts down here,' Byrne said, 'from vents in the rock, or seeping up from the river.'

Drem grunted and walked on. As he did so something floated down from above, landing just in front of his feet.

A feather.
He knelt and picked it up.
It was a dark brown, speckled with white.
Not a crow, then, and besides, it is far too big.
He looked up again.
An eagle, or hawk? One of the guardians that Byrne spoke of?
He tucked the feather in his belt and hurried after Byrne.

CHAPTER FORTY-THREE

BLEDA

Bleda heard the call to halt trickling down from the front of their column and reined in. He was riding rearguard today, the fifth day since they had set out from Drassil.

Where are they? he thought.

The sun was dipping into the west, a red glow above the trees of Forn. They were upon a wide road, broad enough for twenty riders abreast, and still more besides on the cleared fringe to each side. Not that the Sirak and Cheren were proceeding in that kind formation. They rode in neat, orderly columns, four ranks wide, spread out along the road over half a league or so.

After he was attacked, Uldin said he rode hard for five days to reach Drassil. Granted, we have been riding much slower than Uldin's galloping dash for safety, but still. If the Kadoshim were moving on Drassil, we should have met them by now.

His eyes drifted to the skies, a dazzle of blue through the lattice of branches that arched over the road, as he remembered that night in Drassil, Kadoshim flying over the walls, carrying warriors and Ferals in their arms.

He raised a fist, Ruga behind him sounding her horn, his hundred-strong rearguard reining to a halt. Bleda's eyes scoured the forest to either side. It was mostly thick-trunked oaks, their roots drinking the ground too dry for shrubs and thorn, and their branches were high, so the ground was clear; Bleda could see for a good way into the forest.

Good ground and passage for riders.

The drum of hooves, and Bleda saw a rider cantering down the column to him: Jin, looking fine in her war gear.

'We are making camp for the night,' she said. Bleda already knew that, knew that she didn't have to come and tell him. She seemed to make reasons to come and see him, to spend time in his company. It made him feel uncomfortable.

Bleda nodded a thanks to her.

'Any sign?' he asked her, more concerned right now about Kadoshim and Ferals than an amorous Jin.

'Nothing.' Jin shook her head. She gave him a long, lingering look as she turned her mount, came out of the turn with a spray of dirt and set her horse galloping back to the head of the column. It was a fine display of horsemanship, gaining some approving nods from Bleda's Sirak warriors.

'For a Cheren, she is a fair rider,' Tuld said beside him.

Old Ellac gave Tuld a flat look.

Riders began to dismount, setting to the task of making camp for the night.

Bleda inspected the defences of his section of their camp, Ellac, Tuld, Mirim and Ruga around him. All of their horses were picketed within a defensive line on the road, safe from the ordinary predators of Forn Forest, and Bleda paced wider onto the turf between the road and forest, found pairs of guards every thirty paces, torches burning at the mid-point between them. The guards stood in the shadowed point between the reach of each torch.

'Are you satisfied?' Ellac asked him.

'I am,' Bleda said, pleased with the discipline and vigilance amongst his hundred. He looked at Ellac and the other three.

'I have something to do, to ask,' he said. 'I would like you to accompany me and bear witness.'

Ellac and the others nodded, and Bleda turned on his heel and strode along the perimeter of their camp, deeper into their warband, into his mother's section. He found her sitting on a field chair at a fire-pit, her boots off, warming her feet before the fire. Yul her first-sword stood a few paces away, fire and shadow flickering across his face.

'Mother,' Bleda said, dipping his head to her.

'Aye?' she said.

'You gave me my brother's mail, called me a Sirak prince.'

'I did,' Erdene said, 'because you are.'

'Then to me it would seem fitting that I wore the Sirak warrior braid.' He drew a knife from his belt. 'Would you honour me?'

He offered Erdene his knife, held it out, glinting in the firelight as she looked from it to Bleda.

'I will,' Erdene said. She pulled on her boots and stood, taking Bleda's knife and ushering him into her chair.

'Leave us,' Erdene said to them all, 'I would have this time with my son.'

There was some hesitation, especially from Yul and Tuld, but Erdene's word was iron, so they retreated and disappeared into the shadows.

'The Sirak braid is the mark of a warrior,' Erdene said as she stood behind Bleda, unbinding the knot he'd tied his hair in. 'Are you a Sirak warrior, Bleda?'

'I am,' Bleda breathed.

'Have you faced another warrior in battle, looked in their eyes and known that one of you would live, and one of you would die?'

Bleda's mind raced back to the clearing at the woodsman's hut, when he had fought the Ben-Elim. And before that, to the Kadoshim and Ferals in Drassil.

'I have,' he said. It was a solemn burden, knowing that you had taken another's life, that you had stolen all the years they might have had and reduced them to a sack of skin and bone.

But better than the alternative, as Ellac had said to him after his first kill, when tears had blurred his eyes and his hands would not stop shaking.

Erdene took a fistful of hair from the side of Bleda's head and cut it away, shortening the sides, then began to shave the stubble and tufts that remained. She worked around his head in silence, just the rasp of Bleda's knife against his skin. When she had shaved his head, leaving only the portion that would be used for his warrior braid, she placed the knife on the ground and began to braid his hair. Bleda sat quietly, memories sifting through his mind, of his youth as a Sirak prince, living happy and free in Arcona. Of the day the Ben-Elim came, when Kol had thrown his brother's head at Erdene's feet. When he had been taken, torn from his family to become a ward of the Ben-Elim.

'I have always been faithful,' Bleda whispered. 'In here.' He placed the palm of his hand over his heart.

Erdene said nothing, continued to braid his hair, finally tying it with a leather cord. She came and knelt before him, placing a hand upon his.

'I know you have,' she said, meeting his gaze with her sea-grey eyes. 'I will say things to you now that have long been unsaid. We Sirak, we guard our feelings like treasure, and we wear the cold-face like a shield, but there is also a time to speak from the heart.' She looked around, probing the darkness. 'This is for your ears only, and who knows if we will ever get a chance to talk like this again.'

Erdene took a deep breath, holding his gaze. 'It broke my heart, the day you were taken from me,' she said, her voice little more than a whisper. 'And my heart has ached every moment from that day to this.'

Bleda opened his mouth to say something but she held up a finger.

'Ellac has reported to me through the years, and what he told me has made my heart soar. What a man you have become.

You have a rare balance inside you, my Bleda, of courage and wisdom. You stood against the Kadoshim when Jin would not. You took your own counsel and stood for your friend, Riv, against the Ben-Elim, and against Ellac's advice. I know you . . . feel for the half-breed, and yet you would sacrifice yourself. You would do your duty in wedding Jin to ensure peace for your Clan.'

Bleda blinked, knowing that he could not go through with the wedding.

But now is not the time to talk about that.

She lifted his hand and kissed it. 'I am proud to call you my son and feel glad in the knowledge that the Sirak will have a good king after I am gone.'

Five years of worry evaporated at Erdene's words. Bleda had been so scared that Erdene would think him unworthy and a traitor to the Clan, because he had been raised as a ward by the Ben-Elim. There was so much that he wanted to say to his mother, so many things that he had practised saying in an imagined moment like this, and yet it was all like mist, now, fading in the sun. Instead he smiled at her, deep and heartfelt, and she smiled in return.

'There is one last thing I wanted to say to you. You remember when I visited Drassil last year, and I spoke to you on the weapons-field? Do you remember my words to you?'

Bleda did, he had been so filled with a need to please his mother, to earn her respect. For the whole visit Erdene had been under the watchful eye of Israfil and his Ben-Elim, but for a few moments they had been distracted and Erdene had leaned close to Bleda, whispering in his ear.

'I do,' Bleda said.

'Never forget them,' Erdene said.

'But, surely things are different now?' Bleda said, puzzled.

Erdene opened her mouth to speak, then paused, cocking her head.

There was the whisper of wings above them; Bleda looked

up to see shadows flitting across the moon and suddenly Bleda and Erdene were on their feet, swords hissing into their fists. Horns started blaring, Yul, Ellac, Tuld and Ruga appeared, bows in their fists, the camp suddenly alive, like a kicked hornets' nest.

'Friend,' a voice called down from above, and Bleda glimpsed white-feathered wings.

A Ben-Elim dropped low over them, hovering, wings making the fire flicker.

'The Lord Protector is here,' he said, 'you are summoned to a council of war.'

Bleda rubbed his shaved head, feeling the warrior braid that his mother had woven for him. It felt wonderful finally to wear the symbol of his Clan.

And cold.

He was sitting in a circle around a fire-pit, his mother beside him, Uldin and Jin there also, as well as the Ben-Elim captain, Hadran. Kol sat before them all, and Riv sat beside him. Bleda was trying to stay focused on what Kol was saying, but his eyes kept drifting to Riv, thinking about when he had seen her last . . .

Riv's eyes were shining in the firelight, and Bleda could not be sure, but he thought that she was looking at him.

'Where are these Kadoshim and their followers, then?' Kol was saying.

Uldin shrugged. 'We have only covered half of the distance to the site where I was attacked,' he said. 'But if they are moving on Drassil, they should be close.' He looked left and right. 'But this is a big forest and a small road.'

'Yes, I agree,' Kol said. 'Galloping along this road with no ground support is dangerous.'

'Your Ben-Elim stressed that speed was important.' Uldin shrugged.

'It is,' Kol agreed, 'but not at the risk of ambush and anni-hilation.'

'We will not be the ones that are annihilated,' Erdene said.

'I stopped at Drassil first,' Kol said, 'and ordered a dozen units of our scouts and huntsmen to work towards us, scouring the forest as they go. And Lorina is marching up the east way with five hundred White-Wings. A rearguard support in case we need more ground troops.'

Bleda nodded to himself, thinking that was wise. The speed of the Sirak and Cheren was crucial in meeting this threat, but they were not best suited for combat beneath the trees of Forn Forest.

'What if this is a trick?' Riv said, speaking out for the first time. 'An ambush? Or like before, when we marched to Oriens, lured out to empty and weaken Drassil?'

'I have thought that, too,' Kol said. 'Drassil is safe, over two thousand Ben-Elim still there, with Aphra's five hundred White-Wings and more besides. The danger is here. We are at risk of an ambush here, and the Kadoshim have done it before, at Varan's Fall. Which is why we will move more slowly, and if we find them, we will only meet them in battle upon the road, and hold them until the White-Wings arrive.'

Bleda bridled at that, as did Uldin, by the look of him.

'If we bring our enemy to battle, there will be nothing left of them by the time the White-Wings have arrived,' Uldin said.

'The Cheren did not do so well against this enemy when they attacked you on the road,' Kol pointed out.

'We were heavily outnumbered, and taken by surprise,' Uldin growled. 'But with our Sirak kin beside us, victory is certain.'

'We will move slowly, scout the land around us and hold our enemy unless they engage us,' Kol said. 'That is my last word on it. Now, sleep, and we will move at dawn.'

*

Bleda stood in the starlight of a forest glade, waiting. Mirim and Ruga were close by, bows in their fists and arrows loosely nocked.

Not that we can see more than a dozen paces to shoot anything.

They were standing within the trees of Forn Forest, a few hundred paces away from the camp. Bleda could see the flicker of torchlight from the road.

Tuld, Ruga and Mirim had expressed their feelings about him doing this, sneaking out past the picket lines when there were possible enemies in the forest, besides the normal unpleasant predators of Forn.

But Bleda could not stop himself. He had to see her.

And then there was a whisper of movement, soft footfalls, and Tuld was approaching through the trees. He carried something in his arms, and a figure followed behind him.

Riv.

Tuld led her to Bleda, then he put the item in his arms down upon the forest litter.

'Leave us,' Bleda said to Tuld, Ruga and Mirim.

They did not move.

'Guard me, but not so close,' Bleda allowed, and the three guards slipped into the shadows.

And then Riv was in his arms, her lips upon his, her wings enfolding him.

'I have missed you, thought of you every waking moment,' he whispered when they parted.

Riv smiled and caressed his cheek, dappled starlight dancing across her wings.

'There is something about you, Bleda, that calms the storm that is ever raging in my blood,' she breathed.

'There is something about you, Riv, that stirs my blood into a storm,' he replied. Her smile grew wider.

'You have a new coat,' she said.

'Aye. My mother gave it to me,' Bleda said.

'It looks fine on you,' Riv grinned. 'And a new haircut.'

Bleda rubbed his shaven head, the skin stubbled in places, smooth in others. The unaccustomed weight of his warrior braid hung across his neck and shoulder. It felt strange.

'It suits you,' Riv said.

Bleda drew in a deep breath. 'I have something for you.' He looked down at the chest, bent and unbolted it, then carefully opened the lid. He stood, letting Riv see the Sirak bow within.

Riv bent and picked it up, turning it in her hands. It was unstrung, the layers of wood, horn and tendon shimmering in the starlight.

'Here, let me show you how to string it,' Bleda said, reaching inside his surcoat to pull a wax-rolled string from a pouch. Effortlessly he strung the bow and handed it back to Riv.

'Thank you,' she said. 'Did you . . . make this, for me?'

'I did,' Bleda said. 'I would like to test it, but now would not be a good idea.'

'No,' Riv agreed. 'Who knows what I would shoot?'

'Exactly,' Bleda said seriously, though Riv was smiling.

'And there is this,' Bleda said, crouching. He lifted a weapons-belt from the chest, a bow-case threaded onto it, and a quiver full of goose-fletched arrows.

Riv had an expression of joy on her face.

Bleda buckled the belt around her waist.

'I have added some straps,' he said, 'that buckle around your thigh, to keep the quiver and case in place if you are, you know, flying upside-down, or something. And there is a clip, to hold your arrows in place. Unflick it, like this.'

'You will need to teach me how to use this,' she said.

'I will,' Bleda promised. 'Though you are good enough to use it now. Just at big targets. Or close ones. Better if they are standing still and I am standing behind you.'

Riv snorted laughter at that. 'Ah, but it is good to see you, Bleda. The world is too dark and serious a place when you are not around.'

A crackle of forest litter and Tuld was appearing, pointing

into the woods. A hint of movement, shadows within shadows. Bleda reached for his bow, staring into the darkness, and with a beating of wings Riv was in the air, rising and disappearing into the darkness.

Bleda paced to where he thought he'd seen movement, but there was nothing there, and it was too dark to check the ground for tracks.

Tuld, Mirim and Ruga materialized out of the gloom, shaking their heads, and then Riv was returning, landing in a swirl of leaves.

'Nothing,' she said.

'You should get back to camp,' Mirim said, Ruga and Tuld agreeing fervently.

'We should,' Riv agreed.

She unstrung her bow and slipped it into the bow-case.

'My thanks,' Riv said, leaning forwards and brushing her lips against Bleda's cheek. 'I will treasure this.'

'Only string it for battle,' Bleda said, 'or if you think battle is likely.'

'I will,' Riv said, another bright grin from her and then she was taking to wing and merging with the darkness above.

CHAPTER FORTY-FOUR

DREM

'I'm stuck,' Drem said, his voice muffled. He was trying to put on a coat of mail, had seemed to be doing fine when he threaded his arms into it, but now he was having trouble getting it over his shoulders and finding the slit to squeeze his head through. His head and arms were in, but there seemed to be no way forward, just a great claustrophobic weight of steel constricting him.

Cullen chuckled behind him.

'There is an art to getting into a shirt of mail, Drem, my lad,' Cullen said.

Why does he insist on calling me his lad when I am older than him? Not for the first time, Drem resisted his usual urge to correct.

'I'll help you, lad,' Keld said, a reassuring hand on Drem's back. 'Now, lift your arms straight up, and jump up and down. Let gravity do the work for you.'

Drem did, and after a few moments of worry, and a helping hand from Keld, the mail shirt slithered down over his head and torso.

It was heavy, rubbing on his shoulders, a weight on his arms when he tried to lift them, like he was wading through water.

'I don't like it,' Drem said. 'How can I fight in this?'

'A chainmail shirt is a pain, and no denying,' Keld said. 'Takes some getting used to. But this will turn a blow that would slice through your leather jerkin like butter. Better to put up with the sore shoulders and be a bit slower than be dead.'

'But will being slower make me just as dead?' Drem worried.

Keld shrugged. 'Move faster.'

That's helpful.

'This'll help,' Keld said, slipping a thin leather belt around Drem's waist and buckling it tight.

Keld was right, though, as soon as the belt was on, it took some of the mail shirt's weight off Drem's shoulders.

Over half a moon had passed since the night he had entered the tunnels with Byrne. He could feel the scrape of the mail coat on the healing cut on his arm, little more than a dry scab now. He felt a sense of elation when he remembered that night, when he had sworn himself to Byrne. He did not regret it. Since then, each day, more warriors of the Order had arrived, answering Byrne's summons to muster. And on each of those days Drem had trained almost from dawn until dusk. His left arm felt like it was going to fall off, muscles seized and stiff from shield work, something that Drem had been entirely unaccustomed to. Muscles throughout his whole body ached. Not because he was unfit. Living a trapper's life in the Desolation had toned and honed Drem's physicality far beyond what was normal, but these last fourteen nights Drem had used muscles in ways that they had never been used before.

He rolled his shoulders and ignored the aches and pains.

Keld and Cullen were already in shirts of mail, Cullen with a dark leather surcoat buckled over the top, Dun Seren's four-pointed star emblazoned upon it. Keld wore his star in his cloak-brooch.

'Here you go, lad,' Cullen said, passing Drem his weapons-belt. Drem rolled his eyes at Cullen and took the belt. His sword and seax were already scabbarded on it, as well as two empty rings for hand-axes. There was also a pouch with Drem's flint and striking iron, some tinder, and beside it one of the

Order's weighted nets, folded and ready for use. Drem had trained with it, managed to wrap himself in the net a dozen times before finally mastering the art of looping it over his head and releasing.

It had felt like a glorious moment. He liked to learn.

'Well, looks like you're all dressed as fine as can be,' Keld said, looking Drem up and down.

A horn sounded from outside.

Drem felt a stone settle in his gut. They all knew what the horn was for, a weight hanging over them all, though none of them had spoken of it since Drem had opened his chamber door to the two warriors. It had all been light-hearted quips, purposely avoiding what they knew was coming.

They were leaving Dun Seren and marching back into the Desolation. Crow scouts had returned from the Desolation, telling of Gulla's warband marching south from Kergard and destroying all in its path. Drem knew that Byrne had hoped to continue gathering her forces until Kol's White-Wings had arrived, but this news from the north had forced her hand.

'We exist to protect the innocent from evil like the Kadoshim,' Byrne had said to Drem. *'We will not sit idly by while innocents are being slaughtered. Not when I can do something to save them.'*

So, they were marching to war.

The three of them shared a look.

'It's time, then,' Cullen said.

Drem grabbed two short-axes from his desk where he'd been sharpening them and slipped them into the rings on his belt.

They turned and walked from Drem's chambers, through corridors that grew busier with every footstep, and then they were striding through Dun Seren's keep and out onto the steps that led down into the courtyard.

All was noise and chaos. Horses, bears and wolven-hounds, giants, men and women, a swirling, milling mass. Keld led them across the courtyard to a huge stable block, stablehands standing and waiting with three bridled horses. Drem took the reins of his mount, a big roan mare. She whickered as he rested his head against hers, gave her half an apple from his belt pouch, which she crunched contentedly, and then he was swinging himself up into the saddle, a moment as he wavered, adjusting to the weight of his chainmail shirt, and then he was settled in the saddle.

A few moments of waiting, cold breath misting in dawn's chill, Drem patting his horse's neck, and then horns were blowing again and Byrne was riding into the courtyard, Ethlinn and Balur behind her, mounted upon great bears. Byrne reined in before the statue of Corban, a silence settled; her horse dancing a few paces, sensing the excitement and adrenalin that was crackling through the fortress.

'We are marching to kill Gulla,' Byrne cried out, 'to put an end to those that have brought war to our world.' She paused, looked around. 'TRUTH AND COURAGE,' she yelled, and Drem added his voice to the roar that answered her.

'TRUTH AND COURAGE,' echoing from the fortress walls, lingering in the air.

And then Byrne was riding out from the courtyard, crows circling in the air above, squawking a cacophony of '*Truth and Courage.*'

Ethlinn and Balur One-Eye rode behind Byrne, a clattering of hooves and bear claws and iron-shod boots. Two thousand warriors, men, women and giants, a swarm of wolven-hounds loping on their flanks, banners of a white star on a black field rippling in the wind, and the Order of the Bright Star rode forth from Dun Seren.

'Where is everyone?' Drem asked.

They had been riding half a day and had just reached Dalgarth, the bustling traders' village that Drem had passed through on the way to Dun Seren. It was a very different place, now.

Cure had travelled back to Dun Seren from Dalgarth once

since Drem had returned from the Desolation, to tell them that Dalgarth was to be quarantined. He had ridden back the same day, and not been heard from since.

The walls were unmanned, gates hanging open, creaking on a northerly wind, and the streets were empty.

A sense of unease seeped into Drem, and he could see it was affecting them all, warriors ahead and behind looking about, searching for any signs of life. Drem was close to the head of the column and he saw Stepor appear from a side alley, his black and red wolven-hounds with him as he reported to Byrne.

'No one, not a soul,' Drem heard the huntsman say.

'Where have they all gone?' Cullen said, a frown creasing his usual high spirits.

Keld said nothing, but the three of them shared a look. Hildith and the scouts had told tales of the holds and villages in the Desolation laid low by plague and something worse.

Revenants, Drem thought.

He shrugged his shoulders and loosened his sword and seax in their scabbards.

They rode on, through the silent village, even the crows above them ceasing their constant chatter. Slowly the warband emerged from the far side of the village and continued. As they crested a ridge Drem reined in a moment and twisted in his saddle, looking back.

Dalgarth sat like a stain upon the land, unnaturally still and empty, and behind it in the distance Drem could see the dark line of the river Vold, and the walls and tower of Dun Seren beyond.

I have only been there a short while, but Cullen was right, it does feel like home.

He turned, looking forwards, the undulating, cracked landscape of the Desolation before him.

And now we are riding back towards danger, towards Kadoshim and Feral beasts and death. He sighed, feeling the weight of it settling in his soul.

But I am glad to do that, because my father's killers are out there. Fritha, Gunil and you, Gulla, the puppet-master of these dread days. I will kill you all, if I can. I shall take my father's sword back, and then I shall fulfil his oath, and slay your king. I will take Asroth's head.

If I can.

Or die in the trying.

He clicked his horse into a trot, catching up with Cullen and Keld, and they rode on.

Into the Desolation.

CHAPTER FORTY-FIVE

BLEDA

Bleda rode at the centre of their column, his mother riding as vanguard today. It had been Uldin's idea to rotate each day, a way of avoiding bad feeling between the Sirak and Cheren about who led and who rode rearguard. Bleda was impressed with Uldin's straightforward diplomacy, a simple and fair way of avoiding unnecessary conflict. It gave Bleda hope for the future between the two Clans.

If Uldin is this level-headed, perhaps he will be the one to see that my handbinding to Jin is not vital for the Cheren and Sirak to co-exist peacefully.

Then he remembered Uldin's words to him upon his arrival at Drassil.

Are you worthy of my daughter?

Bleda shifted in his saddle, feeling abruptly uncomfortable. He searched the sky for Riv, saw the silhouettes of Ben-Elim high above, but could not pick out the dapple-grey wings that set Riv apart.

This was their sixth day out from Drassil and, as Kol had ordered, they were riding at a slower pace, sending scouts into the fringes of the forest, making the most of the high branches and navigable ground.

There was a creaking sound ahead, horn blasts from the front of the column and riders were reining in. Bleda guided his horse to the edge of the road so that he had a better view down the column. He saw Erdene sitting tall in her saddle, staring at something ahead.

Then Bleda saw it, too. A huge oak on the forest edge, branches swaying as if it was caught in some solitary wind. The creaking sound grew louder, building into a sharp *crack*, and then the tree was falling, branches and trunk crashing down onto the road, a cloud of dust erupting around it, settling slowly.

Bleda reached for his bow, in a few heartbeats had it strung. All around him Sirak were doing the same.

Behind him hooves drummed and Jin cantered up along the line.

'What is happening?' she asked him. 'Why have we stopped?'

Bleda nodded at the fallen tree. 'Ambush. Be ready,' he said.

Jin gave him a curt nod even as she was turning her mount and galloping back down the line.

And then something emerged from the treeline, just in front of the fallen oak, about eight or nine hundred paces before Erdene and the head of the column.

Two auroch, big bulls with huge chests as wide as a wagon and low-curving horns. They were harnessed, behind them was a wain, enormous in its proportions, two shaven-haired men sitting upon the driving bench, reins in hand. Upon the wain was a giant box, or cage.

And then another brace of auroch appeared, pulling another similar-sized wain, two more figures on the driving bench, another massive box upon the wain's back. It stopped behind the first wain.

A silence settled, the creak of wood as the wains strained under some immense weight, Bleda hearing sounds of movement within the boxes.

Scratching, sniffing.

A growl.

I don't like this.

Erdene called out an order and her front ranks shifted, Sirak warriors riding out either side of her, forming a long line across the road, thirty riders wide. More ranks formed in disciplined order behind the first. Bows were strung and in hands, all with fists bristling full of arrows.

Ben-Elim flew overhead, Kol appearing, flanked by a dozen more winged warriors, all of them landing in the space between Erdene and the wains, other Ben-Elim remaining in the sky above. They all seemed hesitant to approach the wains.

Bleda remembered the giant Alcyon telling him of the Battle of Varan's Fall, where the Ben-Elim were ambushed within Forn Forest and suffered serious losses. Alcyon had said that the Ben-Elim had been far more hesitant since then, reluctant to press forward in any situation where they were not certain of victory.

A silhouette flew out from the trees ahead, its wings dark, not white, and Bleda recognized the distinct outline of a Kadoshim.

Fear uncoiled in his belly.

Fear is not the enemy, it is the herald of danger, and that is only wisdom, he reminded himself of the Sirak's Iron Code. *Fear is wisdom, but you must master it, lest it master you.*

The creature landed upon the top of one of the cages, feet spread, and looked down at Kol and his Ben-Elim. Something seemed *strange* about it, different from the Kadoshim Bleda remembered. It looked taller, and a nimbus shadow appeared to edge it, blurring the lines of its movement. Other Kadoshim followed, swirling out from the trees, circling above and behind the wains like a murder of crows, fifty, sixty, a hundred, more joining them as Bleda stared.

'Is that you, Kol?' the Kadoshim upon the cage called out. 'I had heard a rumour that Israfil was dead and you had replaced him. I hoped it was true.'

'Aye, Gulla, it is I,' Kol said coldly. 'I am glad to see you crawl out from beneath your rock. It is a mistake, of course,

because now I am going to send you back to the Otherworld.'
He raised a fist, Ben-Elim swooping up from the back of the
column, speeding over the heads of Uldin's Cheren.

Gulla just leaned down, gripping a huge iron pin on the
cage front and tugging it free. With a squeal of iron and wood
the front panel of the cage fell forwards, crashing to the ground,
a cloud of dust erupting. There was the sound of savage snarling, a cacophony of howls and growls, and then a tide of fur and
muscle and claw was exploding from the dust cloud.

Bleda felt his blood freeze.

Ferals.

But where Bleda had seen a score or so of these creatures
before, now hundreds of them swarmed from the cage and
surged towards Kol, and Erdene behind him, even as another
Kadoshim landed onto the top of the second cage and pulled
the pin, releasing the door in another eruption of Feral beasts.

Kol and his Ben-Elim companions leaped into the air, rushing to attack the Kadoshim swirling above them.

Behind them Erdene was shouting, just noise, but horns
rang out from those beside her and the front rows of her Sirak
began to trot forwards, at the tide of Feral murder surging
towards them. Even in the midst of the chaos and terror that
was turning his veins to ice, Bleda felt his chest swell with pride
for his mother, ordering a charge at these fearsome creatures,
where the first and basest instinct was to turn and run.

Another horn blast, Erdene and her Sirak breaking into a
canter, bows in hand, arrows gripped, and then within heartbeats they were at a gallop, their hooves a thunderous avalanche,
five hundred paces between them and the onrushing, slavering
Ferals, four hundred paces, three hundred, two, and then the
front rank of Erdene's line was breaking left and right, across
the Ferals' path, and their bows were singing, arrows loosing,
the huge power of the Sirak bows hammering into the front
rows of the Ferals' charge, hurling them from their feet, throwing them back into those behind. Screams and howls of agony

rang out, Ferals going down in a tangle, snaring those on their heels, a tumbling mass of limbs and blood.

Bleda saw Ferals claw their way back to their feet, tearing arrows from their bodies, raising their heads to the sky and howling, then breaking into a run again. Some stayed down, a dozen arrows pin-cushioning them, twisted unnaturally in death.

But still the vast tide of them came on.

Erdene and her front row were galloping back along the roadside, reforming behind her last row of riders to continue the manoeuvre in a perpetual cycle, peeling and loosing their arrows in an endless hammer-hail curtain.

They need more room.

Bleda had seen this manoeuvre performed before, upon the open plains of Arcona, where mounted warriors could ride like flocks of birds in the open sky. But here their flanks were constricted by the looming walls of the forest, and they could not endlessly retreat because the road was blocked by Bleda's hundred and then Uldin's Cheren.

We need to get off the road, give them more room to retreat.

A movement on the edge of Bleda's vision, amongst the trees on his left. He stared, arrow nocked, and then saw a Sirak rider burst from the trees, one of their scouts. He was shouting a warning, twisting in his saddle and shooting back over the hindquarters of his mount into the murk.

'Protect the flanks,' Bleda cried out, the cry rippling through the warriors about him, spreading, and he commanded his horse towards the trees. His hundred began falling in on either side of him, a long row facing into the forest.

'Tell Uldin, protect the right flank,' Bleda yelled to Mirim beside him. She nodded and galloped away.

Two bodies crashed into the turf before Bleda, making his mount dance backwards. A Ben-Elim and Kadoshim, wrapped in a tangle of limbs and wings, still fighting, stabbing, biting, even as they rolled on the ground. They came to a halt, a flurry of blows, then a sharp shriek.

The Ben-Elim rose slowly to his feet, blood on his face, wings shaking off grass and dirt, and then he was leaping back into the air, hurtling back into the combat that was swirling above.

And then figures were materializing out of the shadows of the trees, shaven-haired men and women, faces twisted in fanatical rage, screaming as they came running at Bleda's line.

A hundred arrows loosed, the sound a sweet music in Bleda's ears, and all along the treeline the enemy were falling, tumbling to the ground.

Bleda drew and loosed, drew and loosed, grabbed another fistful of arrows from his quiver, but more enemies surged from the trees, pounding across the bodies of their comrades, so much closer now.

A snatched glimpse right and left showed Erdene's Sirak swirling back in an endless retreat down the road, the Ferals surging on, snapping and snarling, the gap between them down to fifty or sixty paces now. Uldin's Cheren on the right flank were facing a storm of shaven-haired enemy, as Bleda was.

Only twenty or thirty paces now between Bleda and the enemy pouring from the forest.

Bleda loosed almost point-blank into the face of a woman, her spear stabbing up at him. His arrow pierced her eye, hurled her back into a man behind her, both of them going down in a heap.

'SWORDS,' Bleda yelled, slipping his bow into its case at his hip, his hand reaching over his shoulder, gripping the worn leather of his sword hilt and drawing, all along the line his warriors doing the same.

'WITH ME,' Bleda screamed and clicked his horse on, riding to meet the enemy rushing towards him.

His trained mount barrelled into a man, threw him to the ground, then hooves were trampling the fallen warrior, cutting short his screams. Bleda struck downwards, his sword jarring on an upraised blade. The blow shivered through his wrist and arm, numb for a moment, he swept a parry, sending a spear-thrust aimed at his chest wide, returned with a backswing from his curved sword, opening a red line across the spear-man's face, and saw him fall away, clutching at bloody folds of flesh.

Bleda rode deeper into his enemy, the treeline looming.

A grunt and scream to his left, a thrown spear slamming into Ruga, hurling her from her saddle. Bleda looked, could not see her, swayed in his saddle as an axe tried to take his face off. He chopped down, a scream, a hand hanging almost severed, dangling by a shred of sinew and skin. He thrust down, into the screaming mouth of his foe, ripped his sword free in a spray of teeth and blood.

And then the enemy were breaking before him, turning and running back into the gloom. Bleda reined in, resisting the urge to pursue his enemy, the blood-rush of victory a sudden surge in his veins. A snatched glimpse over his shoulder and he saw the same was happening to Uldin, the Cheren King spurring his horse after them, his warband following him into the treeline.

'After them,' Bleda yelled, spurring his horse over the bodies of the fallen as he chased after his fleeing enemy.

CHAPTER FORTY-SIX

RIV

Riv tucked her wings and stooped into a dive, slamming into a Kadoshim, the creature grunting as her shoulder crunched into its belly. A flurry of blows were exchanged, steel sparking as swords sought flesh, spiralling in each other's grip, and then Riv's short-sword was stabbing through rusted mail and leather, into the flesh beneath. The Kadoshim shrieked and spasmed in her grip, back arching. With a savage wrench, Riv ripped her blade free and released the Kadoshim, saw it crash into the horde of Ferals that were swarming after Erdene's Sirak, scattering a handful in its ruin.

Hovering in the sky, Riv brandished her bloodied sword in the air, screeching her battle joy.

This is what I was made for, born to do, she exulted, a wild release flooding through her veins as she shrugged off the cloaked weight of normal living, no longer having to think about the rights and wrongs, the moral complexities and consequences of decisions.

She just had to fight, and to kill.

She searched for her next foe.

They were not in short supply.

Hadran had brought a thousand Ben-Elim on this campaign, a number deemed more than adequate to meet any Kadoshim threat, as all knew the Kadoshim numbers had been hit the worst during the last hundred years of war. And yet to

Riv's eyes this aerial combat in the sky seemed equal. It was so hard to tell, the combatants an ever-moving eddy of wings and steel, of feather and dark-leathered skin, but if anything, it looked to Riv that there were more bat wings than feathered in the skies around her.

How can there be this many Kadoshim?

Death screams from below drew her eye and Riv saw Bleda and his hundred upon the left flank of the battle, holding against a tide of enemy that swept out of the forest. Even as she looked, she saw the enemy break and run, saw Bleda rein his horse in, looking back towards the far flank and Uldin. The same was happening there, the enemy fleeing back into the trees. And Uldin followed, disappearing from view, his hundreds of Cheren sweeping after him.

'Idiot,' Riv breathed. Then, to her horror, she saw Bleda doing the same. She shouted out to him, but of course he did not hear her, her voice lost in the din of battle. She tucked her wings to go after him, and then something slammed into her side, and she was spinning through the air.

Steel glinted as a knife stabbed at Riv's throat. She twisted, felt a hot line graze her neck, grabbed the wrist with one hand, saw a male, flat-boned, snarling face, a shaven-haired skull and bat-like wings.

But that's not a Kadoshim.

One of their half-breeds.

The half-breed punched Riv in the face, pulped a lip, the taste of blood in her mouth.

She spat, gave a savage grin and headbutted the half-breed, once, twice across the bridge of his nose, blood and cartilage spraying.

A twist of her arm on the half-breed's wrist and he was spinning through the air. He swung a thick-muscled arm, fist connecting with Riv's jaw, stars exploding, and her grip loosened, the half-breed ripping his wrist free.

Then her assailant was stabbing at her again, Riv shaking

her head clear, wings beating, reversing her away from the half-breed's rush, her short-sword swinging in a looping block, steel grating as the knife stabbed wide, a rotation of her shoulder and twist of her wrist and her sword opened a gash across the half-breed's throat. Arterial blood sprayed, a look of surprise on his face as he dropped like a stone to the ground.

Riv hovered a moment, her wings beating to keep her semi-stationary. She shook her head again to try and clear the fog as the half-breed's corpse hit the ground below.

That is why our numbers are so even. The Kadoshim have been breeding an army to swell their numbers.

While the Ben-Elim have been murdering their offspring, the Kadoshim have been cultivating and training theirs for war.

On the ground Erdene was still retreating in her ever-looping hail of arrows. The twisted bodies of Ferals littered the ground between the two huge cages and Erdene's Sirak, but it looked as if hundreds of the mutated beasts were still powering after Erdene, merely a score of paces separating them now. It was only a short matter of time before the Ferals caught up to Erdene's troops and all became chaos.

Even as Riv looked, she saw Erdene's mouth open wide, yelling orders to a rider beside her, a horn blast and the row of Sirak closest to the Ferals pulled up, twenty or thirty riders, a heartbeat to sheathe their bows and draw the curved swords upon their backs, and then their mounts were leaping forwards, a short charge into the Ferals, hooves rearing, lashing out, swords slicing and chopping.

They are buying Erdene time.

And Erdene used the time her riders were buying her, her warriors reforming and galloping back down the road, opening a gap between them and the Ferals.

Riv felt a wave of respect for those who had charged into the tide of Ferals, knew there was only one fate for them. They were falling already, claws and fangs ripping into horseflesh, dragging the mounts to the ground, other Ferals leaping, slamming into riders and tearing them from their saddles.

A fresh wave of rage swept Riv for those brave men and women. She sheathed her short-sword and lifted her bow from its case, flicked the leather clasp on her quiver and snatched out a handful of arrows, as Bleda had showed her.

He said aim at a big target.

She loosed her handful of arrows into the swarm of Ferals, recognizing the power in the draw of this bow, the smooth snap and twang of the string as she loosed. She grabbed another handful of arrows and loosed them, too, saw one arrow punch into a skull, the Feral collapsing without a sound. Even so, a dozen heartbeats later and the last of the Sirak riders was being dragged from her mount, still chopping about her with her sword as her flesh was torn and rent.

This is useless.

Bleda.

Riv slipped her bow back into its case, tucked her wings and dropped into a dive, sweeping over the ground between Erdene and the Ferals, searching for the point she had last seen Bleda.

It was easy to find, a tide line of dead shaven-haired acolytes marking the spot. She dropped to the ground, eyes peering into the twilight gloom of Forn. Dim figures were moving, riders on horseback, and others on foot about them. The ring of steel echoed out from the treeline.

To Riv's left Erdene was leading her Sirak warband back down the road, to her right the Ferals were bounding, leaping and snarling in their fury as they chased after their retreating prey.

A groan behind Riv, and she turned to see a Sirak warrior try to rise from the ground. A woman, a spear lodged in the meat between her shoulder and chest. It was Ruga, Bleda's guard. Riv ran to her, the rush of Ferals so close now, the ground trembling, the sound of their snarling fury almost deafening.

She tore the spear from Ruga, cast it at the oncoming

Ferals and then swept the injured woman up into her arms, powerful beats of her wings lifting them both into the air, a Feral leaping at her, teeth snapping, claws raking Riv's boot. She kicked out, saw the Feral crash to the ground, and then Riv and Ruga were climbing higher, out of reach of the onrushing river of monsters beneath them as they continued their mindless, furious charge after Erdene.

Riv hovered, taking a moment to assess the battle.

All around her Ben-Elim fought with Kadoshim and their half-breeds, the battle raging, balanced. On the ground, Erdene seemed to have a good distance between her and the Ferals, ever-widening, and on Riv's side of the road the dim sounds of combat drifted up and out from the forest.

Riv was about to fly back into the trees and resume her search for Bleda when a movement caught her eyes.

It was far down the road, ahead of Erdene's retreating warband.

Another huge wain with a giant cage atop it was being rolled out by musclebound auroch. It stopped across the road, cutting off Erdene's retreat, a half-breed Kadoshim alighting on it and reaching down for the gate-pin.

Oh no.

CHAPTER FORTY-SEVEN

BLEDA

Bleda chopped through a raised hand, severing fingers, and then swung his sword into the meat between neck and shoulder. Another blow from Bleda crunched into the man's skull and he toppled lifeless to the ground.

A twist of Bleda's knees, guiding his mount between trees as another foe leaped at him, a woman with a short-sword in her fist. Their blades clashed, the woman's hand grasping at Bleda's surcoat as she tried to heave herself up his horse's side. Bleda hacked into her arm, above the elbow, and she fell backwards, blood jetting. A command and twitch of Bleda's reins and his horse was rearing, hooves lashing out, punching the woman in the chest and face and she was crashing to the ground.

There was a moment's lull as Bleda looked around, trying to make sense of the chaos surrounding him. He had ridden deep into the forest, a wild, heedless charge at first, cutting down all those that were running before him. His line of warriors was broken by trees and melee combat as many of those they had chased into the darkness had turned and resumed their fighting. Bleda blinked, straining his eyes, the gloom restricting his vision to less than thirty or forty paces. He was not even sure what direction would lead him back to the road.

A horse swept past him, Ellac upon its back, a sword in his one hand, a buckler of iron strapped to his other. He was hacking at enemy either side of him, a spear-wielding man closest to Bleda.

Bleda urged his horse forwards. The spear-man heard his approach, twisting and stabbing his spear up, into the chest of Bleda's horse. The animal screamed, stumbled, Bleda feeling it shudder beneath him, biting as its forelegs collapsed, taking a chunk of flesh from the enemy's cheek even as it died.

Bleda fell from the saddle, threw himself away before the horse could roll and pin his leg. He staggered to his feet, saw the spear-man coming at him, blood gushing from the bite on his face, the weapon stabbing for his gut. Bleda stumbled backwards, slashing wildly at the spear, caught it a glancing blow, deflecting it a little so that the spearhead stabbed into Bleda's side, the plates of his lamellar coat holding, turning the strike harmlessly away.

And then the man's head was gone, a severed stump erupting blood. The body fell to its knees and toppled to the ground.

Tuld was peering down at him from atop his horse.

'My thanks,' Bleda grunted.

Ellac joined them, his sword red to the hilt.

They had been left behind in the melee, distant shadows and muffled cries, the three of them seemingly alone in the twilight world of Forn.

Then something changed in the forest around them.

It seemed to get darker, as if night were falling, and yet Bleda knew it could not even be highsun yet. A darkness swelled in the gloom, like a black thundercloud rolling across the ground, deeper within the forest, enveloping the last shadows of those Bleda could see fighting.

Screams, high and shrieking.

They spoke to Bleda of terror, rather than pain.

'I do not like this,' Ellac muttered, his sword pointing at the darkness. His horse danced, ears back.

And then a figure appeared from the gloom, exploding out of the dark cloud that filled the forest before them. A man, no weapons, grey and gaunt, clothing tattered and hanging in strips. Its eyes were shadowed wells, lips thin and blue-black, teeth razored and glinting.

Bleda felt the urge to turn and run.

The man-thing saw them, changed its course and ran at them.

Tuld's horse reared, Tuld falling backwards from his saddle, the horse lashing out with its hooves at this new creature. Bleda heard the distinct sound of bones splintering as hooves connected with the newcomer's chest and shoulder. It flew backwards, rolled. Was still. And then it began to climb to its feet, one arm hanging limp. There was a series of juddering snaps as bones and joints struggled to support its weight, yet still it managed to regain its footing. It looked at them, and lips drew back in a parody of a smile.

It ran at them again.

Tuld's horse bolted, the Sirak warrior stumbling to his feet, Bleda moving to help him.

Tuld swung his sword, perfectly timed to connect with his attacker's neck, but somehow it swayed, Tuld's strike whistling harmlessly over its head, and then it was on him, slamming into Tuld with no thoughts of defence.

They rolled, Bleda running to reach them, Tuld's blade rising and falling, chopping and cutting into the creature's arm and back. And all the while it was biting Tuld, jaws unnaturally wide, crunching down onto whatever part of Tuld presented itself. His arm, his shoulder, hand, the side of his head.

Tuld was screaming.

They rolled to a stop, Tuld's sword arm flailing, Bleda reaching them, stabbing down with his sword into the creature's back. Bleda felt flesh part, his sword-point slipping through ribs into the vital parts of a human's body. He twisted his blade and wrenched it free, felt ribs snap.

The creature's jaws fastened around Tuld's neck. A savage

shake of its head, and dark blood was jetting, Tuld's sword dropping from his fingers.

Bleda screamed his rage, hacked two-handed into the creature's neck, cutting almost to the spine.

It rolled off of Tuld, the Sirak warrior's blood drenching its lips and lower jaw, and it seemed almost to float back to its feet.

The drum of hooves and Ellac was there, chopping down at the creature. It swayed, lightning-fast, Ellac's sword slicing a chunk of flesh from its shoulder instead of hacking into its head.

'Get out of here,' Ellac yelled, and Bleda wanted nothing more than to obey, to turn and run as fast as his feet could carry him.

But this thing had just killed Tuld. His oathsworn man.

Bleda raised his sword, chopped into its side, then drew his arm back and stepped into a lunge, his whole body weight behind the blow, stabbing the creature through its belly, his sword-point punching out through its back.

It looked at Bleda then, a dark malice leaking from its eyes. Then it grabbed the blade of Bleda's sword and began to drag itself along it, towards Bleda, its jaws chomping and gnashing in some kind of paroxysm of fury or hunger.

Ellac was still hacking down at the beast, rocking it, but having no other obvious effect.

And then there was a rushing of wings, Riv appearing, her sword slicing into the creature's neck, once, twice, three times. The head rolled away and bounced on the ground as the thing collapsed. No expected jet of blood burst from the creature's severed stump, just a thick, pale, porridge-like substance. Bleda ripped his sword free and continued to hack at the corpse as it slumped to the ground, where it twitched and spasmed on the forest litter, fading to tremors, a shudder, and was then still.

'What in the Otherworld was that?' Riv snarled.

'I don't know,' Bleda said, breathing heavily. 'But it came

from there.' He pointed with his sword at the black cloud that was rolling closer, filling the forest.

'Quickly,' Riv said. 'Your mother needs you.'

'What?' Bleda hissed, a knife blade of worry twisting inside his belly.

More figures emerged from the dark, the same hollow eyes, thin lips and unpleasant-looking teeth. Five, ten, a score, more shapes shifting into focus behind them. They saw Bleda, Ellac and Riv and moved towards them, breaking into a run, frighteningly fast.

'RUN,' Ellac yelled, guiding his horse in front of Bleda. He raised his sword and buckler at the rush of creatures swarming towards them.

Riv swept Bleda up into her arms and kicked the rump of Ellac's horse, sending it bolting.

'Get back to the road,' she yelled at Ellac as she leaped and beat her wings. 'Gather all you can – Erdene needs you.' And then Bleda was being carried through the air, Riv twisting and turning, weaving through the trees and speeding towards the light that was growing somewhere ahead.

And more importantly, away from those things behind us.

They burst out into daylight, Bleda blinking.

The roadside was littered with the dead, the acolytes that Bleda had repelled. A handful of Sirak horses were grazing on the roadside, riderless. Bleda looked up and saw the skies above were worryingly clear. The aerial war between Ben-Elim and Kadoshim had drifted a long way down the road, back towards Drassil.

The sounds of battle banished any more thoughts.

To Bleda's right he could see the backs of a host of Ferals.

'What's going on?' Bleda said.

'I'll show you,' Riv said, hoisting him into the air.

The road spread out beneath him. The Ferals he'd seen released from their cages were now only paces away from Erdene's warband. The Sirak had formed into a stationary circle, arrows launching out, because their path of retreat along the road had been blocked by another wain and cage. Its gate had been opened, another swarm of Ferals rampaging along the road towards Erdene.

She is finished. Ferals attacking from east and west, north and south blocked by the forest. And there is no escape beneath the trees, not after what I've just seen in there.

Even as he looked, the Ferals that had been released first were slamming into Erdene's warband, a deafening crash as they ploughed through men and horses, the Ferals snarling, biting, clawing in a frenzy as they finally caught up with their prey.

A raucous cheering from the skies drew Bleda's gaze into the distance. To his horror he saw that the Ben-Elim were breaking, wheeling away and trying to disengage from the Kadoshim and their half-breeds. Through the chaos he glimpsed white wings speeding westwards, those that could, Kadoshim jeering and whooping their victory.

They are abandoning us.

Cold rage at the Ben-Elim's betrayal and a deeper fear for his mother filled him.

There will be no help from the Ben-Elim, the cowards.

The only hope is to punch through the Ferals to the west and retreat towards Drassil.

'Riv, put me down,' Bleda said, and she dropped to the earth. Bleda ran for one of the Sirak horses and vaulted into the high-fronted saddle, tugging on the reins and guiding it towards his mother.

Ellac burst from the trees, scores of Bleda's guard at his back.

Bleda grinned to see them. He spurred his horse onto the road, Ellac and the others falling in behind him, spreading to either side, and as one they broke into a gallop towards Erdene. Towards a sea of Ferals.

Bleda took his bow from its case, reached for arrows from his quiver and then he was leaning into the high front of his saddle for balance, loosing arrow after arrow after arrow into the backs of the Ferals, Riv swooping above, her bow in her hand, loosing at large knots of Ferals. They howled and screamed, reaching, tearing at the pain in their backs. Some dropped to the ground, pierced countless times, others turned, enraged, and ran at Bleda and his remaining guard.

One Feral sped ahead of the rest, running low to the ground, almost on all fours, its distended long arms raking at the road. And then it was leaping into the air, its wide jaws a red maw, claws reaching for Bleda's throat.

Bleda leaned in his saddle, drew and loosed, putting an arrow into the Feral's eye, little more than the fletching left visible. It spasmed in the air, a convulsion of limbs as it died, crashing to the ground and rolling in a heap.

Bleda galloped past it.

And then they were too close for arrows, Bleda's bow slipping back into its case, his sword hissing from its scabbard, all those along his line doing the same. They crashed into the rear of the creatures, hooves and horseflesh pounding, trampling, mangling the first line of the musclebound beasts. Bleda and his guard lay about them either side with their swords, hacking and chopping, sending great bloody gouts trailing through the air. Then they were slowing, the press and heave of bodies crushed together halting their advance. Ferals twisted to face this new foe, tearing at Bleda and his warriors. Bleda dug his heels into his horse, hacked and stabbed, but still he could not break through to his mother's warriors. He could see them, hear his mother's voice as she bellowed at her enemy, but there were too many.

A Feral climbed up a dying horse and leaped at Bleda; in mid-leap Riv crashed into it, sending it hurtling back to the ground, a red wound in its chest. She swooped back up, hovering above them to loose more arrows into the Ferals.

We cannot break through to my mother. And there is another mass of Ferals beyond her.

Bleda felt his hope dying, vowed to sell his life as dearly as he could. Close by, he saw Ellac reel in his saddle, claws from a Feral opening up red wounds across his face.

And then horns were blaring, from within the trees to his left. Cheren horns.

Uldin.

He saw riders appear, bursting from the treeline: Cheren warriors with their bows in their fists, hundreds of them. Uldin rode at their head, and Jin at his side. They thundered across the open space between the forest and road, and hope flickered in Bleda's heart.

We may yet break through, with the Cheren at our side.

Bleda's eyes met Jin's and she smiled at him, a cold, fierce thing.

And then the Cheren ploughed into the flank of Erdene's warband and began cutting down Sirak warriors, screaming their battle-cries as they killed.

And his mother's words returned to him, from that day on the weapons-field in Drassil. She had leaned close and whispered in his ear.

Never trust the Cheren.

CHAPTER FORTY-EIGHT

FRITHA

Fritha held her fist up and called a halt. Shouted commands behind her.

Arn rode to her side.

'What's wrong?' he said.

'This is the place,' Fritha said.

They were standing at the crest of a ridge, a long, gentle incline leading down to a crag-strewn plain. Red fern and yellow gorse dotted the landscape, dark scars marking ragged fissures and gullies that wound through the land like old, unhealed wounds. To the right a rocky precipice reared, scattered wood-land before it.

'We will fight them here,' Fritha said.

'Here?' Arn said. He looked around. 'It's too open.' He had raised Fritha on the hit-and-run warfare of the outnumbered and out-skilled. It had done them well, seen their ranks grow and given them countless minor victories.

But this was the Order of the Bright Star they were about to fight. It would be one battle. One huge victory, or one crushing defeat.

They stand between me and my destiny, to destroy the Ben-Elim and their pathetic sycophants, the White-Wings.

The Order of the Bright Star will not keep me from that, no matter what its reputation is.

Besides them Elise rippled on her coils. Wherever Fritha

went, Elise was close by. She looked at Arn, her father, with the hint of a scowl and gave a disapproving rattle of her long, sinuous tail.

That is an interesting development.

'If Fritha saysss we fight here, then thisss is where we fight,' Elise said. Her voice had changed, too, the edge of a reptilian hiss to it.

Fritha liked these changes. And she liked Elise's loyalty, more apparent than before.

Arn frowned at his daughter but said nothing.

Fritha surveyed the land again.

'Here.' She nodded and looked back over her shoulder.

In the distance pinpricks of fire bloomed, scores of them scattered across the landscape, and behind them dark stains of scorched, blackened earth. Holds and hamlets that Fritha had fired on her march south.

'*Draw the Order out,*' Gulla had said, so Fritha had given their crows and scouts something to see, a warband slaughtering its way south, destroying all before it as it travelled.

That should stir the Order's sanctimonious heart, Fritha thought. *Defender of the weak, they swear in their oath. That and the thought that Gulla is here should be enough to draw them.* She had ordered Morn to stay in the sky as much as her stamina allowed, told her to make herself visible to the Order.

Only one Kadoshim for them to see, but where they see one, they should assume there are more. Especially when combined with the tale Drem and the others will be telling.

Closer to her, gathered just behind the ridge, her warband stood waiting.

To Fritha they looked impressive. Five hundred mounted warriors, her Red Right Hand decked in leather and fur and bristling with sharp steel. They were flanked on the left by Gunil upon his bear, and Wrath on the right. He had grown again during their journey south, eating his way through all that crossed his path. Wrath had learned to use his wings, descending upon elk and deer from above. The draig was almost as big as a horse, now. Not as tall, but wider and longer with its thick tail. Fritha suspected that he might be strong enough to carry her into the air.

Morn the half-breed flew in lazy circles above the warband. Fritha's Ferals were nowhere to be seen, but Fritha was not concerned about that. She had commanded them to disperse across the land. They were close, she knew, could feel their presence, a tingle in her blood. They would come when she summoned them, of that she had no doubt.

It had been practical to send them out, an attempt to hide them from the prying eyes of talking crows, and also alleviating the requirement of feeding them. The Ferals could forage for their own meals. Food was what slowed the march of a warband, and reducing that need had contributed much to the speed with which Fritha and her small warband had covered the ground in the ten-night or so that she had been travelling since leaving the mine at Starstone Lake.

She looked at her Red Right Hand again, flanked with a mongrel guard of monsters.

She thought they were a fearsome sight. But she knew the warband coming to destroy her would be vastly larger. Morn had sighted the dust cloud of the Order of the Bright Star, flown close enough to spy great numbers of giant bears amongst their number. Two thousand swords coming against them, at least, Morn had told her. Fritha had expected nothing less. The lure of Gulla, High Captain of the Kadoshim, was too great to resist.

'We have at least a day, perhaps two, to prepare for them. Morn says they're a day's march away from us, at least.'

'But how will we hide from them here? How will we ambush them?' Arn asked, risking a baleful glare from his daughter and another rattle of her white-scaled tail.

'We won't,' Fritha said. 'There is no hope of that, anyway. With their murder of meddling crows in the sky, my guess is that we have already been seen. I hope we have been seen. That is the plan.' Although since Wrath had mastered his wings and had taken to spending more time in the air, it seemed to Fritha that the skies were clearer.

There is a new predator in the skies.

Nevertheless, Fritha had little doubt that her warband had been spotted, even if the crows were too scared to fly closer and spy out the details.

'We may as well let them come to us. At least that way we do not risk them walking around us.'

'We must attack with surprise, it is our only hope,' Arn said.

Fritha looked at Arn, a stern glance. She loved and respected him, but she was becoming vexed by his lack of faith in her.

'We cannot defeat the Order of the Bright Star the way you are used to fighting, Arn,' Fritha said firmly. 'Scattered ambushes, hit and run, it will not work. Their scouts are too good. And besides, it would take too long. We need a decisive win. I must reach Drassil before Midsummer's Day.'

'But we are too few, and are not White-Wings, masters of the shield wall.'

Fritha shouted orders and clicked her horse on.

The warband rippled into motion behind her, following her down the ridge, though every other warrior remained.

'What are we doing?' Arn asked.

I wish you would just trust me, Fritha thought, reining in her annoyance.

'We shall march forward a few leagues to draw the eyes of the Order. They will not think to scout behind us.' She glanced over her shoulder, saw those she had ordered to remain were now dismounting and reaching for their packs. 'There will be one battle to decide this, Arn, but a few surprises will not hurt,' Fritha said with a smile.

'One battle.' Arn frowned. 'Do you think we can win?'

She glanced at her warband, then at Wrath and Elise.

'Just us, no,' she said.

She looked to her left and saw in the distance a creeping mist that coated the lower ground, following the cracks and gullies that spread like a great cobweb across the land. It almost looked as if the mist were following her.

'But with Ulf and his Revenants, yes.'

CHAPTER FORTY-NINE

BLEDA

Bleda knelt in the dirt, spat a glob of blood from his mouth.

His wrists and ankles were bound and he was tied to a stake. A fire-pit crackled in front of him. He saw weapons piled close to the fire, the distinct shape of Sirak bows, and scabbarded swords there, too. Beyond the reach of the fire-pit's light Bleda saw the denser shadows of trees, heard the rustle of the wind in branches.

We are on the roadside, then?

Tied opposite him was his mother, her face crusted with blood, one eye swollen shut. Her jaw was an odd shape, looked as if it had been broken, her lips cut and mangled.

She saw him looking at her, and her lips moved, a croaked whisper coming out of the pulped ruin that had been her mouth.

'Stay . . . strong,' she whispered.

The words hit Bleda, the same ones she had said to him so long ago. The day Bleda's life had changed, the day his brother's head had been thrown at his feet.

The day the Sirak fought the Cheren.

He took a deep breath, trying to steady the anger and fear swirling through his veins.

Figures stood at the edge of the firelight, Cheren guards. They were talking amongst themselves, but Bleda felt their eyes at his slightest movement.

Never trust the Cheren. Mother was right. I hate them, curse their name. If I ever get out of these bonds, Uldin and Jin, I will kill you both.

He had not been conscious long, his last memory of the battle was of a Cheren warrior stabbing at Ellac, Bleda trying to reach him, carving his way through the sea of flesh between them, and then a blow across his shoulders and neck that sent him falling from his saddle, crunching to the ground. And then . . . nothing. Until he had awoken to find himself bound and staked like a goat ready for slaughter.

Uldin must have known of the attack. His idea of rotating the vanguard and rearguard put him in the perfect position to avoid any real conflict with the Kadoshim and their servants.

But what of his attack? His wounds when he arrived at Drassil, and the wounds of his riders? All a ruse?

Bleda shifted, trying to ease the strain on his wrists. His lamellar coat wasn't making moving any easier.

Footsteps: Uldin and Jin walking into the light cast by the fire-pit, a handful of Cheren at their back.

'You're awake, good,' Uldin said.

'I will *kill* you for this,' Bleda fumed.

'You have lost,' Uldin said with barely repressed disdain. 'Tricked and defeated like bairns. At least do not shame yourself with threats you have no hope of keeping. A childlike display. You have little left to you, but you can still die like a warrior of the Horse Clans, with some semblance of honour.'

Uldin's words only incensed Bleda more, a burning rage consuming him that he had never felt or known before. This betrayal somehow struck him as hard as his brother's death. He strained against his bonds, bucking, veins bulging, skin tearing on his wrists. Uldin and Jin stood over him, staring.

'To think you could have been handbound to this pathetic, weak worm,' Uldin said to Jin. 'Even at the last he cannot master his emotions. He is like a child.'

Jin just stared at Bleda, a cold fire in her eyes.

411

'Only a day ago she was still pleading with me to let you live,' Uldin said. 'Until she saw you last night, with the half-breed.'

The noise in the glade – it was Jin.

'I told you not to shame me,' Jin said. She stared at him a long while, perhaps expecting him to say something, but Bleda had nothing left to say.

'You gave your half-breed a gift,' Jin said. 'I have a gift for you, too.'

Jin's honour guard, Gerel, stepped forwards. He held something in his hands, a severed head, gripping it by a Sirak warrior braid. With a contemptuous shrug, Gerel threw the head at Bleda's feet. It rolled, stopped, eyes staring at Bleda.

It was Mirim, his honour guard.

I sent her to ask Uldin to guard the right flank. Never noticed that she did not return.

He thought of standing in his chamber as Mirim, Tuld and Ruga had dressed him for war, thought of the words he had said to them, and to all of his hundred, before they had ridden out to war.

. . . I swear to you all, I will not let you down, I will lead you to the best of my abilities.

Are they all dead, my hundred?

Shame swept him.

And what of Riv?

He remembered her flying overhead, guarding his back as he strove through the sea of Ferals.

The thought of Riv lying dead upon the road, combined with his complete and utter failure to keep his oath to his honour guard, tore at his heart. He felt a deep despair open within him, a bottomless hole draining his strength.

Uldin walked around the fire-pit and squatted before Erdene. One eye was closed tight, swollen and bruised, but her other eye fixed on Uldin fiercely.

'We are old adversaries, you and I,' Uldin said. 'My son

slew your husband. You slew my son. Our war should have decided things between us, but the Ben-Elim intervened.' He shifted his weight, twisted his neck and cracked it.

'Ah, I am old, I feel it in my bones. But today I feel young again, Erdene. Six years since that day. Six years it has taken to best my foe. I want you to know that I respect you, Erdene, for your strength, for your wisdom. How you fought those Ferals upon the road, it was a joy to see. Your battle fame only makes my victory greater and more glorious.' He smiled, a slow, languorous thing upon his face, showing Erdene that there was no reason for him to hide his emotions, because his victory was total.

'Do not think this is over, Uldin,' Erdene said, her voice slurred through her pulped, swollen lips. 'Just because I am in a tight spot right now. All can change on the edge of a knife's blade.' Her open eye flickered for a heartbeat to Bleda.

Tight spot. Knife's blade.

'This is no tight spot,' Uldin said. 'This is your end. Your warband is slaughtered or scattered. You are two hundred leagues from Arcona and your homeland. There is no walking away from this.'

A turbulence in the air above them, all within the light of the fire-pit looking up. Dark shapes dropped out of the sky.

Kadoshim. Seven of them, the whisper of wings in the air above hinting at more.

They were tall, elegant, handsome in much the same way as the Ben-Elim, clean-shaven and fine-boned, though there was something oddly reptilian or raptor-like about them, in the set of their eyes and the way their heads moved, from absolute stillness to abruptly sharp, economical speed. They wore coats of dark mail, their leathery wings furled, arching behind their shoulders like high-backed cloaks.

And then there was one more. Bleda recognized him as the one who had set the Ferals free. He was taller than the others, his limbs longer, and his face was drawn, the angles of his features more extreme, all sharp planes, ridges and hollows, shadows shifting across his face as the firelight flickered. One of his eyes was missing, just a shadowed hole, but Bleda's eyes were drawn to his mouth, which seemed too big for his face, and filled with too many teeth. There was a black edge to him, as if he were etched in shadow that even the firelight could not penetrate.

'You have done well, Uldin,' the tallest Kadoshim said, his voice a scratching hiss that seemed to echo inside Bleda's skull.

'Thank you, my Lord Gulla,' Uldin said, bowing his head.

This is Gulla, High Captain of the Kadoshim.

'Kol and his Ben-Elim are broken, routed. They will flee for Drassil, but they only saw the Ferals. They know nothing of my Revenants, or that you are with me. You did well to hold your attack until they were fleeing, their backs to us. They know nothing of your betrayal.'

'All is as you planned it, then,' Uldin said.

'It is. One hundred and thirty years in the making, and all the sweeter for it.' Gulla allowed a smile to flicker across his face. He looked at Bleda then, and Bleda felt as if a weight had pushed him to the ground and was pressing upon his chest. Terror shifted inside him, Gulla's eyes boring into him, pinning him. When Gulla's gaze moved on, Bleda felt breathless, as if he had been under water too long.

Gulla looked to Erdene, and she met his gaze.

'The queen and prince of your ancient foe,' Gulla said.

'Aye, my Lord,' Uldin answered.

Erdene's words nagged in Bleda's head.

A tight spot. A knife's edge. They were familiar.

Not her words, someone else's.

And then it came to him.

Old Ellac.

He shifted his weight as Gulla spoke with Uldin, the attention of his guards on these two victorious leaders for a few moments.

'I have news, my Lord,' Uldin said. 'Kol joined us last night and called a council of war.'

Some of the other Kadoshim snorted laughter at that.

'There are five hundred White-Wings on the road from Drassil, and there are scouting bands in the forest.'

'All the better,' Gulla hissed. 'The fewer bodies they have to man Drassil's walls, the better. The Ferals are still loose, what is left of them. They are wild, beyond my control, but I imagine they will leave a mark upon these White-Wings and scouts. The rest I shall leave for my Revenants.'

Uldin dipped his head.

'Do not linger here,' Gulla said. 'I need you at the gates of Drassil four days from now. This battle is won, but there will be survivors, and they will try to make their way back to Drassil. My Revenants are scouring the forest, but there is no guarantee that they will find every survivor. We must move fast and reach Drassil's walls soon. Word of your true allegiance must not reach the fortress. My Kadoshim and our children have routed Kol and his Ben-Elim, but there are still too many of them at Drassil. We will not take the fortress from the skies alone.'

'I understand,' Uldin said. 'I will be there, and soon. We will ride hard, using the road. It will be impossible for survivors on foot in the forest to reach Drassil before us.'

'Good. Then enjoy your revenge.'

Gulla glanced from Bleda to Erdene.

'You chose the wrong side,' he hissed. Gulla looked at the Kadoshim around him, and grinned, a humourless distortion of his face.

'We are for some night-hunting. In case there are wounded Ben-Elim out there.' One last look at Uldin. 'I will see you soon. Do not fail me.'

With a storm of beating wings the Kadoshim took to the air, the flames of the fire-pit crackling and hissing.

The Kadoshim horde, flying for Drassil.

'So, to my revenge, as Gulla advised,' Uldin said. He stepped towards Erdene, a hand reaching to the knife on his weapons-belt.

'Gulla did not advise you. He ordered you,' Bleda said with a sneer. If Uldin wasn't afraid to show his emotions, then he certainly wouldn't be either. 'You are his servant, his *whipped dog*. Not slave to the Ben-Elim, no, but you have another master, all the same.'

Uldin stopped, turned and looked at Bleda.

'Not my master, my *ally*,' Uldin said.

'Really? I did not hear Gulla call you *Lord*. Yet that is what you called him. Yes, my Lord Gulla, I will not be late, my Lord Gulla. And you bowed. Since when do the Horse Clans bow to *anyone*?'

'You bleat like a goat,' Uldin said, walking towards Bleda. 'You will stop, or I will make you stop.'

'Best not take too long about it, though,' Bleda told him. 'Or your Lord Gulla will be disappointed you didn't obey his orders.'

A twitch of emotion on Uldin's face, his grip tightening on his knife hilt.

'He is *mine* to kill, Father,' Jin said.

'Oh ho, someone else who gives the great Uldin orders,' Bleda said.

Uldin drew his knife and knelt beside Bleda, close enough for him to smell his sweat, and the goat's milk on his breath.

Bleda slashed the sharpened iron plate from his lamellar coat across Uldin's face, the Cheren King falling backwards with a cry, dropping his knife.

All the while Uldin and Gulla had been speaking of their victory and plans, Bleda had been working at the sharpened iron plate on his lamellar coat, slowly cutting away at the bonds on his wrist and then ankles.

He scrambled after Uldin now, his legs numb but working, threw himself onto the big man as all around him warriors shouted. Bleda's right hand reached to the sleeve of his coat, found the hidden flap, the worn leather hilt. He drew it and stabbed Uldin, low in the waist, Uldin crying out. And then he was hauling Uldin to his feet, his knife at the king's throat.

Jin and her guard had their bows levelled at Bleda, but he was hidden behind the bulk of Uldin.

'Cut my mother's bonds,' Bleda said.

'No,' Jin said.

'Cut my mother's bonds, and give her a horse,' Bleda told her.

'Let my father go,' Jin said, stepping closer to Erdene, 'or I will kill your mother.'

'You were going to kill her anyway. Let her go or I give your father the red smile.'

'Shoot him,' Uldin said. 'Put an arrow in his eye.'

But Bleda knew they could not. Uldin was a big man; Bleda was hidden behind him, only his knife hand visible as he held his blade at Uldin's throat.

'Get behind him, idiots,' Uldin grunted, and warriors around Jin began to move.

Bleda knew it was over, then, that he only had moments until Cheren warriors would have a clearer shot at his body. He dragged Uldin back a step, almost instantly realizing that was futile.

He embraced his death. Wished that he could see Riv one more time.

'Mother, see me,' he cried. 'Erdene, Queen of the Sirak, I am your last son, Bleda. Watch me slay our ancient foe, Uldin, King of the Cheren.' And he stabbed his knife into Uldin's throat, and then cut outwards, severing artery and windpipe together. A dark jet of blood and Uldin was slumping, collapsing to his knees. He gurgled wordlessly and toppled face-first onto the ground.

Bleda raised his arms wide, looked at his mother as the

417

Cheren bows aimed at him. Saw the pride and love in her eyes. He smiled at her.

'He is mine,' Jin cried, taking a step forwards, her arrow nocked and drawn. She stared at Bleda.

'I could have loved you,' she whispered. 'Did love you. But now I hate you with all that I am. Know this, Bleda, that I will slay your mother once you are dead, and her death shall be slow.'

A whistling sound and an arrow slammed into Jin's shoulder, spinning her. Jin's bow-arm jerked, her arrow flying from the string, piercing a Cheren warrior to her left. He fell with a scream.

Another arrow arching down from above, a Cheren warrior stumbling, a goose-fletched arrow sticking from his thigh.

Riv.

And then mounted figures were bursting into the firelight – two, three, more – arrows thrumming, a snatched glimpse of Ellac swinging his sword, and all about him Cheren warriors were reeling, falling, blood spraying.

Bleda lurched into motion, crashed into a Cheren warrior with his bow aiming into the night sky, searching for Riv. He stabbed his knife into the man's belly, ripped it free and threw the warrior away from him, snatched the scabbarded sword upon the warrior's back, continued his staggering run towards Erdene.

Riv swooped out of the sky, plummeting into the midst of them. Her bow was back in its case, a short-sword in each hand, and she was carving a bloody ruin around her, Cheren warriors reeling away. She saw Bleda and flew towards him, weaving in the air, something odd about her flight. He pointed to his mother as he staggered towards her.

Jin appeared out of the chaos, stepping behind Bleda's mother, her left arm hanging limp, a sword in her right fist. She saw Bleda, snarled at him, her face of stone gone, and plunged her sword into Erdene. The blade stabbed down, high in the back, down into Erdene's chest cavity.

Bleda screamed.

His mother jerked in her bonds, Jin twisting her blade, ripping it free. A gout of blood from Erdene's mouth, a spasm through her whole body, and then Bleda saw the life leave her.

The world slowed around him. He heard someone screaming, distantly realizing it was his own voice as he leaped the fire-pit, eyes fixed on Jin. His grip tightened on the blades in either hand, sword and knife.

But then figures were swirling between them, a mounted Sirak warrior, Cheren Clansmen all around her, dragging her from her saddle. Bleda looked around, heard the horn blasts spreading the alarm, saw more Cheren warriors pouring into the firelight.

And then Riv's arms were around him, pulling him, lifting him.

'There is no time,' she was yelling through the red fog in his head. 'We must run, live to fight.' And she was trying to lift him into the air.

'Mother,' he cried, pulling free, and Riv followed him, grabbing him.

'The dead cannot seek revenge,' she shouted into his face. He stopped, the truth of her words hitting him like a blow.

I will have my revenge.

Bleda embraced Riv. As she began to hoist him into the air he sheathed his knife back in its hidden pocket and leaned and lunged at the bundle of weapons by the fire, gripped his bow, and then they were airborne, juddering up and away, into the cover of darkness.

'Ellac, the others,' Bleda said, not willing to leave his warriors again.

'They are running, too,' Riv said. 'Look.'

Bleda saw riders scattering out from the fire-pit, riding in all directions.

419

'They will lead the Cheren a merry chase, but they know where to meet us.'

They weaved through the air, the glow of the fire-pit shrinking below.

'What's wrong?' Bleda asked. Riv was breathing heavily and they were swaying. It felt nothing like when Riv had carried him away from the Revenant in the forest, all strength and weightlessness.

'One of those Cheren bastards put an arrow in my wing,' Riv snarled. 'When Uldin attacked on the road.'

'Thank you,' Bleda breathed.

'For what?' Riv asked.

'For saving me.'

Riv smiled. 'I love you, Bleda,' she said, as if that answered everything.

Bleda looked down at the retreating glare and saw the prone body of his mother. Jin was standing over her, eyes searching the night sky.

'I will see you dead, Jin ap Uldin,' Bleda whispered. 'On my mother's soul I swear it, and on the souls of my people that your treachery has murdered.'

Riv heard him, but she said nothing. As silent as mist they swept away from the Cheren and into the dark of Forn.

CHAPTER FIFTY

DREM

Drem saw the line of warriors upon the crest of the ridge ahead, at least two or three thousand paces away. From down here in the vale it was impossible to tell how many of them there were, just a long line of roughly a hundred swords that disappeared beyond the ridge-line. It could be ten rows deep or fifty.

'Why won't the crows fly closer?' he asked Cullen, who apart from Tain Crow Master seemed to have the closest relationship with the crows of Dun Seren.

'Something's spooking them,' Cullen said. 'And Byrne and Tain are telling them not to fly too close. Because of Flick.'

Flick still hadn't come back, and Drem thought the same as most others. That Flick was dead. Drem was sad about that, he had liked the crow.

'What's the plan, then?' Drem asked.

They had sighted their enemy early, but almost immediately Gulla's warband had made an orderly retreat. The Order had followed, scouts flanking wide and ahead to search out any ambushes they might have been lured into, but nothing had happened. Now the Order was spread along the lower reaches of a vale, the enemy halting their steady retreat and gathering atop a ridge before them. Above the enemy warband Drem saw dark specks in the sky, a handful of Dun Seren's crows circling high. Morning mist still lingered in low-lying spots, where it pooled and swirled. A long, gentle incline rose ahead of them, mostly open ground punctuated with swathes of red fern and clumps of gorse. To Drem's left was scattered woodland that rolled up to a sheer granite outcrop, and to his right the ground was bordered by one of the twisting, cracked ravines that littered the Desolation's landscape, like the ones they had used for cover after leaving the Bonefells.

'Best ask the boss,' Keld said, pointing at Byrne.

She was upon her horse at the head of their loosely ordered warband, roughly a dozen rows ahead of Drem. Balur and Ethlinn were leaning in the saddles of their great bears and talking with her.

Ethlinn's giants, three or four hundred of them, were gathered on the right flank, at least half of them mounted upon bears. The bulk of the Order's warriors were arrayed in a mass in the centre of the vale, Drem glimpsing Utul and his Jehar warriors by the swords jutting over their shoulders. The huntsmen and their wolven-hounds were spread along the left flank. Keld had ignored the order when they'd left camp that morning to gather with the other scouts.

'Why are you not with the scouts?' Drem asked Keld, in his usual diplomatic way.

Keld looked at him a moment.

'Because someone's got to keep an eye on young Cullen,' he said, giving Drem a wink.

'I can look after myself,' Cullen murmured distractedly, eyes fixed on the line of warriors at the top of the ridge.

Drem suspected Keld's presence was more to do with looking after him than Cullen.

'Come on, Byrne,' Cullen muttered. 'Let's just get on with it.'

'Patience, lad,' Keld said. 'See,' he said to Drem. 'If he was left to his own devices, he'd be running up the hill at them right now.'

'The people that killed Sig are up there,' Cullen growled, his face pale, a look in his eyes Drem hadn't seen before. 'I've spent the last few moons running from them, when all I've wanted to do is turn around and carve some vengeance in their hides. And now they're right there. I can't be doing with this waiting.' He looked at them both. 'When I close my eyes at night, all I see is Sig, telling us to strap her to a post.' A tear filled his eye, ran down his cheek. Then his lips twisted. 'They're going to pay for what they did to her.'

He wiped the tears from his face, sniffed.

'Besides, they have the high ground, so they're not going to be obliging and march down here to fight us,' Cullen said. 'So we might as well just walk up there and get on with it.'

'You're not the only one that wants to avenge Sig,' Keld said. 'There's not a warrior of the Order whose life Sig didn't touch.' He squeezed Cullen's shoulder. 'Won't be long, lad.' At Cullen's words there was a new fire in his eyes, too.

He held a hand up over his eyes. 'I can see loads of those shaven-haired bastards, but where's Gulla and his brood?'

That was a good question, and Drem was wondering where Morn was, too. He'd seen her in the sky many times over the last three days, ever since they'd left the wasteground that had been Dalgarth behind them. But now she was nowhere to be seen.

Absently, his hand went to his neck and checked his pulse.

Two crows flew away from the ridge top, sweeping back down the slope towards Byrne. They circled above her; a flapping of wings and they were alighting on Byrne's saddle. Drem could hear squawking, saw Byrne's head nodding. She looked to Balur and Ethlinn, more words passing between them.

'Here we go,' Cullen said.

Byrne twisted in her saddle and said something to a warrior behind her, who raised a horn to his lips and blew.

Ethlinn and Balur rode their bears back to the giants on the right flank.

Men and women dismounted and moved into the open

space before Byrne, shrugging their round shields from their backs. They formed into three groups, each one around two hundred swords strong. Another horn blast and those shields came together with a *crack*, and suddenly they were solid shield walls.

Byrne signalled, and more horns rang out.

Keld looked at Drem and Cullen. 'Be seeing you soon,' he said, dismounted and handed his reins to Drem.

Other huntsmen made their way forwards, threading between the shield walls and forming a row before them.

A horn signal, and the huntsmen and shield walls began to walk up the hill.

Byrne raised an arm and then pointed at the ridge, touched her heels to her mount and followed them.

Drem and all those warriors of the Bright Star still mounted rippled into movement behind Byrne. With a jangling and creaking of bridles and harness, they began to move up the slope, hooves a thudding drumbeat pounding a slow, steady time on the turf. To the right Drem could feel the rumble of three hundred bears and giants following suit.

He felt his heart thumping in his chest, a blend of fear and excitement filling him, all around him. He rolled his shoulders. He was more used to the weight of his mail shirt now, after riding, eating and sleeping in it for four days and nights. Even if the skin of his shoulders had been chafed red raw. The one thing that set him apart from most of the warriors of the Order was the lack of a shield slung across his back. Cullen and Keld had big round shields with the four-pointed white star emblazoned upon them. Drem wanted to embrace the Order, felt he'd learned so much in the short time that he'd spent there, but to use a shield in battle felt like a step too far at the moment.

'*A shield'll save your life,*' Cullen had said to him, and Drem didn't doubt it, but the more he'd trained, the more he'd realized he gravitated to fighting with two weapons in his hands, preferably his seax and axe.

'The best defence is to attack,' Keld had said to him. *'You'll be one of us huntsmen before your training's over.'*

'I'll have to make do with this mail shirt, for now,' Drem had answered.

Seeing their foe lined up along the crest of the ridge, though, he was starting to regret that decision.

They were closer now, roughly six or seven hundred paces from the ridge and their enemy. Drem searched their line for Fritha, but could not see her pale, fair stubble amongst those on the ridge.

Four hundred paces and the huntsmen halted, the shield walls and mounted warriors behind all undulating to a halt. With all of the warriors that had formed the shield wall and huntsmen's line, Drem and Cullen were close to Byrne now, in the row behind her.

The huntsmen began to string their bows, men and women taking a handful of arrows from quivers at their hips and stabbing them into the ground in front of them.

Up on the ridge Drem heard a shouted command and saw shields appear, the warriors up there forming a wall of shields of their own.

They can do that better than I expected.

A shout from the line of huntsmen, arrows nocked, drawn and loosed in one heartbeat, a volley rising high into the sky, arcing down towards the ridge top, drumming into the wall of shields, sounding like hail on turf. A few screams echoed down the slope, Drem spying half a dozen shields tremble and fall. More shields filled the gaps.

Another volley was in the air, and then another, and another.

'It's a hard thing, standing and facing a volley or three of arrows,' Cullen said with a grin. 'Takes some stones. This should soften them up, get them rattled before we even get started.'

A few arrows flickered back at them, flying up from the ridge and down the slope. Cullen slung his shield from his shoulder and leaned to hold it over Drem as well. There was a stuttered thumping as the arrows thumped into turf or wood. A solitary yell, but the arrows did little damage – there were too few of them.

Another volley from the Order's huntsmen, a handful of screams from the ridge, and then Byrne signalled for a horn to be blown.

The huntsmen dropped back between the shield walls, most of them reforming on foot on the left flank. Keld slipped back to Drem and Cullen. Drem handed Keld his reins and the huntsman climbed back into the saddle of his mount.

Byrne's hornsman was about to blow a new signal when a gap opened in the line on the ridge and a giant emerged, riding upon a bear. Gunil. His hair raven black, long moustache knotted with leather, his war-hammer slung across his back.

Drem heard a muttering from amongst the giants upon the right flank, felt his own breath catch.

They helped to kill my da.

Gunil rode his bear down the ridge, thirty or forty paces, then reined in. He leaned down in his saddle and lifted something that was hanging from a harness.

Drem felt a fist clench in his gut, because he knew what it was even before Gunil spoke. He felt Keld and Cullen tense beside him.

'No,' Cullen hissed.

'A gift for you,' Gunil roared, his voice echoing down the vale, and he lifted Sig's severed head and swung it around his head by her long blonde warrior braid, then hurled it down the ridge at them. It arced up into the sky, then descended, bouncing and then rolling to stop a hundred or so paces before the advancing warband.

Gunil sat tall in his saddle, arms outspread.

'There lies Sig, your greatest warrior, slain by ME,' Gunil cried. 'And I ask you: WHO'S NEXT?'

He shrugged his war-hammer from his back and raised it over his head, bellowing wordlessly at the Order of the Bright Star and giants as if he would challenge them all.

A terrible silence settled over the slope, Drem's eyes focused only on Sig's severed head.

'I AM,' a voice shouted in response, right next to Drem.

Cullen gave a wordless shriek and kicked his mount, the horse leaping away. Keld snatched at Cullen's reins but grabbed only air, and then Cullen's horse was breaking into a gallop, threading between the shield walls and pounding up the slope.

Others broke along the line, following Cullen; to Drem's right there was a roaring of bears and a handful of giants burst into motion.

'HOLD,' Byrne yelled, but the ground was shaking and warriors were yelling, Cullen louder than any of them as he pounded towards Gunil.

Keld and Drem shared a look and then Keld was urging his mount on, Drem close behind him.

A black-winged shape rose up from behind the warriors on the ridge, Drem recognizing it as the half-breed, but shouts came up from the enemy warband of, 'GULLA, GULLA.'

Behind him Drem heard warriors roaring battle-cries as they saw what they thought was the Lord of their ancient foe, and then more warriors were galloping up the hill.

To his right Drem glimpsed Balur One-Eye yelling and then joining them in their charge up the slope, or maybe he was trying to stop Cullen. Either way, in a few heartbeats scores of giants were surging after him like water smashing through a dam.

The half-breed swept low down the slope, wheeled high and then stooped into a dive.

Straight at Cullen.

Her arm drew back and she hurled her spear.

Cullen didn't even see it coming.

It struck his horse in the neck, a scream, blood spurting, and the animal's legs gave way, Cullen going down in an explosion of turf and dirt. Drem lost sight of him as others surged past or over him, Drem could not tell.

Keld yelled something, spurred his mount faster, Drem leaning low in his saddle and doing the same. All was dirt and thunder, pounding hooves and warriors yelling.

Then Keld was leaping from his saddle, running to a fallen horse. Drem dragged on his reins, turning his mount to stand between Keld and the riders galloping up the field behind them, waving his arms in an attempt to force them around him.

He heard Keld grunting and heard Cullen's voice shouting, risked a glimpse and saw Cullen had a leg trapped beneath his dead horse, Keld dragging him free.

The riders thinned around Drem, now, and he saw that there was an open space, then Byrne leading the shield walls and those riders close to her who had refrained from the charge.

'Give me a horse,' Cullen yelled behind Drem, and he turned to see the red-haired warrior on his feet, limping towards Drem, frantically searching for a mount that he could use.

'Hold, lad,' Keld was shouting at him.

There were no riderless mounts to be had.

'Here,' Drem called out, offering Cullen his hand. Cullen limped over and Drem pulled him up behind him.

'Go on, Drem, ride on,' Cullen urged as Keld remounted.

Drem paused a moment to stare ahead.

Balur's bear had surged into the lead, twenty or thirty paces clear of the tide of warriors charging up the slope.

Gunil grinned and brandished his war-hammer at Balur, yelling insults.

Balur's bear rushed up the incline, ploughing through red

fern between crags and out onto an open space beyond, forty or fifty more bears powering close behind them, the giants bellowing war-cries, the bears roaring their own wordless fury. The ground trembled with their charge, the sound like a hundred thunder storms rolled into one.

Balur was close, now, only a hundred or so paces from Gunil, the bears behind Balur gaining.

And then the ground beneath Balur's feet just seemed to . . . disappear, opening up into a deep pit.

The giant and his bear fell, crashing out of view, the bears behind him following in a tumble of limbs and fur, other riders bellowing commands, reining their mounts in, but more were falling, disappearing into huge pits that spread across the incline.

A great cloud of dust exploded from the pits the bears had fallen into, expanding and rolling down the slope, closely followed by the screams of giants and bears.

CHAPTER FIFTY-ONE

FRITHA

'My thanks, Drem, for another gift you've given me,' Fritha said, looking at and listening to the destruction her staked pits were wreaking upon the giants and their bears.

She stood in a knot of woodland on the far right of her line, Arn and a handful of her Red Right Hand with her, along with Elise and Wrath. The draig was fixated on the bears charging up the slope, rumbling low growls and snapping his jaws.

'Your plan is a successsss,' Elise hissed beside her.

'The battle's not won yet,' Fritha said.

There were still giants upon their bears tumbling into the pits, as more ran into them from behind, ramming them forwards and over the edges of the pits. But there were still far too many bears and giants left on the slope for Fritha's liking. Perhaps fifty or sixty had been swallowed into the enormous holes, but that still left hundreds of giants moving rapidly closer to them.

'It's a good start, though,' Fritha murmured to Elise.

The death of my Feral in Drem's elk pit does not seem like such a grievous loss now. Every defeat is a lesson learned.

The dust began to settle, screams of pain from bear and giant alike echoed out from the staked pits. Gunil slung his war-hammer back over his shoulder and guided his bear towards Fritha.

430

'That went well,' the giant observed as he reached her. 'Still more to kill, though. Too many.'

'Thank you for your astute observation, Gunil,' Fritha muttered.

Behind him on the slope a hand appeared on the edge of one of the pits, a giant dragging himself up, clawing and crawling onto the ground. He climbed to one knee, then onto his feet, white-haired, with a latticed hole where one eye had been.

'Balur One-Eye,' Fritha whispered.

He was battered and bleeding, blood sluicing from a cut to his scalp, more blood drenching one tattooed arm, but he looked furious more than weakened. He shrugged a war-hammer from his back and hefted it.

'GUNIL,' he roared.

Gunil stared at Balur. Then he slipped his war-hammer into his hands.

More hands appeared on the edges of the pits: giants beginning to climb up from the darkness, dragging themselves onto the turf.

'Wait,' Fritha said to Gunil.

She raised an arm, her Red Right Hand watching her.

'KILL THEM,' she yelled, and with a roar her Red Right Hand hurtled down the slope, five hundred spears, swords and axes glinting in the sunlight.

From down the slope horns sounded, a great roar from the warband of the Bright Star.

Fritha heard their battle-cry echo out, 'TRUTH AND COURAGE,' and the warband surged forwards, giants on the left sweeping wide to circle around the line of pits, some heading for the gaps of turf between the pits that acted as bridges or paths to Balur's side, joined by many riders of the Order, while others veered right, towards the woodland and Fritha, attempting to swing around the right flank of the pit line.

Fritha saw the first of her Red Right Hand reach Balur, his hammer swinging, sending two men hurtling through the air, bones smashed to kindling. Warriors behind began to stab at Balur; Fritha saw blood bloom from wounds.

'Now,' Fritha said to Gunil. 'Go, and make sure Balur One-Eye dies. It will rip the heart from his giants.'

'Consider him dead,' Gunil growled, that manic look back in his eyes, and he urged Claw onto the field.

Fritha drew a knife from her belt and sliced a red line across her palm. She let the blood well, and then put her hand to her mouth, smeared the blood across her lips, upon her tongue.

'*LIOM*,' she cried out, her blood spraying with her spittle, and she felt her summons spread out, like a far-flung net across the land, and in her blood and veins she felt the trembling response. Distantly she heard the sound of howling.

'Ulf,' Fritha said, looking behind her into the woods. A figure emerged, cloaked in shadow.

'Are your disciples ready?' she asked him.

'They are,' Ulf said. 'They hunger.'

'Good. Soon they will feast.'

'*Wrath hungry*,' Wrath grumbled beside Fritha. '*Wrath want to feast.*'

'You are always hungry,' Fritha smiled, scratching Wrath's thick-muscled neck. It was level with her head now.

'*Yes*,' the draig agreed.

'I hunger, too,' Ulf said.

'You must stay with me,' she commanded. 'You cannot be risked.' She gave him a reassuring smile. 'You will feast after. You will glut yourself on their blood.'

That seemed to appease the Revenant, a little.

'Shall I call them now?' Ulf asked her.

'Soon,' Fritha said, holding a placating hand out. She looked at Ulf, saw his dark, predatory eye observing the battle, watching death and bloodshed.

'Do you remember who you were?' she asked him.

He tore his one eye from the carnage and regarded Fritha a long moment.

'Yes,' he said, 'I was Ulf the tanner. It is vague, like a dream.'

Fritha nodded. She wondered if her Ferals remembered, too.

'Do you miss your old life?'

'No,' he said, instantly. 'It was . . . torpid. Life now is . . . rich. Red.' His lips twitched, the hint of teeth beneath.

Screams drew Fritha's attention back to the battle.

Gunil had reached the combat. She saw him lean in his saddle and swing his hammer, crunching into a raised shield from a warrior of the Order. The blow tore the warrior from his saddle and sent him crashing into one of the open pits.

Her Red Right Hand looked hard-pressed though.

'Soon, Ulf,' she whispered. 'Be ready.'

And then there were figures in the woods before her, a hundred paces away, wolven-hounds loping up through the trees, huntsmen of the Order behind them, and following them a tide of riders, picking their way through the trees.

'Be ready,' Fritha breathed, and she pressed the palm of her bloodied hand to the red wings upon her cuirass, leaving a new bloodstain there. She pulled her spear from where she had stabbed it into the ground, hefted it, bending her knees. The imminence of battle flooded her veins, fear and joy mixing into a wild, heady excitement.

The wolven-hounds burst through the trees, snarling and slavering.

One leaped at Fritha, white and grey, its jaws open wide. One of her guards jumped in front of her and the wolven-hound crashed into him, biting and snarling as they fell to the ground. The guard screamed, blood spraying, the wolven-hound's jaws clamped around his face, shaking its head with savage strength. Fritha stumbled back a few steps, daunted for a moment by the ferocity.

The hound stood over her gurgling, dying guard, then looked at her, jaws dripping red. It snarled and went at her. Fritha snarled back, lunged forwards, spear-butt low, almost wedged into the ground, blade high, just as she would do if she were hunting boar. The wolven-hound fell onto her spear-point, its momentum driving the blade deep, and it snapped and growled, a frenzied pain rage, then it was whining and slumping as the blade bit into the hound's heart. Fritha dropped her spear, the weight of the dead creature dragging it from her hands, and she drew her short-sword.

Another wolven-hound was surging at her from the side, but Elise burst forwards on her coils, speed and power a blur, and her sword lashed out. The wolven-hound dropped to the ground, a deep wound in its flank, but it half rose and threw itself at Elise, teeth raking into her coils. She shrieked and hissed at it, her sword rising and falling in frenzied strikes and the wolven-hound collapsed, its head half-severed.

Men appeared, more wolven-hounds with them, and Fritha grinned at them.

'Death smiles at us all,' she yelled as they hefted their weapons and moved towards her.

They came at her with sword and axe, though slowly, the sight of Elise and Wrath either side of her, the draig tearing chunks out of a wolven-hound, giving the huntsmen pause.

There was a rumbling behind Fritha, echoed in her blood, the sound of snarls, howls and growls, and then her Ferals were sweeping out of the trees behind her, a slavering wave of death.

They stormed past Fritha, slamming into the huntsmen. The wolven-hounds howled and leaped at the Ferals, a crashing together of teeth, claw, muscle and fur. The hounds were powerful and deadly, but there were too many of the Ferals, and in fractured, ferocious moments the Ferals had ripped the hounds and huntsmen to bloody ruin and were sweeping them away, tearing at limbs, blood exploding in great gouts, and then they were gone, rushing down, through the woods, and out onto the plain to crash into the flank of the oncoming warband.

Fritha grinned at Elise and patted Wrath's muscular shoulder.

She looked out at the plain and saw that on the far side giants and warriors had reached the point where they could cut around the widest pit and curl in towards her Red Right Hand.

'Ulf,' she called, and the Revenant appeared from the trees where he had retreated.

'Now,' she said.

CHAPTER FIFTY-TWO

DREM

Drem stared at the wall of Ferals that came surging out of the woods to his left and smashed into the packed ranks of Order warriors upon their mounts. He was horrified by the numbers he was seeing, and the sheer volume of this huge battle. There was a roaring all around, deafening, giants and bears and Ferals, merging with the harsh clang of steel and the battle roars and death screams. And the smell, of blood and guts and excrement as people and animals died in enormous numbers. He'd fought before, the battle at the starstone mine was seared into his soul, a memory of blood and chaos and fear, but this was something of an altogether greater magnitude. He felt he wanted to put his hands over his ears and curl into a tight-knit ball.

But he didn't. Instead he took a long, steady breath and tried to work out where he was most needed or useful.

In the saddle behind him, Cullen was shouting and spluttering, urging Drem to charge up the slope.

Drem ignored him and waited to assess what was going on.

Ahead of him battle was raging on the slope, where shaven-haired warriors were swarming around Balur and a score of giants, other warriors of the Order struggling to reach them across narrow spits of land between the huge pits that the enemy had dug. Drem glimpsed Utul and his followers riding across the narrow paths to reach Balur. The warriors of the

Order who had formed the shield wall were reaching the pits now, the shield wall breaking apart as they navigated the narrow channels between each hole. Drem saw Alcyon the giant upon the back of Sig's bear, Hammer. The giant was close to Balur, chopping at the enemy with his two axes in his fists. On the right flank more giants and riders of the Order were circling the pits and curving in to strike on the enemy's flank and come to Balur's aid. He saw the dark silhouette of the half-breed swirling in the sky above, swooping and diving as she flew low, stabbing and slashing with a sword, then rising high to wheel and dip low again.

On the left flank a host of Ferals hundreds strong was tearing into warriors of the Order, riders amongst them, but mostly the huntsmen and wolven-hounds.

He felt he should be there, where the battle raged hottest, and where the huntsmen that he identified most with were being torn apart. He gripped his reins and guided his horse back down the slope, Cullen shrieking in his ear, imploring him to turn and ride back into the battle on the ridge. Drem ignored him.

He dug his heels into his mount and dragged on her reins, guiding her out of the tight-packed press that was piling up against the Ferals and urged her south, back down the slope into more open ground, and then he was cantering, looping around the edge of the Ferals as they ploughed into the Order of the Bright Star, aligning himself for a charge at the Ferals' flank and rear. He heard the drum of hooves behind him, saw Keld burst from the press and follow him. Drem slowed for a moment to let Keld join him.

'What are you doing, Drem?' Cullen yelled. Keld's eyes were wide with confusion. Drem realized they thought he must have been running away.

Drem pointed at the rear of the Ferals. 'No point waiting in a mass to get at them,' Drem said. 'Thought it made more sense to ride around the back and give them a sharp-iron surprise.'

Cullen blew out a long breath, shared a look with Keld.

'Have to admit, I like your thinking, lad,' Keld said.

The huntsman put two fingers to his lips and whistled, and Fen came bounding out of the woodland to their left.

Cullen slipped from Drem's saddle and grabbed the reins of a riderless horse that came cantering down the slope. Favouring his uninjured leg, Cullen swung himself into the saddle.

'Let's go kill us some Ferals,' Keld snarled, and then they were spurring their horses forwards. They broke into a canter, a hundred paces from the Ferals now.

'These nets you use for Kadoshim and half-breeds,' Drem called out, unclipping the folded net at his belt, 'you think they'll work as well on Ferals?'

'Only one way to find out,' Cullen grinned, unclipping his own net and snapping it free.

The rabid creatures heard the beat of their hooves, turned snarling to face them. Five of them at least broke away from the main pack and began to run at the three riders.

Drem flicked his wrist, as Cullen had shown him, setting the weighted balls free, then he lifted the net over his head, holding it by its centre-point, and swung, felt the lead weights swirl around his head, felt their rhythm, conscious of not swinging too fast or too slow, trying not to let the fact that snarling death was hurtling towards him break his concentration, and then he was releasing, not up as he had practised, at an imaginary Kadoshim, but almost straight forwards, just a slight upwards angle to his cast.

His net spread wide and Drem's chosen Feral all but ran into it, the weighted balls snapping around the animal as the net enfolded its arms, torso and one leg, sending it crashing to the ground. It struggled, tearing and biting at its bonds, gaps opening up in the net, one clawed hand ripping through, and then Drem's horse was trampling the creature, hooves crashing down, snapping bones, crushing its ribcage. Drem leaned over, chopping into the Feral's head with a hand-axe.

The creature died in an explosion of blood and bone.

Drem sat tall in his saddle, breathing heavily, saw that Keld and Cullen had snared their Ferals and were dispatching them with sword and spear, and close by, Fen the wolven-hound was rolling with two Ferals, arcs of blood trailing through the air. Drem spurred his horse at them, chopped into the skull of one Feral, saw it stiffen and roll away limp, and Fen had the other one by the throat, a savage shake and it was over.

'No time to rest,' Cullen cried as he urged his horse into the rear of the Feral pack.

'Told you we'd have to watch Cullen's back,' Keld said and shook his reins, his mount breaking into a canter after Cullen. Drem felt a wild grin split his face, laying about him either side with his hand-axe, his horse biting at any enemy flesh it could reach.

Time condensed and blurred for Drem, as he hacked and chopped his way through a sea of fur, snarling jaws and slashing claws. A wild energy raced through him, putting strength and fire into his limbs, and he screamed his hatred and fury at these creatures that were made for one reason only, to kill and rend for Gulla and the Kadoshim.

The battle surged along the fringe of the slope, back in amongst knots of beech and oak, then back out onto the plain.

For a moment Drem found himself free of the battle, and he sat on his horse, blood-drenched, his nostrils flaring, and took a moment to look about.

He had moved further up the slope, closer to the line of pits, but far to the left, almost beneath the eaves of the woodland that fringed the slope.

Keld and Cullen were close by, working together with Fen to pick off Ferals from the pack that still beset the Order. They had come across Stepor and he had joined them in their systematic destruction, his wolven-hounds Grack and Ralla working with them like a pack. Although it seethed and swayed back and forth, it appeared to Drem that the battle was turning in the Order's favour. The Ferals were being held and pressed back into the woodland and, further up the slope, Drem could see Balur One-Eye laying about him with his war-hammer, other giants and warriors of the Order around him, including Alcyon upon Hammer. They had formed a knot and were pushing higher up the slope. Drem glimpsed Gunil upon his bear, but then he was gone. On the far right, giants and riders of the Bright Star were sweeping around the pits and charging into the flank of Fritha's acolytes.

We are going to win.

And then something seemed to change upon the battlefield. For a moment Drem wasn't sure what it was, but then his eyes were drawn to the edge of the slope, beyond those giants and riders who were sweeping around the pits.

A thick mist was creeping onto the slope behind them, boiling out of one of the many ravines that ran through the Desolation.

It did not look natural.

It was dark, almost black, like thunderclouds, and it seemed to bubble and boil, as if there was something inside it, straining to get out.

It crept towards the rear of the giants and warriors of the Bright Star.

And then the screaming began.

Others on the slope paused, some sense of change sweeping over the field, and Drem saw figures in the mist, what looked like a horde of them, some exploding from the darkness to slam into men or giants, other hands snaking out of the mist, grabbing and dragging people back into its dark embrace.

Drem felt afraid, his strength draining.

The mist rolled ever wider, enveloping the slope, moving closer.

No, it cannot end like this, Drem growled to himself.

A voice rose over the din of battle, high and keening, and Drem saw Ethlinn sitting astride a huge black bear, her arms stretched wide, a spear in one fist. She was facing the oncoming mist, even her great bulk looking small before the wave of churning darkness. Drem did not know how he could hear her, but her voice carried across the field, high and otherworldly.

'*Cumhacht an aeir, scrios an dorchadas seo ón talamh,*' Ethlinn chanted, sweeping her spear before her. '*Cumhacht an aeir, scrios an dorchadas seo ón talamh,*' she cried out, again and again.

At first nothing happened, the black mist boiling towards her, but then Drem felt it. A breeze caressed his face, growing swiftly stronger, lifting his hair and swirling it about his face, and then stronger still, a gale that rocked him in his saddle. It swept over the slope, a howling wind that slammed into the mist.

For long moments the darkness resisted, a pressure building in the air, like an imminent thunder storm, and then the mist began to fracture at its edges, wisps and tendrils fragmenting, and then suddenly the fog was lacerated and broken, swept away to reveal what it had hidden.

A host of men and women, even children amongst them, moving in an unnatural, too-fast gait. Drem saw dark eyes and gleaming teeth.

They came on at Ethlinn. Giants and warriors of the Order rallied about her, a dull thud and echo of screams reverberating down to Drem over the general din of battle as the Revenants and giants came together.

Drem saw Ethlinn stab down with her spear, a flicker of blue light bursting as the spear pierced a Revenant. Ethlinn lifted it high, skewered, and blue veins spread through the creature's body. It spasmed and jerked on the end of her spear like a stuck fish, then went limp. Ethlinn cast the lifeless form away.

Drem frowned, not understanding what he was seeing, but he felt a glimmer of hope. It was snuffed out quickly as he saw the host of Revenants rolling over giants and warriors around Ethlinn.

What can we do?

He looked about wildly, and then he saw her.

Fritha, amongst the trees. She was staring at him, warriors and . . . *creatures* about her.

He didn't care.

She slew my father.

He pulled on his reins and urged his roan mare up the slope and into the trees.

CHAPTER FIFTY-THREE

FRITHA

Fritha smiled as the dark mist rolled over the battlefield. Ulf was standing behind her, amidst the trees.

The Revenants will win this for us, Fritha thought. *Without them, even with my Ferals, I do not think we would have triumphed.*

Victory was so close now that she could almost taste it.

She saw a figure riding into the trees, leaping from his horse's back when the branches became too low, and breaking into a run, straight up the slope towards her.

It was Drem.

Fritha wanted to clap her hands and thank whatever fate was smiling down upon her.

Behind him she glimpsed other figures running into the woodland.

Are the Order of the Bright Star breaking already? Have the Revenants won the day?

Then Drem was crashing into the glade where Fritha was. She saw his eyes flicker to Elise and Wrath, saw the shock register, saw his run falter a moment.

He has changed, she thought. He was dressed in fine war gear, for a start, not in his trapper's leathers, a mail shirt that was streaked with gore. He looked older, somehow, less child-like, though his face held that same determined set that she had always liked about him.

443

Once he sets his mind to something, he tries to see it through. Unfortunately, I think this time he has set his mind on killing me.

Let him try. I will take him, bind him in chains and make him into something new, just so he can follow at my heels for the rest of his life.

'Don't kill him,' Fritha snapped to those about her, 'or eat him,' she added to Wrath, who was growling at Drem and licking his lips as if the young man was lunch.

She saw the resolve return in Drem's eyes, despite the odds, and then he was stepping forwards.

Arn and Fritha's other guards moved to meet Drem, six of her best.

Drem drew a short axe from his belt, without any hesitation hurled it at Arn.

It spun through the air, Arn leaping away, the axe slamming into the face of the warrior behind him, a crunch like wet wood being split as the axe blade buried itself in her face, the warrior hurled backwards from her feet. Drem drew his seax and another axe at his belt and ran at them.

Arn swung his spear at Drem, the other warriors spreading wide, trying to encircle him, but he was moving so quickly, his axe snaking out, wrapping around Arn's spear and tugging him off balance. Drem's momentum carried him on, a slash of his seax at another warrior, a red line across the warrior's face, a splash of blood, and Drem was backhanding his axe at Arn, who blocked it with his spear shaft and stepped in close, trying to snare Drem's axe arm.

He's learned a few things from the Order, Fritha thought dispassionately, *but he's not good enough for Arn and the others yet.*

A blow landed across Drem's back, sent him stumbling into Arn, who put his knee into Drem's gut, doubling him over. More blows, and Drem dropped to one knee, twisted to the side, slashing with his seax. A scream, another of Fritha's warriors dropping, clutching his leg, Drem rolling to the side, back onto his feet, crouched, seax and axe ready.

Fritha sighed.

'Elise, take him for me.'

'With pleasssure,' Elise hissed, slithering towards Drem.

Suddenly, more figures were bursting out of the woodland, three wolven-hounds, huge beasts, one grey, one black, one red-furred. They crunched into the warriors around Drem, screams and blood spraying, the sounds of flesh tearing.

Two men ran into the glade, one more limping behind them, setting upon Fritha's warriors. Two Fritha recognized: the young red-haired warrior and the older huntsman from the starstone mine attack. There was another huntsman with them, slim and black-bearded. As Fritha watched, he blocked a sword-blow from one of her warriors, turned the blade and buried his axe in her man's neck. A burst of blood and her warrior was falling to the ground, clutching at the jet of blood that pulsed between his fingers.

'Wrath,' Fritha snarled. 'Kill them.'

'*Yes*,' Wrath growled and burst forwards, a pulse of his wings adding to his speed.

At the same time a figure dropped from the trees above, Morn, her wings spreading, and she was stabbing with her spear at the red-haired warrior.

He shrugged his shield from his back, blocking her spear-thrust, slashing with his sword, but she flew out of reach.

The black-bearded huntsman saw Wrath hurtling towards him, a moment of fear washing over his face, changing to resolve, and he was setting his feet, sword and knife in his fist. He sidestepped Wrath's charge, slashed with his sword at the draig's side, leaving a red line, Fritha feeling a moment of pure rage at her creation's injury. Wrath roared at the pain, his thick tail lashing as he skidded past the huntsman, crashing into his legs, the man going down hard, trying to roll, but Wrath was turning with startling speed and leaping upon the prone warrior, jaws snapping at his head.

Two wolven-hounds appeared out of nowhere, hurling

themselves at Wrath, jaws biting, claws raking as they latched onto the draig.

Wrath just ignored them, even though red wounds were appearing, his jaws clamping around the huntsman's head. The man stabbed and hacked at Wrath's belly with his sword and knife. A sickening crunching sound, a savage wrench, and the huntsman's head was torn from his shoulders, his body collapsing, limbs juddering.

'STEPOR,' the older huntsman cried, hurling his hand-axe at Wrath, the blade sinking deep into the draig's shoulder. Again, it ignored the blow and set about removing the wolven-hounds from its body, both of them frenziedly ripping and biting into Wrath's flesh.

Fritha saw the old huntsman slash at his palm, heard him yelling words of power, and he threw a handful of blood, sparks of incandescent fire appearing in the droplets even as they sprayed one of Fritha's guards and splattered upon Wrath's muzzle.

A sizzle and the stench of burning flesh, Fritha's guard collapsing, screaming, hands gouging at his face.

Wrath roared his pain, charred splotches appearing on his muzzle, wisps of smoke curling into the air. The fire-blood seemed to do little more than irk the draig, though. It gave a violent shake of its body, like a terrier with a rat, and one of the wolven-hounds lost its grip and struck the ground, Wrath scuttling forwards and slashing with a long-taloned foot. The wolven-hound howled as Wrath disembowelled it, entrails spilling onto the ground.

Then other figures were around them.

Fritha looked up, saw that they had moved to the very fringe of the woodland, and the battle on the slope was pressing in upon them. Giants and bears were there, riders of the Order as well as Ferals and her own Red Right Hand.

And Revenants.

Fritha had seen them many times at the mine and on the journey here, but they were different creatures now.

They were killing machines. Fritha stared in a moment of abject awe. They were devastatingly fast, and they were merciless, snatching at warriors, leaping up at horses to tear men and women from saddles, swarming over a bear and rending it with tooth and claw.

A bear lumbered past, a male giant with a long black warrior braid upon its back. He was wielding two long-hafted axes like threshing poles, a constant blur of motion. Fritha saw his axe take the head from a Revenant, a burst of blue light exploding from its neck as the creature dropped slowly to the ground, body spasming, though its hands raked and clawed at the ground for far longer than it should have before it stilled in death.

They can die, then, Fritha noted.

'Frithhhha,' a voice called out and Fritha saw that Elise had Drem wrapped in her coils.

Wonderful, Fritha thought and strode towards her prize.

447

CHAPTER FIFTY-FOUR

DREM

Drem strained with all his might, veins bulging, feeling as if his head would burst, his eyes explode from his face.

But nothing happened.

The giant wyrm-thing with a woman's face and upper body had wrapped him tight in her coils, pinning his arms to his sides. He still held his seax and axe but could not move them. The creature regarded Drem with cold, reptilian eyes.

'No point sssstruggling,' the thing said, and then its coils were rippling and it slithered sinuously across the glade, weaving through the combat that raged about them. Drem yelled, saw Fritha's face smiling at him, growing closer.

'Well met, Drem ben Olin,' Fritha said with a delighted smile, as if the wyrm-woman was giving Fritha a gift on her name-day.

'I will . . . kill you,' Drem said.

'You need to let go of that obsession,' Fritha said, like someone giving their good friend the best of advice.

'You . . . killed him,' Drem wheezed. He felt a flood of emotion – frustration, rage, grief all mingled – blinked the angry tears from his eyes.

'Ah, to be loved as you loved your father,' Fritha murmured.

Drem strained again, the sight of Fritha talking about his da incensing him, wanting only to wrap his hands around her throat and squeeze.

'Kill . . . you,' he grunted.

A ripple of wyrm-muscle and the breath was crushed from Drem's chest, coils constricting tighter about his torso, the beast glaring at him.

'Not too tight, Elise,' Fritha said. 'We don't want a dead Drem, now, do we?'

The coils loosened a fraction, allowing Dem to gasp in a breath.

Elise! It has a name!

Drem stared at Fritha, saw her watching him with fascinated eyes.

All around them the fight was raging. Drem glimpsed Cullen fallen to one knee, blood sheeting from a wound on his scalp, Keld standing over the young warrior, fending off Morn's stabbing spear with his shield as she hovered above them both.

And then a mountain of fur was crashing through the trees into the battle about them, Hammer the bear surging into Drem's view, Alcyon the giant upon her back, swinging his two long-hafted axes.

Fritha jumped and rolled to the side, Elise the wyrm-woman swayed, an axe blade hissing past her face. She lashed out with the sword in her hand, a red line along Hammer's flank, Drem jerked and heaved as Elise's coils rippled, loosening a moment, then constricting, refusing to let him go.

Hammer turned, a swipe of her claws raking the wyrm's coils, gouging red wounds. Elise hissed a scream, her upper body darting forwards impossibly fast, stabbing at the bear's face, Alcyon's axe clanging into her sword, sending it spinning through the air, his other axe whirling, chopping deep into the meat of her coils.

She did scream, then, a high, lilting shriek that set heads turning, her coils spasming, releasing Drem, hurling him through the air to crunch into a tree and drop to the ground. He raised himself on his elbows, saw heads all around the glade looking at the wyrm-woman and giant bear.

Drem climbed to one knee, head spinning, hands scrambling for his seax and axe, which he saw lying close by on the forest litter.

'WRATH,' Fritha yelled, her cry answered by a deafening roar that shook both the ground below and branches above them.

Alcyon tugged on his axe embedded in coils, and Elise's head lunged forwards, jaws unnaturally wide, too-long teeth sinking into the flesh of Alcyon's arm. The giant grunted a yell, let go of his axe and ripped his arm free of Elise's jaws, a splatter of blood arcing through the air.

And then the draig was there, wings beating, lifting it into the air, and it was hurtling at Alcyon, the giant swaying in his saddle, swinging his other axe. The draig's wings shifted, twisting it in the air, Alcyon's axe hissing under a wing, the draig lashing out with long talons, raking Hammer's flank and rump, tearing bloody strips, then it was crashing into the bear. Though smaller than Hammer, the draig's weight and momentum sent the bear staggering, stumbling and toppling to the side, Alcyon hurled from his saddle as they rolled on the ground, crushing figures beneath them, friend or foe, Drem did not know.

Drem shook his head, trying to scatter the black dots that were clouding his vision, heard Hammer roar in agony as the draig ripped into her side with its powerful jaws, at the same time its claws digging, raking at her exposed belly.

There was an answering roar, elsewhere, echoing through the woodland, followed by a thunderous crashing, getting closer, the sound of trees being ripped from their roots, and then the white bear was bursting into the glade.

It cast its head from side to side, saw Hammer and the draig, and roared a challenge, broke into a lumbering run, scattering or crushing all in its way. Drem saw Fritha stand before its rush, wide-eyed and frozen for a moment, and then the wyrm-woman was standing before her, the wyrm's tail wrapping around Fritha and hurling her out of the way. Elise slithered on her coils, trying to evade the white bear's charge, but she was too slow and the bear crashed into her, sending her flying through the air, disappearing amongst the trees.

The white bear slammed into the draig, wrenching it from its attack on Hammer, the two beasts thundering across the glade, swiping and snapping at each other, clawing and gouging.

All was mayhem and madness. Ferals and giants, warriors of the Order and shaven-haired acolytes, Revenants, wyrms and draigs, all fighting for their lives around him.

Revenants spilt across the slope and, framed in sunlight bright across the ridge's crest, Drem saw Gunil atop his great bear, Balur One-Eye finally reaching him. One-Eye swerved around the slash of the bear's paws and then his war-hammer was swinging, high and down with all of Balur's prodigious strength, smashing into the bear's skull. Drem heard the crunch from where he was standing, saw the power of that impact ripple through the animal, from head to claws, and slowly the legs of Gunil's bear crumpled beneath it, its great bulk crashing to the ground, an eruption of dust.

Gunil rose out of the dirt cloud.

'You killed my Claw,' he screamed, spittle flying, and then the two giants were swinging their great hammers at each other, dark iron clashing, huge sparks leaping.

A tide of battle and banks of tattered mist swept between Drem and the two giants, obscuring them from view.

A dozen paces in front of Drem he saw a rider of the Order swing his sword at a Revenant, saw the grey-skinned creature sway away from the blade and leap up at the rider, somehow finding purchase, scrambling up behind the warrior and grabbing onto his head, yanking it to the side and sinking its jaws into the man's neck. The Revenant shook its head, blood erupting, the rider toppling from his saddle, the Revenant falling upon him, biting and tearing flesh in a frenzy. The sight of it turned the blood in Drem's veins to ice.

What are these creatures we are fighting? How is there any defeating this?

All across the slope Drem saw the same kinds of acts, giants, warriors, bears, all trying to fend off the blood-frenzied storm of Revenants. Drem saw a bear engulfed by the creatures, a horde of them swarming over it like ants, dragging it to the ground. A moment of fear as he saw one hurl itself at Keld. The huntsman saw the Revenant flying towards him, instinctively slashed with his sword and cut into the creature's neck. There was a flash of blue light, the Revenant crunching to the ground, rolling. Keld stabbed his sword down into its chest with all his strength, twisting. Blue veins rippled out from the wound, the Revenant spasming and then flopping still.

And then Fritha was standing before him.

She looked like something out of a tale, short-sword in her fist, fair hair stubbled, blood smeared on her face, her cuirass embossed with red wings.

'You're coming with me,' she said.

'Over my dead body,' he said, raising his seax and axe.

'Well, that is the alternative,' Fritha said, looking around her. 'I'd rather have you for my experiments, make you into something that will do my bidding for all eternity. I think I'll leave you with your memory, so you will always remember that I killed Olin, even as you serve me.' She shrugged. 'Or you can have a painful, terrifying death as food for a Revenant.'

He snarled and swung his axe at her.

She stepped back, gracefully, a twist of her wrist sweeping his axe away.

Drem followed, seax stabbing, axe swinging, a windmill of blows, and Fritha blocked and parried and swayed, feet shuffling away, to his sides, ever just out of reach.

'You've got better,' Fritha commented, her face fixed in concentration. 'Your footwork has definitely improved.' She smiled at him, an encouraging sword master. 'But a moon training with the Order of the Bright Star is not better than a lifetime raised as one of Drassil's White-Wings.'

She stepped in, her sword suddenly a blur, sweeping Drem's axe wide, his seax low, knocking him off balance, and then she was closer still, inside his guard, headbutting him across the nose, sending him reeling, staggering backwards, slamming into a tree, dropping to one knee.

'You are mine, Drem ben Olin,' Fritha said as she loomed over him, her sword raised.

A horse crashed into Fritha, sending her lurching away, spinning.

Horse and rider reined in between Drem and Fritha, and Drem looked up to see Byrne in the saddle. She was gore-spattered, a thing out of a nightmare, teeth bared in a rictus snarl, her curved sword blooded to the hilt.

'Get away from my sister's son, you bitch,' Byrne spat at Fritha.

Something crossed Fritha's face: worry, fear.

'I was hoping I'd bump into you,' Fritha said. She drew her sword across her palm, a red line, smeared the blood across her lips.

'*IONSAI*,' Fritha yelled, her blood spraying from her lips, '*IAD A MHARU*,' and all around the glade Ferals stopped their frenzied fighting and threw themselves at Byrne.

Her mount screamed as Ferals' claws raked it in their frenzied rush to reach Byrne, the animal rearing, Byrne leaping to the ground, rolling. She regained her feet, snatched a hand inside her jerkin and pulled out a fistful of what looked like vials, threw them at a knot of Ferals that were swarming towards her, the vials smashing, some kind of liquid bursting across the creatures, soaking into their fur.

'*Fuil agus tine, salann agus lathair,*' Drem heard Byrne hiss, and then blue fire was rippling to life across the Ferals' fur, spreading, engulfing them in flames. The Ferals howled and screamed, limbs windmilling, slapping and clawing at their bodies as they were ravaged by the flames. The acrid stench of seared flesh filled the glade.

Fritha looked at her Ferals, screamed and ran at Byrne. Their swords clashed, the two of them moving through the glade. A Revenant leaped at Byrne and she sidestepped Fritha, slashed at the Revenant with her sword. A wound opened across its chest, a blue light throbbing, and the Revenant screamed, falling away.

Burning Ferals crashed between Drem and the two women, flames sparking on the woodland litter, leaping into hungry, crackling life. Drem scrambled away, into the trees.

All about him the Revenant horde was swarming, ripping and tearing flesh.

We cannot win against them, too many, Drem thought. *It's just a matter of time.* Something nagged at Drem's mind. *I have seen them stabbed scores of times and not fall, and yet Ethlinn and Keld killed them with a blow or two, Byrne's sword hurt it . . .*

Bodies crashed and fell about him, scattering his thoughts. *If I can help Byrne, and kill Fritha . . .*

He rose to his feet, looking for a way around the flames to Fritha and Byrne, but the woodland was becoming a fiery maelstrom. He cast about wildly and saw something behind him, in the shadows. A figure, a Revenant, hunched over a woman, a warrior of the Bright Star. Drem took a step towards them and the Revenant looked up, blood slick on its mouth and jaws.

Drem faltered. Even though transformed, only one eye left in its gaunt, too-pale face, Drem still recognized this creature.

It was Ulf.

Drem remembered watching from a rooftop of the mine as Ulf had offered himself to Gulla, giving himself over to Gulla's fangs, remembered Ulf collapsing, twitching, convulsing as he had been changed, turned into . . . *this.*

Ulf had been a friend to him and his father, or so Drem had thought. But all along Ulf had been a servant of Gulla, spying, scheming. He had betrayed Olin and Drem.

Drem hefted his seax and axe, strode towards Ulf.

The Revenant rose to his feet, a gliding, elegant motion. He cocked his head to one side, regarding Drem with the dark well of his one eye.

'Drem,' he hissed.

'Remember me, do you?' Drem snarled. 'Well, remember this as I send you to the Otherworld.' He struck at Ulf, seax and axe swinging and stabbing, Ulf swaying away, parrying with long-taloned hands that seemed as hard as iron, Drem's blows glancing away. Then Ulf was twisting, suddenly lunging forwards.

Drem's axe chopped into Ulf's neck, a diagonal cut, into the clavicle. He heard the distinctive sound of the bone cracking, but it did not seem to faze Ulf, who shrugged off the blow and reached out grasping hands to grab Drem, claws raking his face, closing tight, raking his cheeks and pulling him close, towards Ulf's distended-wide jaws, razored teeth still dripping with the blood of Ulf's last victim.

Drem screamed as Ulf's foul, bloodied breath washed over him and he stabbed frantically into the creature's belly with his seax, the blade plunging deep into flesh.

Drem felt something in his fist as it was wrapped around the bone hilt of his seax: a hot pulse of heat, and again, and again, like a beating heart.

A blue light burst from the wound.

Ulf screamed, a feral agony, and lashed out, striking Drem across the chest and hurling him through the air, crashing to the ground, rolling through flames. Drem climbed to one knee, still had his seax in his hand, saw that it was pulsing with a fading blue glow, like a fresh-forged blade cooling from the flames. Runes along the blade glowed white-bright, and Drem remembered Keld telling him of Olin's runes, what they said.

Dilis cosantoir. Faithful Protector.

Keld's sword is rune-marked, as is Byrne's, and Ethlinn's spear must be, too.

455

Ulf was staring at him in rage and pain, opened his mouth and hissed a shriek at Drem, and then ran at him.

Drem staggered to his feet, hefted his seax, and threw it.

It flew through the air, the heavy blade and handle spinning, glittering in the fire-flames, and punched into Ulf's chest, hurling the Revenant backwards, against the trunk of an ancient oak, Drem's blade piercing flesh, bark and wood, sinking deep and pinning Ulf to the tree.

An explosion of blue light and sparks as Ulf thrashed and screamed, gnashing his jaws, shredding his own lips in his agony and fury, Drem's seax glowing white-hot within Ulf, the hiss of burning flesh wafting.

Drem stumbled forwards, saw Alcyon's axe lying on the ground, snatched it up and ran at Ulf, swinging the axe over his head, screaming his father's name.

'OLIN!' And he chopped the axe blade into Ulf's neck. There was another burst of blue light as the axe severed the Revenant's head and buried itself in the tree. Drem was hurled away, crashing onto his back.

Ulf's head spun through the air and hit the ground with a thud, rolling into the flames, where it hissed, flesh melting.

All about the glade and slope beyond, something happened.

Revenants froze in their slaughter and feasting, a jerking paroxysm, and then, with a collective sigh, all around Drem, they collapsed.

Drem stared open-mouthed, saw a Revenant almost at his feet change colour, its skin shifting from grey to normal skin-tones as in death the creature reverted to the person it had been in life.

A wind blew across the slope, the sun blazing bright, and the remaining giants and warriors of the Bright Star roared.

Two figures on the slope, Balur and Gunil, were still exchanging blows, battering at each other with feverish fury.

As Drem looked, Balur ducked under a hammer-swing, stepped in and struck Gunil on the knee with the iron butt of his staff. Gunil tottered, his knee bending, and Balur struck him in the mouth with his hammer-shaft, Gunil tumbling over, crashing to the ground, teeth spraying.

Balur raised his hammer high, Gunil's hand reaching out, a pleading scream cut short as Balur's hammer crunched into Gunil's head, shards of bone and brain-matter exploding.

'WRATH,' a voice screamed behind Drem. He spun on his feet to see Fritha standing on open ground, trading blows with Byrne. Fritha was bleeding from fresh wounds, breathing heavily. She ducked and stepped away, rubbed blood over her lips.

'*Sruthán*,' Fritha screeched at Byrne, the droplets of blood sizzling in the air as they sped towards Byrne's face.

'*Cumhacht an uisce, an tine seo a dhúnadh*,' Byrne said contemptuously, waving her hand and the blood-fire sizzled and hissed into steam, evaporating before it came close to touching her.

Fritha shrieked and swung a wild overhead strike, Byrne parrying, sweeping the blow wide and kicking Fritha in the chest, sending her sprawling on her back. Byrne reached inside her surcoat and pulled out another vial, threw it hard on the ground, smashing it, dark liquid soaking into the earth.

'*Fréamhacha an domhain, gabháil agus ceangail*,' Byrne called out.

The ground shifted, moving, as if something stirred deep down. Then roots were bursting from the ground, snaking out, seeking Fritha like a blind man's fingers.

Fritha screamed, crawled away, one of the roots snaring her ankle, wrapping around it while more tendrils sought her other limbs. Frenziedly Fritha hacked and chopped at the root, cutting through it. She rolled away, scrambling to her feet.

Byrne pursued Fritha, stabbing and sweeping, Fritha stumbling away, eyes wide.

'WRATH,' Fritha screamed again, louder, and the draig sprinted towards her. It was ripped bloody from its fight with the white bear, but still full of power. Its wings spread wide, beating, rising into the air, and Fritha was running away from Byrne, leaping, arms wrapping around the draig's neck, and she was swinging onto its back, the draig climbing higher into the air.

A spear whistled past Fritha, and then another winged figure was flying beside her, the half-breed.

Drem watched in frustration as the two winged shapes climbed higher and higher, soon out of range of any spear or arrow, and then they were dwindling quickly to black specks in the sky.

All about them Fritha's warband broke and scattered. Ferals lifted their heads to the sky, howling, and then they were scattering into the woodland, loping away.

Drem blew out a sigh.

An arm wrapped around Drem's shoulder – Cullen, grinning at him through a blood-drenched face.

'Well, that was a fight to write a song about, and no denying,' Cullen said.

Keld snorted a laugh on Drem's other side.

'She got away,' Drem said.

'Aye, well, we've got to leave some fights for the morrow,' Cullen answered, 'or else we'd have nothing left to look forward to.'

Drem looked at Cullen and shook his head, while Keld threw his head back and laughed. Byrne joined them, watching Fritha and Morn fading into the distance.

'Where's Gulla?' Byrne said.

Keld's laughter turned to a frown.

'Not here,' Drem said.

'Aye.' Byrne nodded. 'But if he's not here, then where, and why?'

Drem didn't like where that thought led him.

CHAPTER FIFTY-FIVE

RIV

Riv flew above the trees of Forn Forest. Below her the eastern road cut a line all the way to Drassil, though Riv could see no hint of the ancient fortress and great tree, only a never-ending sea of trees spreading before her.

She grimaced with the pain in her wing, a dull, throbbing ache with every beat of it. The Cheren arrow had caught her high on her wing-arch, the stretch of muscle and tendon that joined her wings to the muscles in her back. She had tried to set out for Drassil the night she had rescued Bleda, but within a score of wingbeats knew that she could not do it. The extra weight of carrying Bleda to safety had been too much for her injured wing. Bleda had tended her wound, cleaned and bound it, and after a night's rest, it had been better, but she was still not recovered, and although she had set out three days ago, what should have been a short journey was stretching into a nightmare of pain.

I must reach Drassil before Jin. Must warn Aphra and Kol of Gulla's plan, tell them all that Bleda heard.

Over three days had passed since she had plucked Bleda from certain death. She had taken him to a safe place and waited with him for Ellac and his surviving guard to appear. They had spent a night in each other's arms before Ellac and Ruga had led a score of battered riders into their glade. Riv had tried to comfort Bleda, who was racked with grief for his mother and fury at Jin.

This world is full of one blood-feud or another, an endless cycle.

Riv knew how that felt.

She flew on.

She missed Bleda, an ache in her chest at the thought of him, but there was no way he could reach Drassil in time. It was too dangerous to use the road – Kadoshim and their half-breeds were patrolling it – and travelling through the snare and tangle of Forn would make it impossible to outpace Jin and her Cheren warriors. The only chance was Riv and her wings.

Something on the road below drew her eye. She swooped lower, saw figures scattered upon the road, dark stains about them.

White-Wings.

Hundreds of them.

Riv landed, scowling at the sight before her.

White-Wings, strewn everywhere. It looked as if they had formed a shield wall, the bulk of the dead gathered in a tight formation. It was clear that many had been torn from the wall and slain.

But not by sharp steel.

They had been torn to pieces, shredded with teeth and claws.

Ferals? Or those other things that I saw in the forest?

She picked her way amongst the dead, saw a few bodies that weren't White-Wings, dressed in tattered clothes.

Not Ferals, then.

Not one of these creatures' bodies was in one piece. Decapitated bodies, amputated limbs.

They are hard to kill, then. I had to take the head of the one Bleda had impaled on his sword.

And then Riv saw Lorina, Kol's high captain.

She was lying beside the headless corpse of one of the creatures, a ragged hole where her throat had been.

Riv had not cared much for Lorina, always thought of her as ambitious and untrustworthy, but she was still a White-Wing, still a comrade-in-arms to Riv. And Riv had respected her prowess on the weapons-field.

She felt she should try and raise a cairn over her fallen brothers and sisters but knew there was no time.

I must fly on, or else all those in Drassil will be needing their own cairns.

Riv leaped into the air, wings beating, a sharp pain in her back. She cursed her injury, and the Cheren archer who had given it to her, and flew on.

In the distance the great tree of Drassil loomed before Riv, branches spread wide, and beneath it the towers and walls of Drassil reared.

One last spurt. She willed her wings to work harder.

She was flying high, just below heavy cloud, moisture like mist dampening her wings. Figures appeared on the road ahead, specks from Riv's great height. With a shift of her back muscles she angled downwards, lower and lower until she was skimming the treetops.

More bodies were strewn on the road, a handful of Ben-Elim, white-feathered wings splayed and twisted. Further on Riv saw what looked like a warband gathered on the fringes of the road, spilling from the eaves of Forn Forest. They were the shaven-haired acolytes of the Kadoshim.

Deeper within the forest to Riv's right, boughs were shift-ing, a rippling motion that wasn't the wind, hinting of something moving beneath the branches. Wisps of dark mist curled up from gaps in the trees.

Riv frowned at that, remembering the dark thundercloud she'd seen, apparently full of the creatures that had slain Lori-na's warband.

Riv flew over it, closer to those gathered on the road.

They were shaven-haired men and women mounted upon

horses. Hundreds of them were appearing, too many to count. And ahead of them were Cheren riders, distinctive with their long warrior braids. Riv was careful not to fly too low, wary of their bows. They were still well ahead, and Riv saw them break into a canter on the road as they approached the point where the road spilt onto the vast plain around Drassil.

Faster, Riv thought. *One more burst of speed and I can still reach Drassil before them.*

And then shapes were rising from the forest beneath her, winged, but not like her, great leathery wings beating hard to intercept her. Three, four of them, making towards Riv.

Kadoshim.

Riv veered across the treetop canopy, glimpsed more Kadoshim gathered beneath the lattice of boughs, half-breeds as well, waiting. A host of them.

Some burst from the canopy and came after her.

Riv reached for her Sirak bow, grabbed a fistful of arrows as Bleda had taught her, in one movement nocked, drew and loosed into the knot of Kadoshim rising towards her.

Her arrow punched into one, a shriek of pain and it was falling away.

Riv grinned and nocked another arrow.

The Kadoshim spread wider, Riv's next arrow hissing harmlessly past them.

She swore, put her bow back into its case and pumped her wings, angling high.

Horn blasts rang out, the high-screeching sound of the Cheren.

On the ground Jin's riders had reached the plain of Drassil and were galloping hard, blowing their horns, not riding in their usual disciplined ranks, but acting as if they were injured and hard-pressed.

The Kadoshim speeding towards Riv broke away, curling back down towards the forest.

Why are they doing that?

The other riders reached Drassil's plain, the shaven-haired acolytes appearing as if they were pursuing the Cheren, both groups thundering across the open space towards Drassil's gates.

Horns sounded from Drassil's walls, answering the Cheren, and to Riv's horror she saw the gates of Drassil creak open. Ben-Elim rose into the air above Drassil's walls and began to fly out to meet the Cheren.

They think Jin and the Cheren are their allies, can see they are hard-pressed and fleeing. This is Gulla's plan, to use the Cheren to open Drassil's gates.

Riv worked her wings harder, felt her wound complaining, muscles failing. Ignored it, thinking of Aphra lying on flag-stones with her throat torn open.

On the ground the Cheren were well ahead of their pretend pursuers, a wide gap between the two groups.

Wide enough for the defenders of Drassil to think they can keep the gates open for the Cheren, and have time to close them before this enemy in pursuit reaches the gates.

Riv saw Ben-Elim reach the Cheren riders, swooping low, heard them calling encouragements to the Cheren, urging them to ride faster.

No, Riv screamed internally.

She swept over the acolytes, outpacing them, narrowing the gap between her and the Cheren, but they were so near to the gates now. Riv saw Jin at their head, bent low over her horse, a bow clutched in one hand.

Ben-Elim were close now, Riv saw one was dark-haired Hadran, and she flew to him. He saw her and smiled, beating his wings to hover in the sky.

'I'm glad you still live,' he called out to her. 'We have had no word since Kol returned. Scouts have been sent out but none have returned.'

'IT'S A TRICK,' Riv screamed, pointing at the Cheren.

'What?' Hadran said, frowning. 'They are our allies, pursued by the enemy. We must help them.'

'The Cheren are allied to the Kadoshim,' she yelled, closer, flying in a tight circle about him. 'Look,' and she pointed back, to the forest, where Kadoshim and their half-breeds were beginning to burst from the tree canopy. Below them, on the ground, a black mist flowed from the trees onto the open plain, spreading rapidly across the ground like spilt ink on parchment.

'Jin and the Cheren are fooling you, seeking to open Drassil's gates for the Kadoshim.'

'No,' Hadran whispered.

They both turned and flew for the gates, yelling a warning, other Ben-Elim in the air now seeing the Kadoshim and the black mist.

Horns blared, voices shouting, sounds echoing out of Drassil. Riv saw Ben-Elim launching from a thousand windows into the sky, the battlements of the fortress thick with warriors.

'CLOSE THE GATES,' Riv and Hadran screamed together, but it was too late; in a thunder of hooves Jin led her warband through the open gates and into the gate tunnel, clattering into the courtyard beyond. Riv reached the gate tower and heard the first screams as Cheren warriors loosed arrows at the warriors hurrying to meet them, a widening arc of the Cheren pouring through the gates, keeping them open, slaying the gate guards.

Riv looked back over her shoulder and saw the air filled with the black silhouettes of Kadoshim and their half-breeds, speeding towards her and Drassil's walls. On the ground below, the warband of acolytes were at the gates, and close behind them the black mist spread across the plain, seething and bulging with the creatures within it.

Archers on Drassil's walls loosed volleys down into the oncoming acolytes, screams echoing on the field of cairns, but the gates were open and already many were riding through them. Kadoshim were close to Riv and Hadran now, the air filled with battle-cries and the beating of many wings. More volleys were loosed into the sky, some Kadoshim screeching and spiralling to the ground. With a snarl, Hadran hurled his spear, skewered a half-breed, then drew his sword and launched himself at a Kadoshim. They crashed together, spinning, snarling, spitting.

Riv hovered, hesitating, unsure what to do. Then, to the south, she saw another black cloud roll out from the forest, surging towards Drassil's gates. And from the west, the trees shook and yet another mist boiled out from the treeline.

They have used the depths of the forest to travel unseen.

A dread settled in her belly, seeing the gates of Drassil already taken and these overwhelming numbers surging towards them.

I must find Aphra.

CHAPTER FIFTY-SIX

FRITHA

Fritha shivered and clenched her jaws to stop her teeth chattering.

She was sitting upon Wrath's back, or more accurately, laying prone upon his back, her arms and legs wrapped tight around him, clinging on for dear life.

Morn flew beside her, in sweeping loops, laughing at the draig's slow speed and lack of manoeuvrability.

'He is like a stone with wings,' Morn called down to her from above.

Any faster or higher and I would die.

Fritha's muscles ached from hanging on so hard, almost three solid days of constant flying from the battleground in the Desolation. Just the thought of that soured Fritha's blood.

We were so close. Victory in the palm of my hand. I told Ulf he had to stay safe. She spent a while cursing and swearing to the clouds above her. There were no birds in the sky, she guessed it was because Wrath's presence scared them away.

And then she saw Drassil in the distance.

She felt a rush of terror at what Gulla would say to her when he heard of her defeat.

I will not tell him yet, not until I have done the deed, and then it will be too late.

She felt a tremor of fear at the risk she was taking, but what else could she do? Flee and live her life in hiding?

Never. I have a destiny to fulfil, a great deed to do, and at the least, my vengeance must be appeased. Kol is at Drassil. She felt a thrill of excitement at that thought, after so many years of planning and scheming, of fighting and dreaming of this moment, and now it had actually arrived. A clouded haze swirled around the towers and walls of Drassil, looking from this distance like flocks of birds wheeling and swooping, but Fritha knew what it was.

Ben-Elim and Kadoshim, locked in their eternal battle. Will this really be its end?

It could be.

The fortress rushed towards them, growing, and below her Fritha saw trees swaying and moving as some great host moved within it. Tendrils of black mist curled from the branches. To the south she saw evidence of another black cloud host surging towards the fortress.

Gulla's Seven with their broods, all converging on Drassil. They have moved at night by cover of darkness, slipped into the deepest, darkest recesses of Forn to avoid prying eyes and crept their way here. But now their terrible beauty can be revealed for all to see. Let the world tremble.

And then Wrath was leaving the forest behind, flying over a plain before Drassil's great walls. Kadoshim and Ben-Elim flew in the air, sweeping and looping as they stabbed and slashed at one another, screaming their aeons-old hatred.

Wrath snapped at a Ben-Elim that swept past them, trading blows with a Kadoshim. The draig snagged a wing, shook it and the Ben-Elim fell spiralling to the ground, its wing ruined.

Wrath spat out feathers.

'*Taste bad,*' he grumbled.

'Soon you'll feast on the finest flesh,' Fritha crooned.

'*Happy,*' Wrath answered.

They winged over the high walls, the clash of arms drifting up to them, Fritha looking down to see the walls manned with White-Wings, but their enemy were already inside the fortress.

There were running battles taking place in the streets, mounted warriors with bows in their hands, swirling hordes of Revenants overrunning all before them, and knots of White-Wings gathered in their shield walls, like rocks in a swirling river. Fritha felt a rush of nostalgia at seeing her old home and the White-Wings she had been raised to be part of.

I was brainwashed, part of the great lie.

She searched the sky, looking for Kol, but the Ben-Elim and Kadoshim were all a too-fast blur.

'There.' Fritha pointed at the Great Hall, a huge domed structure that was built around the trunk of Drassil's great tree. She guided Wrath towards it.

A massive shield wall of White-Wings stood before the hall's gates, four or five hundred strong. Riders were pouring arrows into it, but the shields were soaking them up. Fritha saw a charge of shaven-haired acolytes rush the wall, crashing into it, hoping to break through by sheer press of numbers, but the wall held and the acolytes died, short-swords stabbing.

Fritha whispered in Wrath's ear and the draig swooped upon the courtyard before the Great Hall, sweeping low, and then it was crashing into the shield wall, scattering White-Wing warriors in all directions.

Wrath squatted amidst the destruction he had caused, chewing on a severed leg, and Fritha stood tall on his back. She drew her sword and punched it into the air.

'TO ME,' she bellowed, 'TO ME,' and then she was commanding Wrath on, lumbering through what was left of the shield wall, some White-Wings scattering, others retreating and running through the hall's gates into the chamber beyond.

Fritha and Wrath followed, screaming acolytes charging behind them.

Fritha gasped as they entered the hall – such a magnificent room, a place she knew all too intimately.

Battle was already raging in here, up above, as Kadoshim and their half-breeds swept in through the many fly-holes the

Ben-Elim had crafted. Feathers and blood rained down from above.

They reached the top of the steps that led down into Drassil's Great Hall and the dais before Skald's throne. Fritha commanded Wrath to stop a moment and looked.

The molten-covered forms of Asroth and Meical were as they had always been, locked in eternal battle. Fritha felt a shudder ripple through her belly at the sight of them.

The dais they stood upon was guarded by a half-circle of White-Wings, maybe a hundred strong. More were joining them.

Fritha scowled at them. A thousand would not keep her away from her destiny.

'Onwards,' she said to Wrath, and the draig lumbered down the stairs, here and there White-Wings turning and reforming, trying to hold Wrath with their wall of shields, stabbing and slashing, but the draig smashed through them as if they were so much kindling, and behind them the acolytes rolled over the fallen.

Fritha reached the dais, saw White-Wings gathered before her, the last resistance between her and Asroth the Great. She paused a moment, both savouring this moment and allowing acolytes to gather behind her. A new sound in the building caused her to turn and she saw a dark mist pour through the open gates, Revenants surging into the room.

Gulla must be close.

She turned back to the White-Wings, saw a dark-haired woman at their centre staring at her, staring at the red wings upon Fritha's cuirass.

She recognizes me as one of their own. Good, let them see the hypocrisy of their world that has laid them low.

A winged figure dropped from the sky and hovered above the White-Wing that Fritha was staring at, a Ben-Elim, some kind of shouted exchange between the two of them. Something about the Ben-Elim looked wrong, though.

Fritha frowned.

Then she realized.

Its feathers were a dapple grey, not the bright, pure white of the Ben-Elim.

And it was a woman.

It's a Ben-Elim half-breed.

The implications of that seeped through Fritha.

Like my baby. She could have been my baby girl.

How has this happened? Have the Ben-Elim changed? Repented of the evil they have done?

She was rocked by that thought, shaken to her core, and for a moment she froze in shock and indecision.

She stared at the half-breed Ben-Elim, strong-limbed and fair-haired, hovering above the White-Wings with broad, dapple-grey wings. The sight of her took Fritha's breath away.

Would my Anja have looked like her? A smile touched her face as she thought of that, almost lifted out a hand towards the half-breed as if she could stroke her cheek.

All I have done, fighting against this great crime against us, and now it might have been put right. She felt a moment's relief, even happiness, at the thought that no more Ben-Elim half-breeds were being put to death.

But it is too late for my baby girl. They must still answer for their crimes.

My baby was still murdered by the Ben-Elim, and that crime was condoned by the White-Wings. It was a White-Wing who told me where the cabin was, told me what to do once my Anja was born. To kill her and put her in the ground.

Fritha's gaze flickered between the half-breed in the air and the White-Wings gathered below her.

Slowly, her shifting emotions turned to anger, building to a hot rage that swept through her veins, bubbling like a cauldron coming to boil.

Why was my baby murdered, and this one allowed to live?

470

She felt an irrational, all-consuming hatred for this half-breed Ben-Elim and the White-Wings before her.

'Kill them,' Fritha said to Wrath. 'Kill them all.'

'*Yes*,' Wrath replied, always his answer to this most basic of commands.

He exploded forwards, charging straight at the dark-haired White-Wing below the hovering half-breed.

The world seemed to pause for Fritha as she hurtled towards the shield wall of White-Wings. As if in slow motion she saw the dark-haired woman set her feet, knuckles whitening around her sword. A fleeting respect passed through Fritha for this woman, who could see her death charging towards her in the open jaws of the draig, and yet still she stood.

And then hands were grabbing the dark-haired woman and hoisting her upwards, Fritha slashing with her sword at the woman's feet as she was dragged into the air above her. To either side of Fritha the shield wall was smashed by Wrath's charge, acolytes surging into the fracture and splitting it wide, and then the wall was broken and White-Wings scattered, some running, some breaking into fragmented melees.

Fritha glowered at the half-breed Ben-Elim and woman in her arms, saw them circle and fly towards the Great Hall's doors, the half-breed shouting down to White-Wings beneath them, some of them attempting to follow her towards the doors.

Fritha was tempted to follow them and crush them.

But then she looked at the frozen figures upon the dais.

They were so close, now, Fritha just standing and staring in awe.

'Asroth,' she whispered, dismounting from Wrath's back. He set to ripping chunks of flesh from a dead White-Wing.

Fritha approached the frozen figure of her king and reached out a tentative hand, caressing the stump of his wrist where she had hacked his hand off, which felt so long ago.

A turbulence of wings and she turned to see Gulla alight on

the dais. Kadoshim and half-breeds hovered around him, forming a defensive circle as Ben-Elim and White-Wings tried to retake the dais.

Fritha and Gulla stood there like the calm amidst the storm.

'I am here,' Fritha said, a world of meaning in those three words. She held her hand out.

Gulla stared at her, the Starstone Sword in his fist, dripping with blood and wreathed in a black smoke. Fritha could see the hesitation in him.

'I was chosen,' she said, 'by the Kadoshim Covens and the Acolyte Assembly.' A silent moment between them. Gulla, looking around, saw Kadoshim, half-breeds and acolytes all about him.

He gave her the Starstone Sword.

Fritha turned towards the statue of Asroth.

She touched the black blade against the starstone metal that encased Asroth, then looked back at Gulla.

'Together,' she said to him, and he placed his long-taloned hand over hers, and then they began to chant.

'*Cumhacht cloch star, a rugadh ar an domhan eile, a leagtar aingeal dorcha soar in aisce.*'

Black smoke curled around the Starstone Sword, red veins cobwebbing across the blade.

'*Cumhacht cloch star, a rugadh ar an domhan eile, a leagtar aingeal dorcha soar in aisce,*' they intoned again, and the red veins leached from the blade into the metal that coated Asroth and Meical, spreading like filigree across their bodies.

'*Cumhacht cloch star, a rugadh ar an domhan eile, a leagtar aingeal dorcha soar in aisce,*' Fritha and Gulla chanted again, their voices twining, growing in volume, drowning out the din of battle around them.

The two statues began to pulse, black iron and red glow rippling, as if muscles were shifting beneath them.

And then in one fluid motion Fritha drew the sword away and swung it, crashing into the starstone casing.

There was one long, extended moment where every sound seemed to be sucked into the statues and sword, an utter silence descending upon the hall, and then an explosion, iron-black fragments bursting outwards, a great blast of air hurling Fritha and Gulla from their feet, rolling across the chamber's floor, scattering all before it.

Fritha grunted, a ringing in her ears, dust settling around her, Gulla shifting behind her. She stood on unsteady legs and saw a vision.

Asroth and Meical, ancient enemies, both curled upon the ground, breathing as if they slept.

Meical stirred first, a shifting of his white wings. He was dark-haired, a long scar across his forehead and cheek. He opened his eyes and looked up at Fritha, confusion writ across his handsome features.

Dimly Fritha became aware of sounds around her, a stirring in the hall as all began to climb to their feet and gaze upon the miracle before them.

'Kill him,' snarled Gulla, reaching for a weapon. Fritha looked at the Starstone Sword in her fist and Gulla snatched it from her, raised it high.

An arrow slammed into Gulla's back, sending him stumbling forwards, dropping the Starstone Sword, and then a figure was swooping down, the dapple-feathered half-breed, a curved bow in her fist. She lashed out at Gulla with a boot, kicking him in the face and sending him staggering again, and then she was reaching a hand down to Meical, who was on his knees now.

He looked up at the half-breed.

'Move and live, stay and die,' she snarled at Meical, wings beating, hovering as she grasped for his hand.

Meical reached out and gripped her wrist, and then in a

flurry of wings he was rising into the sky, half-dragged, half-flying.

Gulla rose to his feet, screaming orders, his wings beating, taking to the air in pursuit of Meical and his half-breed rescuer, but Fritha was not paying attention. All she could do was stare.

At Asroth, Lord of the Kadoshim. He was on his knees, but as Fritha approached him he stood, slowly uncoiling, stretching as if he had woken from a deep sleep.

He wore a coat of mail, black and oily. Dark veins mapped his alabaster flesh, his face pale as milk, all sharp bones and chiselled angles, coldly handsome. His silver hair was pulled back and tied in a warrior braid that curled across one shoulder, but it was his eyes that drew and held Fritha. Black as a forest pool at midnight, no iris, no pupil, just a pulsing intelligence. Something lurked beneath those eyes, something wild and feral, a barely concealed rage.

Fritha strode up to him fearlessly.

'Welcome to your kingdom of flesh, my beloved,' she said. 'I am Fritha ap Talgos, and I am your betrothed.' She dropped to one knee and kissed his hand.